Praise for

Rewitched

"*Rewitched* is a refreshing take on magic both practical and elemental, with charming spells that will remind you of your high school Latin and make you wish you could cast them yourself. Belle's journey into the craft will enchant all readers who love witch fiction!"

—Louisa Morgan, author of *A Secret History of Witches*

"I was completely charmed by this delightful and endearing novel about rediscovering your spark. Turning thirty has never been so magical!"   —Sarah Beth Durst, award-winning author of *The Spellshop*

"A dazzling, enchanting read that soothes as much as it entertains. Readers will long to live in this charming wicche world."

—Auralee Wallace, national bestselling author of
In the Company of Witches

Rewitched

Lucy Jane Wood

ACE
NEW YORK

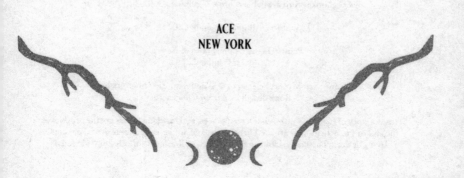

ACE
Published by Berkley
An imprint of Penguin Random House LLC
penguinrandomhouse.com

Library of Congress Cataloging-in-Publication Data

Names: Wood, Lucy Jane, author.
Title: Rewitched / Lucy Jane Wood.
Description: First edition. | New York : Ace, 2024.
Identifiers: LCCN 2024009950 (print) | LCCN 2024009951 (ebook) |
ISBN 9780593820070 (trade paperback) | ISBN 9780593820087 (ebook)
Subjects: LCGFT: Romance fiction. | Witch fiction. | Novels.
Classification: LCC PR6123.O52728 R49 2024 (print) |
LCC PR6123.O52728 (ebook) | DDC 823/.92—dc23/eng/20240308
LC record available at https://lccn.loc.gov/2024009950
LC ebook record available at https://lccn.loc.gov/2024009951

First Edition: September 2024

Printed in the United States of America
1st Printing

Interior art: Mystical elements © Wonder-studio / Shutterstock
Book design by Alison Cnockaert

For the girls who grew up on the wonder of witches, and knew that magic would be found at their own fingertips

1

Something Wicked

A WITCH WILL ALWAYS sense that she is in the presence of another born of magical persuasion. Before any introductions are made, before any actual magic is displayed, she will subconsciously register their arrival for herself. First a witch will feel it on her skin. The tingles kick in, like sherbet and static, dragging up the gooseflesh of her arms to a shiver. She'll taste a shift in the air as it becomes sharper, sweeter, almost coppery. Then comes the smell, distinct like earth and embers and crisp toffee apples, combining to a heady, rich scent of what can only be described as warmth and home. And above all else, the pricking of her ears, as well as her thumbs, will strike a match and fire up the coals of intuition. The very sound of a witch's footsteps will whisper that something is coming her way.

Unfortunately for Belle, such valuable insight into how things worked had proved largely redundant, because at 29 years, 363 days and a handful of hours old, she had yet to encounter another witch at all. Aside from her own mother, of course, and grandmother, who had passed beyond the veil a handful of years ago. There had been a brief, surprising and somewhat awkward visit from a pair of coven leaders, too, who had stopped by on her

fifteenth birthday to begin the long process of her endarkenment.
But Belle had limited recollection of that, as she had found the
whole thing entirely mortifying and hid behind her hair, blushing
and willing it to end, for the majority of the ceremony. She had
shared no contact with the coven at all since her powers were first
instated and had been left to her own devices to explore the possibilities of magic, as was custom.

Growing up with her mother's peaceful, softhearted spells as
part of the everyday meant that an intrinsic sense of magic was always nearby. There was no great moment of recognition, because it
always was. The rush of magic that flowed from Bonnie and washed
over Belle whenever she was around her mother was so normal, she
barely even noticed the hit anymore.

Belle had long since stopped anticipating such a meeting with
another witch. Their kind was rare these days, getting rarer with
every generation apparently, and she had no intention of seeking
them out for herself and inviting any trouble. She lived her life quietly amongst the non-wicche world, and that was more than fine
with her.

"Belle, what have I told you about these loyalty cards? You dish
out stamps willy-nilly, you're costing me a fortune."

Violet was an immaculate businesswoman. Her expensive suits
were always a soft shade of blue or purple (a lifelong habit that came
with a colourful name), her silver hair set and sprayed freshly twice
a week. These days, she walked slowly but with purpose on an elegant silver cane and had always been the holder of an impressive
vintage scarf collection. In all her years of working at Lunar Books,
Belle was almost certain she'd never seen Violet wear the same one
twice. Although still overseeing the goings-on, Vi had slowed down
her appearances at the shop a while ago, popping in only once or
twice a week to slide a finger across the dust, pinch everybody's

cheeks and check that Belle wasn't doing anything as foolish as giving out two loyalty stamps instead of one.

"Vi," Belle called over her shoulder as she slid a stack of new releases into their temporary home, "it's two p.m. on a Thursday, and the place is packed. I don't think you need to worry about me handing out paper bookmarks." She reached up on her tiptoes to the top shelf with a particularly chunky mythology collection, then politely shouldered her way back through the sea of customers towards her boss.

Violet gave her a slightly sheepish look as she handed over a couple of stray hardbacks. "Well, you know I don't mind, really. I rather liked how you used to put them inside every book as a little treat. But Christopher does say if we count the pennies, then the pounds will—"

"Christopher says a lot of things," Belle said. Violet's eyebrows shot up and Belle carefully reined herself back in. "Which is great, always love his input. Obviously." She cleared her throat. "Still just adjusting to him being around the place and making his changes."

"Changes that he says we should have made a long time ago," Violet reasoned.

"Right. It's just that his suggestions . . . Well, they don't necessarily add up to the Lunar Books experience that everybody has always come here for."

"I am well aware that you two have differing ideas about the future of this place. But you also know that if it were up to me, I would never have had to bring my son into the picture in the first place. What choice did you leave me with?" Violet shot her a loaded look from under a poised eyebrow.

Belle sighed. "Come on, Vi. We've been over this. Several hundred times."

"If only you'd stop being so selfish and grant the wish of a feeble old woman . . ." Violet wore a forlorn look but smiled as she leafed through a children's title about a boarding school with her exquisite red manicure.

Belle squinted in her boss's direction. "Nothing about you is feeble. You're a menace to society."

"I don't know what you're talking about. I am an innocent, ailing old lady who simply wishes she could leave her cherished shop in the hands of she who loves it most," Violet said. "You could run things as you wish, I could spend my afternoons at the theatre instead of nagging you about dwindling stock levels—"

"Are you ever going to give this up?" Belle interrupted with affectionate annoyance. She was secretly touched by how keen Violet still was to sell her the shop, having begun the crusade years ago to hand over the reins of her pride and joy.

"Not until we sign the papers. Which we will," Violet said with a knowing nod, now examining the table of Autumn Reads and adjusting a book by millimetres to the exact angle.

"Which we won't," Belle corrected her. "I've told you a million times, there's no way I could run this place on my own." She passed the oak desk, tidying the greetings cards and small selection of seasonal bouquets that lined the till area as she went. They were loaded with miniature pumpkins and dusky bunny tails to mark the incoming start of October, a subtle *Floresco Bellus* incantation lacing the stems and keeping them remarkably fresh.

"Oh, how many times, Belle? You wouldn't be on your own." Violet audibly tutted this time. "You've got Jim and Monica here through the week and that new girl with the unfortunate nose ring at the weekends."

"You know what I mean. I'm talking about taking the reins. Generally not my speciality. I sort of just . . . float around?"

"I haven't done a damn useful thing around here since the

printing press was considered modern technology. Every good idea for years has been yours."

"But it's still your baby. I'm just here making sure books come in, books go out, customers are happy—that's about the long and the short of it."

"And what more is there to it? You and I both know that you practically run the place single-handedly. I'm too old for all of this now, I have better things to do than recommend thrillers to the un-washed masses."

"There's nothing wrong with thrillers. You're a snob, Vi. And you know what I'm like, I'd probably run it into the ground within a few months."

"Less of the self-deprecation, please. I can't stand it. You're a highly capable, knowledgeable woman who I trust implicitly. You've worked your magic here for longer than I care to remember"—at this, Belle choked on the air and spluttered out a coughing fit, earning a thump on the back from Violet—"mostly because it ages me dread-fully. You're just too scared to take a risk, and you care too much about what might go wrong." She pointed a sharp shining nail at Belle.

"You're very good at complimenting and insulting me all at once." Belle frowned, returning to her spot behind the till.

Violet leaned against the green marble countertop and pulled out a pocket mirror to move a single hair back into place. "It is a fine art." She smacked her lips together. "But if you continue to refuse to take up my brilliant offer, then you know I have no choice but to leave Christopher in charge of things. I don't trust outsiders for the job. If I'm to properly enjoy a retirement of luxury cruises and per-sonal shopping, then Lunar needs to be in capable hands. And Christopher *is* capable hands."

"Of course," Belle said placidly, taking a breath to swallow her pride. "The man might not know a paperback from a pumpkin, but he does know his profits and losses."

Belle hoped that the music she'd chosen that morning was enough to hide the not-so-muffled sounds coming from the back office, where Christopher was taking it in turns to either roar expletives or guffaw pretentiously down the phone to an associate. She winced as she spotted a distracted customer turn their head towards the noise.

Profits and losses were seemingly *all* that Christopher knew, leading to decisions that broke Belle's heart a fraction more every day. In the two years since Violet had decided to step down and, albeit reluctantly, hand over the reins to her corporate son, he had been gradually chipping away at the ideas that Belle herself had implemented at Lunar since she had started working there almost ten years ago. Their precious small baked goods and coffee cart had been the first to go, with Christopher declaring that cappuccinos "turned the place into a mothers' meeting." Her annual harvest book festival with other local businesses had him laughing so profoundly that he'd genuinely slapped his knee. More worryingly, just a few days ago, she had overheard him discussing at volume how the younger members of staff were hanging on to the payroll by a thread. This being the final straw, Belle had brought his questionable decisions to Violet's attention. But Christopher had quickly interjected, insisting that Belle was being dramatic, laughing it off, wrapping Violet around his finger as usual. Belle kept the reality of just how bad things had got to herself, like a cold hard pebble to carry around in her pocket.

"Somehow, I blinked and it's a modern world out there now, Belle," Violet said. "I sure as hell can't keep up with the times, but he will make sure this place does just that."

"This place isn't supposed to keep up with the times," Belle said. "It's supposed to exist in its own little bubble of cosiness that's entirely separate from the real world."

"If only," Violet said wistfully. "See you next week. I'll call you about those figures from August." She leaned across to offer Belle a kiss on the cheek, leaving her usual little smear of magenta lipstick behind, a brush of ever-so-slight whiskers and a waft of sugared perfume.

"See you, Vi," Belle said fondly, waving her off as she headed out to the shiny black car waiting to drive her home to her equally perfect townhouse. She was impossibly wealthy after a life spent on-stage as a theatre star of days gone by, before a vocal injury put a stop to things and recovery sent her to the healing world of books. Belle sunk her hands into the pockets of her denim apron embroidered with Lunar moons across the front, and her mind wandered back to its usual battlefield.

Taking Violet up on her offer, to actually buy Lunar Books from her, was a dream that always felt far too big. And every time that Violet broached the conversation and reminded her of the chance she was letting slip through her fingers like sand, she felt herself flinching away even farther.

There was so much that could go wrong. She was clueless as to what the process would even look like, and her meagre savings were too precious to throw at something that wasn't a guaranteed success, even though Violet had made her an overly generous, sentimental offer. Plus, there was the small matter of risking the job that she adored and had worked for, all the way up from Saturday girl to store manager.

Still, she dared to think about it all the time. Dared to imagine herself really doing it, rewarding herself with the bravery that had once been at the root of all her decisions. But she could never find quite enough courage to light the taper, to find out whether the explosion would be a controlled one or a wildfire. And so life had unfolded. The wheel stayed in hands that weren't her own, and she continued watching out the window as the road sped past.

A woman in a salmon pink cardigan reached the till, juggling an armful of picture books with a roll of rainbow wrapping paper and a toddler attached to her right hand.

"This is a lovely one, it might be my favourite," Belle told the little girl as she wrapped up the book on top of the pile in brown paper. "Did you choose this? You did so well." The girl nodded shyly, then promptly buried her face in her mum's skirt.

"Thanks for all of your help with finding the right ones. Should keep her busy for a while." The lady smiled gratefully.

"Of course." Belle rang up the total. "Sorry I couldn't stay with you longer. It's a bit crazy in here today. This weather makes everyone want to curl up with a book."

On perfect cue, a flash of bright lightning split through the bruised evening sky, cracking through the soft lighting that kept Lunar feeling warm and welcoming no matter the conditions outside. A loud thunderclap followed quickly behind, so intense that it rattled the top floor's stained-glass windows. The woman gathered up her shopping, stowed the books underneath her jumper and pulled up her child's hood before reluctantly heading out into the rain.

A BUSY EVENING unfolded. Life at Lunar, locally loved for its charm and indefinable specialness, swung chaotically from calm and quiet to unstoppably busy. Belle would often receive a call on her days off from a frantic Jim, tearing out what remained of his halo of fluffy hair while attempting to simultaneously refill shelves and man the till. Their tiny team had been struggling to keep up with Christopher's schedules, each day understaffed and overcommitted.

Ringing up another customer, she glanced over at the kids' section. As always, it had been completely ransacked, despite Belle setting up a neat little *Libri Liberi Ordino* incantation for the soft books and toys to return themselves to their boxes when nobody was looking. It was safe enough magic to pepper about the place amongst the other incantations she had strung around. Children didn't question it if the odd picture book tidied itself away and, of course, adults never noticed.

Closing time grew tantalisingly near. While Jim and Monica dealt with the debris of the day, Belle was run off her feet with a queue of shoppers that remained as relentless as the rain outside. In the back of her mind somewhere, she registered the sound of the brass bell above the front door ringing for the millionth time that day. She rubbed at her forearms as a layer of goose bumps swept over her skin with the gust of chilly air from the open door.

"Would you be interested in taking home this week's Stellar Read? It's a really . . ."

Belle felt her breath catch short. A feeling like a warm wave breaking over the crown of her head, strangely pleasant but forceful, slipped over her from top to toe and almost sent her reeling in the swell. She gripped the countertop for balance. If she didn't know better, she'd have said . . . Well, she'd have said it was magic.

"Are you okay?" A customer gave her a concerned look.

Belle swallowed hard, then flapped her hands dismissively. "Oh, fine, fine. Sorry. A bit dizzy. Means it's time for another coffee."

She laughed dryly and composed herself, ignoring the potent feeling that had appeared one moment and washed away the next. It had been a long day. Sliding the stack of sold books into a bag with a hasty, stressed smile that Violet would not have considered signature Lunar service, she called for the next customer.

The man waiting on the other side of the desk caught her off guard. She noticed his height first, tall to the point of feeling slightly looming. And he was—she couldn't help but also acknowledge—intimidatingly handsome. The kind of handsome that would have her reporting back to Ariadne when she got home and had her instantly wondering why she hadn't done something better with her hair that morning. He was wearing belted trousers, a rust-coloured shirt tucked in over a white T-shirt and round wire glasses, which he removed when their eyes met. He popped them into the inside pocket of a long black leather coat that hung across extremely broad shoulders, and a curl of shaggy, shoulder-length dark hair fell into his eyes as he looked down. A silver thumb ring glinted with an amber stone as he pushed it back, placed a hand down on the counter-top and leaned ever so slightly towards her. She forced herself to break eye contact almost instantly, unable to hold it as her face flushed hot.

"I'm wondering if you can help me." He spoke with a deep honey voice, like burnt caramel, and a twang of a London accent. "I'm looking for something rather specific. A little special."

Belle blushed so fiercely that the tops of her ears prickled with heat. A strange, barbed sensation travelled to the ends of her fingers as she rested them on the counter, then in her pockets, before finally settling on grabbing a pen, sending ink splashing across the counter.

"Sorry, sorry." She hastily mopped it up with the end of her sleeve. "Sounds interesting. How special are we talking, exactly? Is it a gift?"

The sides of his mouth perked up almost imperceptibly. "It *is* a gift."

Belle quickly gathered her remaining composure, distinctly embarrassed by her own embarrassment.

"Great. That sounds great. You could take a look at our Special Editions section, there's some signed copies which might go down well for a present. Or we have some great popular titles on the Stellar Reads table if you're looking for a more recent—"

"*Malleus Maleficarum.*"

Belle's face blanched from flushed red to stark white in a moment. She must have misheard. "Sorry, it's been a long day, I think I'm going mad. Which is good." She laughed politely, shaking her head clear. "Pardon?"

"*Malleus Maleficarum.* Not saying I agree with the message, of course," he mused. "That magic is evil or wrong. But tracking down witches is an interesting concept, don't you think?"

Belle's vision flickered. *Malleus Maleficarum*, the most notorious text from history on the origins of witchcraft, the infamous witch-hunter's guide on how to spot a witch.

A coincidence. It had to be a coincidence. But then she felt it, as though a switch had activated something intuitive inside her. She forced herself to make eye contact with the man again, and it was instantaneous. Her skin turned to pure static. A coppery taste flooded her tongue. He leaned his forearms on the countertop, interlacing his fingers, and a scent of woody bonfire smoke and spiced sweetness hit her. Belle noticed the muscles of his jaw lock a fraction of an inch, the smallest flash of a knowing smile. Realisation hit with the weight of a wrecking ball.

A witch.

Jim dropped an enormous cardboard box of hardbacks behind the front till with a loud thud, and Belle snapped back to reality.

"Don't mind me," Jim chimed, sauntering back towards the cookery corner while he whistled at an unbearably high pitch.

"Interesting choice." She let out a painfully awkward laugh, tucked her hair behind her ears, then inexplicably fired finger guns at the man opposite. Panic had now evidently taken control of all of her limbs. "Not something we stock, I'm afraid. Such a shame. Sorry. Thanks for popping in."

"That *is* such a shame," the man echoed.

It was only then that she registered his tongue poking firmly into his cheek, a deep dimple etched into the other side. His eyebrows raised knowingly, as though waiting for the penny to drop. He beckoned her to match his lean across the counter, bringing his voice to a whisper just inches from her neck.

"I tried the Hecate House library, but it would seem their editions are all on loan. They said to enquire with a Belladonna Blackthorn. That she'd happily oblige and lend me her copy?"

No one ever called her Belladonna. She hated her full witch name with a passion and always had. So much so that not even her mum used it anymore; it was reserved only for when she was distinctly disapproving of something or other about Belle's major life choices.

The world spun in slow motion, but Belle somehow managed to paint on something like a professional smile. Her first and only thought was simply to remove this man from public view. She had spent a lifetime protecting herself from this exact scenario, from the moment her magic would be revealed to a non-wicche world after everything she'd ever done to keep it a secret.

Monica shot a quizzical look across the floor in Belle's direction, silently asking if everything was okay as the queue began to grow behind the man.

"Actually, of course." Finger guns again. "Silly me, it's through here, in the back . . . Right this way. If you'll just follow . . ." She gave the man a desperate look, spun on the spot and said a silent plea to any forces who might be watching in pity. Anything to hide whatever this conversation was about to be.

Signalling to Monica to take her place, Belle shot to the rear of the shop towards the dimly lit stock cupboard piled precariously with boxes and cut-out characters from window displays. She frantically manoeuvred a large cardboard dragon aside and beckoned wildly for the man to follow her away from the customers. Mainly from the handful of women who had been surreptitiously lingering around him, watching his every move since he entered Lunar Books like he was the last slice of cake. The man followed her diligently but with an unmistakably mischievous smirk as he strolled nonchalantly behind, hands clasped behind his back.

She tugged on the cord light in the cupboard, kicked a heavy box out of the way and, after a distraught glance at the shop floor to ensure that Christopher was nowhere to be seen, yanked the door behind them. Fortunately, she was too consumed by dread to bother feeling embarrassed anymore as she stood eye to eye with a complete stranger in extremely close, warm proximity.

"Cosy." A glint flashed across his dark eyes.

"Who are you? What is this?" Belle asked in a furious, hushed voice. She had already begun to make assumptions. It occurred to her that his arrival could only signify a limited selection of bad news. "Is it my mum?"

"What? No, of course not. Nothing like that," he replied instantly.

Belle felt a rod of tension across her shoulders bend.

"I've been sent by the coven," he went on, looking down at her with a heavy brow. Having always been fairly tall herself, it was rare that she felt like the short one in the room.

"I gathered that much from your hilarious introduction," she snapped, stress still bubbling to boiling point.

"I wasn't really going for hilarious. More mysterious, maybe alluring." Evidently finding the whole thing very amusing, the man crossed his arms and leaned back against a shelf of Ordnance Survey maps.

"But Selcouth has never sent anyone to me before. Or communicated with me at all in almost fifteen years of witchery, for that matter. Did I do something wrong? Am I in trouble?"

"Trouble? You tell me." He smirked, apparently finding far too much enjoyment in her teetering on the verge of a breakdown.

Belle gave him a distinctly unimpressed look, then risked a glance around the door to check for wandering bosses. "If you hadn't noticed, I am working," Belle said, her voice getting gradually more high-pitched. "And if my boss finds me in here with a customer, I might as well just say goodbye to my life now. I haven't got time for whatever it is that you're meddling in."

His face dropped, and he rolled his eyes at her refusal to play along.

"Well, you're no fun. And I do *not* 'meddle.' Do I look like a meddler to you?" he said hotly. "Look, you've been ignoring our correspondence." His voice softened a fraction, a little more serious. "You know you can't do that—"

"Correspondence?" Belle interrupted.

The man's eyebrow cocked sharply. "Right. The birthday letter? On the rare occasion that the coven does deign to contact you before completion of your endarkenment, it's up to you to confront it. You can't run away from magical problems, even if—"

"Sorry, sorry." She held up a hand to stop him, brushing against his coat in the small space. "If it wasn't clear already from the way that I'm about to spontaneously combust at any moment, I have absolutely no idea what you are talking about."

"The letter," he repeated impatiently. "Frankly, you should be a little more grateful. It was either coming here to check up on you or raining down a batch of hell-fire to catch your attention. Your record stated that you live with a non-wicche housemate, so it seemed like hell-fire might have given your game away somewhat. First you ignore me, now this."

"I wasn't ignoring anything," she said exasperatedly, starting to find his demeanour particularly grating combined with the lack of answers. "What are you talking about?"

His face shifted, one eyebrow raising again in doubt. "You haven't received it?"

Belle blinked.

"Black envelope? Gilded edges? Sentient presence spell? Ability to manoeuvre itself in front of your attention when ignored . . ." he reeled off.

"Not ringing any bells. Maybe your spell doesn't work."

"What?"

"I'm just saying." She shrugged. "Nothing's *manoeuvred* its way to me."

He looked incredulous, blinking. "It's a traditional *Vocare Attentio* spell, specifically crafted for coven correspondence. Used since medieval times. Of course it works."

"Sorry to break it to you, but your spell must be dodgy. I haven't seen anything."

The man thumbed his sharp, square jawline, now matching her exasperation. "Oh, that's right, it *must* be the fault of an ancient and nigh on foolproof spell cast by the United Kingdom's esteemed coven. There's simply no way that a witch as neat and organised as yourself could possibly have misplaced any important magical correspondence. Looks like you've a well-kept hold on things around here. Running a real tight ship."

He gestured with a sceptical nod to the heaps of books arranged across every inch of shelving in the small chaotic cupboard, all further blanketed with scattered receipts, literary magazines, trade newsletters, bookmarks and shopping bags.

"You know," she replied, throwing her hands onto her hips, "you're very rude for someone who's apparently representing the 'esteemed coven of the United Kingdom' on a rare, honoured visit. And an uninvited one, might I add."

"Selcouth doesn't wait for an invitation."

"I'm trying very, very hard not to have a meltdown here. You could be a little more understanding."

They both stared, silently daring the other to back down.

"Apologies," the man finally said through gritted teeth, relenting.

Belle eased off a fraction to match. "This letter, then, if there is one. What do I need to know?"

"No can do." He shrugged. "You have to read it for yourself. That way there can be no denial of knowledge. Too many witches, warlocks and wicchefolk feigning no prior awareness to the trial over the years. I'm sure you understand," he added formally, twiddling the silver ring on his thumb while he eyed her.

"Trial?"

His eyes widened for a just a moment, but his unbothered demeanour returned in a second. "Pretend I didn't say that."

Belle took a steadying breath, attempting to retain a single inch of reason. She crossed her arms, mirroring his pose.

"Let me check I've got this straight. You come here, to my place of work and my life amongst non-wicche folk, potentially putting me and my whole existence in danger of exposure, to tell me that I specifically need to find a very important letter. I tell you that I have not received it, and rather than giving me another letter or just telling me what that letter actually says, you're going to leave and tell me, again, to read the letter."

If Belle hadn't known better, she could have sworn the faintest pale flush bloomed across the tops of his cheekbones. His cool faltered the tiniest fraction again, a frustrated furrow appearing between his eyebrows.

"You're making this seem a lot more foolish than it felt on my way from Hecate House."

"Oh, not at all, it's been a treat. Your journey is much appreciated. Mystery, allure, lack of hell-fire noted, etcetera. Now, as thoroughly enchanting as this meeting has been, can you please leave before anyone notices that for some entirely insane reason, I am suspiciously bickering with a customer in the stock-room?"

He smirked, as though trying to stop himself from giving away a real smile. Belle noticed the fine lines crinkle at the edges of his dark eyes.

"But I'm having such a lovely time. And I worked so hard to set the mood."

Realisation dawned. "Wait, was this storm your doing, too?"

He sunk his hands into his pockets, seeming a little self-conscious. "Might have been. Don't you like it?"

"I forgot my brolly, and I have to walk home once my shift is finished, so no." She grabbed the door handle, keen to get herself out of the confined space and away from this man's irritating arrogance. "Will that be all?"

He sighed, equally unimpressed. "Not that this visit hasn't been incredibly welcoming thus far, but on second thoughts . . ." He snapped the thumb and middle finger of his right hand. In a fraction of a moment, a black envelope was summoned neatly between the two with a dusting of golden sparks. "So I don't end up making a second trip, more than anything." He offered the paper to her. "Read it. Don't ignore it this time."

"I told you, I wasn't ignoring anything." Belle pinched the letter from his grasp. "Thanks," she added curtly, turning the paper over in her hand. "Will there be anything else?"

"Yes, actually. Any beach read recommendations? Something light, something fun, a little spice?" he asked, a wide grin escaping which almost split his face in two, entirely giving the game away for just how much he was relishing stealing her time.

Belle glared at him. Reluctantly, she stuffed the letter into the pocket of her apron for when there wasn't a five-person-deep queue requiring her immediate attention. How bad could a letter be? If it was urgent, they'd call. Did covens call?

She pointed a finger at him. "Do not go past the office. If Christopher sees a customer coming out of the stock-room, I'll never hear the end of it. Follow me. But not yet. In a minute."

Her instructions seemed to amuse him greatly, and he gave her a small salute. Without glancing back at him, Belle flung open the stock cupboard door, dusting down her apron and speed-walking back towards the till. The man hung back for just a moment, intently watching her leave before eventually heading out behind her, ducking his head to avoid the door-frame.

A short while later, and with the queue under control, Belle returned to the back of the shop with her arms full of books. Shocked, she stopped. There he was, still lingering between the shadows of the classics and contemporary shelves, all long limbs and unkempt hair. He shot a covert glance in her direction and quickly looked back to the book in his hands when their eyes caught, as though he'd been found up to no good.

Belle's hands went to her hips. "You're still here?"

"Can't a man enjoy a browse anymore? I came all this way and you're not going to let me take advantage of the offers?"

"By all means, browse away. In fact . . ." She gestured for him to hold that thought while she dove into an adjacent corner. She returned to find him looking intrigued. "A personal recommendation. This would be perfect for your next read," she said with a sickly sweet smile, thrusting her suggestion against his chest. She caught a flicker at the side of his mouth, as though pleased with himself for winning her over.

125 Magic Tricks for Young Magicians: With Free Gifts to Astound Your Friends!

"There might even be something in there to improve your little envelope spell." Their eye contact burned: his a strange combination of fury yet faint amusement, hers entirely indignant. Belle held it this time, adamant not to buckle under his stare again.

"Please do not come back here again," she said. "Or at least warn me next time so I can leave the country first."

"Excuse me, do you work here?"

Belle transformed her expression back to genuinely friendly in a fraction of a second, turning to a bespectacled lady who was approaching her with a stack of brightly coloured romance covers.

"Sure do. Are you okay there? Let's get those in a basket for you."

As she steered the woman towards the till while reeling off a list of author names, Belle couldn't help but notice a flutter of movement from the corner of her eye. Only a string of faint golden sparks remained, trailed between the shelves, and that crackling scent of bonfire smoke that ignited her senses again. In the chaos of his arrival, she'd forgotten to even get his name. Probably something as ridiculous as he was. Gandalf maybe? Fortunately, she highly doubted that he would make a habit of visiting Lunar Books.

2
A Witch's Home

MAGIC IN THE mundane can be difficult to find, but it is always waiting patiently somewhere, snuffling quietly, curled up like a sleeping animal and ready to be found by those searching hard enough. Flat 31 was one such enchanted place. Small and shadowed, with wonky cupboard fronts that didn't quite fit properly and a temperamental back right hob ring that had needed fixing for months, the kitchen inside was nevertheless filled with magic. Every inch of it was covered with the stuff, from the heap of used teabags on the drainer to the mixing bowl in the corner. Even the butter dish was charged with magic, because this was the home of a witch. Albeit a humble one.

"... talking about losing that magic in a relationship, you know? That real, enchanting kind of magic between the two of you that can only be considered witchcraft. For many couples it—"

The radio clicked over again.

"Goal! That magic left foot of his once again, some kind of sorcery from the boy in—"

"You've got to be joking."

"Good morning, Jane. Yes, Londoners will no doubt be disap-

pointed to hear that the unseasonably warm spell is officially over for us. That dry, sunny, altogether rather lovely late summer spell—"

"Oh, for . . ."

The button was pressing of its own accord to anyone who happened to be watching. Finally settling on a station, music quietly hummed alongside bubbly splashes coming from a sponge working diligently against last night's plates, which positioned themselves neatly on the drainer. Across the worktop, a stack of post shuffled itself into tidy piles. One was for brown envelopes demanding money, another for shiny flyers from pizza places and window cleaners. The most important pile was across the room, a rainbow of brightly coloured envelopes, which had been busy lining themselves up on the coffee table for several days. As an orange one addressed to Belle Blackthorn landed on top, ready for her birthday tomorrow, the kettle boiled itself with a soft babble.

"I swear I literally just paid this," Belle muttered, ripping open a particularly uninviting-looking water bill and immediately casting it aside on top of the microwave to deal with another day. Only the most astute of eyes would have noticed the neat flick of her finger that guided a teabag from jar to mug.

"Considering one member of our trio uses their own spit and tongue to wash, we don't half get through a lot of water." Belle spoke to the cat at her feet, who was weaving her way in and out of her ankles with a purr. "All right, Jinx, all right. Greedy guts."

The cat was distracted from her quest for food by a rogue spark of magic that flittered by, weightless in mid-air like the translucent wings of a moth. She frantically batted at it with her paw.

"I really need to hoover. That stuff gets everywhere."

A handful of reliable household charms aside, Belle was a dab hand at keeping her unique abilities largely to herself. It wasn't that she was ashamed to be a witch. After possessing her powers for very nearly fifteen years to the day, her home was packed with telltale signs of the truth. They were quietly proud but subtle enough to not invite unwelcome questions or complicated answers. Crystals were positioned for charging in all the right sun spots (although there weren't a lot of those, because she would have been paying double the rent for a south-facing terrace). Her bookshelf was lined with a few almanacs and rune guides passed down from her mother, now wedged inconspicuously between childhood favourites and splattered cookbooks. Bottles of moonwater, peacefully powerful. Coloured candles for all requirements. Dream and shadow work journals. All small signs of a quiet witch, like whispers woven here and there, but the secret largely kept itself these days. Nobody ever noticed the magic, dusted through all corners of her life like dewdrops caught in cobwebs, because nobody was ever looking for it.

Magic for Belle was a comforting constant, which felt like home on the occasions that she did call upon it. It was just that, when working long hours through the week and living in a small maisonette above a café, the faint smell of espresso lingering from dawn until dusk against the clockwork sirens of London traffic, she found there wasn't a whole lot of use for practical magic.

Belle's powers were not completely dormant; they were just a little sleepy. Running a small and somewhat chaotic bookshop hardly required creative hexes or mystical menageries to be whipped up on request. She did now throw together the weekly horoscopes for the Lunar newsletter after the team discovered her knack for surprisingly accurate predictions, but even that only required a quick side glance into a miniature crystal ball that she'd deftly disguised as a paperweight. She certainly wasn't bothering the natural order or creating too much divine chaos when she miraculously managed to fix the broken photocopier or match a customer to their perfect historical fiction with a quick *Lectio Adaperio* incantation. In fact, the most sparks that ever flicked from Belle's forefinger probably came when the end of the tax year rolled around. It was complicated, time-consuming magic, squaring it all with *Pecunia Tributum*, but it saved her from wading through the chaotic records she failed to keep on top of at Lunar and was therefore worth the effort. Cheaper than an accountant, too.

Belle gave Jinx a scritch behind her inquisitive ears and received a quiet meow in return.

Even as a fifteen-year-old sorceress with fresh powers at her fingertips, those powers hadn't had a chance to display themselves with too much exciting fanfare, given the setting of a sleepy northern town and an all-girls school. A new haircut here, a vanished spot there, some particularly great cakes with colour-changing icing for friends' birthdays. An underrated highlight had been using her powers to implode a tape recorder to avoid the beep test during a PE lesson.

Then, magic had been actively difficult and painfully awkward to handle. Belle had always been a force of calm, physically recoiling at the thought of causing a fuss or drawing attention. And if you're trying to avoid the spotlight, it's a bad idea to get bold with your magic around teenage girls, who are finely tuned into spotting that sort of weirdness in a heartbeat. The whole witch thing had been largely mortifying, often showing itself of its own accord before she had mastered keeping her magic in check. Eventually, she had learned to control it. Even embrace it.

But the chance for her magic to prosper and shine had continued to dwindle ever since. Once, the purposeful dimming of her powers had been through shame of being different. Now, at one day before thirty years old, it was instead a case of magic slipping into the shadows, barely noticed, forgotten and neglected over time.

Belle flung herself down onto the green sofa covered with layers of blankets and a small fort of cushions that she shared with two flatmates: one human (allegedly) and one tortoiseshell feline. The latter leapt with a chirp onto her chest and settled with contentment on her shoulder.

It wasn't that she was too dull or boring or unadventurous for magic. She had her fair share of adventures and travels under her belt; she had largely done what a girl in her twenties was supposed to have done, as far as she could tell. But as life had begun to unfurl like two silk ribbons, one in front and one behind her, Belle had learned that following the non-magical ebb and flow without too much resistance tended to make things easier. While trying to tread through life successfully, she fought to keep magic subdued: ticking boxes, making everybody happy, never causing a fuss.

And realistically, what does one even do with magical powers, anyway?

Lying flat with the cat balanced under her chin like a warm, only slightly suffocating beard, Belle flicked out her left index finger in the smallest of gestures and aimed it over her head at the kettle, which swiftly poured itself into a kitschy cauldron-shaped mug. Her finger absent-mindedly wound three clockwise circles in the air, and a teaspoon echoed her movement. Infusing her intentions was one of the old habits that she'd picked up from her mum. Stir clockwise to bring positivity, anticlockwise to banish negativity.

The mug floated gently from the kitchen to park itself on a coaster. As it approached through the air, steam billowing from the rim, the bedroom door across the living room flew open, and Belle leapt up to slam her hand down onto the mug. She winced as droplets of scalding tea splashed over the sides.

"Right, I'm going, I'm going. Don't talk to me, I'm late."

Ariadne, wrapped in a thickly padded coat and a giant scarf that could have doubled up as a duvet, hurtled out of her bedroom, always a matter of minutes from mattress to door.

"And I mean it. Don't you dare eat that last croissant. It's got my name on it, and the thought of it is giving me one vague ray of hope to cling to through my meetings of death."

Belle's heart thumped from the adrenaline rush. Luckily, Ari continued to spin like a whirling dervish from key hook to shoe rack, entirely oblivious to Belle's flash of panic.

"That croissant is all that's good in my miserable, hideous life right now."

"You're being ridiculous," Belle called.

"I will murder you in your sleep."

"All right. Staying away from the pastry. I hear you."

Ari's constant faffing at any given time was a contributing factor to Belle's witchery having remained secret for so long. Her hair was wet and hastily braided, leaving damp shadows on her coat as she grabbed the coffee cup waiting on the side, filled earlier by Belle as part of their finely tuned daily routine.

"You better. Late meetings this afternoon, but I'll be home for tea. Love you, love you, bye bye bye bye . . ." Ari's voice trailed out into the corridor as she slammed the front door behind her.

Belle audibly exhaled as she collapsed back on the cushions. One day, her blood pressure would learn to handle the rush of disguising magic at the last possible second. Blowing on the remaining contents of her mug that wasn't now splashed across the carpet or her pyjamas, she slotted the stack of birthday cards up against a vase. Glancing at the clock, she grimaced. She should probably get a move on, too.

Escaping her attention in the morning's rush was one unassuming matte black envelope which, in her hurry, caught on the door's breeze and flew from the table. It had escaped from her apron pocket when she shut up shop the night before, cleverly gliding inside the paperback at the bottom of her handbag. Arriving at Flat 31, the envelope had shrewdly manoeuvred itself onto a folded blanket on the bed but remained unnoticed when a cat parked her furry stomach directly on top of it for the evening. It really had tried its level best that morning, determined to follow her back to work in her coat pocket, but acted a fraction too slowly and slipped from sight again. Sent sailing under the sofa, it bore a silver star illustration, entwined with three words.

Tonitru, Fulgur, Pluvia. Thunder, Lightning, Rain.

＊·＊·＊·＊

LATER THAT DAY, Belle pushed her thumb into her forehead in an attempt to stimulate the wilting brain on the other side of her skull. The three-o'clock haze was kicking in, the pixels of the computer screen blurring in front of her eyes as she catalogued copies of a shiny celebrity autobiography in the stock cupboard. The need to procrastinate was seizing control. Sentences were crashing into the ends of each other, hanging precariously off the end of her computer screen. Caffeine would probably help. Or chocolate.

She kicked back on the wheels of her chair and spun to glance out of the stock-room and onto the shop floor, hoping to spot an unsuspecting colleague who might volunteer a snack run.

Her line of sight was invaded by an enormous autumn wreath. An army of vibrant reds, oranges and golds marched towards her periphery, Monica's tiny height and chestnut hair struggling somewhere behind it. Belle maintained that her colleague was the coolest person she'd ever met, covered head to toe in a patchwork of colourful tattoos, as well as a constant rainbow of paint swatches all over her clothes and fingers, residuals from her art coursework. She was something of a mythical creature to Lunar's youngest customers, who always left gleefully covered in the never-ending supply of stickers that were drawn from the pocket of Monica's apron.

"Where do we want this, Belle?" Monica asked, holding the wreath at arm's length. "It smells a bit weird."

"It probably just needs airing out," Belle said uncertainly. "It's for the front door, there should be a hook in the big box, too. Actually, make sure there's no mice in—"

"Belle Blackthorn. How's my favourite wonder woman?"

Monica's face, poking through the hole in the foliage, plummeted as she clocked the man to whom the roaring voice belonged. Suddenly overtaken by the urgent need to decorate as quickly as possible, she shrugged apologetically as she made a swift exit. Belle shot her a scowl that she hoped effectively communicated the meaning of *ruthless traitor*. Training her face to the picture of professionalism, she leapt up.

"What can I do for you, Christopher?"

Without bothering to get any closer or even to glance up from the pager in his hand, her boss shouted across the bookshelves. As always, he was oblivious to the many heads nearby that had turned in frustration at his lack of volume control against the peaceful hum of the shop. His corporate presence in Lunar always felt wrong, unnatural and jarring, like the full-body jolt that shakes a sleeper from a dream. Belle bolted through the shop to meet him in an attempt to lower his volume, knocking over a stack of magazines in her haste, with apologetic half-smiles to the customers.

"Mind jumping onto this call with the bank for me, darlin'? Got held up at the gym this morning, so haven't had a chance to read the files that Mum dug out. Waste of my time anyway, to be honest. Not showed up today, has she? Wish we could all be bloody part-timers," he guffawed.

Belle felt the anchor of her stomach plummet.

"You're all right to step in, yeah? It's the big one, they're not happy," he continued loudly.

"Well, no. I mean, yes. I can. But I'm just in the middle of a stock check, and we've got the author signing this evening, so there's a lot to—"

"Brilliant, thanks, sweetness. They're expecting you. I'll be back later." Having landed the reply he always knew that he'd hear, Christopher had already started to retreat to the personal office that he'd somehow wangled on his arrival, sacrificing their old staff room for his own private space. At no point had he looked up at her from his pager during their conversation.

Belle's eyebrows almost reached her hairline. "You're leaving? Have you got any notes? What's it about?"

She mentally ran through her immediate to-do list. Working her usual shift, obviously, but the children's entertainer wanted to discuss the Halloween party, too. Although she couldn't think about that until she'd finished the personal reading recommendations with customers that were booked in for the afternoon. Jim's performance review was pencilled in for sometime around five o'clock, and that had already been pushed back last week. Then there was double-checking those numbers that Violet had requested and a visit booked in with a potential new supplier for the stationery corner. Belle had wanted to give some time to an idea she'd had for evening craft classes, too.

Christopher obnoxiously batted his hand to dismiss her, his shirt straining across his chest. "You'll be fine, kiddo, you always are. Something about predictions, might be a few investors listening in, the big family names that Mum won't want to disappoint. Just run them through the outlook for the quarter. Fire any feedback over to me to handle, but if you could let them know about the drop in profit across the board. They won't like that one. It is what it is, yeah?" Still looking down at his pager, he shot her a dismissive thumbs-up over his head while walking away.

"Yep."

"Oh, and do something about all that orange crap in the window, yeah? It looks like a jumble sale. What were you lot thinking? Get the financial stuff on display, business autobiographies, entrepreneur guides and that. A bit of aspiration for the blokes who need it."

"Really? Your mum gave it the thumbs-up," Belle said quietly, trying to swallow the bitterness in her voice. She had spent days putting the suitably spooky window display of Halloween horror reads together, inking the lettering on the glass and hanging the paper decorations. She had forced Ari to carve several large pumpkins with her, making the entire flat stink of gourds in the process. They'd carried them all the way to the shop in a collection of bulging bags to sit them amongst the scariest reads she could think of on a bed of dried grasses, along with a scattering of plastic black cats, bats, rats and a handful of witch hats for good measure. It looked particularly perfect when the sun went down, the windows giving out a warm glow against the chilly evenings.

Christopher snorted. "The woman's lost it, so that sounds about right. This place is a joke. I keep telling her she's wasting money on all this novelty nonsense. I want it gone by the time I'm next here, no arguments."

Once he was out of earshot, Belle retreated to a quiet corner of the shop and promptly booted the display board to her right with feeling, making a woman reading just behind jump a foot from her armchair. Belle apologised hastily, then knelt down to pretend to tie her lace as she fixed the damage with a disguised flurry of *Turbamentum Reversio* sparks. She crouched against the nearest shelf, picked up the last of the scattered drawings and papers and dug the heels of her hands into her eyes.

Monica sidled over and leaned above her, offering out a steaming mug as some kind of consolation prize. Herbal teas were her cure for all and were always accompanied by the biscuit tin, too. "He's an arse. Sorry for abandoning you."

"You're a turncoat, but I won't hold it against you." Belle accepted the mug gratefully. "Once again, we step up to do every part of that man's job for him, and somehow he still manages to ruin everything."

"No, *you* step up to do it for him. We step in to help when you look like you're about to go insane or land yourself in prison."

"Don't worry, it's not like he's on all of our salaries combined while hoodwinking his lovely mum, out of office three times a week, mocking the bestsellers, mistaking the authors for the postman, all while taking credit for anything we've ever created and simultaneously turning this wonderful place into some kind of corporate wasteland. Oh, no, wait, we are in fact in hell. And it's all my fault."

"Maybe. But look on the bright side," Monica chimed. "At least he's moved on from talking to us directly from the neck down. Now he stares at the pager instead, which is a huge improvement in my mind."

Belle scowled.

"Just think. We could have been existing in a Christopher-free world with you at the helm if you'd accepted Vi's offer. We might even have Mrs. Abbott's cupcakes back on the coffee cart again," Monica said, chancing a lack of tact as she glanced gingerly at Belle.

"Thank you for that."

"I know you had your reasons." She sighed. "Although you know we think they're completely wrong ones."

"Well, if it's any consolation, I can confirm it feels categorically awful to turn down your dream."

"I still don't really understand why you did," Monica said.

"Because I'm not ready. I couldn't do it. There's a lot that could go wrong, more than could go right. And I don't deserve it, anyway." They drained their mugs in unison. "Although, having said that, I'm not sure I deserve a man coming in and turning my favourite place in the world into what's starting to feel like an after-work bar in the financial district, either."

"At least then we'd be drunk," Monica offered. "Still, promise me you won't leave. No one else here is weird enough for me to eat my lunch with."

"Thanks?" Belle snorted, then pinched the skin at the bridge of her nose. "Well, I need to do something. He walks all over me, takes the credit for the fact we're somehow still afloat despite all of his awful decisions. And there's literally nothing I can do about it. It's my own fault. Every time I so much as mention it to Vi, she just rolls her eyes and says that he's a businessman."

"What does that even mean?"

"I think it means he wears a suit. How do we stand up to a man who allegedly 'knows business,' when we're just the silly little guys actually selling the books?"

"We attack at dawn? Or at the morning meeting, anyway," Monica suggested, tilting back against the wall above Belle, who was still slumped on the floor in defeat. "Or, I guess, we leave before we watch the whole place burn."

"I won't leave, don't worry," Belle said, then hesitated. "Maybe I will leave. I should leave. Should I leave?" She searched her friend's face for an answer, then sighed heavily. "I can't abandon Lunar." She offered her hands to Monica, who tugged her to her feet.

"Life really loves to chew you up, doesn't it?"

Belle nodded. "And then rather than spitting you out and giving you any kind of escape, it slowly digests you until you're a rotted, relenting piece of your former self. Just covered in enzymes. And Christopher's effusive sweat."

Monica shuddered. "So much sweat."

3

The Unexpected Invitation

ARIADNE PULLED AT her slice of pizza, wrapping the strings of melted cheese around a finger while they entirely ignored the Halloween film that they'd spent a considerable amount of time selecting.

"So leave." She was always so matter of fact, so logical, that it came across as harsh if you weren't familiar with Ariadne's heart of gold. "I keep telling you. You could get another job so easily."

"How about vampire's wife? Tiny frog in a forest dwelling? Seductive keeper of the underworld in a ghostly wedding dress?"

"All of the above." Ariadne nodded. "Anywhere would be lucky to have you."

"Why should I leave, though? I love Lunar. It's special. I just don't like being taken advantage of over and over by a man who is a walking midlife crisis, has no talent that I've ever witnessed other than an impressive skill for ruining joy and yet earns double what I do while accepting all the credit for . . ." Belle chewed and swallowed. "Wow, I should leave."

"Thank you. Now we just need to find you something that's worthy of your time and general excellence."

Rewitched 33

"You think I'm much more excellent than I actually am," Belle said, dipping a crust.

"Well, of course I do. I'm your best friend. I believe you are a perfectly excellent idiot."

"And I you."

Excellence had once been something that both the girls considered a given. Growing up with slightly terrifying determination, they had both been certain that the curse of ordinary would simply never happen to them. It wasn't meant to be that way. But time changed things and brought a dose of reality with it.

On paper, Ariadne had ticked the boxes of "successful" a little more effectively. People took her seriously, working in an office with floor-to-ceiling windows and swanky free lunches from which she regularly snuck extras home for tea. Healing from a long-term relationship that had simply faded through no one's fault, she was even testing the ghastly waters of online dating for the first time in over a decade, unexpectedly embracing it, finding all new facets of herself. Belle was constantly in awe of the way her friend grabbed plot twists by the lapels and always found the excitement in them.

"You've been talking for so long about buying the shop from Violet, I don't understand why you won't just go for it. It's what you've always wanted. And she must be getting on for—what?—197 years old now. She'd be grateful for it," Ari said, picking off a piece of pineapple.

"She does keep telling me that I made a big mistake, to just say the word," Belle admitted.

"There you go."

"I know, I know. It's just terrifying. If I'm in charge and blow it and the shop goes under, I lose everything. I've plugged so many years into getting to this point. Imagine if the dream job isn't the dream, that I picked the wrong thing. So much could go wrong," Belle said, ripping pizza from crust. "It's not the right time."

"It's never the right time. Ever. If you're waiting for all of the stars and planets to align before you make decisions that'll make you happier, you'll be waiting forever."

Belle sighed. "I'm so behind already. We're supposed to be leading empires and bringing down the patriarchy by now. It was on the calendar for last week."

"I told you, I had that epiphany. We're past the point of having to think we can take over the world. We can just exist happily if we want to. As long as it pays the bills. And you would be happy, which is really all that matters. You could be spending your days recommending fiction to old people in your own bookshop, reading stories to sticky-fingered kids, stressing over barely making ends meet but loving the quiet day to day. That's the dream right there, Belle."

Belle gave a thoughtful "Hmm." What would happen if she really did allow herself to seize it with both hands? She always felt embarrassed when she was confronted by her own cowardice like this, but the fact was that it was less disappointing and much less painful to refuse to give your heart and soul to any one thing for fear of an imperfect result.

"It's just about breaking the spell," Ariadne added. Belle sniffed under her breath at the irony. "Ow! What the . . . ? Oh look, you dropped a birthday card." Ariadne yanked a slightly crumpled black envelope from between the sofa cushions, where it had surreptitiously tapped a sharp corner of itself against the back of her arm to interrupt. "If that has cash in it, then it's now rightfully mine." She closed the pizza box and placed it on the patterned rug.

Maybe it wasn't a totally failing spell. Thankfully, only Belle noticed in that moment how the handwriting shone with a distinctly magical glint: *Tonitru, Fulgur, Pluvia.*

* * ✴ * *

SEPTEMBER NIGHTS HAD been drizzly and dark in London, the storm from yesterday leaving petrichor stuck to the streets and the sky, but tonight was exceptionally still. Everything outside seemed to be waiting with a held breath. The moon sat silver like a milk top.

Ariadne slunk off to bed once the movie had finished, taking the final piece of pizza for luck. Belle knew that touching wood, salt over the shoulder, rabbit feet and wishing on eyelashes were all well and good, but the best results she'd had with luck-related magic always came from their own bizarre, superstitious inventions. The final piece of pizza had long ago become a talisman between the two of them.

Since her mystery visitor at Lunar yesterday, Belle had been doing her level best to pretend that the whole encounter had never happened. With the chaos of the day, it had been easy to ignore. But once Ari uncovered the letter, Belle spent the rest of the evening sitting on her hands, attempting to focus on the television, her gaze practically boring a hole through the paper. Who on earth (boldly assuming they were even of this plane) had been in touch from Selcouth, and why? She had no magical contacts, no colleagues or friends or wizened old mentors to speak of.

Only when Ari was fast asleep and snoring at rhythm through her door did Belle allow herself to finally reach for the envelope. She curled her feet up underneath her and adjusted Jinx on her lap, pulling the blanket closer as a chill wove itself through the notches of her spine. The silver star on the stamp felt distantly familiar, lingering in the back of her mind like a dream.

Maybe Selcouth was sending birthday cards now, although that would make mystery man's insistence on delivery a little overblown. This one *was* a milestone birthday, or so everyone kept reminding her with dramatic knowing looks. Belle blew her hair out of her eyes and lifted the deep purple seal. A stack of pale papers tumbled into her lap from an intricate fold, and as her eyes scanned the letter, each word lit with a warm glow perfectly in

time with her reading. Magical texts tended to do that, words illuminating like fireflies trapped in amber when met by the eyes of a
witch.

Ms. Belladonna Blackthorn,

*An abundance of the happiest returns on your thirtieth
Orbital Completion.*

"Happy Birthday . . . probably would have been fine," she muttered before reading on.

> *In accordance with the ancient and binding rules of
> Selcouth, which claims you by birthright, it is with much
> pleasure and pride we inform you that you will soon
> complete your inaugural Hecate House visit for the
> EquiWitch trial hearing and manifest assessment.*
>   *Saturday, October 1, 11:30 ante meridiem*
>   *Hecate House, Highgate Cemetery, London*
>   *All witches, warlocks and wicchefolk between must
> adhere to the EquiWitch trial to suitably mark their equal
> years of non-wicche existence versus years of holding
> sacred sorcery powers. Following your hearing, a jury of
> Selcouth's esteemed membership will conclude whether
> you have behaved with suitable mysticism and fervour
> since said sacred powers were first instated.*
>   *The overwhelming majority of wicchefolk pass their
> trial and assessment with flying technicolours. However,
> in the unlikely outcome that your esteemed power is
> agreed to stand as underused, abused or entirely
> neglected altogether, your magic will be regretfully
> removed with immediate effect and returned to Selcouth.*

Please bring with you to your hearing your bestowed sooth stone for the Selcouth endarkenment presentation in Hecate House courtroom following the (assumed) successful hearing.

With all the best on your thirtieth birthday! Cheers!

In thunder, lightning and in rain,
Caspar Strix
United Kingdom Coven Balancer
Tonitru, Fulgur, Pluvia

Disclaimer: Selcouth will not be held responsible for feelings of fatigue and lethargy following magic removal on possible expellation. We politely request that all witch familiars are left at home following the infamous toad incident of 1962. Your cooperation is well appreciated.

Belle gazed blankly at the letter, looking at the words elegantly inked on the paper. They seemed to loop themselves into one big tangled knot as she read them again. And again.

Your magic will be regretfully removed with immediate effect.

"You have got to be kidding me."

Belle stared at the unfurled papers, chewing relentlessly at a cuticle until it bled. Obviously, this didn't mean what it appeared to mean. It couldn't. Could it? She willed her mind to slow down, but her nervous system said otherwise. October 1 was tomorrow. Her first thought was that her birthday plans were almost certainly ruined. But a larger feeling of pure, burdensome dread began to brew up through her insides, an awful, anxious dismay bristling across every nerve ending like a wire broom.

She threw off the blanket and jumped up from the sofa. Jinx, disrupted from her nap, slunk away in a sulk to find an alternative bed. Belle shot to the phone and quickly made a call. The same call she always made whenever there was a major, minor or medium crisis unfolding in her life.

"Pick up. Pick up . . ." She was grateful to hear a click as the ringing stopped, followed by a lot of noisy fumbling at the other end. "Hi, Mum."

"Hello, love. So glad you called, didn't want to interrupt. I'm out with the dog to collect my moonwater, and I've lost my glasses again somewhere in the woods, so the signal might not be great."

"What do your glasses have to do with the signal? No, that's not the point. Mum, I've had this letter . . ." Belle was interrupted by a triumphant cheer from her mother.

"Oh, it came? I'm so relieved, mainly so that I don't have to keep the secret anymore. You wouldn't believe how many times I've nearly spilled. More to the point, I can't believe I'm old enough to have a daughter reaching the EquiWitch. Oh no, Wolfie, bad girl. Don't eat that . . ."

Belle sighed. She loved her mother more than life, but talking to Bonnie Blackthorn on the phone sometimes felt like a trial in itself: one that tested for levels of superhuman patience and stoic mental stability.

"Listen a sec, Mum. What is this? It's got to be a mistake." Belle turned the letter over again, as though expecting the message to have changed in the last few seconds to something that made sense.

"Darling, it's in the book," Bonnie said casually.

Belle steadied herself against the wall, appreciating the coolness on her clammy palms. "The book? This cannot be happening."

"Besides," Bonnie continued breezily, seemingly not overly concerned about her daughter's unfolding breakdown at the other end, "elders of the coven aren't allowed to tell you about it. As much as I might have wanted to, we can't interfere. We can't push you to be doing special things with your magic. The EquiWitch is supposed to be a nice surprise, a party of sorts for celebrating your powers having blossomed in full. You can't have your mad mother being all embarrassing and pushy about it, nagging you . . . Oh, Wolfie, put that down."

"A subtle shove in the right direction might have been nice," Belle said.

"And how would I do that without being seen to be 'meddling, guiding or assisting your witchery and discovery,' hmm? As the book specifically dictates against."

"I don't know, Mum . . . Maybe an 'Oh, hello, Belle. Any plans for your birthday? Have you got a cake? And have you done a bit of reading up about the fact you're about to be inexplicably stripped of all of your magic and cast out into the dark abyss of nothingness?' Something along those lines." She spoke in an emphatic whisper so as not to wake Ariadne, but Belle could hear herself getting more frantic.

"Belle, it's the law of Selcouth. The law of every coven across the world. You must be left alone to explore your own endarkenment. From the minute you left home and were no longer considered to be learning under my roof, I had to take a step back, let you out into the world. And this is the final stage of it all. You can't be guided through it, told how to make magic your own. Endarkenment is your journey to embark on, your responsibility, for the young witch to discover herself."

In the distance, Wolfie barked with enthusiasm. Likely at an unsuspecting duck, which the enormous hairy Irish hound, her mother's familiar, had something of a penchant for.

"Wolfie, leave that poor duck alone," Bonnie continued, confirming Belle's suspicions. "The fifteen years of the endarkenment journey are about you and your powers growing, how they both blend together naturally. The process of finding yourself in the magic. Getting into the groovy groove of things . . ."

Bonnie was attempting to calm her daughter, but words like "endarkenment," "finding yourself" and "groovy" were not helping. Belle gave a resigned sigh, tapping her head against the wall. Her mother carried on anyway in between calls for Wolfie, who had a habit of sprinting off into the woods and returning from the bracken with something furry carried carefully in her chops. Thanks to Wolfie's ability to track down injured creatures, Bonnie consistently had her greenhouse full of recovering, blanket-wrapped squirrels, hedgehogs, baby badgers and birds while she charmed them back to full health with her arsenal of curative concoctions.

"I tried to drop some subtle hints, keep reminding you to pick up the grimoire once in a while, but—Wolfie!—I kept forgetting until after I hung up. And I wrote a note on the fridge to remind *myself* to remind *you* of the consequences, and I started, but then there was all that business with the cobwebs in my big bottle of eel scales on the top shelf, and . . . Wolfie, there you are! Oh, stop harassing the ducks, will you?"

Belle wedged the phone between her head and shoulder, wrapping the spiral cord like a finger trap. "So, this is really happening?" Her voice cracked. "I'm going to lose my magic?" The uneasy brewing in the pit of her stomach swilled. She felt a little lightheaded.

"No, Belle, you are not. Of course you're not. You're an extremely capable witch," Bonnie said matter-of-factly. "I take it you didn't see it mentioned in the book, then? You haven't had a little read recently?"

Belle could tell her mother was trying as hard as possible to sound airy and unbothered, not judgemental or concerned, which in turn always made her sound entirely judgemental and acutely concerned. The book she was referring to was looming in the corner of Belle's eyeline. If it had been a person, it would have waggled its fingers and raised a captious eyebrow.

Of course, she had not read the book.

In fact, she'd barely touched the book for several years, and it stood ominously in the corner of the bookshelf now like a neglected beast grown too big and too dangerous to touch the longer it was left alone. Belle had always told Ariadne it was a poetry anthology from university. In actuality, it was the sacred grimoire of her coven, but that would have been a more complicated conversation.

"I . . . must have skipped that chapter," Belle said, lying through her teeth. Better than disappointing her mother.

She tore her regretful gaze away from the grimoire to grasp at her last ounce of balanced logical thought. She needed to get off the phone as quickly as possible to silently stew in her own despair. Her mother's advice was always welcome—until it wasn't.

"But it's fine, it will be fine. So fine, Mum. My life is obviously . . . suitably magical."

Belle glanced over at Jinx, whose back leg was currently in the air at a right angle while she washed in a very unladylike way on top of a pile of Jim's overtime sheets. To the left, an empty sharing packet of crisps that she and Ari had demolished the night before sat amidst a selection of tea-stained mugs. To the right was a cactus that had possibly started rotting. How they'd managed to kill an unkillable plant, even with an assortment of floral magic available to her, she wasn't entirely sure.

"What exactly does the coven expect from me, though?"

Belle heard the line muffle loudly again, followed by a distant swear from her mum and a noise that she recognised to be the sound of an active spell. Like TV static but more focused, like the crack of a whip.

"Sorry, love. Tried to siphon off a little moonwater and dropped my phone straight into the pond. Bloody mobile telephones. Think

I've managed to save it with a quick *Exsarcio Electri*. Although if you hear any muddy-sounding splashing on the line, I might have to turn it off and on again."

"Mum, tell me. What am I supposed to have done with my life? And I don't mean that in my usual existential crisis kind of way. In a magical way. What is Selcouth expecting of me? Should I have used magic to do something special by now?"

"It's not a case of a checklist, darling," Bonnie said. "The trial isn't a clear-cut test with right or wrong answers. It's a feeling, an instinct. The trial examines how the real Belle lets magic exist within her, how you allow it to flourish and trust it to guide your life. It's a gift, but it comes with responsibility, and this is just to prove that you can look after it."

The very dead cactus caught Belle's eye again. In reality, when was the last time she'd used her powers for anything more exciting than . . . quick caffeinated drinks? Did conjuring a last-minute Friday night table at the nice Italian up the road count?

"You've lived fifteen years as a non-wicche and fifteen years as a witch now," Bonnie continued. "They only want to check that your powers aren't being held by you for nothing."

Belle bristled at that. "Surely they're mine to keep and do with as I wish."

"Of course they're yours. But the privilege of retaining them has to be earned fairly. There is only a finite amount of magic in this world, after all."

Belle dusted away a rogue spark of her own powers, which was sitting alone on the kitchen countertop, left over from when she'd reversed the little patch of mould on the bread that morning.

"I basically just make a lot of long-distance drinks while I'm lying down."

"Don't be silly, darling. You create wonderful magic on a daily basis, probably without even realising. You're talented and bright and fabulous. You have nothing to worry about."

Belle couldn't help but feel, not for the first time, that her mother's unwavering confidence in her abilities was perhaps misplaced. "Nothing to worry about . . ." She repeated dubiously, wrapping the phone cord in a complicated cat's cradle.

"You've embraced it all as I taught you, and as your nan did, too. She was so proud of you." Bonnie's voice caught, wavered.

Belle glanced back at her bookshelf and chewed the inside of her cheek until she could taste a faint tang of blood.

"I know you, Belle. You always do anything and everything to the best of your ability, magic or non-magic. In thunder, lightning or in rain. You'll tick all of their silly coven boxes, sweetheart, and your manifests will shine through. I have every faith in you, always do."

Manifests? Suddenly, the Christopher problem, the burn-out problem, the life purpose problem, the perpetually single problem—all felt like distant, insignificant baby hiccups. Jinx flipped over onto her front and retched up a slug-like hairball with grotesque sound effects. Absolutely, suitably magical.

While her mum chatted on, now something about quiche in between shouts at the dog, Belle stretched on her tiptoes and pulled the thick leather-bound grimoire from the top shelf. Across the cover, she saw the star illustration that she'd recognised on the envelope. That was where she knew it from.

Selcouth Coven Grimoire: A Witch's Counsel for Endarkenment.

Under its own weight, the book fell to the floor with a thud. Belle froze, spun to the door across the way, prayed the noise didn't wake Ariadne, but a quick snuffling and a snore indicated otherwise. Belle traced the etched title with her finger, carved deeply into the timeworn violet leather, and heaved the book open over the carpet. A fine cloud of dust plumed from its pages.

"Daily Rituals, Practice of . . . , Dragon Ownership, Safety Regarding . . . , Draught Brewing, Beginners Guide . . . , Elixir Lore . . . , EquiWitch Trial. Here it is. Wow, I should have read this . . . well, fifteen years ago."

"I promise, petal, you'll be fine. You are my daughter, magic runs through us like a river through a mountain. Show them the real Belle. I'm just sorry I'm not allowed to be there to watch you sock it to them."

Bonnie revelled in her supernatural abilities and was, without question, born to be a witch. Her cottage in the quiet northern town where Belle had grown up was enveloped in wild flowers and grasses, a pocket haven of flora and fauna, each carefully cultivated for her passion: Earth Sorcery. Neighbours simply thought her to be a slightly eccentric green-fingered lady. But she spent her days in a small greenhouse at the end of her garden, Wolfie for company, brewing spells of protection, hope and appeasement for others. Her abilities were something of a whispered legend around the town and would often bring neighbours, superstitious mostly through desperation, knocking with trays of flapjacks or bunches of tulips in exchange for a moment of her time and a bath-friendly mix of her latest for luck, a tea blend for attraction or a lotion specifically for confidence.

Belle's father had left a long time ago, two strong-willed witches too much for him to handle, and Bonnie had always been certain that her daughter would follow in her footsteps. That Belle would find solace like she had in the potions, elixirs, draughts and tinctures. The joy and art of magic—always the beauty of it rather than the power.

But, of course, the modern witching world wasn't how it was

when she had been a girl. Whenever she'd asked about Belle's progress with magic, Belle reassured her that she'd get round to it just as soon as something else more pressing was out of the way. Friends, exams, deadlines, dates, trips, work . . .

Belle found the paragraph in the grimoire that she needed. Ending their call after something about a risotto recipe and someone from school that Bonnie had bumped into at the supermarket, Belle knocked the phone receiver to her forehead. All she'd wanted to do to celebrate the final precious evening of her twenties was eat pizza, watch a film and get an early night. But here she was plummeting into an abyss of contemplation on her own pointless existence and her stupid, selfish waste of powerful potential for her entire adult life.

Thirty was everything she'd been warned about.

With crossed legs, she flipped through the long-neglected pages. Her early study of magic had been diligent, excited and eager. Then, over time, it had dwindled. Nightly became weekly, weekly turned to fortnightly, often to sometimes to rarely. Belle couldn't remember the last instance that she'd dedicated any kind of time to her own potential.

With vague recall, she studied the pages covered in painstakingly detailed illustrations sketched in ghostly black and brown.

EquiWitch Trial, The

On a thirtieth celebration of life in the non-wicche realm, all wicchefolk are bound to undergo the EquiWitch trial, with strictly no exceptions to be made through nepotism or otherwise. This examination, metaphysical in its decision, delves thoroughly and intimately through manifest viewing into the personal history of the magic holder, beginning at the conception of their powers on their fifteenth celebration of life through to present day. This passage of time is known as the endarkenment process, and such an assessment brings endarkenment to completion and conclusion. An exact balance of one's experience, action, perception and truth will be taken into account to judge whether the witch is deemed worthy by their coven of maintaining their sacred power and position in the world of sorcery.

If successful in passing their Equi'Witch trial, and in having proven themselves to be suitably pragmatic, shrewd, courageous and bold for the coven, the magic holder will be granted permission to keep their powers until their final mortal breath. If unsuccessful, and deemed unworthy, the magic holder will be stripped of their powers with immediate effect and the magic returned to Selcouth. (See Expellation Ceremony on page 439.)

The words lit up amber across the pale pages as if to only emphasise her lack of the aforementioned qualities. Sinking against the sofa, Belle pointed her forefinger at the flame of a candle burning on the fireplace. Feeling the familiar comforting warmth that filled her whole body when she was holding a spell at the end of her fingertip, she made the small flame dance, hypnotising herself into deep thought as she contemplated what she would, could, should do about this whole mess.

Casting any magic—even this tiny, insignificant spell—felt like a tender, caressing swell. The feeling spread like melted butter on warm bread from the top of her head to the tip of her toes. It was like covering uncertain spring seeds in sun-drenched earth. Like nourishing soup in the winter. A hot water bottle wrapped around cold toes. It felt good. Come to think of it, it felt right. One of the only things in her life that did feel entirely right.

What did the coven expect a girl in her twenties (still . . . just . . .

currently twenty-nine, thanks) to be doing with this kind of power when residing in an uneventful, overpriced borough of the non-wicche world? Was she supposed to be creating earth-shattering magical fusion from her two-bedroom flat? She had to go to work. She had bills to pay and friends to hold on to, relationships to attempt, decisions to second-guess, imposter syndrome to fight . . . The fairly certain knowledge that she was about to brutally disappoint her mother, having already thus far failed to find a dashing husband or produce an adorable babbling heir, was the cherry on top of the cauldron.

A memory burst into Belle's mind. The candle went out with a breathy puff the moment her focus snapped to an immediate pinpoint. She quickly flipped back to the first leaf-thin page, which she remembered writing on shortly after receiving her powers on her fifteenth birthday. The book was inked with one important question, asking its holder, *What do you hope this new blessing of magic means for you, witch?*

Underneath, in a faint and ghostly string of pencil letters now faded with time, her fifteen-year-old self had written, *To be special. To like myself and be confident. To be happy.*

Belle felt an ache in her chest, raw with sadness and affection for that young girl. But the ache also brought with it a brilliant clarity.

She had to pass the trial.

Not just for her mother or her grandmother. She had to do this for herself, too. For herself more than anything, actually. For reasons unbeknownst to her, complicated histories, rites of passage, all the women who came before her, the universe had decided that magic was a fate to bless upon her all those years ago. Her magic was the glue that strung everything else together, like a fine stretch of honey clinging to every other fibre of her, joining the dots that growing up and growing older had drawn in more definite ink. This was something precious. A treasure of glass and gold, buried in sand but glinting in sunlight, waiting to be uncovered and held tightly in her palm.

These powers weren't to become a memory, wasted and abandoned. Magic was meant to be hers, and for the first time, Belle would fight to prove it.

4

Forgotten Gifts

BELLE BLACKTHORN WAS officially thirty. It had happened. Before yesterday's events, she had expected to wake up either one of two ways on her milestone morning. With her birthday sunrise, she might feel surprisingly at peace, quietly confident and hopeful about a new decade of possibility. Or (she had tried to tell herself that it would be a reasonable feeling) she would wake up and find that it had somewhat crept up on her, the disappointment that her life was meandering off in directions that her younger self hadn't hoped for.

Instead, thirty was neither of the two. Belle's mind was entirely elsewhere after a night of staring at the ceiling with heavy, gritty eyes, feeling a sickly mix of determination and dread over her looming EquiWitch trial. She squinted against the brightness bleeding through the curtains and was stirred by a tap on her bedroom door.

It started with a gentle whisper. "Belle . . . Belle . . . Are you awake?" A pause. Then a vigorous shake of the handle with a rattle. "Are you awake? Belle?" Ariadne bellowed.

Belle's pointing finger gestured in mid-air to unlock the door, peering out from the duvet pulled up to her nose.

"Sorry, I'm dead," Belle groaned, shoving a pillow over her head.

"That's the spirit. Happy birthday!" Ari barged into the room unceremoniously and belted out the song in her strong northern accent so loudly that Belle was pretty sure the neighbours would be round to complain. Again.

Ariadne stood with her long, lanky arms outstretched, laden with a selection of pink balloons tied around her wrists. Wedged under her armpits and between the legs of her dungarees was a selection of oddly shaped gifts and what looked worryingly like a birthday cake shoved into a Tupperware, a birthday banner wrapped around her shoulders like a scarf. She looked ridiculous, joy personified. Belle couldn't help but snort at the pandemonium of balanced birthday goods.

"You're actually thirty. What the hell is happening?" Ariadne said with an enormous grin, shuffling forwards so that presents fell from between her legs like a strange birth.

"I cannot believe this curse is upon me. I thought the gods would hear my cries." Belle stretched her forearm over her face in mock despair, the feeling of being cursed hitting far more realistically than her friend could possibly realise. Was Selcouth into curses now? Maybe that's what was happening, just a friendly coven curse.

"I have to say that as your extremely young and sprightly looking friend . . ."

"Sorry to be the bearer of bad news, but you are also hitting this decrepit milestone in a mere matter of weeks."

Belle gestured for her friend to join her. Ari dumped everything on the floor with her usual inelegant flair, balloons still attached awkwardly to her arms. A trailing number 3 bashed Belle right in the face before almost garrotting her.

"Are you decent under there? Any roguish gentlemen stashed away? Let me in, woman." Ari and balloons climbed under the duvet next to Belle, seizing the covers for herself. Belle wiggled along the mattress to make room.

"No gentlemen, roguish or otherwise. Just Jinx."

"My joining you in a new decade may soon be true," Ariadne lamented. "But for now, I am going to enjoy the fact that I am your extremely young hot friend in her twenties, and you are my withering old crone in her thirties." She wrapped Belle in her enthusiastic, double-armed hug that always came with a smell of sweet vanilla conditioner from her curly hair and a comforting extra squeeze at the end.

The unpleasant feeling of impending doom faded, just for a moment.

"My favourite crone, though, so it's fine. How are you feeling?" Ari asked, grabbing the cushions to shove behind her after tying the balloons to the bed-frame. "Do you feel different? Older and wiser?"

"I currently feel hungry and in dire need of caffeine, so I'm not sure all that much has changed as I cross the bridge into old age."

Belle, wrapped in her blanket shroud, hair up in a slightly mad-looking bun, reluctantly got up to trudge to the kitchen to make two cups of coffee. She had been dreading this moment since last night, when she double-checked the finer details of the letter. She prepared herself for the inevitable volume of Ari's reaction and seized her chance as she splashed in the milk, calling back to the bedroom.

"I have news that you're not gonna like and must preface it by saying please don't kill me."

She rebalanced her blanket cloak and grabbed the two mugs, then slunk back into bed with the steaming drinks.

"I can't join you guys today anymore. Something's . . ." Her voice trailed off reluctantly. "Something's come up."

She glanced warily over the brim of her cup. Ari laughed before realising that her best friend wasn't kidding and froze mid–cat stroke.

"Oh, come on! You're joking. Your own thirtieth?"

Belle winced.

"You can't not turn up to your own birthday picnic, weirdo. It's your thirtieth! I made you a bloody pavlova, look in that lunchbox. I was on the tube with giant helium balloons, and one got caught when the doors shut, and I nearly died. All for the grand cause of your birthday celebrations. What am I going to tell the stripper?"

Belle spluttered on coffee, horrified.

"Okay, the last bit is a lie, but the rest is true."

As feelings went, this one was particularly awful. Not only cancelling plans that they had all been excited about for weeks in exchange for one that she was dreading but also lying to her favourite person about the reason.

"I'm so sorry. I am the saddest person in the world. It's a . . . work thing."

"Please? You have to come." Ari sounded genuinely upset. Belle shrunk back against the pillows. She stretched her pyjama top over her knees to her ankles and racked her brain for anything that might sound plausible.

"You know what Christopher is like. He's a demon, wanting the stock check completed, like, yesterday. And there's his general zero respect for my having an actual life . . . You know I'd get out of it if I possibly could."

Ari gave her friend a cutting, unimpressed look. "I don't understand your loyalty to that place, especially with him at the helm."

In fairness, Belle had never understood her friend's job, either (something about pensions?). Although they'd been friends for what might as well be forever, the two girls had grown up polar opposites, with Belle diving into the world of words and Ariadne opting for systems and numbers. Confident and instantly charming, she walked the line between chaotic day-to-day disorganisation and being keenly logical and focused when her mind was put to something important. Unfortunately, that meant that she could spot a lie from a mile away, which was somewhat inconvenient for her magical best friend.

"Just don't cancel the whole thing, okay?" Belle pleaded. "Have a good day with the others. I can call you when I'm done and see where you guys have ended up crawling to. You won't even miss me."

She tried to wave a white flag. How long could a magical hearing take, anyway? She might be out by lunchtime.

"If this isn't the final straw for you to tell Christopher to take a hike and grab Lunar for yourself, I don't know what will be." Ariadne sounded distinctly peeved.

Belle's guilt rattled. She wanted desperately to explain the real gut-wrenching problem currently ruining her birthday. It was exactly the type of scenario that Ariadne would be able to offer some solid reassurance on. But somehow "I was so excited for my birthday with my best mates today, eating all the fancy packets of tiny autumn picnic food, but now I have to go and see a coven about procuring a magical destiny" felt a little much to get into.

Her powers were the one and only secret (albeit a big one) that Belle had ever kept from Ariadne since they met on their first day of school. They'd been inseparable since Ari had gone home and told her mum about the strange girl with the silver hairband, Belle sharing the same encounter with Bonnie while standing on tiptoes to peer over the kitchen cauldron.

There'd been a close call when Belle had almost blurted out the events of her fifteenth birthday, the day after her endarkenment debut. The girls had been three hours deep into a film marathon, and she'd spent the whole evening falling down a dark pit of overwhelm. Shy wallflower teenage Belle was desperate to share with her closest ally, seeking a crumb of precious reassurance.

She'd stopped herself from spilling the secret, even to her best friend, after remembering the sage witches' warnings of non-wicche knowledge, of sharing the truth with non-powers. Bonnie, too, had sat her down with a cup of soothing velvety hot chocolate to talk about the dangers of their potentially world-shattering secret. Even with those who were closest to you—*even* Ariadne, Bonnie said—it was never a good idea. It was a sad fact of life that those who you would trust with your life were often the ones who could inflict the most damage when put to the test. Selflessly holding on to the secret of magic when you cannot partake in it yourself was a torment that even the strongest non-wicche could be driven out of their mind by. History had proved that non-powers couldn't typically exercise much restraint when presented with close proximity to magic. Something about torches and pitchforks.

"I'm not going to pretend this isn't dreadful," Ari said, cutting straight to the point, "but"—she sighed and held up a finger—"do not stress, for it is your special birthday. We will just have to celebrate on your behalf because we are very good, noble friends."

Belle felt herself physically relax just an inch.

"Birthday cake breakfast?"

They fell into their usual talk, most of it indecipherable to anyone but them, between generous slices of sweet Victoria sponge, a cloud of dusty sugar on their fingertips, the red jam bright and nostalgic. For a while, Belle almost forgot about what lay ahead.

Eventually and reluctantly, Ariadne headed out to enjoy Belle's birthday without her, taking the mash of pavlova in a Tupperware under one arm and a bag full of tequila under the other. The balloons were left tied at various intervals around the flat, much to the horror of Jinx, who was convinced that they were out to fight her. Belle shut the door behind Ariadne and tilted her head back heavily against it with closed eyes. The outright lying never got easier.

She flicked out her spell finger at nothing in particular to release the pent-up block of magic that had been aching to escape all morning. As a stream of tiny stars cascaded across the room, like leaves carried on a gust of wind, Belle felt instant relief. The fringed lamp flickered on and off, the drooping peace lily stirred itself to a freshened state and curtains billowed dramatically as magic filled the room. Resisting the urge to cast always felt like an itch that she couldn't quite scratch. She crossed the room, cheering herself with small tasks. Reviving the wilting sunflowers in their vase for a few more days. Sending the heaped fresh laundry into the right bedroom. Refilling the cat food bowls. Abandoning balloon enemies for biscuits, Jinx chirped a thank you.

Belle hauled herself in the direction of the shower, feeling like the worst person in the non-wicche world and probably the magical one to boot. Did Selcouth really have to host the trial on her actual birthday? A little inconsiderate but, knowing the coven's nature, probably a wildly old tradition that inflicted some kind of generation-spanning curse if broken. Plus, Belle imagined, medieval folks probably didn't do much to celebrate their thirtieth birthday. There was dysentery and the plague to worry about. Not to mention witch accusations getting in the way of most party plans. Maybe her own hand wasn't so bad.

In her bedroom, filled with a jumble of yellowing second-hand books alongside bright brand-new ones, Belle sat lost in thought on the bed. All great thinkers knew that contemplation came best when wrapped in a towel, with another precariously balanced on one's head. Jinx giving her a headbutt on the shin eventually snapped her out of it.

"I need to get my act together, don't I?"

She glanced at the clothes in her wardrobe, the alternative heap draped over the armchair. One spell that she did cast every day without fail was to bring forth the clothes that she should wear for whatever occasion was on the agenda—her nifty *Idoneus*

Indumentum incantation that teenage Belle had perfected as a priority within a few weeks of gaining powers. It saved a lot of indecision in the mirror, but probably wouldn't qualify as proof of full endarkenment.

With a flick of her finger, an old favourite sailed towards her. An emerald green dress, suitably witchy but nothing as to garner strange looks on a packed train. It was comfortable, reliable. Plus, it had pockets.

She would shove the required coven cape and hat in her backpack once she remembered where she'd put them. Noticing the time, she zapped her wet hair dry (*Capillus Aura*, another useful one) and grabbed a pair of boots.

"Jinxy, wish me luck."

Jinx glanced up with her usual catty mix of affection and disdain.

Sliding aside the clutter on the coffee table, Belle pulled out the letter. The writing, a little crumpled now, glowed like embers as she reread the words off almost by heart. The *Cheers!* at the end was starting to grate.

> *Please bring with you to your hearing your bestowed*
> *sooth stone for the Selcouth endarkenment*
> *presentation . . .*

She sighed. She'd nearly forgotten.

It had been a long time since she'd seen that thing. Finding it now would be nothing short of a miracle. While she wasn't quite up to conducting those yet, she did have a quick *Perdita Invenio*, a lost-and-found incantation up her sleeve. With a small finger turn, she completed a circle of tiny stars. In moments, she heard the stifled rattling sound of something trying to escape.

"Well, I would never have found you in there."

Rummaging in the corner of her dresser drawer, delving amongst bottles, tubs and endless hair bobbles, Belle felt her fingers wrap around a small bundle of silk scarf tied into a knot. She unfurled it carefully to uncover the brooch hidden away inside. It fitted perfectly into the palm of her hand, the delicate case carved from shell that framed a pebble-sized jewel, a chunky shard of lacklustre grey glass. A little underwhelming in all honesty, considering its apparent status as a mysterious, magical artefact.

It had been years since she'd seen it. She tossed it over in her hand. The glass was always murky, inky, but the inside moved and swirled slowly like smoke behind glass, like tiny storm clouds gathering. It had been a strange birthday gift from her grandmother fifteen years ago.

"When the time comes, you'll appreciate it," Alvina Blackthorn had said, closing her granddaughter's fingers over the gift with a gentle tap. It had gone unexplained and unsurprisingly unworn, teenagers not usually being big on brooches. The glass was forgotten about, shoved into a jewellery box before she could think to ask much more about it. Now, with her grandmother gone, it was another souvenir of unasked questions, unspoken conversations. Belle's questions about the stone had joined the pile, insignificant compared to other words that she longed to speak with her nan. She pinned the brooch onto the strap of her dress.

"I'll take all the luck I can get today."

Although it was instantly hidden by her dark hair, Belle was taken aback, bolstered ever so slightly by a warm feeling. Something that once belonged to her grandmother, her precious and caring and cherished nan, tying them together as soon as it rested against her chest. The small, quiet reminder of an ever-loving presence.

5

At the Willow

AS IT TRANSPIRED and as should have probably been expected from a witchcraft high headquarters, Hecate House was not easy to find. The letter only gave sparse detail—Highgate Cemetery, London—which Bonnie explained in another frantic phone call was to be expected. The exact entrance to Hecate House regularly incarnated, changing every full moon so as to minimise the chance of non-wicche folk stumbling across it. It was left to a witch's intuition to locate it for themselves again and to figure out how to open the entrance, which Belle quickly decided was extremely unhelpful and stupid.

She emerged from the humid Underground to find autumn giving a sleepy sigh across the city. Leaves skipped like skimming stones, and a damp breeze rippled silkily at her ankles. It was welcome after a sticky journey across almost the entire breadth of the city. A drizzle slipped down from the sky and threatened to soak her from head to toe in a matter of minutes, so she hastily threw an umbrella over her head. Rainy London could be a miserable feeling—heads down, socks soaked, arms folded fiercely across chests—but it fit this time of year like a glove, the smell of damp ground and muddy earth tailored to the place.

Belle snuck her first glance at the entrance to Highgate Cemetery, elegant and sombre, framed by a pointed Gothic arch. The entryway was cloudy with damp and centuries of soot on a street that was quiet and peaceful, save for a handful of passersby wrapped in waterproofs and clutching takeaway cups. Belle, feeling as though she may as well have hung a sign around her neck declaring "Lost Witch," gave them an awkward "nothing to worry about" wave for inexplicable reasons.

She had hoped that when it came to it, Hecate House would call to her. A carried voice on the air, a beckoning finger. She'd heard stories of the cemetery whispering with a disembodied voice, enticing people to look back over their shoulder, only for them to see nothing and nobody behind them. With no such helpful spectres presenting themselves post-breakfast, this was evidently where Belle's intuition and abilities were supposed to take over. It seemed to be happening increasingly often—this moment where she'd look around for the responsible adult to guide her with a hand at the small of her back before the gut-punch realisation that she was on her own to make the call. The creased, well-thumbed pocket A–Z sticking out of her bag could only take her so far. Magic had to point the rest of the way, along with a few aged signposts.

Belle tried to trust that instinct was pulling her feet in the right direction amongst a landscape of thousands of gravestones, jutting from the gums of the soil like chipped teeth. Weeping angels looked down over those below, one sweetly sleeping on the job. Sombre obelisks, looming crosses and veiled urns depicted snakes swallowing their own tails for eternity. Everything was coated in a watery sheen, speckles of rain flickering the picture like old film. The minutes were ticking by alarmingly quickly on Belle's watch, but time in the cemetery felt halted. In perpetual memory, in loving memory, in precious memory . . . all gulped down by the silence.

Doing her best to follow the weathered signs, she eventually found herself at the grand dark tunnel of Egyptian Avenue and took a moment to hold a stitch that was blooming above her hip. The main path was flanked by a pair of looming obelisks that could have touched the sky itself. Then appeared a shady, circular avenue, lined with delicate sunken tombs like tiny terraced houses. The vaults, built around the roots of an ageing cedar tree up high, looked oddly welcoming with their cold, moss-cushioned eternal rest behind front doors. A rest sounded great, frankly.

One step farther, and Belle felt it. That crest of a wave breaking, the force upon her senses that told her others of magical persuasion were nearby. Of course Hecate House had to be here—the most revered, supernaturally charged part of the cemetery. She followed the trodden path around the grand circle like a lasso, past ancient family crypts and tombs of the historic London elite, scanning for a possible entrance. A caretaker sweeping an enormous pile of wet leaves into a neat mountain remained oblivious to the witch who was looking a little unhinged and very unsure.

"Please. Please. Please tell me I don't have to break into a tomb. That does not feel like a good thing to do."

Belle glanced at the dark doorways of each vault. The darkness, the ice cold, whatever else might be inside. "Why would a high witch headquarters be anything to do with a tomb? Of all the places. You're magic. You can choose *anywhere*. Next time, choose a Maldives water villa, guys."

She stopped in her tracks at what had appeared on the path. She'd done a full loop, and the Victorian lamp-post in front of her, the only one, standing alone in the circle, had not been there before. Had it? It was unassuming enough to go unnoticed—if you didn't happen to be looking for an undisclosed entrance to a witch headquarters.

Belle hesitated, questioning herself. The lamp-post reminded her of stories that Bonnie had read to her before bed when she was young. Inevitably stories of witches, in so many forms and worlds. There'd been a matching lamp to this one in their local church graveyard, where they'd walked together in all weathers, hunting down specific weeds, rare crabgrass, downy thistles and oily feathers for Bonnie's brewing. Bonnie would remind her daughter, long before powers came into play, to never doubt that wise lions, powerful witches and mystical wardrobes were all very, very real and waiting to be found. To venture past the lamp-post in the story had always led to strange adventures and great changes in fortune. It had always led to witches.

"This has to be it."

Her instincts said *fire*. Belle focused on the unlit tinder inside and tipped her finger up towards it, a nest of tiny sparks conjuring a small flame behind the glass. Instantly, the iron frame filled with tawny light, pleasant against the damp grey air. The lamplight landed simply and selectively on just one weeping willow tree, which covered the opposite walls in a cascade. Against the drizzle, the glow coated each sweeping leaf like a cobweb, falling as if to spotlight that tree alone.

Glancing over her shoulder to check that nobody was taking any notice of the mad girl staring at a thicket of a willow, Belle reached out and parted the dense wet greenery, soaking her sleeves. As the darkness shrunk away, the warm light revealed a wooden door pressed deep into the stone circle wall of the cemetery. It couldn't have been there before. Even behind the willow, she would surely have spotted the heavy dark oak door strapped with aged metal. Or the weighty knocker shaped like a celestial moon. Or the intricate carvings of stars in the grain, along with three single words: *Tonitru, Fulgur, Pluvia.*

6

The First Test

THE DOOR WAS locked, of course.

Luckily this was a spell she did have in her arsenal, having used it frequently when she still lived at Bonnie's house. It had been worth committing to magic to avoid knocking in the middle of the night every time she forgot her keys. Belle flicked a finger of *Ostium Resigno* stars towards the heavy bolt. It opened with a click followed by the flurry of a brown mouse scurrying into the musty darkness that breathed out of the passageway.

Belle let out a loud laugh of sheer disbelief.

She dropped her bag to the ground and tugged at the bundle stuffed inside. Rushing to straighten out her cloak, she batted at the creases before throwing it over her shoulders and fastening the silver clasp at her collarbones. Although not exactly a frequent choice from her wardrobe, Belle had a soft spot for the coven attire. The fabric billowed around her right to the floor, black at first glance but revealing rich tones of plum, amethyst and violet when it caught the warm light of the lamp-post. It wasn't until the cloak was admired more closely that it revealed the best part—delicate, exquisite embroidery of constellations. Stars, moons, planetary alignments and zodiac signs, all in fine lucid threads like spider-silk woven into the fabric. Each witch's cloak was uniquely personal to them, the pattern designed to their own birth chart: the way the night looked the moment they arrived into this world, the plotting of the sky that the universe had crafted to welcome a witch's first breath. Even when Belle had been somewhat mortified by all things magical in the early years, she had known the cloak was something to behold.

Belle pulled out the crumpled hat to match, which was scrunched underneath a water bottle and a notepad. While she had always loved the cloak, the hat could get straight in the bin. No one looked good in that thing. Although the coven had voted to give their classic hat a much-needed refresh a couple of decades ago, shrinking the towering height and banning all unbecoming cliché cobweb detail, it still sat tall in the classic point. The wide brim flopped down as she popped it from inside out, shoved it haphazardly onto her head and blew her fringe out of the way. It looked ridiculous. Belle hastily snatched up the rest of her things, steeled her nerves and rushed inside.

She found herself in a pitch-black corridor, save for a smattering of burning torches pinned to the walls. They lit the way in pools of meagre light and heat, just enough to vaguely make out a long stretch ahead. Enough to see a corridor slope downwards and disappear into an unwelcoming nothing. It smelled hot and dark, like scorched earth at night.

"Well, this seems like a wonderful idea."

Taking a step forward into obscurity, Belle jumped what felt like ten feet into the air as the door slammed behind her. With it went the last trace of daylight. The outline of the outside world faded to nothing, as though it had never been there at all. She was alone.

Squinting to make out anything at all, she attempted to yank one of the flaming torches from the wall before quickly realising that a *Lux Vegrandis* spell to turn her finger to torchlight was a slightly more refined option. She felt her way along the walls, following the path that uncoiled like a hibernating snake underneath London.

It had only been a few metres of careful treading when the whole corridor shuddered suddenly and violently. It seemed as though the floor would give out beneath her, that the tunnel would collapse entirely, debris and dust crumbling onto her shoulders. Belle cried out and clung to the wall. An earthquake in an underground witch's tunnel felt like an unfortunate way to go but was about what she deserved.

It took a moment for her wits to register that the tremors came from a tube train rumbling past just on the other side of the stone walls. She gathered herself and walked on.

With a growing feeling that this was probably the end of it all, Belle eventually came to an abrupt stop with a hard, painful smack against both knees. The small light from her finger extinguished in an instant, and she found that it couldn't be reignited, forces bigger than her now blocking her meagre magic. She thought her eyes were tricking her, still adjusting in the swallowing darkness, but a firm stone wall gradually formed into view a foot or so ahead, shutting off the way, like the shadows themselves had turned solid. A dead end. She must have missed a turning, a hidden corner or an entry in the walls, and walked straight past the door that took her to the courtroom. She sighed and spun to turn back.

The winding corridor was gone. It had been silently closing up behind her as she walked. The once stretching, endless space now pressed up close, the solid stone only six feet away. Her heart skipped double, rebounding off her ribcage.

She was trapped. A sole torch was giving out watery light that barely lit her own hand in front of her. She swallowed over and over again. A firm stone lodged itself thickly in her throat. *Don't panic.*

She gazed around again, noting every possible inch of the space but finding only an echo of her own unsteady breathing. A spell was required, that much was obvious, but the possibilities were too many to know where to even begin.

"If anyone is listening, if I get out of here, I promise that I will never try and improve myself ever again."

She took a moment to steady her breath, to push away the claustrophobia stroking at the back of her neck with spindly cold fingers. Desperate for stability, she leaned against the wall in front to steel herself. She flinched. The contact of her skin against the stone sent static energy through her, unpleasantly shocking like brushing an electric fence. With a hiss of pain, Belle could only stare with dreadful realisation as the stones began to crumble to a fine dusty powder at her touch. And once they'd started, they didn't stop.

Sand began to gather at her feet, slowly but definitely pooling. It was piling up as the wall disintegrated. Some kind of chain reaction from her touch.

"This cannot be happening. Why? Why are you doing this? Please stop, stop, stop."

She tried to shove the rapidly multiplying sand back into place, scooping it feverishly from the floor into the holes of the wall. But as quickly as the stones crumbled at her feet, they refilled and rebuilt themselves, leaving the dust to pile higher around her toes. A horrifying thought of quicksand crossed her mind. Trapped, inside her own personal hourglass.

"I cannot die in here. Mum will kill me," she spat, trying to clear the flying grains of sand from her lips.

She was struggling to loosen her feet now, but the tip of her boot hit against something solid with a dull thud. The top of a glass bottle bobbed up through the sand. A flicker of frenzied relief and hope flooded her heart as she noticed a small scroll inside. She grabbed at the bottle. Real-life buried treasure. It had to be the right spell. An answer or instructions. Some kind, any kind, of help. She frantically uncorked the bottle with her teeth, shook the contents out into her hand and unfurled the scrap. The sand tightened just below her knees. She couldn't read the words fast enough as they glowed like fine embers against the paper.

No soul shall pass untrue in purpose.
This wall unmoved for those superfluous.
Key nor hammer break illusion.
Transfigurate this path's conclusion.
While time's relentless sand does flow,
Face those fears that you well know.
Pragmatic, shrewd, courageous, bold,
Remain of mind for fate foretold.

She rushed to say the words aloud and fired a desperate finger at the wall, anticipating the flurry of sparks to follow that would end the unfolding nightmare.

Nothing. The feeling of magic that she knew so well stayed dormant. There was no rush. No warmth—other than the rising real panic making beads of sweat form damply at her temples. It wasn't even a spell.

"You have got to be kidding me. A riddle? A fun little brain-teaser? Now?"

Belle yelled in between gritty mouthfuls of sand, kicking out to try and loosen her legs under the vast, thick weight. She stared at the piece of paper, willing her brain to work it out. But every thought spluttered and stalled the same moment it began. Spells only worked with full understanding of what was being cast, full comprehension of cause and effect. She had to know what she was casting before any kind of magic could successfully happen. She tried to centre her mind, line by line.

There couldn't be another hidden door involved if a key wouldn't work. Nor could she smash anything down—frustrating, because destroying the place sounded particularly appealing. *Break illusion . . .* So it wasn't real? Good to know. The wall was a glamour, a false reality, however realistic it might look or feel in the moment. But that didn't help much, either, while her very real claustrophobia insisted on believing otherwise.

Transfigurate this path's conclusion. Transfiguring was somewhat in her arsenal, the basics at least. Usually turning a soggy forgotten bag of salad into a fresh one or a pair of old jeans into a one-size-bigger pair of jeans, but still. The same principle surely applied when it came to transfiguring stone walls into something else. Anything else.

That cold tapping finger of panic was back again and now felt all the more real.

In the pitch black, a parched whisper reached her ears. "I knew you'd amount to nothing."

It didn't just speak. It reached inside her skull, breathing at the bone.

"Everything I sacrificed for you."

She recognised it. "Mum?"

It was Bonnie's voice, but stretched out to a different, painful octave. It sounded low and tortured, choked with tears and thick, opaque revulsion. Speaking everything that Belle could ever fear, had ever feared.

Face those fears that you well know.

"I loved you so much when you were small. You were so special, so clever and so beautiful."

Belle's hands flew to cover her mouth, disguising an appalled disbelieving sob.

"You were gifted. And now look at you. Never daring to try. Nothing special, tumbling behind everybody else. A burden to everyone. In my nightmares, I couldn't have imagined facing such a disappointment. So much promise and potential, wasted over and over. I'm ashamed of you."

"It's not real. This is not real," Belle murmured on repeat, hands against her ears, headache thrumming.

"You are no daughter of mine."

Remain of mind.

It didn't even matter anymore, the sand. She couldn't focus on the rising pressure of it clinging to her skin and cementing around her. The voice stole her from the physical. Bonnie sneered a vicious, howling laugh that morphed into a piercing, ear-shattering scream.

And then it changed.

"How could you lie to me?"

Belle's eyes snapped open wildly.

"Ari?"

"And for all this time. Do you hate me that much? Do you not trust me?"

"Ariadne . . . What is happening?" Belle yelled.

"How could you do this to me? Keeping such a giant, ugly secret from me. We're supposed to be friends. Best friends. It's us."

She knew it wasn't Ariadne. It couldn't be. It had to be a trick, a spell. She knew that voice laced with so much poison and hatred did not, could not, ever belong to her best person. The girl she'd grown alongside, from seed to tree, two intertwining branches blooming in parallel through decades of shared seasons.

This Ariadne was not hers. It spoke with a knife edge, a monster that echoed deepest, darkest thoughts Belle never dared to dwell on, if only to protect herself.

But on it went, the furious hatred.

"You never think of anybody but yourself. You never cared about me, not really. You think you're special with this . . . whatever it is. This magic. But you can't even control it. You don't share it, you shut it away, so what's even the point? You don't know what you're doing, about anything, ever. You're such a *mess*."

Tears flowed uncontrollably, wetting and warming Belle's burning cheeks.

"You're strange, you're selfish. A burden. And you chose all of this over me."

"I never would, never, ever, Ari. I would always choose you."

Remain of mind. Remain of mind. It's not real.

"You're unlovable."

"I know this isn't real. You're not real!"

Then came magic.

Pure, unhindered magic. Flooding from her fingertips so that the space filled with light, so suddenly bright it was blinding against her eyelids. It cascaded around her, billowing satin, the warm arm of a friend swooping in to hold her up.

Candescence rushed through her veins, the warmth like a bathtub filling, rising, flooding then overflowing. Golden sparks flew in ribbons of sunshine. And slowly but definitely surely, the solid stone in front of her began to liquidate. It melted. For a moment Belle thought that her tears were playing tricks on her vision. But the sandstone rippled in shades of dove and fawn and ivory around her, turning to watery reflects. The solid wall became a rolling waterfall in front of her.

A thunderclap boomed against the waterfall, shuddering every part of her body as a lightning bolt struck in brilliance. It sent a mighty soaking tidal wave through the tiny space on a gust of bullish wind. The force of water knocked her to the floor and washed the tower of sand away. With it went the waterfall. In its place, a grand floor-to-ceiling velvet curtain the colour of dark silver adorned with bronze rope tassels hung in front of Belle.

She slumped against the solid wall still behind her and gulped down the clean, fresh air in greedy mouthfuls. Shoving her wet hair out of her face, she untangled herself from the swell of velvet and reached out on hands and knees to move the heavy curtain aside. Whatever waited on the other side was welcome, because it couldn't be worse than the hell that she'd just fought her way through.

She furiously wiped away the tears clinging to her eyelashes. She had saved herself, remained of mind. Just about. She had found the way.

For fate foretold. This was Hecate House.

7

The Gowden Sisters

AH. GOT THERE in the end, I see. Some might say stale, un-inspired, predictable . . . And who *doesn't* strive for stale when armed with infinite magical possibility."

In front of Belle stood a rather formidable-looking woman. Belle scrambled to her feet as quickly as she could, her limbs screaming with exhaustion.

"Ultimately successful, I suppose," the woman's drawl contin-ued. Her lips were pursed as though she could smell something par-ticularly displeasing lingering on someone's shoe. "Others tend to favour something altogether more impressive, you understand. As-tral projection, bending elements, mythical creatures—you know, something with a little more pomp and production. Always appreci-ated after a long morning; these EquiWitch trials are such tiresome work."

The woman sounded bored and lowered her disapproving stare to admire her own long fingernails, sharp and polished to a crimson reflect. "It got you here in one piece, I dare say. Although judging by the sight of you, I may take back that observation."

A shock of silver-grey hair against the woman's complexion re-minded Belle of bare, bleached parchment. It was coiffured elegantly underneath the brim of her coven hat, with a single victory curl furled with immaculate, measured precision. She bore razor-sharp cheekbones that stretched up to her temples and wine-coloured lipstick made for a dramatic ghostly contrast.

Belle swallowed down the embarrassment of being chastised, a mixture of mortification and fury that left her unsure how to respond.

"Oh, right, well . . . Sorry about that. Sorry for keeping you waiting. I think I did just nearly die, but all right."

The woman raised one sharp angled eyebrow in scepticism. "We are not in the business of murder, Ms. Blackthorn."

"Marvellous. Glad to hear it. Just a healthy dollop of torture instead, is it?" Belle asked, shaking out the water from her sleeves.

The woman pointedly brushed a droplet from her lapel. "One only experiences the full tests of Hecate House if one isn't quick enough to produce astute magic," the woman snipped, as though it were entirely obvious.

"Tests? You call that a test?" Belle said, gesturing back at the curtain behind her. "I'm pretty sure I just went through an exorcism."

Belle's scorn was caught off guard as she glimpsed the unwelcome sight of herself in an enormously tall gilded mirror across the entryway. To say she looked feral would be a tender compliment. Her skin was red and blotchy from the hysterical tears. Wet, sticky sand clung to every inch of her soaked dress and cloak, she could even feel it between her toes. Her hair hung in damp, knotted rattails. Her legs weakened underneath her as she stood, pure adrenaline having flushed everything else away.

The woman glanced across to meet her eyes in the reflection and looked Belle up and down in the mirror. With a barely perceptible but distinctly disdainful flick of the wrist, along with an unguarded eye roll, the woman quickly cast a spell that left Belle immaculately clean and freshly pressed. She felt a welcome warmth flood her body again from top to bottom, more revived and awake than she'd felt for years. As though she'd woken up from the best sleep ever and eaten the most filling meal.

"Thank you," Belle muttered. "The quick trip to hell and back was a nice touch. Who doesn't love a bit of drama?" she said, straightening her shoulders.

"A bit . . . A bit of drama?" the woman said, enunciating purposefully. "I can only assume you are referring to the sacred Selcouth ritual of facing your most intimate fears to push your magic to its limits to commence an endarkenment ceremony?"

Belle gulped. "That's the one. It was . . . great. Now that I think about it, I mean. Enjoyed it, actually."

The woman's arms fell into a firm condemning fold.

"Sorry to have disappointed you thus far, Ms. Blackthorn. Did you expect passing from realm to realm to be a quick hop-skip? What were you expecting would be involved in a process so aptly named as endarkenment? A sleepover, buttered popcorn, a bouncy castle? We can arrange a face painter for your next visit, should it be to your liking."

"That won't be necessary," Belle clipped back, blushing. Reluctantly, she considered that the woman may have a point. Endarkenment was so far what it said on the tin.

"Although any thought of a further visit is perhaps presumptuous," the woman said. A painfully awkward moment of silence and eye contact passed. The woman widened her eyes expectantly.

"Oh. Right. I'm . . ." Belle offered out her hand.

"Belladonna Blackthorn, yes. You're also rather late."

Was this woman for real? Moments ago, Belle had stared death, nightmares, her own personal hell itself in the face—and, she might add, battered it into submission. Eventually. Yet here she was, this lady, concerned about a slight delay?

"I'm dreadfully sorry about that. All of the, you know, demon voices, sinking sand"—she reeled them off on her fingers—"thinking I was about to expire inside a stone broom cupboard, my loved ones declaring their undying hatred for me. Torture does dreadfully get in the way of things. Let alone how awful the trains are at the moment."

"Just the"—the woman consulted a pocket watch from the inside of her cloak—"nineteen and a half minutes of lateness, though. We thank you for that courtesy. A remarkably organised record for the Blackthorn family."

Belle let out a snort but quickly realised it was the wrong response.

"It's no wonder the house decided to deliver a lateness punishment for your arrival. You have no one to blame but yourself, Ms. Blackthorn."

"That"—Belle gestured a thumb back to the chamber—"was all for being late?"

"I would assume so, judging by the sand that was decorating your eyebrows," she replied as though Belle were entirely foolish not to know, "you faced the hourglass hex. Hecate House does not take kindly to poor timekeeping. It's a perfectly reasonable addition to the process."

"Of course. Nothing says 'perfectly reasonable' like death by quicksand."

The woman pursed her lips. "Be glad that you remembered your coven uniform. Caught on a bad day, the house has been known to turn one's clothes to dust for incorrect attire, which has made for some rather unfortunate arrival scenes."

Belle couldn't hide the horror on her face.

"And the rest of it? The traumatising ghostly apparitions and voices? Which hex was that?"

"No hex. Delivered as standard on first visit to the house," the woman said dismissively. "A revered tradition for any wicchefolk of Selcouth thirsty for the chance to prove themselves worthy."

In a gesture of reluctant, optimistic truce, Belle sighed and reached out to shake the woman's hand again. She offered a smile to try and reset their introduction in the humour of their ridiculous meeting. A fraction of a second too slow to be considered polite, the other witch returned the gesture, offering slim, sharp fingers. Each was adorned with an ornate silver ring, all embossed with rich, dark stones and jewels. The one on her index finger, Belle noticed, bore a streak of glass swirled with misty smoke—a sooth stone.

"I am sorry for the wait," Belle said. "I think this means the only way is up."

"You haven't changed a bit since we last saw you fifteen years ago. And you look so like your mother."

It was not a comment delivered with affection or nostalgia. The woman's icy blue eyes looked Belle up and down with brazen dislike. Belle pretended to ignore the frost and smiled still but couldn't stop herself from blushing. She clutched her hands onto her bag straps to stop them hanging awkwardly at her sides.

"I don't think I caught your name?" Belle asked. "Although I feel like I remember your face. I guess that would be from my endarkenment debut all those years ago."

With a quick turn of her wrist, the woman produced a parchment which unfurled smoothly in a sprinkle of sparks, along with a plumed black quill. Both levitated importantly next to her, then sailed gracefully towards Belle to tap at her chest.

"Sign this," the woman said, ignoring Belle's request completely.

Belle eyed it suspiciously. "What is it?"

The large jet-black feather promptly leaked three thick, viscous drops of blackened, raven ink from its point onto the hem of her dress. She watched the syrupy liquid seep into the fabric, spreading slowly like black clouds.

"Standard EquiWitch contract. You shan't hold Hecate House responsible for the manifests chosen at random, nor any loss of magic as a result of the outcome of your trial."

"How about for the inflatable assault course of horror I just completed? Can I sue you for that?"

The woman simply stared. Belle sighed resignedly, reaching for the quill. As soon as she completed the "n" of "Blackthorn," the contract tore from her hands and flew high into mid-air. It spun in a whirlwind, then burst into radiant purple flames. Within seconds, it had vanished in a flare of fire.

A loud bell clanged importantly from somewhere in the distance. The toll seemed to fill the whole space in a resounding echo.

"Saved by the bell from this arduous small talk, I'm sure we can both agree." The woman adjusted her perfectly crisp hat and smoothed her sharply tailored trousers. "I wish you luck, Ms. Blackthorn. I suspect you may need it." She paused for a moment, and Belle hoped she misheard her final words. "You shouldn't have come."

With a needle-pointed clicking of her heels against the stone floors, the woman turned and headed through an archway at the back of the room. Belle watched after her, mouth agape, until the final trail of plum-coloured cloak disappeared with a stretch of shadow.

The withdrawal of such an intimidating presence was palpable. Belle exhaled all formalities and let herself flump down onto the long wooden bench that lined the wall. The trial hadn't even begun yet, and she was exhausted from the peaks and crashes of sheer adrenaline. She'd nearly drowned, or whatever the sand equivalent was. Touched the brink of madness, the sound of her own deepest nightmares come true. Unleashed wild, intuitive magic that she'd never seen herself show before. And that was all irrelevant anyway, because she had just been eviscerated by a simple conversation.

She gazed around the entryway she now found herself in. Like the corridor approach, the foyer was lit by flickering torches, although these flames had definitely been enchanted to a larger size than normal to cast a luxurious, balmy glow. Handsome patterned rugs in jewel colours stretched out through the room, and the bleached stone walls loomed high, huge slab stacked on huge slab. The walls were carved with patterns of archaic words, moons and stars in plinths and cornices at the ceiling. The cascading curtain which she'd accidentally transfigured hung down elegantly, and opposite was the archway through which the mystery woman had made her exit. It stood beneath an enormous serif inscription that read **HECATE HOUSE**.

"Ms. Belladonna Blackthorn, please proceed to the courtroom, post-haste. Thank you!" a voice rang out, then switched off abruptly, like a school hall megaphone.

She headed the only way that was available, through the shadowed archway, which held another heavy door.

Now Hecate House truly began. She stumbled back a few steps and shielded her eyes as the next room instantly flooded with golden light like a sunset, revealing something that could only be described as . . . wonderful.

The space was a gigantic and perfect circle, a rotunda with towering high walls that rose up into an elegant domed ceiling. Sweeping reams of deep violet velvet adorned the height all around, and each impressive curve was buttoned smartly with enormous elegant depictions of the twelve zodiac signs, all cast imposingly in bronze. A proud ram, which must have been ten feet tall, was hanging high. A Herculean bull, a regal lion, fish the size of whales triumphantly splashing. Each stood above a corresponding wooden door as though guarding it, twelve of them at intervals around the circular room like the points of a clock.

But the ceiling was what caught Belle in awe, and she nearly lost her balance as she craned her neck and held on to the brim of her hat to gaze straight upwards. Melting into the bows of velvet, the whole expanse was charged with lightning. Live electricity, a parachuting blanket of what looked like television static, crackling and popping as sparks flew in all directions, crashing and bouncing off one another, stars that were alive and flying. Rainbows of lights reflected like the most extreme disco ball, a mirrored mosaic of colour and energy. She recognised the glittering, firefly-like movements from her own finger, but this existed on a much larger hypnotising scale. The ceiling of Hecate House's atrium was lined with pure magic, a woven tapestry of the precious power that ran through her every day. It was mesmerising to witness.

She only broke away her gaze when she caught sight of the floor, equally beautiful at her feet. Below her boots, vividly painted tiles of navy, cerulean and slate slotted together as an intricate puzzle to form a floor that depicted the night sky, wild and stirring with the smallest of details, just like the coven cloaks. An astrological sun and whimsical moon were woven together and surrounded by all of the stars imaginable, constellations and planets gilded with gold and set against the rich blue. She hardly dared walk across it.

Belle's trance snapped as the loudspeaker sounded again with the same click. "Ms. Belladonna Blackthorn, courtroom, posthaste."

She had entered from the twelfth doorway, the poised bow and arrow of Sagittarius above the doorway behind her. The tenth doorway had a looming set of swinging bronze Libra scales poised above it. Balance, harmony, decision, fairness . . . Her instinct decided that it made a certain amount of sense for it to be the courtroom. Taking soft steps over the beautiful floor, spinning as she crossed to catch every detail in the art that she could, Belle crossed to the tenth doorway.

A wall of excited chatter exuded the moment the door opened, but the thrum of noise shrunk back when her arrival was noticed. A sudden silence fell, cut through only by one or two throat clears. The courtroom of Hecate House stood proudly in front of her.

"Hi. Hellooo, hi." She waved, then cringed. "I'm here for my EquiWitch hearing . . . trial . . . assessment . . . interview?" Belle made a conscious effort to straighten her spine and raise her gaze.

"We were beginning to think you must have expired along the way."

The acerbic voice came from the same lady who had met her with winter's frost earlier. She sounded distinctly disappointed that her suspicions had not proven correct.

The courtroom was almost entirely lined with hundreds, if not thousands, of richly coloured old books, shelved tightly together from floor to high concave ceiling, a mixture of jewel-shaded spines turning the background into a quilt of muted colours. A carefully placed brickwork of history and knowledge and magic. The heady scent of aged pages, the same smell as Lunar Books, was an unexpected comfort.

Nevertheless, her attention was drawn straight ahead of her to the centre of the far wall, where a magnificent golden pendulum spanned the entire height of the room. It swung heavily and grandly from the ceiling side to side, second by second, with an audibly deep whoosh, like a crash of distant waves. Beneath and behind it, a grand fireplace tiled in rich purple roared with dancing flames.

To the left and right of the pendulum were rows of dark wooden pews. Each seated a selection of wicchefolk who appeared to make up what would be the jury. Her coven. *There could be a hundred of them*, Belle thought, *maybe more*. They sat packed in so closely that they jostled shoulders, all wearing cloaks and hats that mirrored Belle's own coven uniform, the glints of their personal constellation detail reflecting in the firelight, hat points dancing at all angles. Some were clutching papers, glancing at watches, reading books, while levitating pens and notebooks hovered patiently next to their wrists, poised for action. One man even had a grey typewriter floating over his lap, which clicked while diligently making notes on his behalf. All had simultaneously stopped their gossiping and turned their heads to peer at the flustered witch who'd burst through the door.

Belle could feel her cheeks burning.

"Oh, Morena, you are too harsh on these younger ones. Be nice, for once in your life."

Belle was so relieved to finally hear a kind voice, that it wasn't out of the question that she might burst into tears. Again. Instead, she gave a desperately grateful smile to the face it belonged to, which was suitably kind-looking to match.

"Hello there, love. Belle Blackthorn, is it? Of course it is. You don't half look like your nan, and your mum for that matter."

Directly in front of the pendulum were two women who couldn't have been more chalk and cheese. Behind a grand wooden podium, intricately carved with the coven star at the centre, they looked comically opposite.

On the left was Morena, surely six feet tall, straight as a broom and just as bristling. And on the right, barely visible over the top of the podium, was maybe the kindest-looking, roundest face that Belle had ever seen. This witch looked as though she'd give a wonderful hug. Her once red, now greying hair was bluntly cut under her chin, which only added to her pleasant shape, and unlike Morena, she looked to be having a lovely time. She smiled proudly at their newest visitor with her hands on her hips. A flush of pink was spread across her cheeks and button nose, and Belle was amazed to spot a tiny brown mouse sitting perfectly calmly, watching on with its paws curled over the front pocket of her cloak. She thought back to arriving at Hecate House, when she'd spotted the mouse by the willow. She should have known.

"Come on in, there we go. Don't be scared, lovey," the second witch said with beckoning arms.

She tottered over, her little legs hidden underneath her long skirt, giving the impression that she was gliding. She guided Belle farther into the courtroom with a reassuring arm, towards a three-legged stool in front of their podium.

"You're going to take that seat in the middle, there. And then we can get started, petal." She beamed.

Belle had barely dropped her bag and touched the seat when Morena spoke again, loudly and impatiently.

"Belladonna Blackthorn, your presence was summoned here today, as is the practice of—"

The pink-cheeked witch, having tottered back towards her place behind the podium, promptly whacked her sharp-nosed colleague on the arm with a tut.

"Hold on a minute there, Mor. Let the girl gather her thoughts. Let's have a proper introduction. It's an overwhelming experience, being in front of us old fogies. No offence, everyone." She chuckled to herself, gesturing to the juries to her left and right.

Several members tittered graciously like old friends.

Morena prickled, folding her arms crossly.

"Belle, would you like some tea, dear? Talk amongst yourselves for a moment, folks," the kind witch instructed the jury.

Before Belle could answer for herself, a pretty pink teapot appeared from the air in front of her with a burst of bright sparks and poured itself neatly into a matching teacup, complete with saucer, teaspoon and chocolate biscuit on the side.

"That's kind of you," Belle answered. "And I really am so sorry. It was a bit of . . . an adventure, finding the place. I'm sure my blood pressure will return to normal one day."

A smell of honey wafted from the spout. The teaspoon stirred and tapped itself with a clink. Grateful for the sugar, Belle quickly drank the comforting chamomile and instantly felt soothed. She suspected that a particularly well-brewed calming potion might have had something to do with it.

"Yes, we should probably do something about that entry test," the kind witch pondered, sipping her own tea nearby. "It's supposed to be a callback to what those who came before us were forced to endure. If there's one thing you can count on wicchefolk for, it's a few theatrics. One does wonder why we're so obsessed with tradition when the past was so bloody awful for everyone involved."

"Once we've finished having our picnic and discussing the forecast for next week, it would perhaps be prudent to begin business. Before the next ice age lands upon us, preferably." Morena stared down stony-faced from the height of the podium, her fingers tented in front of her in a stiffly drawn fail of patience.

"Sorry. Yes, absolutely. I've taken up enough of your time already this morning." Belle inwardly cringed. Why did she feel the need to be so constantly polite? The only reason she was late was because these people had half dragged her to the brink of death this morning, and here she was, still determined to be liked by them.

"Don't you worry, deary," her new favourite person said, fanning away her apology. "We have put you through rather a lot this morning, it's understandable to be a bit flappy. But if you are feeling ready, then we shall certainly proceed. Would you like to introduce yourself?"

No, thank you. Belle stood up hesitantly. Each of her limbs felt excessively long, like they were made of noodles. How did she normally stand? She shifted from one leg to the other. Every pair of eyes in the room was focused intently on her.

She coughed. "I'm Belle. Blackthorn. Belladonna, but I mean, obviously no one calls me that because . . . it's a lot. Thanks for having me. This is great. Really . . . great. I'm thirty today. Thanks for coming to my birthday party. I live in London. I'm a Libra. I like piña coladas, getting caught in the rain." She scratched at her forearm. "I'm not sure what else to say."

"You can just state your name, dear. It's for the records."

"Oh. Well, Belle Blackthorn, then."

The pleasant witch clapped her hands together twice and gave a happy nose scrunch. She cast her hands towards the sky, and with a bright beam of her magic, the enormous presence of the pendulum stilled mid-swing. Within the fireplace, the flames ceased to dance. Dust particles hanging in the air began to float at only the tiniest fraction of their normal speed, as though time itself were standing still entirely for everyone and everything in the world except those present in the courtroom. Belle wondered if, perhaps, it really was.

The bright lights came down to a sulking darkness, and the rustling of murmured chatter came to an unnerving, perfect quiet. Morena cleared her throat importantly, gripping the edges of the walnut podium to glare down at Belle. She had evidently been chomping at the bit for her moment.

"Belladonna Blackthorn, your presence was summoned—"

"Oh, rubber ducks and bat whistles, Morena! *Our* introductions! We forgot! You'd think in all the years we've been doing these blasted hearings—"

Thunder flooded Morena's gaunt face. She looked entirely affronted, as her short companion interrupted the beginnings of her speech with a cheery chuckle and a palm to the forehead. The pendulum began swinging again in its slow heartbeat of a rhythm, and the lights lifted as though someone had yelled "Cut!"

"I tell you, Belle dear, I'd forget my head if it wasn't screwed on. And a headless witch is never going to be too popular mixing amongst the non-wicche. I think they might spot something was afoot." The short witch chortled. Her rambling received another generous rumble of jury laughter. "Belle, I believe you've already met my sweetness and light sister, but this is she. Morena Gowden, as we all live and breathe."

Morena had still not quite managed to compose her indignation. She looked thunderously at her sister, shooting daggers with her eyes and quite possibly wishing she had a real one to use. Belle hoped there wasn't any kind of spell which created looks that could kill, because if so, she was about to witness sororicide.

"And I am the better half of the Gowden sisters." The small witch winked. "Bronwyn Gowden," she said, tapping her chest vigorously and only just missing the mouse in her pocket.

8

Meeting of Minds

BELLE DID A less than great job of hiding her sudden understanding, the realisation painted across her face. The Gowden sisters were legendary. Even she, with her limited knowledge of the world of witchcraft, instantly recognised the names. In her defence, they were older now than their iconic portraits in the grimoire. Although saying that, it was almost guaranteed that the sisters had taken the pledge of the cauldron, an esteemed decision presented to Selcouth's elite, to stretch the normal passing of their human years in the name of bettering their magic for the good of wicche-kind. Age really was just a number in this realm.

It was well known that the sisters, while not the slightest bit similar in appearance, were equally matched in their unrivalled levels of magical ability. In passing chats with Belle about coven history over the years, Bonnie had told the inspiring story of how the sisters had swiftly risen from obscurity to the top of the coven, thanks to clear skill and natural prowess, following the untimely death of the previous sage. The coven had fallen into turmoil, but these two women raised it from the ashes in a united front of sisterhood. They were widely respected and admired, revered even, by any and all who encountered them. Their grasp of the magical arts was said to be exceptional, bending usual boundaries to their will. She'd heard many times from her mother that, although they often bickered over anything at all—tradition versus modernisation, spell lore, tea readings, soap operas—they always stood together for the coven. They had steered it through uncertain times of history with an unyielding stance. The Gowden sisters could always be trusted to do what was right for Selcouth. That included, it would seem, delivering final verdicts on its future via EquiWitch trials.

"We will be conducting your hearing today. You may even enjoy yourself, love. We do have a laugh here, we do get a bit silly," Bronwyn said, as she gestured to the rows of jury members quietly observing.

"You've got Cas there, Caspar Strix. Balancer here at Selcouth, the one to make sure everything is conducted properly and fairly. A useful man to butter up, aren't you, Cas?" Bronwyn gave a tinkling wave to the man at the front left of the jury.

He sent a grand and kindly nod in Belle's direction.

"There's Andromeda there, and Felix and Wilmott. I probably don't have time to introduce everybody, or Morena will have me strung up. But if you stay for the lunch spread once we've wrapped up, then you're sure to meet us all properly for a natter. We're a friendly bunch, Belle. Oh, and Elspeth, she's your girl if you're in need of any winter recipes. Makes a smashing cheese soup, does our Elspeth."

Elspeth, with tight dark ringlets underneath her hat, gave a quick wave to make herself known and replied, "Yoo-hoo!"

"Wow, great. Cheese soup sounds . . . great," said Belle, trying to seem enthusiastic.

"And Aoife and Ike and Spottswood. And that handsome devil to the back is Rune. The coven's rising star, that one. I believe you two are already familiar. Maybe you can give him a run for his money, Belle," Bronwyn said proudly.

Belle startled. Bronwyn was referring to a man who'd seated himself at the back of the right-hand jury. Bronwyn wasn't wrong about the handsome part. He leaned against the side of the pew with long limbs, all angles and presence, an air of distinct, detached boredom but passive grace. Dark hair brushed the shoulders of his long black leather coat, a single curl falling forwards, and a shadow of stubble added to the angles of his face. He played absent-mindedly with the silver ring on his thumb. He was the warlock who'd appeared at the bookshop—of course.

"You're too good to me, Bron," he replied, and gave Belle a nod, faintly amused. Rune removed his glasses, breathed on them to fog the lenses, and began to polish them with the untucked tail of his shirt, all while keeping his eyes firmly on her.

"Hi, birthday girl."

What felt like several slow-motion moments later, Belle tore her gaze away from Rune and his ridiculous coat straight back to Bronwyn, listening intently and decidedly not letting her eyes wander anywhere else. Belle hoped that the burn she could feel in her cheeks wasn't visible under the low lighting.

"It's lovely to meet you. All of you, finally."

"This is your coven, Belle. All except your lovely mum, of course. I'm sure you understand that family members are not permitted to sit for an EquiWitch. We've no time for nepotism. But I'm sure Bonnie is waiting to hear all about it. We are ready to welcome your endarkenment with open arms."

Belle took a second to glance across the jury again. This was it. The entire gathering of witches, warlocks and wicchefolk alike in the United Kingdom. Those who had been found or sought out or had openly declared themselves, anyway. There seemed so few of them in the grand scheme of things and yet more than she'd ever considered before. Unexpectedly, she found herself longing to be a part of it. Properly. To know them. Some more than others.

"You see? We don't bite," Bronwyn added. "Unless you're a biscuit, then I'm afraid you are in trouble."

"I am so glad I've spent vast years of celestial existence on this planet only to wither and die while waiting for this wretched hearing to finally begin," Morena interrupted, shuffling a stack of papers atop the podium.

Bronwyn ignored her, only smiling wider at Belle. "It'll be more of a . . . lovely chat. A reintroduction after fifteen years. All right, poppet? Wonderful, wonderful. Go on, then, Mor." Bronwyn wrapped a firm arm around the side of her sister, who instantly went rigid and leaned away at a sharp angle. "Do your thing, all of the dramatics. I know you do so enjoy making the children cry."

Morena rolled her eyes so dramatically that it seemed to Belle she could probably see the back of her own skull in great detail. She clapped twice with long, spindly fingers to summon silence in the courtroom before casting her hands towards the sky. All sound and movement seemed to cut from the air once again as the pendulum froze mid-swing, taking out the fire with it. The lights faded to eerie dimness.

"Belladonna Blackthorn, your presence was summoned here today, as is the practice of our preternatural kind, to deliver you unto a life of true eternal magic."

Morena read from an unfurled scroll levitating to her right, but she clearly knew the ceremonial speech by heart and was delivering it with marked enthusiasm.

"We congratulate you on your thirtieth orbital completion within the non-wicche realm. This feat brings with it myriad trials and questions upon yourself, your mind and your existence."

Dramatic but not wrong, Belle thought. Her late twenties had indeed been constant, incessant trials and questions about herself, her mind and her existence.

"This, the greatest and most important of traditions, shall mark the conclusion to your endarkenment, and be held here today, the first day of the month, Winterfylleth. Do you agree to submit to your trial with truth, certainty and bravery in thunder, lightning and in rain?"

It seemed to Belle that Morena was enjoying her role a little too much. Belle shuffled uncomfortably on her hands, perched on the rickety wooden stool, then realised that Morena was waiting for a response. "Oh, of course. Truth, certainty and . . ."

"Bravery, dear," Bronwyn said, nodding enthusiastically.

"That's the one." Belle clicked. "Yes. Bravery."

Morena practically snarled at Belle's delivery, ruining the rhythm of her own, but continued her speech with added vigour. "It is a fact of magical life, as proven and evidenced through history, that witches, warlocks or wicchefolk will be challenged by their co-existence with non-wicche society."

"Hear, hear," the jury echoed in ceremonial manner.

"The monotonous world of the non-wicche will strive to crush, to beat and to flatten the magic out of any soul who deigns to explore or reveal their own power."

"Hear, hear," they chanted again.

This seemed a little much to Belle. It was only working with Christopher, really, which ever left her feeling particularly crushed, beaten or flattened. The rest was okay. Witches clearly enjoyed a bit of show more than she'd ever realised, perhaps a fair compromise for spending most of their lives hiding their magic.

A deep, dark crimson red overcame the last of the light in the room, and Morena's shockingly pale complexion glowed translucent against it.

"The non-wicche people, oblivious to the potential for wonder that surrounds them, fear wildness. They fear the power that our proud and present kind represent. They see in us what they cannot and never will see in themselves. Ashamed and bitter, knowing that their own magic could never, and will never, dare to show itself."

Belle's brow furrowed.

"Within them, magic withers. Within us, it shines."

"Hear, hear," the jury echoed again.

Belle thought of her friends. She would argue that they each had their own version of magic to share with the world. She wasn't sure that they should be considered ashamed or bitter. As a witch who mixed in the non-wicche world, she couldn't help but bristle at the criticism of those whom she loved. Neither Bonnie nor her grandmother had ever expressed sentiment like it, never attempted to divide the two sides of life.

Morena, looking satisfied with her performance, cast a quick hand over the scroll at her side, which re-rolled itself up tightly and vanished.

"You don't half commit to that, Mor. Very good." Bronwyn gave her sister a quick round of applause as the lights rose.

Belle swallowed a snort.

"If you're not going to do it by the book, Bronwyn, then it's not worth doing at all," Morena hissed, her lips so firmly pursed together that her dark lipstick disappeared.

Again, Bronwyn ignored her. "Belle, if you're ready, poppet, we'll begin your manifests. Let's get those out of the way, and then we'll be done and dusted with this palaver. And you can get home to enjoy the rest of your birthday. Have you got a cake? I'm always partial to those caterpillar—"

"Is this really the time?" Morena snapped.

"Oh, and I've got my sooth stone here," Belle said, fumbling at the pin on her strap, struggling to unhook the clasp with nervous fingers.

She approached the podium and reached up to hand it over to

Bronwyn, who took it in the palm of her hand. Belle could have sworn the elder witch inhaled a tense breath as she took it, her eyes fixed on the small stone. Belle noticed what must have been Bronwyn's own stone sitting on the end of a chain around her neck, misted grey behind the glass.

"I don't know much about this little thing," Belle said fondly. "Is it important?"

"Important? Oh, well, perhaps . . ." Bronwyn's voice trailed off as she examined it gingerly.

"Do I need it for the—what do you call them—manifests?"

Morena let out a cutting bark of a laugh, startling Bronwyn. There was a disconcerting murmuring amongst the jury, who began to shuffle and fidget. To Belle's shame, the words "clueless" and "foolish" distinctly simmered above the whispers.

"No matter, Ms. Blackthorn. This historic and prestigious moment is clearly no concern of yours. Never bothered to memorise the grimoire, I take it? Otherwise you'd know that a sooth stone plays a sacred part in the final moments of endarkenment rites. I dare say, not something *you* need to worry about. Perhaps we should forget this whole ceremony. I truly haven't the patience for this today." Morena viciously massaged her temples.

"Oh, Mor, please," Bronwyn tutted. "Don't pretend that you have any patience at all, today or any other day."

"I think I have, in fact, been very patient while you both prattle on with—"

"You're about as patient as a lion cub getting its claws clipped. And you're nowhere near as cute or fluffy, so you can't get away with it, I'm afraid."

"Bronwyn, I warned you that this would not run smooth." Morena's temper flared. "There is quite clearly no natural witchery exhibiting from Ms. Blackthorn. No skill of note has shown itself, no preternatural instinct developed—"

"Madame Sage and Madame Sage." A deep gravelly voice boomed from the jury and echoed across the books that lined the walls, making both the sisters and Belle jump in unison, as well as several jury members. The lights and the pendulum were snapped from the spell's effects, returning to normal.

The man who Bronwyn had introduced earlier as Caspar rose confidently from the first seat of pews on the left. Thick silver-streaked locs reached down to his elbows against his cloak, which he'd paired with a burgundy suit. His handsome aged face seemed irked by their bickering, but his poise remained positively regal, calming. He was evidently well practiced at intercepting Gowden squabbles.

"Madames Sage, if you please," he repeated, indicating for them to steady themselves. "It would be unfair to lead Ms. Blackthorn into this ceremony without some further clarity. She is evidently feeling anxious. Perhaps the honourable jury will grant some time for additional discussion."

Belle, wanting to immediately die on the spot, jumped in. "Oh no, honestly . . . I don't want to cause any—"

"Please, Ms. Blackthorn," Caspar said with gentle assertion. "We are in no rush; time waits for men of magic if we so wish it to. I'd invite you to accompany me, and perhaps Bronwyn would be so kind as to join us for a moment?" His words were not a suggestion.

"And what would you have the rest of us do, Strix? All wait here patiently while you enjoy a quick 'get to know me,' I suppose? I truly despair," Morena said.

"Yes, please, Mor. Shan't be long!" Bronwyn called. "Oh, Rune, you come along, too, lovey."

Rune slapped the thighs of his trousers as he rose to make his way down the pews. Belle did her level best to ignore the faintly mocking smile that he was exhibiting, as though he knew that Belle would be annoyed at his inclusion.

"Why does he have to come?" Belle followed uncomfortably after Caspar, trying to keep pace as he strode towards the back of the courtroom.

"Rune Dunstan. A protector of sorts. Newly ordained, but certainly worthy of it. Exhibits a level of magical skill that you'd expect to see in someone a generation or two above," Caspar told her, heading through a door hidden amongst the bookshelves which seemed to materialise from nowhere with a quick rotation of his palm. Bronwyn toddled behind to catch up, Rune walking with his hands in his pockets beside her as they spoke under their breath.

"I really am so sorry about all of this. Have you got a busy afternoon?" Belle said, trying to patch awkwardness with politeness.

"Hecate House Athenaeum. Also my office, incidentally," Caspar announced.

Rune closed the door behind them and leaned against the fireside, his arms crossed in front of him. The remaining trio each took a seat in one of Caspar's wingback chairs. Belle admired the portrait in a large gilded frame above the mantel, a likeness of Caspar standing proudly next to a beautiful woman and two witches around her own age with curly hair, whom Belle also recognised amongst the jury, presumably the Strix daughters. A towering set of balanced scales and a huge sword were positioned at their feet in the painting.

With an elegant wave, Caspar cast a fire into the hearth, and the warm light bounced from the vast collection of shining telescopes positioned through the room. Huge rolls of detailed sky maps bound around wooden handles were stacked against the walls. A central table, which seemed to be a golden globe opened in half, depicted some kind of planet model and was covered in a scattering of carefully arranged cool-toned crystals. His specialist branch of magic was evident.

"Pardon my interruption on your special day, Belle. The energy of the courtroom felt in need of a reset," Caspar said. "I merely thought it best we take a moment to make sure we're all on the same page. It's my role to ensure all things remain even-handed, and that often requires rebalancing."

The fire crackled behind his words.

"Hence the title," Belle said.

"Indeed. As balancer, treasurer, gatekeeper at Selcouth, I'm here—along with Rune, of course—to keep you safe and well, and to keep things fair and measured. To make sure the spellwork is by the book, to make sure your jury is attuned to your true circumstance, that sort of thing."

Caspar seemed like he'd have any and all answers for her, probably to questions she hadn't even thought to ask yet. Belle nodded, making a conscious effort to not let overwhelm take hold. She glanced over at Rune and found that, despite his disinterested body language, his gaze was firmly fixed on her but darted to the fire when their eyes caught.

"And where do you come into all of this?" she asked him, finding herself bristling, unable to drop the lingering combative tone from their first encounter at Lunar.

"Wouldn't you like to know," he said with a raised eyebrow, spinning the ring on his thumb.

"Rune," Bronwyn said in a warning tone. He rolled his eyes in response.

"Watchman for Selcouth. Not something I volunteered for myself, but Bronwyn here was adamant that I accept."

"Well, who else were we going to ask to keep us all safe? Ruddy Elspeth?" Bronwyn replied.

"It's a protective role," Rune went on. "I monitor magic use across the coven for red flags, unusual activity, keep an eye out for anyone attempting any spells that they shouldn't be using."

"And acting as the coven's personal postman, too?" Belle asked.

"Only for you," he responded with a head tilt.

Caspar coughed pointedly, snapping the string of tension in the air. "The point is that some of our elders forget that younger coven members have not witnessed hundreds of these jury trials as they have. They forget all too soon what it's like to be at the crucial, vulnerable point of endarkenment. Thus, I am determined to ensure things proceed fairly. For anyone, of course, but particularly for the daughter of such a good friend."

Belle's eyebrows shot up in surprise. "Oh, you're friends with my mum?"

Caspar smiled fondly, beaming right up to his eyes. "Indeed. We were at university together. We faced our EquiWitch hearings together, and both specialised in Earth Sorcery. Bonnie followed her heart towards the nature of the land, while I found my solace amongst the skies."

"Belle, my love." Bronwyn spoke slightly too pitying to be comforting. "Maybe it's best we . . . spell it out. Leaping lizards, my terrible puns. I don't even mean to do it." Bronwyn adjusted herself in the deep armchair. Her feet didn't quite touch the floor. "All will be fine, I do promise you that. But as your elders, it is our duty to remind you officially that there is the chance that this verdict will change . . . well, everything."

"That'll make you feel better," Rune quipped, feigning innocence when Bronwyn shot him a look.

"I might not have exhibited a whole lot of flair or special talent," Belle said, "but I also haven't done anything terrible. I've never upset the balance, I've never touched time or death or true love. All the golden rules."

Caspar straightened his burgundy blazer, smoothing the lapels. "Which certainly works in your favour."

Belle frowned. "How do you decide if I'm . . . worthy? If I'm enough?"

"The trial begins when the coven recites the EquiWitch incantation together," he explained. "Once we begin, the pendulum at the back of the room . . . I'm sure you noticed it? That pendulum is a force of greatness. Its presence is no decorative choice. It stands on a precise nexus point. I don't mean to patronise you, Belle. Are you familiar with the word?"

"Nexus? It's a crossing point. Full of elemental energy," Belle said, relieved to have an answer.

"Exactly. Earth, air, fire and water all merge at those exact coordinates. And magic theory dictates that nothing is more powerful than that. Crossroads in the ley lines of magic itself."

Belle nodded keenly.

"In the wrong hands, the presence of the nexus can be manipulated towards dark magic, too. It's why the coven came to be in Hecate House, and one of the reasons why the place is guarded by the unpleasant challenges you faced earlier. The pendulum is a huge resource which we only call upon for this traditional, sacred ceremony of endarkenment to cement magic in its rightful place for good. The coven only leans on the abilities of the nexus when huge numbers of us are present together for fairness and protection. Otherwise, it is best left well enough alone."

"That pendulum holds access to time itself," Bronwyn said. "It resets magical balance, essential for completing endarkenment, cementing magic where it belongs and welcoming a witch fully to the coven."

"The nexus also allows us to bend time as needed, which is how your manifests will be shown," Caspar added.

"It'll call on the elements to show crucial moments from your past," Bronwyn said. "Key milestones from your life that have made you who you are and when you've notably used your magic to the benefit of yourself or others. Your highlight reel, so to speak, lovey."

"The jury will review the selection of manifests that the nexus creates and, with the advice of Bronwyn and Morena, decide whether your past history and present self meet the expectations of Selcouth, in truth, certainty and bravery," Caspar said.

Belle swallowed hard, feeling neither truthful, certain or brave. On reflection, maybe she never felt those things.

"What could possibly go wrong?" Rune said, tossing some kind of orb that he'd lifted from Caspar's display into the air and smoothly catching it with a grin. She ignored him.

"Thank you, Rune," Caspar said shortly. "Again we must stress that an expellation, a full removal of magic, hasn't happened in . . . well, a long time. I'll have to check the records. Certainly not in my lifetime, or in yours, Bron?"

"Only one banishment I've ever known of. But the circumstances were different. You're not about to break that record, Belle," Bronwyn continued. She leaned forwards and patted Belle's hand, which was still stress-gripping the arm of the chair.

"Told you, nothing to worry about, eh?" the elder witch chimed. "You'll get your coven colours, and then it's time for chocolate and buttercream."

Belle tried to offer a smile. Walking head first into the blaze with the blindfold removed wasn't all that much of a comfort when the flames were still licking at her feet.

"It's just that I'm not absolutely, entirely convinced at this moment in time that my historical use of the craft is going to be up to scratch. I mean, to reiterate, I've never done anything bad," Belle clarified, waving her hands. "World domination attempts have not been in the cards. It's just that I'm a bit . . . I'm more of a back-seat witch, I guess. A wallflower. A witchflower?"

"Nonsense!" Caspar bellowed happily. He clapped Belle on the back, making her cough, and dusted down invisible lint from his carefully pressed trousers. "All we're doing is taking stock—considering what you've achieved, the decisions you've made, the responsibility you've shown, celebrating the milestones."

Although he meant well, this made Belle feel even sicker.

He flashed her a dazzling smile and gestured for Belle to exit. "All protocol, you understand." He clearly considered the matter closed.

Bronwyn locked her hands over Belle's and grasped them with a tight grip. "You'll be gone before you know it."

Belle rose to follow Caspar and Bronwyn back into the courtroom, gathering her cape around her. Rune held the top of the doorframe. He reached for her shoulder as she passed underneath his arm. Belle looked at his hand as though it were a foreign object, then their eyes locked again.

"Seeing as no one else around here seems to have properly said it," he murmured, "happy birthday, Belle."

9

Belle's Manifests

"HOW CONSIDERATE OF you all to rejoin us. I hear the sun is in its last moments of burning, the final reckoning should be upon humankind any second." Morena rifled through a stack of papers on the podium, peering over the top of a pair of reading glasses as she addressed their re-entry into the courtroom.

"Third time's a charm, Ms. Blackthorn," she continued with dripping sarcasm. "Unless you have a further tête-à-tête to bring along to the court today. I can grab my knitting, if you'd like? Help pass the time a little."

"Now, now, Morena. Play nice," Caspar warned.

With the short break, the jury seemed to have settled back to something more neutral, marginally less side-eyes and curt looks being thrown in Belle's direction. Bronwyn took her place beside her impatient sister, and Belle regretfully returned to her precarious stool. As Rune found his seat again, adjusting the thighs of his trousers as he lowered himself, Belle was surprised to notice him give her a small expressionless nod of what she assumed was supposed to be encouragement. Belle returned the gesture and did her best to entirely ignore the small swell of appreciation in her chest.

She fiddled with the clasp on her sooth stone, now pinned back onto her dress.

"No knitting needed, thank you. I'm ready."

Bronwyn gave Bélle a wink and a keen thumbs-up, like an enthusiastic parent watching their child in a school play. The mouse in her pocket adjusted itself to get a better view of the courtroom scene, its tail peeking over the hem.

"We'll pick up where we left off, eh, folks? No need to rehash the boring stuff," Bronwyn asked the jury, who murmured in approval. Morena looked disappointed that her speech about withering death did not require a reprise.

Bronwyn clapped twice to bring the lights low and the pendulum to a languid halt once more. Belle could feel her own pulse raising the skin at her temples in an emphatic rhythm.

Recognising their cue, those able amongst the jury rose to their feet with a flurry of cloaks and a rustling adjustment of hats. Hands were raised in unison, poised in personal shapes, gestures and statures. Belle was grateful she had instantly selected the simple finger point fifteen years ago without much thought, drawn to its minimal margin for error. Other magic folk chose options with a little more flair when first receiving their powers. Raised open palms like both Gowdens were common, claps and clicks like Rune also popular choices, but any gesture was a possible option to accommodate all physicalities. Nose twitches had their day, intentional stares were considered a power move, wands were sometimes favoured by traditionalists but widely considered clunky in the modern magic era. She'd heard of a warlock who burped to cast his magic, which seemed like a choice that a fifteen-year-old boy would find funny and later grow up to deeply regret.

Speaking in one galvanising voice, the coven began to chant in unison, and the words washed over her in a wave of solid magic. She shut her eyes.

Our grandmothers wait for the truth to reveal,
Equidistant existence, thine secrets unsealed.
Ten nine fifty days to span decades three,
Transcend limitation, and thus shall it be.
Experience, action, perception and truth.
This coven now claims you for life, so in sooth.

For a moment, nothing happened.

Belle dared to peep through one eye while keeping the other firmly shut, half expecting everything around her to have vanished. To wake up with a start but safe in her bed.

Instead, everyone present in the courtroom had turned completely still, all held under the same blanketing trance. Their eyes closed, the slightest of movement only in hair caught on a slow breeze, and steady sleeping breaths seemed to come at a fraction of normal intervals. Everything in sight was motionless. Frozen in time.

"Oh . . . god." Belle swayed on the spot, gripping the edge of the stool. "Please don't have all died. Please, please don't have all died."

Bronwyn stood at peace, a pleasant smile on her face. Morena, deathly still, could have been a glamorous corpse. Belle chanced a glance at Rune, somehow expecting his attitude to be immune, but he, too, was entirely stationary, though still leaning unruffled against the wooden pew with one hand in his pocket. Belle's internal panic was reaching interesting new levels of chaotic. How best might one begin to escape an underground witches' lair full of the mysteriously deceased, with no exits known or available? All of the true crime documentaries in the world couldn't help her cover it up.

The ground beneath her jolted in a giant tremor. She grabbed the flopping brim of her hat, losing balance. An enormous deafening clap of what could only be thunder boomed so loudly that Belle felt it rattle through her legs and chest and all the way up to the domed ceiling. The walls shook so hard from the noise that books tumbled from the shelves. The fireplaces burning at each end of the room were instantly extinguished.

The courtroom ceiling began to disappear from view as looming layers of opaque grey clouds rolled in thickly from the shadows and knitted themselves densely together. Several hundred feet under London, a storm was coming to Hecate House.

There followed three blindingly bright bolts of lightning, which slashed through the air with startling white light and wrapped the pendulum in a live, sparking current. All the while, through cacophony and chaos, the entire jury and the Gowden sisters remained absolutely motionless, frozen and floating in time.

And then came the rain. Sheets and sheets of it, relentlessly pouring down from the clouds which had formed inside. The heavens—or wherever she'd found herself for her birthday—had opened, and Belle threw her pointing finger out instinctively to conjure an umbrella.

But it wasn't needed. Rather than drenching her from head to toe, the rain slid right over her. It felt like a ream of chilled soft silk, the water skimming over her clothes and skin, leaving no trace. Yet the rain pooled at her feet in translucent floods, reflecting rainbows like a petrol spill. The rainwater rippled like invisible pearlescent cloth across the floor, while the sparks and shocks from the lightning bounced and crackled haphazardly through the air, falling like a snow flurry. Rather than sticking as snowfall would, the sparks hovered in mid-air above the floods, from snowflakes to fireflies. It was breathtaking to see, the lightning dust reflecting off the torrents of rain. Belle couldn't look away. It was beautiful and terrifying.

As suddenly as the thunderstorm arrived, it passed. One final grand thunderclap shook the room and seemed to break the spell. The rain slowed in a moment. The clouds above parted and dissolved to nothing, as candyfloss vanishes in water. The iridescent flood remained pooled across the ground, and the fireflies of lightning stayed floating.

The jury were awoken from their trance in unison as though they'd been napping and jerked themselves awake. The Gowden sisters jolted back to consciousness, Bronwyn so startled by her return to the room that she dropped like a sack of spuds into her chair with a snuffling snore. Morena simply shook her head elegantly as if to brush away the cobwebs, returning to perfect composure in an instant.

"Bravo, everybody! Bravo, folks! All okay back there?" Bronwyn called cheerily, as she dusted herself down.

She was answered with a murmur from the jury that didn't sound entirely convinced that they were okay, actually. A few looked wobbly on their feet, like they'd had one too many. One lady covered her mouth in panic to stop herself from throwing up. Another person was attempting to wring imaginary water out of their ears. Caspar simply straightened the lapels of his blazer. Rune casually pushed hair back from his face and looked straight at Belle.

"Oh, isn't it pretty?" Bronwyn said, gesturing to the dance of stars and rain now in front of them. "Well, that's the easy bit out of the way."

"The easy bit? I thought you'd all died," Belle exclaimed, any fragment of composure long gone.

Bronwyn, double-checking that the mouse in her pocket had survived the events, didn't seem to hear. "And on with . . . What's next? Ah, yes, the nine manifests of Belle Blackthorn. That's you, dear," Bronwyn said.

The sisters turned away from their view of the witch in question and spun to face the pendulum, its huge brass form reflecting in the flooded floor.

"We begin the Manifests of Belladonna Blackthorn. Thunder, lightning and rain, come together with the magic of Selcouth." Morena spoke firmly and clearly.

She held out her hands so that they hovered over the iridescent floods of storm-water surrounding their podium with rainbow reflects. At her words, sparks of magic flew magnetically from Morena's palms and joined the thousands of tiny lightning bursts. Like a whirlwind, the magic and lightning began to fly in great tornado circles. Belle could only watch in awe as the sea of storm-water then rose to meet it all in a great tidal wave that towered over everybody. Sparks and splashes flew madly in a cyclone together as Morena's palms conducted the spellwork. Together, the powers were forming a shape. A pattern. A picture.

"Is that . . . me?" Belle was astonished.

With chaotic elegance, the elements formed what was undeniably an image, a live dot-to-dot made of magic and cascading water, of her younger self. Bronwyn turned back to her, nodding excitedly but placing her finger to her lips to shush her.

1

Belle recognised the moment almost instantly. It was her fifteenth birthday, and she stood around a family-sized cauldron with her mother and her grandmother. The three of them were dishevelled and filthy, having spent the day in Bonnie's greenhouse picking flora for Belle's first ever cauldron-based spell. They'd decided on something simple, a comforting brew of *Solatium Quies* to help Belle feel at home with her newly acquired powers. It was one of her most treasured memories, the three of them selecting the right flowers and herbs and mushrooms together. She remembered the potion, like sipping on the feeling of stepping out into a warm day, feeling the sun's rays on her skin as she drank. Her heart could have burst to hear their trio of female laughter in a chorus, the clinking of bottles and flasks a balanced harmony. She suddenly wished desperately for her mum and ached with the familiar raw grief for her grandmother who, even now, made herself known like a weary visitor seeking a home for the night.

"Touching. It comes so naturally to the Blackthorns. Undoubtedly truth," she heard Caspar say.

"The power of mother and daughter magic—threefold, too," offered a jury member with colourful hair knots, who clapped with sheer joy. They all sounded thoroughly pleased with the first manifest. After moments that Belle wished would last longer, the sparks and splashes tumbled back down, sending deep ripples across the floor before rising back again in a wave.

2

This time, they merged to become the image of a later teenage Belle, when her hair was longer and her jeans were, frankly, terrible. She sat cross-legged in front of her single bed and a floor-length mirror to practice, a tiny kitten Jinx nuzzling at her chin as Belle pored over a book in her lap. She was trying (failing but trying nonetheless) to master a basic levitation spell straight from the grimoire without Bonnie's supervision. She'd managed to raise the unsuspecting cat about a foot off the ground for a handful of seconds but hadn't got much further. She persisted for hours, much to her floating furry friend's confusion, before finally succeeding in continuous levitation.

A murmur of fond laughter from the jury at the floating, pawing kitten bolstered Belle a little. So far, shockingly, so good. A sentimental moment with her highly esteemed witch mother and grandmother followed by an example of dedication to learning her craft and an Animal Affinity to her familiar. Not only were these precious moments to relive, but they were earning points from hardened coven critics. She smiled as her own manifestation scooped Jinx onto her shoulder and gave her a scruff on the head, receiving a headbutt in return.

"Look, Mor. A natural and loyal familiar. The sign of a born witch." Bronwyn pointed to her sister with a told-you-so expression. Morena rolled her eyes for what must surely be the hundredth time that day.

"Oh, please. Anyone can have a bloody cat, Bron."

3

The picture cascaded back down into the water, and the elements remerged in a triumphant dance into a third manifest. Now they painted Belle and another figure.

"Ariadne!"

They must have been no more than seventeen, Belle thought, trying to recognise the scene that was crafting itself in dots. The sparks became a picture of the pair at university all those years ago, when they'd been the true meaning of the word "inseparable." Ari had been dumped by a particularly foul boy (Belle couldn't remember his name anymore) and was inconsolable.

On the grey day that the manifest had plucked from obscurity, they'd skipped university and parked up in front of the river in Ariadne's second-hand car to lament her broken heart. In an attempt to cheer up her best friend, Belle had performed magic that she hoped would spark a smile. She'd thrown together a nature summoning spell, entirely doubtful of its success, but after she'd chucked the contents of the bottle out of the car window, it had ended up attracting all of the wildlife within a ten-mile radius.

The girls sat in disbelief, watching as deer, rabbits, badgers, hares and foxes emerged from the shrubs and woodland—even seals and otters glided by on the river. Ariadne swore that she'd seen a unicorn. Belle had tried to convince her it had been a dog with a stick. Their hysterical laughter and delirious shrieks from the memory rang around the courtroom. With the joy of magic, she succeeded that day in putting a smile back on Ari's face, even for a few minutes, and watching the scene again made Belle remember the pleasure in magic for magic's sake. Each new animal, depicted like shadow puppets in the magic, brought gasps and compliments from the jury.

"Wonderful, wonderful!" Bronwyn said, clapping. "Beautiful magic. I remember my first fauna summons, there's nothing like it. Did end up bringing a dragon wandering into Donnington Service Station, though—bit of a ruckus . . ."

It felt to Belle like watching a film she didn't want to end. The moments brought a nostalgic ache to her chest, both hollow and full at once. Magic really had shone inside her once, with a genuine love and desire to make life more wonderful.

4

Ariadne stayed in the picture for the fourth manifest, the image twisting and contorting to new strings of stars.

They stood together, shoulder to shoulder, ponytails swinging, in the corner of the college. Pieces of paper were lined up regimentally across tables, and both girls reached out for the one with their name on a neat square sticker. The brown envelopes contained what had felt like the be-all and end-all, the outcome of their final exams and the verdicts from universities.

Ariadne had been frantic all morning, chewing on the ends of her hair and stopping to be sick in a drain on the walk. She'd known that she'd botched the higher maths paper earlier in the summer and had been plagued with self-loathing ever since, knowing that it would spoil her chances of following the path she'd been set on.

Belle, much less of a fixed plan in mind, had been more nervous for Ariadne's results than her own. Unable to handle the months of waiting, she had finally caved and reached for Bonnie's crystal ball in the middle of the night. Her stomach had plummeted as the clouds behind the glass revealed Ariadne's second choice university printed boldly across the paper. She'd cried for Ari and the thought of her broken dreams at eighteen.

Belle saw her manifest's hands working unnoticed. She vaguely remembered turning to the grimoire to find a transformative spell to change the typed letters on the page inside the envelope. It was only what Ariadne deserved.

"That's rather thoughtful," pointed out a jury member wearing a frog-patterned jumper.

"Helping friends in need is a happy part of our position. We hope to see magic shared sensibly for the non-wicche who needs and deserves it," Caspar said.

The jury seemed appeased.

"Some might call it meddling." Rune thumbed his jawline, leaning languidly on the pew, dragging his gaze from the manifest performance back to Belle. She could have sworn a tiny smirk twitched across his lips. Belle's face flushed like fire; she was furious with him. She shot back an indignant look.

"Well, I . . ."

Someone else interjected, "Ms. Blackthorn was in turn benefiting from the result of enchanting her friend's future; it was she who couldn't bear to face the reality. For all we know, the non-wicche girl would have handled it well. It could have been the making of her."

"In fact, this spell changed the trajectory of her friend's life entirely . . ." a blond witch pointed out.

"And we certainly never encourage cheating," added the soup lady, Elspeth. "Using magic on others for one's own advancement or unfair advantages."

"Hang on a second," Belle interjected, rising from her seat. "I wouldn't go that far. You don't know her. Ari is pretty much a genius. It wasn't 'cheating.' She buckles when the pressure gets too much, and it's not fair. I was just righting a blatant wrong."

"Pardon me, Ms. Blackthorn." Morena raised her voice sharply. "Interruptions are not welcome. You will have the opportunity to plead your case when all nine manifests have been presented."

Belle promptly shut up, feeling like a scolded child.

Rune at least had the grace to offer her a sheepish look the second he caught her eye again, mouthing a brooding "Sorry" across the courtroom. She only squinted a scowl in return. For a charismatic "rising star" warlock, the man was particularly skilled at inadvertently putting his foot in it.

5

As it transpired, the spell for Ariadne twelve years ago seemed to have been an inadvertent catalyst for Belle's magic losing its footing. With each graceful tidal crash of water and lightning dust, she was filled with a little more rising dread.

Next came the fifth manifest, a moment from a university night out which was entirely mortifying to witness. Reliving it in front of a jury of esteemed wicchefolk just seemed plain cruel. Belle had rolled home late—or early, to be more accurate—and failed miserably at reading texts for the morning's seminar. She had already spent the whole term feeling like the least knowledgeable person in every room she entered, sliding from consistent top grades and praise to someone distinctly mediocre in all her work.

The manifest revealed how she had attempted a messy potion brew, a rather desperate *Brevis Eruditio* knowledge spell in the sink of her tiny room. A few weeds she'd plucked from campus which seemed the right colour, some substitute kitchen ingredients only slightly out of date. The lazy spell had unsurprisingly led to limited success: uncontrollable babbling about Shakespeare to her professor and, worse still, relentless chatter about John Donne at a party. She'd later discovered that people knew her until she graduated as the "intense Renaissance fan."

This one attracted horrified looks.

"We *never* drink and conjure," one witch said with vehement disapproval, as though her decision had just been made.

"And magic is never to be a substitute for effort. It is not to be contorted into crooked short cuts for sheer laziness," another outraged older witch cried.

Several icy glances were exchanged.

Belle flushed, unable to defend herself even if she was permitted to.

6

Belle smarted as she watched the sixth manifest reveal a time, one of countless despondent times, that she'd tried to use magic to change herself.

Altering clothing and outfits multiple times a day back then, haircuts and hair colours, helping her skin to play ball when it refused. But more than that. With Ari at the opposite end of the country, she'd been painfully lonely, desperate for a true friend. Even just one. As the loneliness at university grew and felt overwhelming at times, when she should have been poring over textbooks or pouring drinks with new friends, there'd been nights that she'd shut herself away for shame, landing on her own body in lieu of anything else to blame. How the fabric hung and clung, how her silhouette went this way instead of that way. How everybody else around her seemed to be exactly as they should be at twenty-one, while she felt intrinsically wrong in every way possible. On bleak, desperate nights, after food and tears and loneliness, she'd grown obsessed with trying, without success, to create magic that would make her smaller. To take up less space, to shrink as much as she possibly could. Defying the very point of being a witch, losing all pride in her own unique self.

The convoluted words of the spells, spoken desperately through tears and hiccups, had resulted in nothing except ruining several pairs of jeans and making her bones and throat ache while plunging her self-esteem to what felt like unrecoverable lows. A decade of slowly improved kindness and gentleness had since taught her that even magic was not an answer to something so deeply burrowed under skin.

"Thousands of years of magic at your fingertips, and you decide to use it for the sole purpose of insignificant vanity?" An older warlock with thick eyebrows barked his opinion.

Belle answered quietly. "Obviously you've never been at war with your own body. At the time, nothing else mattered."

7

The seventh manifest recreated the day that she'd concocted a particularly rotten stomach bug for Christopher, who had patronised her to an even worse extent than usual in front of everyone at Lunar, heckling during a sold-out author Q&A that Belle "had her knickers in a twist" over the popular banshee romance series. It had brought considerable satisfaction to see him sprinting from the office to the toilets while clutching at the seat of his trousers.

She stuck her nose in the air. "I'm not apologising for that one."

"Madames Sage, I have seen everything I need to see here. So have many of us, I suspect. Selfishness, short cuts, superficiality. Strix, you can't let this continue," called a wicche with a floral headscarf wrapped underneath their coven hat.

"Revenge should never fuel magic." Caspar sighed and nodded slowly, reluctantly.

Belle couldn't bring herself to catch his eye.

"Is this really what the future of our coven rests upon? Absurdly disappointing," spluttered a furious older lady.

The jury called out and bickered amongst themselves.

"We cannot deny that truth of magic exists here. She is a Blackthorn."

"Family name can only carry her so far."

"But this jury cannot negate the other qualities. Experience? Her magic remains largely unexplored, usually ignored entirely."

"What of action? Hardly commendable. This witch has barely ventured to imagine what she's capable of."

"Even perception is questionable. It cannot be said with confidence that these manifests come from entirely unselfish magic."

8

As soon as the next scene began to play out, rain and lightning transported her back. As everyone had already witnessed in glorious technicolour, Belle had previously used magic to try and change herself in several different ways, but they had always been appearance-based. This particular time, she had decided that magic would change the aspects of herself that nobody else could see, which she wrestled with alone.

Violet's offer took her by surprise the first time, years ago at twenty-seven. The fear had been too great. Curiosity and excitement were displaced by dread of what might happen if she dared to make the leap. She almost resented her boss for putting her in that position. It wasn't the right time for change. It never was. She couldn't trust herself to do it. And she didn't deserve it.

The potion that she had created to make herself braver and bolder, make herself steadfast with confidence, had burned in her chest. As she attempted to swallow down the vile mix, trying incantation after incantation to manipulate who she was, it had become clear that magic could not be relied on to change that. Confidence potions and nerve tonics were complex but valid magic, but something to change her intrinsic gifts, her innermost make-up, was to dabble far beyond her skill set. She wasn't ready to be brave, even with the help of magic. So she had stayed scared, turned down the chance and watched her opportunity drift instead to somebody else's snatching hands.

"She started out with such promise . . ."

"Decisions from fear, every time. I certainly can't respect it."

"Superficial and selfish."

Belle's shoulders were so tense that they felt glued to her ears, the brim of her hat pulled down so low that she could barely see anymore. She felt exposed to an extreme, a light being shone into the darkest nooks of her magical history. It all felt so unfair, but perhaps there were no better options for the fates to choose for her manifests. This was, at its crux, an accurate painting of her potential. She had remained stuck, stayed living small. Fading from favour, magic wilting away while the years passed.

The dancing sparks and splashes had lost all of their earlier beauty. They turned her stomach as they painted their last picture.

9

She saw two figures side by side again, and at first, she couldn't work out what was happening. It soon dawned on her, however, that there couldn't have been a worse, more private moment for Selcouth to see. The memory came from a long time ago.

Unable to sit with her secret anymore, Belle had ventured timidly to open up the conversation and reveal her magic to a non-wicche soul. And, foolishly, she hadn't chosen Ariadne. She had been proud and excited to share it, tender with the blush of first love.

"Do you believe in magic?" she'd asked nervously, creasing the corner of a page between her fingers as she thumbed through a paperback.

In response, he'd sneered. "Don't tell me you're getting into that. Anyone who goes in for that stuff is embarrassing."

"You don't believe at all?"

"It doesn't exist, obviously."

"But not everything can be explained in black and white, so surely it must exist," she'd chanced, used to having to defend her joy to him by now.

"No, it doesn't. And it's kind of pathetic to think it does."

"But—"

"Why are you even asking me this? Stop being weird."

Although some buried part of her had known to expect it, his response had shoved her hard in the chest, sent her curling back into a closed shell. He had always been repulsed by her wonder and naivety once the initial novelty of them had worn off, so she had trained it to stay hidden afterwards. That was the one and only time she'd attempted to share her magic with a non-wicche.

The manifest showed, too, what followed after that conversation. Somewhat bewildered by her own stupidity and strangeness, she'd made an effort at the cauldron. She had aimed to bind her own powers. Unthinkable now, but the obvious, only possible answer to her then. Magic had shown itself to be more of a curse than a blessing, and his response had only confirmed everything she already suspected about herself.

But she'd cut corners and hurried to finish, desperate for her magic to never have happened at all, desperate to eliminate the element of strangeness that she could blame for it all. From the first unnatural sip, her slapdash incantation had sent her flying backwards with such force that she still had a scar on her shoulder.

Trying to run from who she truly was had left its own scar, too. A seed of shame had been planted then, and from it, a deep-rooted oak of self-doubt had grown unchecked ever since. Not enough, yet somehow too much. Easy to leave behind, so she had to work twice as hard to keep people loving her. To this day, it held her back, wrapped its shadowed arms around her waist and locked its hands.

Belle watched as the young manifest of herself, tearful and strung together by sparks, summoned her cloak and hat, books and bottles, even her sooth stone. They all flew to her grasp in unison and were stuffed into a crumpled ball, shoved into the corner of a cupboard.

Everything special, unique, rare was left behind. The wonder-seeking girl she had been was no more. And shame of her own magic would not be excused.

10

Just Visitors

FOR WHAT FELT like the entirety of forever, no one said a word. As the shards of lightning and crystal raindrops cascaded to the floor one final time, they took with them all hope that Belle could possibly be leaving Hecate House with her powers intact. The pendulum began swinging again, slicing through the silence, and Belle's head fell into her hands.

She heard her own voice crack precariously. "Please . . . Please, can I say something?"

"I hardly think it's worth bothering," replied Morena.

"Mor, now is not the time for rubbing salt into the wound," Bronwyn scolded. "Have some heart, for the divil's sake. The girl deserves a chance to speak her truth." Bronwyn looked and sounded distinctly less chirpy than she had before.

"I think we've seen enough of her *truth*, sister. And it's not something I wish to see again. She's wasted enough of our time—the past fifteen years, for that matter. I've never seen anything quite like it," Morena said. "Bitterly disappointing. She has not used her powers, barely scraped their surface. Worse, she is ashamed of her magic."

Morena's condemnation was met with murmurings of agreement from many of the jury. But Belle's defences shot up simultaneously.

"With respect, if I'd known I was being watched by a jury of high wicchefolk, I might have done things a little differently."

It stung to acknowledge the memories that had been played out so publicly. This coven's apparent determination to flay the deepest, most vulnerable parts of a person made her feel queasy.

"But these are choices that I've made along the way, whether I like it or not. Nothing about my life looks how I thought it would when I was fifteen years old, holding fresh magic. Thinking about the space between the two, between her and me, then and now, feels like standing on the doorstep like my grandparents used to and waving off endless versions of myself. The ones you planned to be as they leave and disappear off into the distance."

She pressed a hand to the base of her neck, trying to cool her flushing skin. The brooch brushed her arm, and she blamed the intensity of her emotions when she could have sworn she felt a rush from it, what felt like a whisper, a touch to her shoulder. *Keep going.*

She could hear that she was already rambling, getting defensive and brittle. But she didn't care. Belle saw Morena's mouth move to respond with venom, but Bronwyn quickly clapped her around the arm before she had the chance.

"Trying to be a vaguely normal person in the non-wicche world, who can just about function enough to get the washing done and pass a performance review while also having all of this terrifying, overwhelming potential at your fingertips? *Who* can navigate that well? You know it's there, but you're terrified of what it could mean for you, where it might take your life, how much it would hurt to fail. So it's easier to forget it, fall back to what feels easier and what you've always done before."

She could feel herself careering with speed sharply away from the point, whatever the point was. The point was somewhere far behind in the rearview mirror. She sighed in surrender.

"Somewhere, I don't know where, the magic slipped. And for a moment, I was ready to accept that the manifests and all of the wrong turns that I've made were the sum of who I am, but that's not true. I am worthy of this power. I know my potential. Maybe I've neglected it for a long time now, but it's still there. It has to be. If you could just give it time. I'll show you."

She turned to the jury directly.

"I go through life constantly feeling like the moment right after lightning strikes but before the thunder hits, when you aren't sure if it will even come or how loud it will be when it does. It's all stored up so tightly and loudly in here, pressure and promise."

Belle took a moment to steady herself.

"But the prospect of losing my magic is infinitely more awful than trying to use it to its fullest and failing. My mum always says that perfection stops progress, and she's right."

Belle choked on something between a sob and a hiccup, and blew out a breath to stop herself.

"At least I will have tried this time. For the first time in a long time. I need to learn how to let myself do it all, do everything and not be scared of letting myself down or being too much, not be scared of failing and falling behind. I want magic to lead my way again.

"Okay. That's all I have to say." Belle bowed her head low and exhaled long and loud. She sank slowly back down into her seat but then shot back up again.

"Oh. Except also, let's be honest, the first of those manifests were good. You *know* they were good. They were great, actually, when I had time to dedicate to it. And that girl is still inside me. It's just that life got in my way. Being a grown-up is relentless, exhausting and is not conducive to wonderful magic, but I need to work on that and figure out how the two can live together. Okay, *that's* all."

She sat down, then stood back up a third time.

"Also, I would argue that we have a bad enough history with trials as it is, so maybe this shouldn't be the way that things work anymore. The last time you saw me, I was wearing a T-shirt with a tie printed on it, for god's sake . . . Just give me one more chance. Please."

Now it was over. Surrendering to the inevitable, she finally burst into tears. The uncontrollable kind. She could hear her own sobs noisy against the still courtroom, a cruel echo slapping her around the face. But she didn't care now. There was nothing left to lose.

A gentle hand squeezed her shoulder. "Come, dear. Perhaps a cup of tea to calm us all down. I'm sure we can find some kind of compromise, there'll be something in the grimoire that . . ."

"Actually, I do not believe we *can* find *compromise*."

The jury froze, as did Belle.

Morena stepped down from the podium with purpose and slammed her hands onto the wooden pews in front of the jury. A warlock in the front row with a twiddled moustache visibly jumped in his seat.

"Not only is it clear as solstice morning light that this jury has already reached its verdict and that you, Bronwyn, and you, Ms. Blackthorn, are actively defying Selcouth's deciding word"— Morena gestured to the rows of magic folk who were each showing varying measures of agreement, disagreement and exasperation— "but it seems to me that you are also suggesting that we allow this witch, seemingly incapable of the most base-level spells, to—"

"That seems a bit—" Belle went to interrupt the rant, but Morena lifted a firm hand to silence her. Nothing would stop her.

"—let me check my notes. Ah, yes, break all structures and traditions that this historic coven has upheld since the beginning of magic itself. The very foundations that Selcouth is built upon: the importance of upholding worthy magic and not letting it rot within people who insist on wasting their own wonder. Did I miss anything? Or am

I to believe this is the legitimate direction in which you are steering this trial, sister?"

She patted at the elegant victory curl under her hat, which had begun to fall looser as her rage grew.

"Hear! Hear!" A few indignant murmurs from the jury members who were clearly on Morena's side rumbled behind the Gowden sisters.

"Mor," Bronwyn responded calmly and turned to speak to the room. "Dear sister and dear jury alike, I am only speculating that perhaps an alternative approach, a . . . loophole! That's the divil's onion. A loophole. I am certain that a loophole—"

"I won't stand for it! I told you, Bronwyn."

"But Mor—"

"Enough." Caspar, like most others in the room, looked like he had lost the will to live.

The coven balancer raised his palms to bring a hush to the debate and took charge of the room with ease. Belle couldn't help but watch Morena, who was glaring at Bronwyn. The sisters were locked in silent battle. Morena parted her lips but closed them when Caspar gave her a look that dared her to try.

"In all my years with this coven, I have not witnessed a debate as divisive as this—perhaps it has never been. The energy in this courtroom is frankly fraught. As balancer, I am bringing this hearing to a close to reset the energy within Hecate House as a matter of urgency. And I will hear not another word on the subject."

A moment of quiet passed, no one quite knowing how to respond. It was Morena who broke it.

"So, what happens to her magic?"

Bronwyn gathered her long skirts and remounted the podium, the mouse in her pocket emerging to her shoulder as though sensing the importance of her next words. "I will personally consult the grimoire over tonight's moon and see to it that we find a solution. Belle may return home with her magic intact until then."

Morena interjected, sharp and shrill. "But—"

"We are unprepared for this. My decision is final," Bronwyn said, uncharacteristically solemn. She spoke to Morena directly. It was as though they had forgotten anyone else was present in the room, the tension between them so palpable that it didn't seem entirely impossible that the air itself would burst into flames.

Morena shot Belle a venomous look, fists balled at her sides. "You don't know what you've done."

Before Belle could bite back, ask why exactly she'd decided to loathe her from the second they had met, before she could even straighten her hat, Morena turned on her heel and crossed the courtroom, the cascading ripple of her cloak trailing behind her.

She ascended the podium, Bronwyn cried out "Mor, wait!" and Morena banged the wooden gavel down with livid force.

⋆ ✦ ⋆ ✦ ⋆

BELLE BLINKED AND opened her eyes to her own front door. A wink of creamy light from the evening street lamps outside illuminated the little glass panes and brass letterbox.

Had she lost the plot? Maybe that sushi yesterday at lunchtime hadn't been right. Or was it a fever dream? Had too much caffeine finally knocked her over the edge into insanity? Knees buckling, she fell with a thud against the front door. Her coven hat was still on top of her head, her cloak still fastened at the collarbone. Then, hurrying to snatch the former and push it deep into her backpack, struggling with the clasp of the latter before one of the neighbours came out to find her in full witch attire, Belle noticed the dark ink stains on the lap of her dress.

It *did* happen, as disconnected as it felt, like a dream she was scrabbling to recall. The furious bang of the gavel had transferred her back home in less than an instant. She'd barely felt her feet lift from the floor of Hecate House.

"Coming, two seconds, sorry, hang on! Don't take any packages!"

Belle's clumsy crash against the door must have sounded like a knock. She heard Ariadne shouting and footsteps as she dashed to answer the front door.

"Oh jeez. Stop, Jinx . . ." Ari peeled back the door to their home, using a carefully placed ankle to keep the cat from sprinting out. They had skipped the small detail of Jinx from their landlord's contract several years ago and were skilled in the art of hiding their illegal flatmate.

"Belle! Thank god! Where the hell have you been?" Ari hissed through the crack in the door. "I've been trying to reach you literally all day. I thought you'd—Jinx, will you please hold on a second?"

While Ari was temporarily distracted by four nimble paws, Belle seized the opportunity to stuff the point of her hat as far down into her bag as possible before stumbling across the threshold and into their flat.

"Ari, I'm sorry, so sorry. It's been . . . a day."

"Oh, I'm gonna need more than that," she said crossly. "Monica and Jim said you hadn't been at the shop, pretty sure they now think I'm crazy, so I know you were lying about that. And your mum chatted my ear off for half an hour about her trip to Isle of Skye, so that was helpful."

"To be fair, that one is not my fault. That's what you get for ringing my mum." Belle sighed. She slumped down immediately, falling face-first into the familiar hug of the sofa.

As she nestled into the lumpy cushions, she already felt a little better. Ari always had the heating on. The candles were lit across the hearth. The fireplace was stuffed with bundles of fairy lights. A repeat of their favourite sitcom played quietly on the television. It felt familiar and right, after the longest day of everything being distinctly, extremely wrong.

"I thought you'd been abducted and shipped off and trafficked and brutally murdered and held prisoner and thrown into a canal, or something. I was ready to fight. I thought I was gonna have to be one of those people on the news holding up some bloody photo of you on the telly, which would make you die of shame anyway, even if you hadn't already been murdered."

Belle stretched her arms out wide as Ari stood over her with a maddened look. She rolled her eyes dramatically and reluctantly dove into the hug, flopping on top of her friend with merciless brute force. When Belle surrendered, insisting that she couldn't breathe, they sat side by side under a blanket instead.

"Thank you for worrying that I was dead, and thank you for preparing to avenge my demise. I had to go and . . . see someone about . . . something. I'm fine."

"Ahh, someone about something." Ari nodded, giving a sarcastic thumbs-up.

"Honestly, it's nothing. Well, it is something; otherwise, I wouldn't have disappeared for the day and missed my birthday plans, but . . . Ari, I wish I could tell you. You know that I would if I possibly could. And I will, at some point. It's just that right now, I can't."

Belle cringed at her own lack of explanation. Ari was even less impressed, her right eyebrow sitting at such a dramatic, stabbing angle that it could have been used as a weapon.

"Are you embroiled in a deadly drug war?"

"No drugs."

"Living a double life with a millionaire businessman?"

"No such luck."

"So, what, then?"

Belle grabbed at easy solutions, like she always did. "It's . . . an

NDA thing. At work. Contracts and agreements and secret publisher meetings, you know. And I won't go back to prison again, Ari, they can't make me!"

She grabbed Ari by her shirt and pretended to shake her. In honesty, the part about contracts and agreements and secret meetings wasn't *not* the truth. And the joke worked. Ari snorted a laugh and seemed to have already lost interest in the questioning.

"Fine. Want some birthday toast?"

"My love language. Two pieces, please." Belle raised her hands in grateful prayer, suddenly realising that her stomach felt like it was eating itself. "When I tell you I am beyond starving . . . Is there any picnic food left?"

"Over there. Help yourself, but all the booze is gone. The pavlova met a terrible fate in the park involving someone's Jack Russell. At least he enjoyed your birthday."

Belle padded over to the kitchen. She began rummaging in the Tupperware from the birthday picnic that had happened without her. A pair of sausage rolls were practically inhaled.

"Belle. I am serious, you know." Ariadne spun on the spot to face her friend, chewing on a piece of toast. "What is going on with you? You haven't been yourself for days, but now you're a no-show at your own birthday plans. You lie to me about needing to work. Whatever it is, it's only the 'not telling me' part which makes you an arse by default. I can read you like a book. Something's up, I know it. And we do not keep secrets. That's always been the rule."

She brandished the toast in Belle's direction threateningly.

"Besides, you always explode with stress eventually, so we might as well get that out of the way and arrive more quickly to the part where we fix everything together."

Belle picked at the pastry on a third sausage roll, avoiding eye contact, feeling the temptation to spill everything once and for all.

Ari rolled her eyes and gesticulated with toast dramatically at Belle's lack of response. A moment later, she spun back around on the spot as an epiphany crossed her mind. "This is about a man, isn't it?"

"What?" Belle laughed, looking at her friend like she was mad.

"You're seeing someone. A man."

That wasn't entirely wrong. She had seen many men today. Warlocks, but still. It wasn't *quite* lying to say that this whole mess at least involved *a* man. Because it did. Technically.

"Yes." Belle threw up her hands in defeat. "A man. It is a man. I am seeing a man." She gratefully clung to the lie like a life raft, a compromise solution to the questioning. From past experience, she knew that Ariadne wouldn't rest until she got an answer that made sense, and this would have to do.

"And I couldn't come to the picnic today because I was . . . sorting some things out with him. Making arrangements with him. The man. It's complicated. With the man," she added quickly.

"That goes without saying, when is it ever not complicated with you?" Ari scoffed, generously buttering yet another round of toast. "Is he treating you badly? I'll fight him."

"We just needed to talk today, to . . . make sure we're on the same page." Belle carefully navigated the hairline cracks she'd visited so often, wobbling between truth-telling and lie-avoiding. She scuffed her socks against the kickboards.

"Is he not a good communicator? Don't go down that road again, no more emotionally unavailable losers for your collection. Or is this about your birthday? Don't let thirty stress you. I keep telling you, it's not a big deal. Don't rush into anything."

"I know what I'm doing . . . I think."

"All I'm saying is, if it's this complicated this early on, then it's not going to end well. It sounds like he's taking you for granted, whoever he is. I hate him already." Ariadne shrugged and finished off her last bite, brushing crumby fingers across the butt of her jeans. "What's he like, then, this mystery man?"

Belle cringed. "Different. Magical?"

Ariadne cackled at high volume. "Excuse me while I vomit."

Belle couldn't help but laugh, too. Looking at her friend, familiarity and security personified, filled her heart. But it also brought back the nipping memory of the voice she'd heard in the Hecate House tunnels.

How could you lie to me? Do you hate me that much? Do you not trust me? We're supposed to be friends. Best friends.

Belle swallowed hard. "Ari?"

"Yup?"

"Sorry for lying. I should have told you. I would always choose you."

Ari gave her a half-smile. "Get some sleep, you look knackered. See you in the morning."

Heading into her room with a piece of toast in hand, Belle called goodnight back to the kitchen. Bed would solve all of her problems. Pushing the door closed with her hip, Belle vanished her contact lenses with a flourish and pointed towards her glasses resting on the side table. They glided through the air and came to rest on her nose, a trail of delicate sparks in a kite tail. She gave a sigh of instant relief, dead on her feet. She summoned her last ounce of energy to kick off her boots, circling her finger to unlace them magically—lazy but necessary. Finally, today called for her cosiest pyjamas, the soft tartan slipping itself over her arms and neatly buttoning up with a whirl of sparks.

She pressed her forehead against her bedroom window and exhaled, feeling the cold touch of wet condensation cool on her skin. Her breath fogged the glass as she looked down at the road below. The path was covered with a carpet of soggy scarlet leaves, turning soft like stewed apples in the drizzle. The autumn sun had long retreated into slumber for another evening, but the streetlights wavered like birthday candles behind the beaded raindrops on the glass, their pockets of gold breathing a lullaby over the street. Home.

That was it. Her thirtieth birthday over, certainly not one to be forgotten.

And now she had to wait for fate to find her.

11

Safely Near the Dead

THE MEMORY OF the trial paired with the dread of what was still to be decided had Belle a nervous wreck the following day. Even the usual peace and comfort of Lunar Books fell short, failing to measure up to the size of her worries. She couldn't focus, her attention unravelling at any given moment. Pushing the loaded brass trolley towards the Sci-Fi and Fantasy section, Belle tried to console herself with the knowledge that at least somebody inside Hecate House was on her side. Bronwyn would be doing what she could to find an answer, seemingly set on making sure that the coven saw her again, thanks to whatever it was she saw in Belle. There was Caspar, too, who had expressed a fondness for her and her mother; that surely counted for something. She wondered idly if Rune might even be lending them a hand, then, blushing, dismissed the thought as unlikely. He would probably see little point in that without her being there to mock mercilessly with that infuriating side smile of his.

She loaded herself up with a stack of particularly dense hard-backs that were flying off the shelves ahead of Halloween, something about feral werewolves and a team of ladies who knew how to tame them. She struggled under the weight, balancing them beneath her chin as she manoeuvred them one at a time onto the display, but it felt good to be doing the usual after the most unusual of birthdays. At least Lunar existed, her bubble of contentment, wrapped in a cosy blanketing quiet that separated her two worlds and the two realms definitively.

"Hello, lovey." Bronwyn appeared behind the stack of hardbacks as if from nowhere. "Appeared" being the operative word, and almost certainly from nowhere, too.

Belle was so surprised to see her—her high sage witch—in her bookshop, her distinctly non-wicche-realm-residing bookshop, that she leapt into the air, and her hands flew to her mouth, sending the remaining books in her arms to the floor with a crash. Heads spun in their direction as Belle stood motionless, all thoughts instantly draining from her brain. Bronwyn didn't seem to notice that her arrival had caused mild chaos.

"What a lovely spot you have here! And I sensed the beautiful little incantations you've set up around the place, you should have told us all about them yesterday, you silly goose!" Bronwyn wagged her finger at Belle, who was fairly sure her heart had stopped the second the witch cried the word "incantations" in close proximity to customers.

"Ha. Ha. Right, Mrs. Gowden. You're talking about that . . . that fantasy book I recommended last week? I knew you'd love it. Ha." Belle spoke exaggeratedly and pointedly, hoping to hook an understanding Bronwyn. No such luck.

"Fantasy? Grizzled goatweed, not likely. They never get the magic theory right, they always overcomplicate things. More of a romance girly myself, Belle, the more swoon-worthy the better."

Belle clutched at where her heart used to be, trailing behind Bronwyn, who remained entirely oblivious as she wandered through Lunar Books.

"Oh, but of course today is official coven business," the sage witch continued, as she examined the pair of cat ears and bin bag cape that Belle had draped around a cardboard cut-out in the children's section. "The fate of your magic and the like. Though remind me to share with you the neat little charm I have for permanently plumped cushions. Some of the armchairs in here do look a bit sad, and you'd really—"

With that, Belle threw an arm over Bronwyn's shoulders and guided her with speed and precision towards the front door. She hastily untied her apron and threw it down onto the desk towards a baffled Monica as she passed. "That's break for me, Mon. I'll be back. Hold the fort."

Belle ushered Bronwyn out of the shop, under the tinkle of the doorbell and around the corner onto a quiet cobbled street in an impressive matter of seconds.

"What is it, deary? You look as though you've seen a ghost, and I have it on good authority that they're largely at peace in this borough of London, at least until Halloween, and then there's no stopping—"

"Bronwyn. Hi." Belle stared at her sage witch, incredulous.

"Hello, Belle. It's wonderful to see you again," Bronwyn said gleefully, scrunching up her nose with a chuckle. "And this is all rather exciting, isn't it? I don't much consider myself a city slicker, but here I am, adventuring to the other end of London! Oh, poppet, you look dreadful. I bet you've been worrying yourself ill over all this EquiWitch business, haven't you?"

"Something like that," Belle muttered. "How about we go and find a cup of tea rather than standing out here in the cold?"

Belle guided Bronwyn the few streets down to Jitter Bug, the coffee shop below her and Ariadne's flat. The girls were such consistent regulars that Mr. Ricci came straight over to deliver coffee without so much as a glance. It took him a moment to realise that Belle had taken the crimson leather booth not with Ariadne but with an old woman in what seemed to be a witch's costume. He paused for a moment, his walrus moustache bristling in confusion.

"Thanks, Mr. Ricci. This is . . . This is my . . ."

"I'm Bronwyn, lovey. I'm Belle's coven leader."

He stayed motionless for a second. "'Course you are," he grunted before tossing his dish-rag over his shoulder and heading back to the counter.

"Tea for me, please, my good sir. And crumpets, if you've got any. If not, I'll conjure my own," Bronwyn called after him.

Belle's head fell into her hands. "Bronwyn, what are you doing here? I really wasn't expecting to hear from you so soon, let alone see you. Here. In the non-wicche realm. Asking for crumpets . . ."

"I have news. Good news. Or interesting news, at least."

Before Belle could stop her, Bronwyn directed a stream of sparks from her palm to the silver metal tabletop, and an enormous book materialised between them, sending the sugar dispenser flying. Gasping in horror at the flagrant display of magic for all to see, Belle frantically grabbed two menus from a neighbouring table and flung them up around the book like a protective wall. Luckily, only a child tucking into a stack of blueberry pancakes seemed to have noticed, mouth agape mid-bite until his mother told him to stop staring.

"Bronwyn, please," Belle reminded her desperately.

"Sorry, poppet," she said with a dismissive chuckle. "Rune did warn me that you're a non-wicche for all intents and purposes around these parts. The moment your trial came to an end, I started searching the grimoire like a madwoman. Dotty as a box of frogs, I was, hunting for something we can use to our advantage . . ."

With great difficulty, she eased open the thick cover of the book that took up most of the table and emitted a chalky cough of dust as the pages were turned.

"If one needs answers . . . Now, where the blasted heck did I . . ." she muttered to herself.

"But Bronwyn, I thought the EquiWitch rules were about as certain as it gets. They've been written into coven history for generations. Otherwise, what was the point in the trial at all?"

"Life is for loopholes, dear." Bronwyn gave her a wink. "This thing has never steered me wrong, in all my years leading this coven, and I knew your predicament would be no different. When you get to be this old, lovey, you know that there is always another turn to take. It's never a dead end."

"Well, Morena wants to have me burnt at the stake."

"Oh, pay her no mind." Bronwyn batted away the subject of her sister. "She was born on the wrong side of the bed and has never since managed to find the right one. I'll have her to answer to, but the divil to her. She doesn't know what's best for the future of the coven."

Belle chewed nervously at a cuticle as Bronwyn examined the book with squinted eyes, licking a finger now and then to pass through the pages at speed.

"Is this the coven's first grimoire?" Belle asked curiously.

Bronwyn nodded. "The original. High sages have added to it and contributed their wisdom to Selcouth lore since the day it was first created."

"Have you and Morena added things to it?"

"Of course. We're not just a pair of pretty faces. Morena certainly isn't."

"So you can just change the rules of magic? If it can be edited and added to over the years, I mean."

"Yes and no. Got a bit of a mind of its own, this thing, by way of complex, historical enchantments. Legend goes that the pages of the Selcouth grimoire will accept contributions written in raven black ink that are valuable and true magic lessons to benefit the coven. The grimoire itself decides what can remain within its pages as coven lore, some form of twisted, ancient sorcery that even I don't fully understand, love. Everything in here is valuable and necessary."

"And the one I have at home?" Belle asked, curious. "The copy that's presented when a coven member is given their magic, I mean. It's the same version?"

"It's an abridged almanac that everyone is given, but yes. Yours will update itself when this big old lump decides a new lesson is worthy. Doesn't happen often, mind. Plenty of our suggestions have been rejected over the years. The rest of you have the handy pocket-sized version."

Belle thought back to her own grimoire, which would require the world's largest pocket to be transportable anywhere.

"Sort of a witch's bread and butter," Bronwyn added.

Mr. Ricci reappeared with a giant mug of milky tea and two plates of crumpets glazed with burnished blackberry jam. He delivered the order unceremoniously and gave a side-eye to the giant book that Belle's menus were attempting to disguise.

"I won't ask," he grunted in his endearingly strong accent, and promptly walked away.

Belle gave him an apologetic and grateful half-smile.

The pages of the grimoire were chaotic, dirty and well thumbed, folded every which way. Not all of them were even attached to the spine anymore, and all were filled with notes, quick jottings, thoughts of witches past, all tied together through time. The edges of the binding were frayed, the golden embossing long worn away and chipped into shards on the cover. The words on the original pages were intricately inked in dark, detailed calligraphy barely decipherable to a modern reader. Belle wondered whether it was even a known language. The margins were richly coloured with jewel-shaded borders, side by side with sketched illustrations that reminded Belle of da Vinci's anatomical studies, eerie but beautiful still.

"Surely the grimoire is just going to tell us what we already know about my disaster of a trial. I might as well have come into my Equi-Witch with a rabbit in a hat and done 'Izzy whizzy, let's get busy.'"

"Izzy who, love? Oh, cursed capers, where is it?"

Bronwyn was barely listening, lost in deciphering the mess of helter-skelter scrawls and loose leaves of papers, hunting for something in particular. Belle dropped her crumpet when her sage let out a sudden shriek.

"Good gladioli and graveyards! The divil dance on it. I knew I hadn't imagined it. I told you! I knew I'd seen something . . . Look, Belle, look. Ha ha, ho ho, hee hee!" The high witch sprang to her feet and did a little jig from one foot to the other.

Belle lunged over the table for the scratchy lace of ink that Bronwyn was, for some reason, so thrilled to have discovered. In tiny writing, barely legible and scrawled into the margins like a footnote, was a passage that must have been somebody's afterthought. A rushed addition, but written down in raven black ink and evidently accepted by the omnipotent book.

In the extraordinary circumstance that a jury stands divided on the outcome of an EquiWitch trial, the wicchefolk in favour of preserving the membership may put forth a suitable and unbiased mentor from the venerable archives guarded within Hecate House, if said trial should fall in the hallowed month of Winterfylleth (October).

For the duration of the month until Halloween falls, this figure may ready their student to complete six challenges, created by the esteemed coven grimoire for recompense. All six challenges, reflecting the fundamental branches of magic, must be completed to the grimoire's satisfaction. Adequate success in each branch shall be indicated to student and mentor when the paired allegory within the grimoire lights to an amber glow. A second hearing shall be held and a final verdict given on the night of All Hallows' Eve to decide whether the subject shall retain their neglected or maltreated magical abilities.

Refer to Hecate House Ossuary for the available guardian archive.

The two witches looked at each other, one in confusion and one in unmistakable triumph.

"There's always an answer to every problem," Bronwyn murmured quietly, a glint in her eye.

"A mentor for October? Until Halloween?" Belle turned, wide-eyed. "That's . . . Well, that's actually perfect. Can it be you? I would love if it could be you. Or at least, please can it not be Morena?"

Bronwyn chuckled as she closed the book, leaning on it with her elbows and lacing her fingers together. "As much as I would love to be your teacher, I cannot. As coven sage, my position holds too much influence to be considered unbiased. Fortunately, the same does also go for Morena."

She reached out to Belle and gave her hand a comforting squeeze.

"In fact, we may find this tricky," she added thoughtfully. "Any coven member present at your trial has to be ruled out. They saw your manifests and will have already formed opinions. Your mother, of course, also cannot be rightfully unbiased. That leaves us with anyone who may have been absent, ill or otherwise engaged."

Belle chewed at the inside of her cheek as Bronwyn rattled through her thoughts out loud.

"But we'll have a little look-see at the register. The courtroom was rather full yesterday. But maybe someone's got the runs or at least the sniffles. There's bound to be some wonderful wicche name who we can call upon. Let's see, with this loophole in mind, we have twenty-nine moons remaining for a mentorship . . . Of course, this will require you to return with me to Hecate House."

Belle frowned, then jumped up from her seat. "Give me five minutes to check that Monica can cover for me. Stay here, have some more tea. Please, do not do any more magic. And *please*, do not drink the Jitter Bug espresso, it's enough to wire a normal person for a week, so I'm unsure what it would do to . . . well, to a woman like yourself."

✦ ˙ ✳ ˳ ✦ ˙ ✦

TEN MINUTES LATER, the floor disappeared from under Belle's boots, dropping out from beneath her like a trapdoor, and a forceful feeling encased her whole body, like being whipped up inside a vacuum cleaner.

Bronwyn had transferred them both in an instant to what seemed to be her own space within Hecate House. While Caspar's office had the opulent feeling of classic luxury and professional academia, the sage witch's looked remarkably like a living room: terracotta textured wallpaper with stencilled grapes along the border, chintz floral armchairs in bold apricot-and-green patterns, and chunky wooden shelving adorned with magic memorabilia, including several plastic pumpkins, even more plush ones with happy little faces and small ceramic ghosts.

Bronwyn's office also played host to an extensive collection of Clairvoyancy tools, the array of equipment and paraphernalia revealing her specialism. Scrying mirrors in various gilded frames on every surface, crystal balls of all sizes, corked bottles stuffed with shards of pastel-coloured crystals and dustings of herbs. The room felt chaotic but cosy in its clutter. A patterned rug was placed underneath a table bearing a brightly filled fruit bowl. The mouse that had perched happily in Bronwyn's pocket hopped down from its home in her cloak and began nibbling contentedly on the side of a peach.

"There, now. Turns out you're a good companion for a swift transference spell, too. Staying calm under magical transference isn't easy. Although you do look a bit green."

"Calm? I've been about as calm as a cat getting in the bath. I feel insane." Belle wiped her nose in a slightly feral fashion, eyes streaming from the force of the spell.

"Yes, a visit to Hecate House can have that effect on you on a good day."

"Could someone not have collected me like this yesterday?" Belle asked, dusting down her jeans. With Belle remembering Morena's threats of house hexes for incorrect attire, Bronwyn had just about granted her the time to summon her cloak and hat. "Just to avoid the little trip to hell and back?"

"We're not a taxi service, Belle. And anyway, it's—"

"Tradition. Right."

Bronwyn scurried to her shelves, struggling under the weight of the grimoire, and reached on her tiny legs to wedge it back in between a set of glow-in-the-dark plastic fangs still in their packaging and a pop-up vampire which gave an electronic laugh as she approached.

A pointed cough came from the entryway. "Pardon me for breaking up the party." Morena had transferred. She brushed down her tailored trousers after announcing herself, then stormed farther into the room with a flourish of her cloak and hands on her hips. "I trust you have a suitable explanation for your sudden disappearing act this morning, Bronwyn." A vicious look was fired in Belle's direction.

"Don't you know that nothing keeps an audience on their toes quite like a disappearing act, sister? For my next trick, I shall be sawing Ms. Blackthorn in half within a wooden box."

"I would take great pleasure in completing that task myself, sister."

The Gowden sisters glared at each other, frozen in an unspoken staring contest. Reluctantly breaking eye contact, Bronwyn turned back to Belle.

"Please excuse us for one moment, dear. Step out, take a breather. I'd better fill Morena in on our lucky findings. I'm sure she'll be as thrilled as we are that there's a perfectly legitimate loophole for us to take a chance on."

With a nod and an awkward smile at Morena, who, unsurprisingly, did not return the favour, Belle excused herself from the office, grateful to not have to play witness.

The door led back to the main atrium of Hecate House, with its twelve possible entries and the astounding ceiling that flickered with its canopy of magic. Bronwyn's office lay behind the Gemini door. Two silhouetted witches wearing pointed hats were cast in bronze above—fitting, both for the star sign and for the two Gowden sisters. Belle leaned back against the door with her eyes closed. She could still see the bright flecks of the ceiling crackling behind her eyelids.

A mentor. This was exactly what she needed. She couldn't believe her luck and sent her best vibes of thanks to whichever imaginative, ancient mystic had taken the time to jot down that offhand idea in the margins. Her magic might flourish now, with help from someone who knew what they were doing. Someone who knew better, who could show her the way that she was meant to go.

She almost toppled backwards as the door swung open without warning. Morena, radiating palpable fury, shoved past her without a backward glance. She crossed over the tiled moon and stars, cloak cascading behind her like a bird in flight, before disappearing through the eleventh door underneath a giant brass scorpion. Also rather fitting—sharp pincers, a sting in the tail.

Belle peered her head back around and saw Bronwyn staring

straight into her fireplace. Her fists were clenched tightly at her sides, a fury of magic crackling across her knuckles. Belle cleared her throat, and the elder witch immediately released the angry tension, dropping her shoulders and smoothing her expression.

"Wonderful, wonderful! It's all settled, Belle."

Belle suspected that, in fact, nothing had been all settled or wonderful and that Bronwyn had merely refused to lose the argument.

"My sister has gone to share the developments and make necessary arrangements with those who need to know. So without further ado, we shall get to choosing you a suitable . . . well, a suitable suitor."

Belle hesitated. "I really am sorry to have upset Morena so much. I don't seem to have started out on a good note with her at all, and I'm not entirely sure why she—"

"Don't take it personally, lovey," Bronwyn interrupted. "There *is* no good note with my sister. Only flat ones, caterwauls and hideous violin noises."

Belle dared to let the tiniest ounce of hope take seed in her mind, that maybe this could and would be resolved soon. All was not lost.

Bronwyn was refastening her cloak and adjusting her hat as though preparing to leave. Belle took it as an invitation to follow suit.

"The grimoire said we should refer to the Hecate House glossary for the archive. How do we find that?"

"Not 'glossary,' dear. Ossuary."

"Pardon?"

"It's where we keep the bones," Bronwyn replied.

Belle choked. "Bones?"

"Yes, love. Bones. Of the coven members who've passed on," she said airily, as though explaining where the bread was kept in the kitchen. Sensing Belle's horror, she added, "Oh, don't look so aghast, you ninny. Renting space in London doesn't come cheap, as

I'm sure you know all too well. The above-ground cemetery is well out of our budget, even as supernatural beings. Having the coven ossuary means we can give our wicche family a final resting place together within Hecate House, if they so choose. It's not unusual for members to be cast out of their families, for friends to turn their backs when truths are revealed, for lovers to decide it's all too much. This place becomes both their home and comfort when nothing else remains."

"Home sweet Hecate House."

"Quite. It's not obligatory, nor as frightening as it sounds—particularly when you remember that half of this blasted city is built on top of plague pits, anyway."

"And if you've got something precious that you want to keep hidden from prying eyes, like an archival register of coven members' names and locations . . ." Belle started to fill in the blanks.

"Which could cause revolutionary chaos in the wrong hands," Bronwyn nodded knowingly. "Then you keep it safely near the dead. They tend to be the best at keeping secrets. People who are alive get too spooked to go poking around."

"Right. So, where is this ossuary?"

"The library, of course. Anything of importance is always in the library, dear."

12

Artorius Day

THE LIBRARY OF Hecate House looked similar to the court-room but was darker, sleepier and mustier. The smell was sort of coffee, sort of chocolate, earthy and dusty and sweet. Like the bookshop, if it had been operating underground for a few centuries. There must have been thousands upon thousands of books inside. They left little room to even shuffle oneself between the corridors of endless pages and waxy spines. Belle and Bronwyn were forced to repeat their steps more than once, bringing a whole new meaning to getting lost in a good book. Belle noticed several piles heaped so high that they swayed precariously, only holding their balance through the presence of an invisible enchantment stringing them up to the ceiling.

The single sound was the turning of pages against the soft crackle of burning fireplaces. Some of the books seemed to be reading them-selves, unless their readers were invisible, which, Belle thought, was entirely possible.

Leading the way through the library's maze, Bronwyn cast out her palms, each hand emitting an illuminating beam like a torch and leaving a trail of glittering magic dust in their wake. Belle followed the magic like breadcrumbs, attempting to find her footing. In her clumsiness, her elbow knocked a clothbound copy to the floor. She stooped to pick it up. *Merlin-Worthy Millinery: Stitch a Modern Take on the Classic Sorcerer Hat.*

"Plenty of time for browsing later, deary. We're over here, in the Lore and Resources section."

Careful to keep both elbows in, Belle stopped in her tracks. Once her eyes adjusted to the darkness, she noticed reading nooks nestled deeply between the towering shelves. Each nook, with desks and armchairs and lamps poised to help escape into someone else's words, was in front of a large window. One showed the rolling countryside. Another the bustling city. The beach, the desert, the night sky, the morning sunrise. A woodland, a glen, a cottage, a poolside. The past, the present, the future.

"A neat little bit of bewitching, don't you agree? Something Rune rustled up . . . For himself more than anyone else, I think. Don't tell him I said that. Fixed to transport the reader to wherever they may wish to go. The magic adapts to reflect the pages they're reading."

Bronwyn carried on ahead as Belle stared in wonder at the window to her left, which showed an inviting forest cabin, and made a mental note to try it for herself if she ever returned. She hastened to catch up as the sage witch beckoned her to the main desk, which lay at the centre of the library. Behind it stood a lady who Belle could only assume had been living down there for several hundred years and not missed the fresh air enough to leave at any point.

She was bent almost double in her old age, a huge knot in her spine protruding through the form of her cloak. Although stitched with the coven's constellations, the brilliance of the thread was fading, dimmer and fainter than those of her younger peers. She was hazardously leaning her frail frame against a gnarled walking stick while she catalogued a pile of titles in slow motion. Belle felt like she should run over and lean her back the other way to stop her from toppling straight over. Smoky grey hair reached her knees in a thick plait, with wilting flowers and thistles the colour of tea stains entwined through the braid. She herself looked translucent and brittle, like she may be fading away before their eyes.

"Bron!" the old librarian croaked, and creaked as she turned, pivoting dangerously on her stick. "I've put a stack of new romances to one side for you. One about a captain and a scullery maid which is right up your street, and . . ."

"Not today, thank you, Sybil. Although do keep that to one side, it sounds a bit of me. I need to fetch the Lore Key from you, please, my love."

Sybil's eyebrows shot up in surprise with a la-di-da expression. She spoke with a strong Welsh accent. "All business today, eh? Oh, is this the EquiWitch I've heard so much about? Bonnie's girl? Lacquered lizards, don't she look like Alvina? Got the nose and the nervous fidgeting and everything."

Sybil grinned at Belle, revealing several missing teeth. Belle, instantly self-conscious, dropped her hands from picking at her cuticles and held them firmly at her sides.

"Syb is the long-time librarian here at Hecate House. She's your woman for any book you could ever need. Potion recipes, incantation writing, Earth Sorcery theory . . . Or a spot of fiction. She knows I'm partial to a swashbuckling sex bomb. Spent a summer with a handsome pirate once. Never got over him, truth be told."

"Lovely to meet you," Belle said quickly to the librarian, who continued to look her up and down with curiosity.

"The Lore Key, Syb?" Bronwyn reminded the woman. While Bronwyn spoke to Sybil, Belle absent-mindedly picked up a copy of *Thine Newborn Toad*. It croaked a wet belch as she opened the cover, which, to her horror, was thickly slimy to touch.

"Ferns and figs, the Lore Key? That old thing. Now, where did I last see it?"

Belle privately marvelled that these two were the perfect example of "the ones you least expect."

"I tell you, it's been a long while since anyone's dug that out, Bron. I haven't got a clue where it is, I won't lie to you. Let me concentrate for a moment. Pardon me for a second, Ms. Blackthorn. Much obliged."

Belle expected Sybil to start searching through the drawers and cupboards set within the desk, which curved around her in a rich oak crescent. But instead, Sybil simply closed her eyes. Wobbling dangerously as she righted herself onto her stick, she waved one palm over her other. A small ball of silver light formed in her fist and opened to reveal a tarnished key.

"Knew it was in there somewhere," Sybil muttered to herself. "Not as easy for me to conjure these days as it once was."

She handed the key to Bronwyn, who wrapped both her hands around Sybil's to shake it with gratitude. "Many thanks, Syb. That's good of you." There was a pause as the old witches smiled affectionately at one another.

"Oh, Bron! Wasn't expecting you today. What can I do for you?" Sybil's glassy eyes suddenly seemed to glaze over. She turned back to Belle. "And who's this young thing? My, you don't half look like . . ."

Bronwyn smiled sadly. "You come by my office for a cup of tea when you've finished for the day, Syb."

The old woman waved the pair away, already forgetting their brief encounter.

"One of life's kindest and cruellest gifts, old friends. Anyone's Achilles heel," Bronwyn said sadly. "I miss her and she's still here. Love does leave you vulnerable, if you allow it to endure."

Moving through the endless aisles again, the pair finally reached an intricate iron structure buried in the shadows. A gate stretched all the way up to the high ceiling and was wide across. Its bars of iron

twisted and turned together like immovable roots of ivy, marking off
a separate chamber. Its branches sprawled out all the way across the
roof overhead and wound downwards like an unnatural twin to the
willow tree above. The ossuary stood like a giant birdcage but de-
void of any life inside.

"An unlocking spell won't work?"

Bronwyn was roughly digging the small key into a thick lock on
the cage's gate, wiggling it about with great effort. She laughed aloud
at the apparently ridiculous idea.

"Heavens and hell's bells, girl. Safely storing sacred magical information requires a good old lock and key. Any witch or warlock
can work out a spell if they think about it hard enough. But the Lore
Key is one of a kind that only Sybil can mind safely. No one stands
a chance."

With a satisfying click, the lock opened. The key vanished from
Bronwyn's grasp as soon as it had completed its duty, leaving no
trace but a few miniature sparks amongst her fingertips.

"Oh, where did that come from?" Belle heard Sybil across the
library, sounding faintly far off in the distance as she received the
key back in her possession.

"Foolproof," Belle muttered in amazement.

As the ossuary gate swung open, a cold breeze sent Belle's hair
flying backwards, and she only just managed to catch her hat from
sailing several shelves behind. The coldness carried the scent of
winter. Crisp frost, misty rain, pine needles.

Belle felt her breath catch in her chest as more of the space came
to light. A blanket of pale, blanched bones covered the entire back
wall. It must have contained hundreds if not thousands of skeletons,
all artfully arranged and thoughtfully positioned in an eerie but undeniably joyful way. A startling chandelier of bones of every shape
hung hauntingly from the ceiling, swaying slightly in the cold air
amidst draped garlands. The sight was all at once both deeply

horrifying and strangely beautiful, bringing an awareness of the skeleton under her own skin, which was a feeling she wasn't sure she loved. Despite the sentiment Bronwyn had described—lost souls finding friends and chosen family to rest beside—she couldn't help but shiver.

"That's the badger!"

As well as the macabre decor, the ossuary also held a vast selection of chests, trunks, cabinets and cupboards slotted together like building blocks. It looked like the most cursed Lost Property Department of all time. Finding her footing on various knobs, handles and jutting drawers, Bronwyn climbed up to one particular cabinet. With a huff, she shoved aside a box brimming with newspapers, a plinth holding a golden cauldron and an inexplicable statue of a screeching cat head. Eventually giving up and clambering back down to instead direct Belle with hands on hips, the pair brought down what looked like an ornate library card catalogue system.

"This," the sage witch began as she pulled out the first drawer with a flick of magic and immediately began rifling through the contents, "is the coven archival register. Hasn't been updated for a while, in truth. But I'm sure there's some folk in here who'll be keen contenders for your mentorship, lovey."

Belle frowned. "And if there's not?"

"Then it's Plan B, I suppose. Although, actually, *this* should probably be considered Plan B. Plan A was that you pass your hearing and head off for a lovely birthday dinner. I think we're past that one. Plan C remains unconfirmed as of yet, poppet."

She replied brightly, as though Belle's powers were not hanging by a fine thread. Bronwyn continued rummaging through the drawers, pulling out from each oddly shaped compartment a stack of what looked like old sepia postcards with a holographic quality to the film.

"In this archive is every single member of this coven, past and present, who, in different ways and circumstances over the centuries, have proven themselves to have the hallmarks of legendary Selcouth magic. As the note in the grimoire plainly said, they would all make worthy mentors."

Bronwyn shuffled through the cards, glancing fondly at each as she went.

"You could put all of this on a computer, Bronwyn. It might be a bit easier to keep on top of everything," Belle said, trying to be helpful.

"A what, love? Ahh, see, I would have loved you to meet Elagoria. Fabulous, she was," Bronwyn said affectionately. She extracted the card in question from the archive stacks. It showed a grinning woman with her witch's hat covered in tropical flowers and a few pieces of fruit. "So gentle. Loved animals above all else. A perfect magic mentor—if she hadn't met an unfortunate end a couple of years ago. Poor Elagoria. That's what happens when you try to moisturise a dragon's tail. They don't like to be groomed."

Bronwyn handed her the card for a closer look. Elagoria's photo featured a bold red line, which looked alarmingly like blood, slashed right the way through.

> *Name: Elagoria Tippleton*
> *Last known location: Leeds, United Kingdom*
> *Special arts: Animal Affinity, incense burning*

Next to "Status," an updated detail had been written: *Deceased. Dragon fire.*

Bronwyn sighed. She dove back into the cabinet, trying the next drawer along.

"Arjun Christophate . . ." She flashed a picture of a man with piercing eyes and a dense black beard. "The less said about what happened to him, the better. All I can say, Belle, is never trust a siren when you're on holiday. It never ends well. His poor wife." Belle, aghast, caught the phrase *driven to madness, drowned* at the bottom of Arjun's card.

Things didn't brighten up from there. Once they'd removed everybody with a vested interest in her trial, the pool of potential mentors dwindled drastically. The handful of remaining Selcouth members seemed to have followed one unfortunate fate after another. Poor Lira Draculite had suffered a miserable demise from something that Bronwyn would only mysteriously describe as "the pox . . . but not *that* pox." Ethellius Hartingham had attempted a transference to Hull, but had ended up in hell thanks to his strong Scottish accent, which seemed particularly unfortunate luck. Marigold Drefus had fallen down the stairs. Her family swore that spirits had been to blame.

"You can say that again. Always on the drink, that one" was Bronwyn's cutting assessment.

When they finally reached the end of the archive, Bronwyn clutched just one solitary card.

Belle reached for it. "Are they still kicking? Can I take a look?"

Bronwyn hurriedly stashed the card in her cloak pocket. "This one should have been removed a long time ago. I've only kept it with me so Sybil can make sure he's stricken for good."

"Who is it?" Belle asked.

"Trust me, Belle," Bronwyn said, uncharacteristically stern. "You do not want this person as a mentor. Bloody Sybil needs to update things more than once a century. Remind me to tell her—"

"Bronwyn, please."

The witches locked eyes.

"I need to make this work," Belle said, panic in her voice again. "Otherwise, that's it. Like you said, we don't have a Plan C. I'm going to lose my magic." Saying it aloud again felt terrible. "Whoever it is, they can't be that bad. If they're a member of Selcouth and they're technically still alive, then I'll take it. In fact, I'm not even too bothered about the last part. I'm open to the undead at this point, now that I've seen the ossuary. They have a great eye for interiors."

The elder witch paused for a moment. She hesitated, poised to say more, but something changed her mind. Bronwyn sighed and pulled the card from her pocket. She took a long look at the photograph, examining the face in the picture. "Artorius Day."

Belle glanced down at the photograph on the card as Bronwyn offered it to her. In tones of sepia brown was a young man with dark eyes, slightly too big ears and a lost look.

"Oh, that's him all right. Categorically the most good-for-nothing weasel of a warlock to have ever stumbled his way into this coven."

Belle was surprised to hear the hard tone in Bronwyn's voice. Artorius Day, like a rabbit in headlights, seemed to stare straight back at her from his photograph. His hair stuck up all over the place, as though he'd quickly dragged his fingers through it the moment the camera captured him. His round face was covered with a healthy smattering of freckles. Whether it was the lost expression or the fact that this warlock was her last hope, Belle found herself instantly warming to him.

"Not who I would have chosen in a million years, Belle. But like you say, this may be your last chance, and this is what the universe seems to have presented to us in its infinite wisdom."

"The universe seems to like keeping me on my toes at the moment. Can you tell me more about him?"

Bronwyn gave a resigned sigh. "I think we're going to need some more tea."

13

Cauldron of Fire

"WHAT I AM about to tell you is widely known but rarely discussed."

Back in her office, Bronwyn leaned towards Belle in the armchair opposite, the mouse in her pocket hopping up to her shoulder and burying itself in her wiry hair.

"It is a story which has brought great shame to this coven for many years. It is the ink-blot on our proud history, and there are many folk around here"—Bronwyn gestured to the door—"who would not approve of me passing on this tale to you. Selcouth tries to forget it ever happened, but there's no scorning history. And I would never leave you to make any decision like this without having all of the facts presented to you, dear. The truth always outs in this coven."

"I appreciate that," Belle said. The cold of the ossuary had chilled her, and she inhaled the sweet scent of honey gratefully as she sipped her tea. "But how bad can he be?"

"Artorius Day is a villain. A warlock with blood on his hands."

Belle choked on scalding hot tea. "Bad, then."

"The blood of a respected, much-loved high warlock of this

coven, no less. Selcouth can forgive many things. But it cannot forgive magic with evil at its heart."

A BOY, SMALL *for his age at fifteen years old, stood between a cauldron bigger than him and an older brother even bigger again. Savaric had grown to over six feet tall, and the boy had concluded the only logical explanation was that he was secretly part giant. Maybe an unknown uncle or a grandfather somewhere up the family tree. More than a decade younger than Savaric and constantly overshadowed by his impressive magical achievements, the boy struggled to walk the tightrope between envy and admiration towards his older brother. By the minute, it changed from one to the other— hatred, then adoration. Adoration. Hatred.*

"Sav, look, look. It's turning, it's turning!"

With brown eyes and ears that he still hoped to grow into, the boy leaned over and gazed in awe at a complex, rich potion that had been steeping for the last seven days straight. The brothers had checked on it fastidiously since their work began, waking up through the night with the changing patterns of the moon risings. They had monitored its progress with unwavering determination to ensure their creation was developing exactly as planned.

"Artorius, calm down. Don't get your face too close. Mother will kill me if it does any damage to you."

Savaric dashed over to his side and plunged a rusty ladle deep into the concoction. He dragged it through the sludgy mix in laborious clockwise motions.

"This stuff will be bubbling any minute now, and you don't want to see what happens if it touches any part of your skin. Scales wouldn't be a handsome look on you, lad."

Artorius scoffed, frantic and over-excited. "Is it time? Can you try it? Oh, go on, just a sip. Let's see what happens, Sav. You're being an awful bore."

Artorius's grip was so tight that it tipped the cauldron at an angle, sending a splash down to their feet. The boys yelled and leapt backwards simultaneously, narrowly avoiding it.

"Careful! Patience, little brother. Any warlock worth his salt knows that you cannot rush good magic, idiot." Savaric grinned smugly and ruffled his sibling's sandy hair.

Artorius scowled up in his patronising direction. He hated being called "idiot," "stupid," "fool"... But the worst was "little brother." He was a warlock now. The coven said it was so, officially, because his powers had finally been instated last month for his fifteenth birthday. One day, he'd be thought of as the man of the family and would fire insults back at Sav with relish.

"First light tomorrow," Savaric reassured him, not realising that his gentle tone was grating on Artorius's last nerve. Both brothers peered down with almost identical freckled faces, one with the faintest etching of worry lines, preparing himself to take on responsibilities that he wasn't sure he was ready for. In a matter of weeks, on his thirtieth orbital completion, Savaric would step into the role that his father had left waiting for him and become high sage of Selcouth. The idea terrified and thrilled him, although he'd never admit the former to anybody. Not even to his younger brother, who was his closest ally despite their constant bickering.

The liquid in the huge pot simmered and smoked as though it could come alive. The colour of a sunset melting from daytime into night, the potion was blending from a peachy shade of inviting orange into a much darker blood-like hue. As Savaric had anticipated, an enormous bubble suddenly filled out like a creature surrendering a deep breath underneath the surface. It popped with a slow, gelatinous splash.

"Oh, go on, Sav. Do we have to wait another night? How much more can it possibly steep?"

"I've told you a million times that there is no nobler branch of magic than Alchemy, it's patience and artistry combined. Real magic comes in the study, the art, the patience of waiting for it to knit together properly."

Artorius sighed as he heard the snobbish resolution in his older brother's voice. "Fine, fine."

Savaric rolled his eyes, then hesitated. "I suppose a small extra sprinkling of spearmint wouldn't do too much harm. Some extra fire for this one, little brother? Let's make sure we put on a show for Selcouth."

The younger boy punched the air, thrilled that Savaric was taking a rare risk for their secret project. Sav had had no choice but to share his plan when Artorius stumbled across him brewing up a literal storm in the dilapidated barn, the smoke already choking as it leaked out under the doorway.

His plan to perform the most complex and impressive of magic to mark the beginning of his coven leadership began when Sav discovered the spell stored away in his father's grimoire, the original of the coven. Incandesco Caelestis. Wings to span across the sky, impossibly tough scales of iridescent armour, a breath of the wildest fire. Normally a man of level head and sensible shoulders, he could barely contain himself at the idea of dragon transformation for his sage ceremony. It would be the perfect majestic display of power for Selcouth and the promise of unflinching leadership—especially for those who had doubted that he would be able to fill his father's shoes. Savaric had sworn his younger brother to secrecy, allowing him to help and promising a ride on his transformed back in return for keeping the secret. Since learning of the plan, Artorius had spoken of nothing else, and not always quietly.

Savaric crossed the barn and rummaged through the ingredients cabinet. *Second shelf, behind the dried dandelions.* He pulled out a stoppered jar of shredded spearmint leaves, emptied a little into his palm and passed the offering to his brother. Artorius immediately took one to chew on, then threw the leaves into the potion. It swallowed the sprigs of green into its murky depths.

"Come on, muggins," said Savaric as he loomed over and squeezed his brother's shoulders. "The sooner we sleep, the sooner the spell is ready. It's going to be quite a day tomorrow. We'll both need our strength." Savaric laughed as he pretended to give a boot to the bottom of his young sibling to hurry him out.

Artorius scowled. "Don't do that, Sav! I hate you sometimes."

* • *• •*• *

NIGHT FELL. PARTICULARLY dark, with so many stars overhead that Artorius wondered whether each one had arrived especially to see his brother's sacred show tomorrow. The song thrush had not yet shared its singing, but scuffed shoes appeared at the barn door all the same. Tiptoeing noiselessly across the weathered floor, creeping to the ingredients cabinet filled to burst. Grubby fingers reached inside. *Second shelf, behind the dandelions. Spearmint, for extra fire.*

The tin of bonfire ash, charred and filthy. The jar of fireflies, beads of flame. The bottle of black salt, earthy, sharp and jagged. A combination of ingredients for an unbridled inferno, gathered and carried with difficulty by young freckled arms to the cauldron. Lids opened and cast aside, each element was thrown into the cauldron unmeasured and unchecked. Almost instantly, the promising layer of bubbles ceased, and instead smoke breathed out from under the surface.

"Let him burn."

Jars and bottles were hurriedly discarded. The latch was closed *again. Scuffed shoes scurried like mice back to bed, and then the song thrush began.*

"BURNED INSIDE OUT, he was," Bronwyn said. "A potion of pure flame, pure fire, liquid ember and ash created while Savaric slept. Oblivious to the changes, he consumed it that very next day, pulling the stoppered bottle from his cloak pocket as his endarkenment and sage ceremony came to its conclusion. Unaware that Artorius had tampered with it in the night, ignorant of its guarantee of grim death. It killed him without warning in front of the whole coven."

Bronwyn rose to her feet and went to the grimoire. From it, she pulled out two loose leaves of paper, which had been placed between the back pages for safekeeping. One small cutting was torn at the edges, ripped from a newspaper.

MYSTERY FARMHOUSE MURDER

Laverlett Village woke to shock and mourning on Monday when the death of 30-year-old farmhand Savaric Day was confirmed. Day, popular and well-loved amongst locals, is said by devastated family and a sweetheart to have howled in pain and dropped dead before their eyes under most mysterious of circumstances. While Day's body appeared unafflicted to those who witnessed his death, a post-mortem later revealed severe burns throughout Day's inner and skeletal form. Sources tell the *Globe* that Day's younger brother, Artorius Day, has been missing since the tragic incident occurred. A formal investigation is currently under way by Laverlett police.

Belle felt sick to her core. A boy with murder on his mind, and another meeting a dreadful death. "What happened to Artorius?"

"Nothing, to begin with. He never came to his brother's endarkenment, slipped from the scene, wasn't found again for years. He couldn't be linked to Savaric's death by the police, by the non-wicche community, because how could he have had anything to do with it? A freak accident, they said. Blamed it on 'internal combustion' in the end, would you believe?" Bronwyn said with air quotes.

Belle sunk back into her chair, reeling. The pair sat in silence for a few minutes, sipping every now and again at their cups for unconscious comfort.

"To die like that. And at the hands of a family member, too . . ." Belle said. "But he *was* a child, Artorius? Only fifteen, only new to his powers. It had to be an accident. There's no way he could have known it would turn out the way it did."

"No accident, Belle." Bronwyn shook her head regretfully. "When Artorius was eventually found three years after Savaric died, Morena and I had only just found Selcouth ourselves, only just learned the history. He was barely alive, hiding in an abandoned outhouse through a bitter winter. He'd used complex magic to keep the coven from finding him for all that time, remarkably skilled for his age—dangerously so. He confessed immediately to killing his brother. He was brought to Hecate House, and he told the coven outright that he'd committed the murder. Guilty as sin itself."

"But why would he do it? Sure, Savaric wound him up, but to kill him . . ."

"Who can say? He researched it in their late father's coven grimoire, gathered all of the ingredients that he knew would turn their potion into darkest magic and threw them into the cauldron with one thought: to kill Savaric."

"A boy that young, murder their sibling? It makes no sense."

Bronwyn sniffed, stirred what remained of her tea and clinked the silver spoon against the saucer in deep thought. "For revenge? For jealousy? For power?" she said. "Perhaps it was the only way he'd ever feel powerful, taking something for himself."

"Surely not. For coven rule?"

"Coven rule is a funny thing, Belle. It may seem as though it's neither here nor there as to who takes the sage role. But coven rule in the wrong hands could mean disaster for us, for wicche and non-wicche folk alike. Access to the grimoire, for one. It's powerful stuff."

Belle was silent, her lips a thin line.

"Maybe it was merely to prove something, to others or to himself," Bronwyn continued. "Maybe even for no reason at all, but simply a want to hurt. To be noticed, to be heard."

Belle and Bronwyn locked eyes, the atmosphere tense and thick.

The tiny brown mouse emerged for a moment, eyed up its surroundings and then promptly scurried again into the mass of hair underneath Bronwyn's hat. She stroked its bottom absent-mindedly. "You and I could never understand a mind like that, Belle."

Belle slumped backwards against the swell of the armchair and allowed her shoulders, which had been so tense against her ears throughout the story, to fall with heavy relief.

"I'm sorry to have to share such a story," Bronwyn tutted. "Not in my character, stuff like that. If it were up to me, I'd have lent you the romance that Sybil's got saved for me downstairs." She chuckled and reached out to pat Belle on the knee. "But now you know the truth. And I'm confident that you can make the informed decision that's best for you and you alone. I don't wish to influence you. I understand that you're between a rock and a hard place."

Belle gave her a weak smile in return, remembering only then that Artorius Day was a decision that she had to make and not just a story. She tried to pluck one of the hundreds of questions that were flapping through the front of her mind like birds.

"Where is he now, then? Artorius, I mean. What did the coven do with him when he was found?"

"Non-wicche police couldn't prove a thing, but his confession to the coven was enough. He was kept here at first, in the dungeons beneath Hecate House. Oh, they're not around anymore, my love," Bronwyn added hurriedly, seeing the horror on Belle's face. "Out of action these days, health and safety. We use them to store the hoover and the toilet paper."

She cleared her throat and continued. "After the loss of Savaric, Selcouth was left largely unprotected for a handful of years, and chaos reigned. Various attempts to seize it, stolen magic, coups and breakaway covens. That's when Morena and I stepped in to take the reins as shared sage. It seemed the fairest option, to start all over again. The vote was unanimous. And our decision for Artorius, right or wrong, was that he should be kept close, at least for a time."

She handed Belle the second scrap of paper she'd slipped from between the pages of the grimoire. This one was a photograph. "Taken on the day of his expulsion, for coven records."

Belle could barely believe it. Whether it was the act of killing or his time spent in the dungeons, the years since the first photo of Artorius had deeply altered him. Deep shadows pocketed a pale face underneath angled cheekbones, skin stretched taught. A beard clung to his jaw, which had changed shape from boy to broken man. He looked out at Belle through the paper with sunken eyes, lifeless and hopeless, and dark like the bottom of a well.

"Oh . . ."

"A long stint in Hecate dungeons probably doesn't help matters, but what were we to do? Nothing like this had ever been put upon the coven before. We had to be sure that he wouldn't act again."

As though she couldn't bear to look at it anymore, Bronwyn snatched the photo quickly from Belle's hand and tottered back to the grimoire to put it back within the binding.

"We settled on expellation. Previously unheard of without an EquiWitch trial, but he hadn't yet reached thirty."

Belle's gaze shot up. An unwelcome puzzle piece slotted into place. "Artorius Day was the last to fail his endarkenment before me."

"Yes and no. Technically, he was stripped of his powers before his endarkenment could even arrive."

Belle's brows knitted together. "Would it even be safe for me to work with him?"

"The coven has kept a close eye on him since banishment," Bronwyn explained. "He's in the very same house that he was sent to when his expellation was decided. And, in the man's rather limited defence, he has shown no sign of danger since his confession. We would reinstate him with only the basics to ensure he can provide mentoring to your magic, allow him to knit simple spellwork together without reaching significant heights."

Belle groaned. "I don't know if I can do this."

"You won't accept the mentorship?" Bronwyn asked with raised eyebrows.

"Well, surely I can't? Not after everything you've told me. I can't expect this guy to help me in good faith with anything, let alone provide lessons in magic. All he notably used his powers for before they were expelled completely was murdering the good guy who everyone loved."

Bronwyn nodded. "I must say, I'm somewhat relieved. But . . . that's not the decision I was expecting from you, Belle, to be frank."

Belle felt defensive. "Can you blame me? I thought Artorius was going to be a bit of an eccentric. A few too many whiskies with breakfast in his old age or something. I wasn't expecting you to say he was a brother-killing murderer. Plus, my mum will kill me even if he doesn't."

"I must in good faith remind you to consider again what you're giving up. What you're letting go of, Belle. On reflection last night while pondering the grimoire, I noted that almost all of your manifests slipped up thanks to a lack of faith, a lack of self-belief, a worry of what others would think. You've turned down chances, allowed yourself to remain unhappy, simply because you were afraid of the changes and even the successes they might bring."

The two witches held each other's gaze for a long, unspoken moment.

"I want this to be entirely your decision, Belle, let it be known. But I know what you are capable of being and capable of becoming." Bronwyn continued earnestly, "Your magic is meant for you, if only you'd claim it."

Belle buried her head in her hands, elbows on her thighs as she tried to pull focus. Bronwyn chuckled sympathetically.

"Decisions, decisions. I was vehemently against the idea at first, Belle, I was. But I confess, after our talk, that I do wonder . . . Artorius is powerless now. He holds no magic that can be used to hurt or harm you, without the coven being aware of it before it even happens."

Belle looked at her, taken aback by the change in stance.

"And still, as a descendent of Day, one of the oldest magic families in library record, he and his brother were known by the coven to be naturally gifted warlocks, even as teenagers pre-endarkenment. He would be an adept mentor, with the restricted powers that we would return to him for the occasion."

Belle sighed. "I should have stayed at home, where literally nothing ever happens."

Bronwyn chuckled again. "I'll give you a moment to gather your thoughts." She stepped out of her office, leaving Belle alone in front of the fire.

Belle closed her eyes for a moment, taking a breath. What else could be done to save her magic? This was her last chance.

Her hair was suddenly unbearable, falling in her face. She hastily pulled it back with the bobble on her wrist so she could think straight.

"Ouch!"

She started. As she gathered a ponytail, her forearm had brushed against the brooch that she'd been wearing as a kind of talisman since the trial. She snatched her hand back, recoiling in surprise. The sooth stone had turned blisteringly hot, and the pale smoke inside the glassy pebble was moving. She seized the fabric of her blouse for a closer look. The misty smoke twisted like a drop of dark ink in water, a languid swirl. It was brightening, awakening. Careful to touch only the shell casing, she hastily removed the pin, held it cautiously in her palm. Watching the blooms of smoke serpentine together behind the glass, Belle felt a hypnotising, all-consuming feeling.

Ignoring all logic, following the instinct of something else entirely, she clutched her fist firmly and fearlessly around the whole brooch. This time, rather than scalding her skin, the warmth travelled instantly through her, filling her whole body from head to toe. It was the most powerful, emboldening feeling. The same sensation as performing a spell but on an even greater, visceral scale. The essence of magic itself seemed to travel through her from the stone.

I'm here. It seemed to speak. No noise, no voice, but she heard it again, just as she had yesterday. *I'm here. Keep going. Make the right choice for yourself.*

There was no question in Belle's mind that it was a sign. The same as the moment during her EquiWitch trial when she had been at her lowest. A nudge, a nod, a glow. Just when she needed it most.

14

The Watchman

"YOU'RE ALL SET. Let me know what you think of the ending next time you pop in, Mrs. Rollings. It's a good one, I think you'll love it."

Belle gave the till a hard shove with both hands, the cash drawer jarring awkwardly against the frame like it always did. After years of offering advice for what to read next and unfailingly ringing up books as a result, she'd mastered the tricky knack of making it shut properly. Slightly to the left, push until it feels extremely broken.

The doorbell tinkled as the last customer of the day headed out the door of Lunar Books. The humming rush of the high street flooded in and faded out. Finally. The day preceding her first night of mentorship had dragged in the sleepy shop. Even on regular days, the quieter times made it feel as though time stood still between those shelves, like the shop's own nexus pendulum hidden somewhere in the fiction department.

She seized her chance to start the familiar closing routine. Scooping up discarded copies of this week's *Stellar Read* strewn across the wrong tables, Belle locked the front door, giving it a secure shake for good measure. She flipped the sign from Open to

Closed, and dimmed down the lights. A quick flick of sparks tidied up the chaotic children's corner. Her final job was manually inputting the sales into a calculator and jotting down the numbers into a lined notepad. Lunar Books was yet to arrive into the modern age, and Violet had no plans to make the journey anytime soon. She insisted it was part of the charm.

Belle's head swam slightly, the tips of her fingers pricking a little, dizziness washing over her. Probably a headache brewing at the thought of what was to come later in the evening. Clipping back her hair to concentrate, she hunched over the counter and scribbled down the sums under the light of the stained-glass lamps. A quick flick of her finger had the pencil-written numbers dancing across the page, arranging themselves into the correct order while she totalled the day's cash. The soft tinkle of the front doorbell rang out against the silence of the shop.

"Sorry, we're closed. Back tomorrow at ten."

Her concentration snapped like an elastic band. Didn't she just lock that? She did, she definitely locked it. Her head shot up. Someone was waiting inside. Barely lit but leaning tall and calm against the door-frame, one hand stretched up to tinkle the bell above the door and the other plunged into a coat pocket. Her hand instinctively reached for the keys on the counter to arm herself with something more quickly than debating a spell.

"I was hoping for after-hours service."

She squinted more closely at the customer. Was it? His face lit up with a smirk as he stepped out of the shadows. "Rune."

"I'm looking for something that I won't be able to put down. Something that'll keep me awake at night. A plot that'll drive me crazy."

Slamming her pencil down and clutching her chest, Belle groaned with relief and frustration. He smirked at her reaction. "With absolutely no due respect, what the *hell* are you doing?"

"Just browsing," Rune said innocently, thumbing titles on the front table.

"That was the single most creepy entrance that anyone has ever made. What is wrong with you?"

Rune faltered. "Oh. Well, I was going for suave and mysterious."

Belle rolled her eyes, gathering up her paperwork and placing it in the drawer for tomorrow's shift. "You skipped both of those and went straight to terrifying."

His mischievous look quickly changed to abashed. "Sorry, I didn't—"

"Fine. It's fine. I only thought you were going to kill me. And if you hadn't heard the news, I'm on high alert when it comes to murderers this evening. Next time, please just knock rather than transferring unannounced into my workplace behind a locked door when I'm alone in the darkness."

"Well, when you say it like that, I feel like an idiot."

"Good."

They stood in charged silence, staring at one another.

"Well? Now that you've revealed yourself to be a total weirdo and I'm traumatised for life, what can I do for you?"

"I told you, I'm book shopping. The plot that'll drive me crazy?"

Belle rolled her eyes again. "Take a look in that Romance section right there, and every one of those books will include a handsome man saying lines just as corny as yours."

"Well, you sure know how to make a guy feel special." Rune smiled. "I'll take the handsome thing, though."

Belle scowled at him as she felt her face flush.

"I've been waiting for you to leave," he went on. "I was starting to think you might have bottled it, decided this wasn't worth all of the hassle."

"No, I've been at work." Belle gestured around her. "You can't rush people when they're choosing books . . . Sorry, did I miss something? I didn't realise I was supposed to be meeting anyone tonight other than Artorius."

"And I didn't realise I'd been roped in until this morning."

"Roped in?"

He stepped a little closer to her. "Watchman duties. Looks like today is full of lovely surprises for us both," he replied coolly. He was trying and failing to keep a grin under wraps.

Belle attempted to rearrange herself in a nonchalant way to match his own posture. She was suddenly overly aware of her arms hanging at her sides and her feet standing at weird angles. She pressed both palms against the cool marble countertop, just to give them somewhere to be. "Lovely surprises," she replied doubtfully. "So, you're the muscle at Selcouth, hey? Come to meet with Artorius to make him an offer he can't refuse?"

This time, Rune laughed openly. White teeth flashed, and he shook his head. Rune approached the counter and mirrored her posture, placing his hands on the counter outside of hers and leaning forwards. She cleared her throat awkwardly, shuffling the loyalty cards as an excuse to break the eye contact.

"Why are you here, Rune?" It came out more abruptly than she'd intended. "Not that I don't appreciate you coming down to . . . Be my cheerleader? My bodyguard? Whatever this is," she said, leaning under the counter to pick up her backpack and hoist it onto her shoulder. "But I need to get a move on. I have a mysterious, hopefully reformed, warlock to go and hang out with."

That smirk again. "Don't worry, I'm not sticking around. But thank you for such a warm reception as always. I'm only here to reassure you that the coven is . . . aware of your whereabouts."

Belle's brows knotted together sceptically. "Are you always this ominous?"

"I try to be." He grinned again. "For reasons unbeknownst to both of us, the Gowden sisters—mostly Bronwyn," he corrected himself, "decided that I should be the one to make sure you showed up for your mentorship. To be honest," Rune said, taking a sweet from the bowl by the till and popping it into his mouth, pulling her attention to exactly where she didn't want it to be, "I think she was a little concerned that you might have done a runner."

Belle instantly bristled. If Selcouth had already decided she couldn't even be trusted to successfully meet with Artorius, what was the likelihood of them giving her a fair assessment on her return?

"That's thoughtful of you. Them. Her," she stuttered. "But as you can see"—she came around the counter, tugging her backpack farther onto her shoulder—"I'm fine. I'm getting this show on the road."

"And I for one look forward to seeing how the show turns out. Quite the drama already. Plot twists, ancient lore loopholes, a hung jury, banished murderers . . ." Rune said teasingly as he followed her through the shop, reeling the points off on his fingers.

She gestured to the door to encourage him out as she unlocked it.

"All right, I can take a hint." He laughed softly. "This wasn't what I had planned for the next few weeks, either, but whether we like it or not, Bronwyn's decreed that I'm yours. For twenty-eight moons."

Belle gave him a blank *You have to be kidding* look.

"And I can see why they chose to match us together," he added. "The chemistry here is . . . truly palpable."

Big on eye contact, this guy, Belle thought to herself. She ushered him through the open door. "I don't love the idea of having a 'watchman.' It sounds horrendously outdated, like I should be living in a turret and playing the lute while you charge around with a sword. Can't we call it something else?"

"Sure." He nodded agreeably. "How about protector? Keeper? Handler?"

"On second thought, let's stick with 'watchman.'" Belle grimaced. "What does the job really involve?"

"I thought you'd never ask. Traditionally, it tends to involve bringing down some great evil, an endeavour on behalf of Selcouth. Spending the weekend trying to prevent the inevitable end of mortal existence itself. That sort of thing."

Rune cleared his throat as a woman walking a terrier turned the corner and shuffled past them apologetically.

"So you've got off pretty lightly with this one, then," Belle said. "Watchman for little old me, meeting and greeting a man who's going to bring my homework up to scratch. Probably not the most immediate threat to mortal existence . . ." She was struggling to remember what one normally did with their hands when speaking normally in a normal conversation.

"I wouldn't speak too soon."

"True. Maybe my great villain origin story is just around the corner. Alas, I knew it was inevitable."

This earned a side smirk.

She switched off the lights, leaving the spotlights on the suitably spooky display that she'd purposely neglected to take down. The windows gave out a glow against the chilly evening.

"Look, as much as I appreciate you swinging by unannounced, once again, despite me literally begging you to never come here again . . . I don't need a 'watchman,'" Belle told him, with added emphatic air quotes. "In fact, I actively hate the idea."

"I'm not huge on it, either, trust me. There's a million and one things I could be doing with my time instead."

"Like what? Brooding in the shadows of some underground vampire den? Or wherever it is you pass the nights?"

"I do not live in a den." He sulked. "If anything, it's more of a lair."

"Right."

"You won't see me much. Most of the watchman duties are done from Hecate House. I'm only here to point you in the right direction," Rune assured her, his voice a fraction softer and more sincere. "I just wanted to make sure you know that you can reach me. All you have to do is ask."

"I think your hero complex is showing," Belle scoffed.

Yes, maybe she was feeling a little defensive, still licking her wounds after the EquiWitch trial, but she'd never relied on anybody for anything—particularly not a man. Now she had inadvertently found herself relying on *two* of them to help her keep hold of magic that was rightfully hers, anyway. Her pride prickled like heat rash.

But as frustrating as it was, if the coven considered her to need an extra, *extra* helping hand, the reasonable part of her brain debated that it wouldn't hurt for it to be someone like Rune. One of their most promising warlocks, rising up the ranks, specialising in forms of protective magic. The idea of him keeping an eye on her was unsettling, awkward. But maybe practical. She'd be stupid not to take all of the help she could get.

"I can tell you're not convinced, and I'm trying not to take offence," Rune said, as though reading her mind. "But trust me. They're your lessons to learn. I'll just be around if you need anything. Extra protection, guidance, advice . . ."

Belle gave him an overly dramatic side-eye. This guy. "Only if I ask for it?"

That smirk again. This *guy*. "I've cleared my schedule, just for you."

"I'm honoured to hear it."

"Trust me. I want to help." He looked surprisingly sincere. It was maybe the first truly genuine thing he'd said to her so far, delivered without any attempt at mystery or bravado.

Belle defrosted a fraction. Perhaps sensing her thawing, Rune held out a hand to shake hers, which she accepted. A crackle of magic snapped between their palms as they connected, his grip warm and strong. Belle wasn't sure, but she felt as though he held on a moment too long.

"Well, thanks for stopping by and scaring the good grace out of my soul."

"Anytime. I'll leave you to meet the infamous Mr. Day. And I'll check in with you in a couple of days. Hey, Gowdens' orders. Don't hex the messenger." Rune held up both of his hands in mock surrender.

With a swift glance over his shoulder and around the corner, he shot Belle a quick wink, snapped his forefinger and thumb together languidly and vanished. Where he'd stood, a few rogue sparks of magic tumbled between the cracks of the pavement.

"Bye, then." Belle spoke to thin air.

Batting all lingering thoughts of Rune and his annoying dimples away, Belle pulled a small card with Artorius's address from her pocket. Caspar had provided the necessary information, a second letter from Selcouth arriving on her pillow that morning in a flurry of sparks, much to Jinx's distaste. Heaving her stuffed backpack farther up onto her shoulder again, she stumbled on the cobbles under its weight. She hadn't been entirely sure what to bring to meet her new mentor, so had packed everything possible as a sensible compromise, including her own hefty grimoire, which accounted for the weight of a small boulder.

She turned down a street lined with tall trees. The fiery leaves were a painting of autumn. A confetti of buttery biscuit browns, almond and amber, chestnut and chocolate. The colours canopied, hanging overhead against an evening sky of blended purples and blues.

This was how the coming nights were going to be. She already felt drained after being on her feet for hours at Lunar, but evenings of carbs and falling asleep on the sofa were off the cards for a while. For twenty-eight moons, specifically.

The leaves crunching underfoot reminded Belle of walking in the woods with her mum when she was little. A deep dip between two particular trees would fill with fallen leaves every year, and they'd called it the cornflake bowl. They'd meticulously choose the most perfect shades of orange and brown in every variety to take home for Bonnie's flora collection and would later toss them into the swirling potions of luck and guidance that were constantly brewing atop the stove.

Shaking off the memory, Belle was grateful to spot a black-and-white weathered sign for Quill Lane in block letters. Artorius lived at Number 8.

Behind the trees were regal Georgian houses stacked tall in orange brick and bay windows. Immaculate gardens sat outside every one, the last of the summer roses still clinging on. Carefully carved pumpkins of all shapes and sizes, done by perfectionist parents after their children got bored of scooping the guts out, sat plumply on porches.

She stopped. Ten Quill Lane was now on her left. It wasn't even a house; it was a mansion. Six Quill Lane was a little farther along in her eyeline, another beauty with spotlessly plush hedging—so pristine that Belle reckoned it must have been cut with a spirit level balanced on top.

Number 8 Quill Lane stood alone.

It felt like the other houses had taken a swift step away from it, sensing something strange. The grubby penny at the bottom of the street's shiny piggy bank, the house almost seemed to be lurching back from the road, desperate to retreat into the shadows. It must have been beautiful once but had been long neglected and left to its own devices. The place looked like a faded, forgotten memory, a shadow of its former self. Although still a tall house like the rest, Day's home stood rickety and unsure, with a dingy round window in the pointed eaves hinting at an attic room perched precariously on top. Yellowed lace curtains hung across the panes inside, moss sprouting in every crevice of the frames.

"Of course. It's the one that's filled with the spirits of the damned," Belle muttered to herself.

She took a few cautious steps towards the house. Amber tree sap was dashed across the pathway, and matching rust coated the gate in dark orange icing. Parched brittle brown stems had grown up from the ground and snaked their way towards the door, a carpet of weeds between the cracks of the broken driveway slabs.

Apprehensive, doubting her decision to go ahead with the mentorship, she thought of her mum again. Belle had called Bonnie to fill her in on what had unfolded, recounting the entire day's events (minus the voice in the tunnels), and had wanted to turn inside out with guilt. Not that Bonnie had *tried* to make Belle feel bad. She had done everything she could to reassure her daughter that she wasn't upset about her obvious lack of magic prowess and that everything would still be okay in the end (otherwise it wasn't the end), but Belle had felt too miserable to take much cheer from the pep talk.

"Come on. Get a grip."

Steeling herself, Belle gingerly reached for the gate. The metal gave a shrill wail, impossibly loud against the peaceful evening street, and Belle cringed, scraping rust against rust as it clanged shut behind her. The photo that Bronwyn had showed her of Day before his trial was imprinted in her mind. The haunted expression on his face, the soulless look behind his eyes. Now she was about to meet the man. A wriggle of fear hooked her under the ribs, anchoring her to the spot.

She forced herself down the driveway. Faced with a navy blue door, paint peeling in shards like a shedding skin, Belle reached for the heavy brass knocker and banged thrice. She hoped that nobody was home.

A second dim light came on through the door panes of frosted glass. A scuffling of chain and handle. A heaving creak of old hinges. And then . . .

"Oh, my dear. Welcome!"

15

Quill Lane

"HI . . . I'M LOOKING for Mr. Day?"

"Why yes, that would be me."

Belle's mind went blank with shock. The hand that wrapped itself around the edge of the front door was pale and bony, with thin, mottled skin stretched across the tendons like crepe paper.

Artorius, several inches shorter than Belle, was wearing a beige jacket at least two sizes too big for his frail frame. Grey slacks and a striped button-up shirt fitted with about as much success as the coat, as though the man inside of them had significantly shrunk. There was a pair of tartan slippers on his feet, bobbly and well worn. The thick glasses sitting on his nose magnified his brown eyes into a smiley, puppylike stare. Tufts of ashy grey hair stuck out at all angles above ears that were still unusually large. Perhaps the most unexpected part of his appearance was the pastel pink woolly hat perched on top of his head.

Surely not.

"Oh!" she spluttered, then managed to compose herself. "Right. Hi there. Hi. Well, I'm . . . here to be your student, I think."

"Of course, Belladonna! Yes, hello, hello. I've been expecting you, been most excited about our meeting. It's a great pleasure to host you. I hope you weren't too chilly out there."

The old man opened his front door with what seemed to be great effort. He peered expectantly and warmly at his new student.

"Do come in, Belladonna. There's a cup of tea waiting with your name on it."

Belle stepped into the house, still utterly baffled. "Please, call me Belle."

"Right you are."

It would seem that Bronwyn had missed the small, crucial detail of when Artorius's story had actually taken place. Bronwyn had told it as though it were freshly painful, but judging by the man in front of her, Belle estimated it must have been around six decades and a couple of generations earlier than she'd thought to be the case.

Artorius moved down the long hallway with an unsteady shuffle, his scuffed tartan slippers brushing across the patterned carpet of his hallway as he hummed a little tune.

The walls were lined with floral wallpaper, which seemed to have largely given up on sticking where it was supposed to. A scattering of old portraits and photographs were hung so clumsily that it seemed they'd given up, too. But despite its shabbiness, the house felt undeniably welcoming. Small trinkets and ornaments were across every surface, each room bathed in warm light and the sweet, musty smell of age, mingled with what seemed to be freshly baked bread. It was, despite appearances, evidently a well-loved home.

"Have you eaten this evening, Belle? I'm afraid I've already had my supper. The bread's not quite ready yet, but there's definitely a few fairy cakes in one of these cupboards that you're welcome to tuck into," Artorius called back to her. "Might be a little old now, mind. But what could go so wrong with a little flour and icing, I wonder?"

Inside the kitchen, lined with dark wooden cabinets and tiles that featured tiny coloured fruits, the old man pulled out a folding stool. He climbed it precariously to reach a high shelf above the cooker, straining for a tin, and Belle rushed to his side to help.

"Let me grab that for you."

Artorius chuckled to himself. "Thank you. It will be handy to have some long limbs around the house. You can do the dusting for me while you're here."

Belle smiled kindly. "Of course. I'm grateful that you were willing to take on a student, especially so out of the blue like this."

Another chuckle. "Well, yes, I was rather busy this week, had to move a lot of plans around. Three cancelled parties, a romantic tryst or two, several important business meetings all down the drain," Artorius lamented. "Joking, of course. About the dusting, too. I dare say it'd take a little more than a feather duster to spruce this place up. Not quite as spritely as I once was, you see, and it's a rather big house to look after on my own. But I promise you'll find the place clean enough and warm at least."

Belle offered him a smile again, faltering at the instant connection she felt with this man. "Why don't you have a seat while I make the tea?" she insisted.

"Move the books out of your way. There's a lot of them in this house. The pages provide the most golden company when one feels the pestering tap of loneliness. Two sugars for me, please," Artorius chimed in a sing-songy voice.

This could not be the evil man Bronwyn had described. It couldn't be.

"It is nice to have a visitor," he carried on, chatting happily. "I can't remember the last time I had reason to take more than one mug out of the dresser at a time. I was rather surprised to hear from Selcouth yesterday, I must say. Delighted but surprised, and the news that I would get to undertake a mentorship role? I've been hoping for so long . . . I never dreamed . . . It was quite a day, I'll tell you."

Artorius gave a contented sigh as he sat himself down creakily. "What a treat to have a new friend."

Belle crossed the kitchen with two cups of tea, placing one in front of the old man. She clasped her own mug, a chunky freebie from a sports store, and soaked up its welcome heat.

"I thought I'd gone doolally, seeing that letter appear on the armchair as I did the crossword. It's been a very long time since I was called upon by Selcouth for anything at all, let alone trusted to pass on knowledge or magical capability. I never thought I'd see the day . . ." Artorius trailed off as he sipped at his own cup, with the words *Good Morning, Handsome* printed in swirly letters.

"I'm not sure how much they told you about what happened," Belle said warily. "But, in a nutshell, I failed my EquiWitch assessment. Pretty spectacularly."

"And I am sorry to hear that. These blasted traditions . . ." Artorius said with what seemed to be genuine sympathy.

"Thanks. The manifests did not work in my favour," she continued, shuddering at the memory. "And that would have been the end of it, but it turns out that for October and Halloween, a witch can be mentored through the branches of magic to strengthen their craft. That's where you come in." She gestured to the old man in front of her, who beamed.

"There weren't many options for mentoring. Most of them had met a rather unfortunate end, sadly," Belle added. "But there you were. And here we are. Drinking tea."

Artorius simply nodded. The combination of Belle's nerves and his apparent lack of socialising meant that the pair sat in silence for a time. But it was already a strangely comfortable silence. A charitable silence, allowing the other to think and adjust. Light rain was now falling outside, drops tapping at the thin windowpanes like glass marbles.

Belle wondered whether it was best to get the rest of the difficult conversation out of the way first. But it didn't feel quite right to launch into questions about murder and vengeance and banishment. She was here for herself, after all. Maybe it was in her own interest to keep the peace and complete the list, tick off all the boxes as quickly and as painlessly as possible. Maybe she didn't necessarily need the answers yet. She was safe, Rune had made that clear. She was grateful when Artorius took the lead again.

"First of all, I imagine you may be feeling great disappointment in how your trial concluded. But I for one am glad that Selcouth has reached out the hand of second chances to you. Sometimes a second chance is all one needs." He looked at her thoughtfully.

"Even a witch as useless as me?" She gave a breathy, awkward laugh.

"There is much, much more to a witch than simply her technical abilities. Magic is in your spirit, Belle. It makes up your body and soul, like blood and sinew and muscle. It is not a matter of separation, if you ask me, not something that can be weighed or measured for judgement."

Belle was taken aback by his spirit.

"Before we begin our studies, and earn you the result that you rightfully deserve, I must insist that you allow no doubt to hinder our efforts." He rattled a determined finger at her. "Or, if you do feel it, as is inevitable in this life, you must not let it win," Artorius said firmly.

She nodded, touched by his considerate words.

"Good. And so, to the kettle of weasels at hand," the old man continued, drumming on the table. "I think this calls for treats. After all, we are celebrating the start of a wonderful adventure. For both of us, I'm sure."

He raised a frail arm and cast his palm out. In a moment, the tin wriggled itself away from the counter and flew to the table with a couple of uneasy rattles to match his unsteady hand.

"Must feel pretty good to have that back in your system," Belle said.

"Hmm?"

"The magic. Having your powers reinstated after all this time."

"Back in my . . . Oh! Yes, very good. Rather a novelty, of course."

Artorius prised open the tin to reveal four fairy cakes encased in pastel-coloured papers, looking altogether squashed and sorry for themselves.

"I beg your pardon, Belle. The fairies at the bottom of the garden would be most ashamed of me, embarrassing their delicacy like this." Belle suppressed further questions, only adding more to the pile every moment that passed. "Perhaps past their best, but nothing that a little magic can't fix." Artorius lifted a cake into his palm, hovered his fingers just above it for a moment and unfurled them to reveal a fluffier, perfect version with a rainbow of hundreds and thousands set in sticky icing. "Freshly baked today." He winked at Belle and handed her the snack.

"Now, that is worthwhile magic."

"I respect the art of powerful witchcraft to the utmost, especially when it comes to reviving stale snacks." He busied himself, carefully peeled away the paper like he was uncovering a treasure and raised his fairy cake. "To your birthday. To new friends. And the adventure of self-discovery."

Belle bit into the golden lightness and felt the sweetness squash between her teeth. The familiar taste took her back to evenings at her grandmother's house after school. Sugar and blankets and TV and armchairs.

"Frogs and martens! The grand tour!" Artorius leapt from his seat with surprising amounts of energy. "I'm a little out of practice when it comes to being the host with the most. Please, Belle, do come with me and I'll show you around."

She followed behind Artorius as he showed her the rest of his home. A ramshackle but cosy living room sat at the front of the house. Shag carpets. Two armchairs. Worn upholstery, brash floral patterns clashing dramatically with everything else in the room. A small boxy television that didn't seem to ever be switched off and showed a picture that flickered with the wind speed. Every surface possible bore a cream-coloured doily, which Artorius proudly informed Belle that he'd crocheted himself. It was comfortable and inviting but frozen in the past, pulled together by someone who'd tried their best to hold on to a sense of home. The fireplace, constantly roaring and (Belle suspected, magically) stoked, helped a great deal.

A study of sorts lay behind it, less a place of work and more a jumble sale, mere hints of a desk buried under piles of documents and discarded reference texts. It felt like what would be an accurate physical representation of all of the knowledge within an old warlock's mind, spilling out in a clutter of loose pages and scribbled paper under an array of glass paperweights. Belle cupped her hand against the back window and peered out into the thick black London night. She could make out the silhouette of a wildly overgrown garden lying in wait. Thickets, brambles and weeds knitted themselves together, droplets of rainwater caught in the moonlight like gemstones.

Up the creaking stairs, Artorius's bedroom sat at the back of the house, overlooking the garden and next to a bathroom with a slightly alarming avocado-green colour scheme. A second winding spiral staircase towered in one corner of the landing, which Artorius explained led up to the attic.

"For us to visit another night. And best to not head up there without me. It's a room that can be unpredictable, to say the least."

"That's a bit ominous."

Artorius didn't respond, either unhearing or pretending to be.

"We merely make our acquaintances tonight, Belle. Of course, our limited moons are precious, but I also think that it's important to begin with fresh eyes tomorrow."

Artorius had insisted on escorting Belle to the end of the path as she headed out with the moon hanging high and heavy. They had to stop several times as he made various exclamations at plants poking their heads through the ground of his front garden and to give a quick scratch behind the ears to a fox who seemed to be a faithful friend. Maybe even a familiar.

"This one stops by most nights for dinner," Artorius explained. "Although I can't tell you how marvellous it is to have a little human company again."

Their meeting could not have been further from what Belle had anticipated. It seemed impossible that this man, so kind and gentle, could be the same figure that Bronwyn had spoken of with such loathing in her voice.

"I'm looking forward to working with you," she said. Something compelled her honesty, and she felt the need to share it. "I actually have a weirdly good feeling about this, something I haven't felt for a while." She sounded as surprised as she felt.

Artorius politely lifted his pink hat to Belle. With a grateful nod, she headed down the broken driveway. She turned back to lock the gate, expecting the old man to have vanished back inside. Instead, she found that he remained, a few rogue sparks of magic lingering around him like biscuit crumbs, to wave his hat the whole way behind her until she turned the corner.

16

A Warlock's Home

SCOOPING A BLOB of whipped cream from mug to mouth, Belle bounced back against the booth as she missed her aim, spilling onto the thigh of her jeans. Cursing under her breath (not an actual curse—she wasn't one to meddle with those), she frantically rubbed at it with a serviette while using her elbow to keep the page of the grimoire open. She heard a stool across the table scrape backwards as Ariadne plonked herself down unannounced.

"Finally, here you are. I thought you might have been out with Mr. Magical when you rolled in late last night, and then I couldn't find you all day to grill you. But of course, giant book and an equally giant coffee. Should have guessed."

"Huh? Oh, right." Belle threw her arms over the grimoire, quickly dashing it underneath her jacket on the seat. With sleep not wishing to linger past sunrise, she had followed her nose towards the caffeine and spent almost the entire day cooped up at their usual table, bent double over the pages in front of her, curious as to whether the EquiWitch challenges would make themselves known in the grimoire. They hadn't.

"He's more of an evenings and nights visit kind of guy," Belle said. "I do not mean it like that! He . . . works a lot," she continued hastily as Ariadne danced her eyebrows suggestively.

Mr. Ricci appeared to deliver Ariadne's Americano (cold milk on the side) and slid two plates onto their table from the crook of his arm.

"Some cinnamon rolls for my best customers. Most sane people have stopped with the caffeine by this time of day. They're yours if you're hungry," he muttered, always gruff but secretly kind and generous with the leftover pastries. Once, he'd stood behind the counter for almost half an hour, drying the mugs with a rag while Belle cried about how she had no idea what she was doing with her life after a terrible day at Christopher's beck and call.

"No one knows, girl. If they say they do, they lie," he'd said matter-of-factly, sliding a shiny cherry Danish across the countertop for her woes.

"I love him as if he were my own father," Ari said sincerely as Mr. Ricci headed back to the counter. She added a few drops of milk from the small jug. "In fact, probably more. Fancy that new Halloween film tonight? There's a midnight showing."

Now that their initial meeting was out of the way, Belle's lessons with Artorius were to properly begin that coming night. Her nerves were shot, so she'd been attempting to distract herself with reading up, but the feeling had been made entirely worse by all the caffeine. She could already see the slightest scratch of a crescent moon in punctures between the café shutters, silver and misted in the dark late afternoon. By sheer luck it was a new moon: the perfect time to begin anew, to embrace a fresh start.

"Can't," Belle said reluctantly.

Ariadne gave her a disgusted look. "I knew this day would come, and yet I did not expect it so soon. Belle, you cannot abandon me in singledom. I forbid it. You can't leave me in solo spinsterhood."

"I promise it's not like that. We took a solemn vow to grow old and become haunted beldams together while everyone else gets happily married and has delightful chubby babies. I respect the vow."

"And don't you forget it. Matching warts, waist-length grey hair, clacking spinning wheels, the lot."

"It was sealed in blood," Belle said. "I take it very seriously."

"I don't know, I feel treason in my bones. Two nights in a row sounds pretty 'reformed spinster' to me."

"And that is precisely why you have commitment issues with everyone but me," Belle said, snapping her chocolate flake in half to offer out, as was the rule.

"I'm actually so happy for you. This feels kind of exciting. I think I want you to meet someone more than you do. But if Mr. Magical is keeping you out every night until the wee hours of the morning, I should at least know his real name. What if he murders you and I have to come and avenge your death?" Ari asked, chocolate crumbling over the table.

"Why are you so obsessed with avenging my death?"

"Because we are in love. So go on, what's his name, then?"

Belle chewed at the inside of her lip. She could not offer up the name Artorius. For one, it was synonymous now with a smiley old man, and it felt wrong on many, many levels. For two, it was a name that Ariadne would rip to absolute shreds.

"Rune." Not much better. She presented it as an answer before she could stop herself.

"Pardon?" Ariadne attempted to keep a straight face. "Rune? That's not a name, that's a noise."

"You're being rude."

Ari snorted. "You are dating a man . . . who is called Rune."

Belle nodded indignantly, spinning her coffee cup in an attempt to appear nonchalant. Where did that come from? His was the first face that popped into her head. She instantly regretted the impulsive answer. Ariadne pushed again.

"Rune? As in those little stones with symbols on them. As in 'room' but not. As in 'rhymes with spoon.' As in 'the Rune in spoon stays mainly on the ploon'?"

"The ploon? You had me until the ploon."

"Is he a son of Gloin?"

"Shut up, please." Belle folded her arms on the tabletop. "I think it's, like, German or something," she muttered under her breath. Why she was getting so defensive, she wasn't quite sure.

"I can't believe the man who's finally going to steal you from my grasp is named . . . Rune. I'll never get over this. He had better be alarmingly hot." Ariadne was no longer even trying to stifle her laughter and cackled loudly.

"Did you want a cinnamon roll?"

"Don't change the subject. Where do you find these men?"

"They seem to find me all by themselves," Belle said grimly, rummaging for her purse.

"It must be serious, though? With *Rune*." Ariadne bit her tongue, emphasising the name while ripping off a chunk of sticky cinnamon dough. "You're sneaking in way past your bedtime, cancelling our plans for him, and you look like you haven't slept in months. No offence."

"Wow, thank you for that."

"Sorry, but it's true. You can't keep this up. Working all day, then spending all of your nights at his place, travelling back to ours, begin again, repeat. It's ridiculous. Why is he making you do all of the work?"

Belle raised an eyebrow. "You can buy me more caffeine if it makes you feel better."

"Why don't you ask him to come to ours? I'll be good. Or I can make myself scarce for a few hours," Ariadne answered her look.

"Thanks, but it's fine. I'm fine. It's only going to be for a few weeks."

"You've put a time limit on this thing already? That doesn't sound particularly healthy."

"It's not that. I've decided to give it the month and see what happens. If it works, it works. If it doesn't, it doesn't. But I want to give it the time that it deserves."

Ariadne sighed. "Just try and put yourself first, okay? Please? You're crap at it."

"This time I am. I really am. It's something I need to do. Now, can we talk about something else?"

"Yes, but only because I can tell you're tired and you'll probably cry otherwise."

"It's likely."

✦ ˙ ✳ ˳ ✦ ˙ ★

BACK IN HER bedroom, Belle hunched over so acutely that her nose was almost touching her folded ankles, her spine resembling the posture of a prawn. The grimoire sprawled in front of her across the rug. It was nearly time to head to Quill Lane, with just a few final minutes to remind herself of the task ahead.

In spindly letters, the book spelt out the basics: the six branches of magic to explore during her mentorship, each one feeling more challenging and distinctly failable than the last.

Luckily, with Jinx refusing to sit anywhere other than draped across her legs and currently purring euphorically, she considered that the first, Animal Affinity, was a probable done deal. Her familiar for over ten years, the link was one of the strongest in her life.

"Actually, Jinx, I can probably thank you for not being thrown out of Hecate House sooner," she told the cat as she absent-mindedly stroked her tiny soft chin.

Earth Sorcery was next, Bonnie's distinct area of expertise and specialist art. Belle felt reasonably confident that a refresh of the craft would bring back what was once a fairly solid understanding of natural ingredients, the power of the earth itself, the qualities it could wield in the right hands. It was a relief, as she pulled at the early saplings of learning buried somewhere deep in the earth of her mind, to feel memories already unfurl small green leaves.

When was the last time she'd actually learned something or challenged herself? She was surprised to feel a tingle of excitement brush her spine at the thought.

Incantation, of course. Spells, enchantments, charms, the branch she used on a daily basis, even if only in their most humble, unadventurous form. She could see potential there, but it was a vast subject, the challenges limitless. Nonetheless, three out of six branches that weren't entirely starting from scratch. Those weren't terrible odds.

She turned the next page of the grimoire to be met with the branches which would require most of her attention. Alchemy, or potion practice. She'd barely dipped her toes into these artful waters and, even worse, this branch came loaded with a . . . complicated history for Artorius.

Clairvoyancy was fifth, the connection to the mind and harnessing the power of it. Premonition, meditation, telepathy, divination, spiritual contact. Notoriously challenging and certainly the most visionary, but one of the most rewarding powers to harness. Apparently.

A brisk October wind breathed through the open window and blew the page aside to the next. The grimoire reminding her, all by itself, of the sheer size of the challenge that lay ahead. Sixth and finally, the book revealed, came Necromancy. Communication with the dead.

✦˙✳˳✦˙✦

QUILL LANE WAS damp and drizzly when Belle stepped off the bus, treading carefully over a blanket of slippery leaves. Arriving back at the house, she was struck by the finer details that she hadn't noticed yesterday. The smattering of blackberries tangled in bushes that lined the front window. The deep cherry red tree that reclined over the driveway in a sweep of shyness. The fox had returned, just as Artorius said, and was curled up in a perfect amber circle in a corner of the front garden. He opened one eye drowsily to see who'd interrupted but quickly nuzzled back down into his leaf quilt.

Following her arrival, which Artorius seemed entirely surprised and thrilled about—"I wasn't sure I'd be seeing you again, I fretted all day that I may not have been a welcoming enough host"—he had plied her with strong tea and wedges of toast buttered so thickly that pools of sunny yellow sat on the bread.

She was surprised when, afterwards, he led her to the top of the house, to the "unpredictable" attic that he had specifically warned her not to enter yesterday.

"I was nervous to show you. But after much deliberation, I think we are best to dive in together with both feet. This is where the magic happens, as they say. In my case, you understand, I do mean that entirely literally."

The moment his palm rested over the brass door handle, it unlocked with a soft click and a fizzle of sparks.

As a witch who liked to keep her own tricks and tools hidden from prying eyes, it had only occurred to Belle over their tea and toast that the house seemed to be largely void of signs of a magical existence. It made sense, given that he had been stripped of his powers until now, although it was clear that he enjoyed researching his magical heritage, magical theory and the like. The decor was a little eccentric and rough around the edges, but there were no spell books or almanacs that she'd noticed. No rogue wands lying around or undisguised potion ingredients. No cauldrons perched on the draining rack. Just carriage clocks, commemorative china plates on stands, a small statue of a flamenco dancer that read "Minorca 1979" on the mantelpiece.

But it was now apparent that every sign that Artorius Day was something of the supernatural persuasion had been stored up in this attic room. It was a glittering treasure trove bathed in silver moonlight, alive with every possible strange and unusual ingredient lining the eaves. Shelf upon shelf of apothecary jars, bottles and vials in every shape and size and shade made up his collection. They stood in vast numbers, a patchwork of glass as they captured the outside moonlight and inked it in new colours. Peeling labels in scratchy lettering had been carefully assigned to them all. Each one was stoppered tightly with a cork, an ornate lid, or simply stuffed with rolled-up newspaper to make do in a hurry.

Amongst stacks of books piled in every corner were tons of haphazard cardboard boxes, all full and scattered across the floor, much like a promising jumble sale. Old-fashioned suitcases and trunks, too, some filled with cauldrons like Russian dolls, ranging from pocket-sized to the biggest at the centre of the room in front of Artorius, who had instantly busied himself with what looked to be a pot of snail shells. A beautiful brass telescope was pointed to the sky at the window, and next to it, to Belle's amazement and admiration, a full orrery, gracefully spinning on its own heliocentric orbit, to show the motions of the planets and moons. Selections of crystals, wax-sealed jars and discarded tarot cards. The perfectly preserved skeleton of some kind of small winged beast. A rainbow of candles, scattered tapestries and carpets, not to mention a lot of objects that Belle failed to recognise. Everything in sight glinted with a faint sprinkle of magic, like a dusting of icing sugar that caught in the thin, watercoloured light.

"This is beautiful," Belle marvelled.

A few bigger objects remained unseen, splattered dust sheets thrown over their hulking forms. A tall, sagging armchair was angled next to Artorius, evidently his thinking spot of choice. Things whirred soothingly, buzzed quietly and floated peacefully all around her, igniting every sense as though the room itself was alive with possibility. It was truly a wonder. An inventor's workshop, a magician's box of tricks, a collector's cabinet of curiosities. A warlock's home.

"Oh, do you think so? It's not much. Everything that I've accumulated over the years, with no particular rhyme or reason. Not that I could use any of it, of course . . ." Artorius hurried to reassure her. "But I suppose many people collect things that remind them of the past. Nostalgia is a powerful thing."

"Why do you keep everything hidden up here? You could fill your whole house with wonderful things."

"I'm a private man. Unwanted attention is not something I seek. And it's important that you create a space like this for yourself, Belle. It doesn't have to be a whole attic. But all wicchefolk need their own altar dedicated to practice of the craft. 'Altar' makes it sound rather fancy, but it's just a personal space of one's own. And this is mine," Artorius said, gesturing proudly.

"Again, not that any of it is in active use," he swiftly corrected himself. "Only my studies through my non-wicche life. Merely curiosities that I like to peruse to remind me of . . . of the magic of it all, I suppose." His expression turned watery for a moment before snapping back into consciousness.

"Besides, I dare say the neighbours already think I'm mad enough. The last thing I need is for one of them to come knocking and find me dabbling in the eye of newt jar, looking for a juicy one. Mr. Nuttall next door is already convinced I'm a lunatic."

Belle thought to herself that Mr. Nuttall must have seen and heard some things from 8 Quill Lane over the years and probably had a good case for his point.

Night pushed its way through the attic eaves to mark their first

lesson, and Belle sat studiously as Artorius embarked on a refresher
course on magical theory, the cornerstone of what made a successful
spell of any kind.

"Vision, courage, tenacity. Plus benevolence, for good measure," Artorius repeated, rapping his knuckles at each of the points
on a levitating pyramid that he'd crafted from magic, counting off
the qualities as he went. "And I have no doubt in my mind that you
possess each one in abundance."

It was odd. She hadn't felt this particular kind of contentment for
a long while—it reminded her of time spent with a beloved grandparent. An abundant love, with no conditions put upon it. Unwavering belief and support and admiration, as though she were a precious
thing. It had been years since she'd lost her, but that presence was
something that she missed every day since Alvina had passed away,
her magic returning back to Selcouth. The years without her had
softened the grief, worn it down to a bluntness. It was no longer
sharp or stabbing or severe. Instead, it was as though a silk scarf was
knotted around her chest, permanent and solid but existing tenderly,
tugging her backwards with a gentle pull every now and again with
news or stories that she wished she could share.

Perhaps not to the same extent, but Artorius's words plucked at
the nostalgic chord of that beloved company. Unwittingly, her hand
reached for the warm familiarity of her sooth stone.

As though someone had opened the sash window with a sudden
force, Belle felt a shiver travel from the top of her spine, a current
along each vertebra like dominos. A biting breeze spun through the
gaps in the window frame. The musty smell of the attic, like crisp old
pages and tobacco, filled her nose as it picked up on the wind. Her
gaze was snatched towards her grimoire resting on a music stand.
The pages swiftly began to fly, whipped up in the frenzied wind that
left Belle pushing hair from her face and Artorius clinging to his
pink hat. It dropped as suddenly as it had begun, and the grimoire

seemed to settle on the page that it desired. The pair shared a hesitant glance before Belle rushed to approach the book, seizing the leather cover in her hands.

It had been opened to a page that she had certainly never found before, and she wondered whether it had even previously been a part of her grimoire. Artorius followed and peered around her side on his tiptoes.

The title of the page simply read *Incantation* and was followed by an inked paragraph.

> Conviction in thy words must hold,
> Speak a truth that's brave and bold.
> Be thy assured all shall be well,
> A fortune magic cannot tell.
> So to prove good thine incantation,
> Rewrite the mind's own dark narration.
> Spirit, soul and spell to start,
> Summon that which is thine heart.

"What is it with magic and undecipherable, unhelpful poetry?" Belle sighed.

Artorius grinned. "And so begins your first grimoire challenge."

17
Incantation

"BRILLIANT, BRILLIANT! ONTO our next task. Unless . . . crikey, liver and onions—'tis almost morning! Belle, I have kept you so many hours. You must get some sleep. The effects of new magic practice can be exhausting."

Belle did feel wiped. The fifth moon had been a brutal one. She'd arrived tired but heartened by a confident start with incantations. After two nights of successful incantation in many of its forms, Belle had seemingly exhausted most options in Artorius's house, animating, manifesting and transferring so much chaos that it now resembled a museum run by a madman. Artorius was unbothered by the mess and thrilled by the progress, while Belle was caffeinating so much that she could feel her eyelashes vibrating. A personal triumphant highlight had been the notoriously tricky *Vividus Animo* incantation, bestowing real life to the inanimate. To her own surprise, she had successfully enchanted the small flamenco dancer from Artorius's mantelpiece, much to his delight, and animated an overcoat, which he'd thoroughly enjoyed as a waltzing partner during their snack break. Minor chaos ensued when the statue then began instructing Artorius and the overcoat in their own flamenco routine.

Tonight had seen the pair jump to another huge task: magical transference, effectively teleporting from one space to another. It was magic that she'd been determined to perfect as a teenager but had given up on after a while, neither patience nor the motion sickness really her forte, along with a characteristic frustration when she didn't prove to be instantly successful at something. The craft of transference was often painful and bruising, leaving joints relentlessly bashed and limbs overstretched like overworked dough.

Aided transference with a grip on Artorius's skinny forearm had proved fine. She'd managed that successfully in and out of Hecate House, too. But that only served to make smooth solo transference (or the lack of it) even more infuriating. After hours of failed attempts, Belle had almost managed a solo transference from kitchen to attic and back again. Nearly, but for some reason, she couldn't seem to manage it while retaining both shoes. Now, her temples were throbbing with a constant eye-splitting pulse, and her newfound confidence was suffering.

"Our first real hiccup in proceedings!" Artorius exclaimed with confusing glee, as though the failure itself was a milestone to mark. "No matter, Belle. We shall but return to it with added vim and vigour in a few moons time. Now, as I said, you should head home and get some sleep."

Belle, so exhausted from the constant presence of magic flooding her system, simply looked at him despairingly.

"Let's try one last thing, we should end on a good note," she suggested, pushing down her shoulders to try and ease the solidifying tension.

"Perhaps something a little softer. No less challenging, I'll wager, but gentler, more encouraging magic."

"Yes, that," Belle said gratefully.

"Very well. While planning our lesson today, I thought perhaps the art of protection circles would be interesting to visit. It's good practice to avoid interference and simple enough. That feeling when in tune with your magic, I'm sure you know what I'm referring to. The balmy glow that feels like a blanket or honey or warm milk. Impossible to describe, but the feeling of magic itself . . ."

Belle nodded with familiarity.

"There now, draw the circle around you, expand that feeling of warmth and magic. Let it flood your mind entirely . . ."

Belle concentrated intensely, feeling the glow melt from the tips of her toes all the way upwards.

"Envision that feeling physically, see it fill every inch of this attic. Imagine it passing around you, circling you and through you and . . . Ah, wonderful! Really, truly wonderful! Perfect, in fact!" Artorius's exclamation surprised Belle.

She opened her eyes and saw instantly what he was so delighted by. A radiant circle had formed brightly around her like a lasso at her feet. It was encompassing her, levitating inches above the floor. Just the sight of it made her feel instantly powerful. She felt safe in her own body. A strength that Belle had never allowed herself to feel was suddenly brimming within her.

"I already feel better."

"Confidence will do that for you, but a circle of protection will also help. This will safeguard you from negative entities which may otherwise like to wreak havoc and run amok."

Belle was still marvelling at the gorgeousness that beamed around her when her attention was stolen once again by the sooth stone, hot to the touch in her pocket. She pulled it out. The stone, like the circle, was glowing impossibly brightly, as though it were a tiny piece of the sun itself. She glanced at Artorius, wondering if he would be able to offer up an explanation. His eyes were wide, and he looked as baffled as she did.

"Newts and thimbles . . ." he marvelled quietly. "May I?"

Belle handed Artorius the stone for him to examine more closely.

"It happens sometimes. No particular rhyme or reason to it, as far as I can figure out," she explained. The warlock faltered as he took it between his fingers, a puzzled look flashing across his brow for only a moment. It was evident that his busy brain was working at a million miles an hour.

"Sooth stones themselves are funny things. Something of a family heirloom among witch families. Some are more precious than others, recorded so far back in history that they were said to be cast in fires at the birth of magic itself."

"And they all do this? The light-up glow-in-the-dark thing?"

"Can't say I've seen that before. But I have read about it . . . Tell me, was your sooth stone a gift handed down from your mother?"

"My nan," Belle said quietly.

"*Praesentia Pretego . . .*" he whispered.

Belle looked at him blankly. "Excuse me?"

Artorius shuffled with as much enthusiastic speed as he could muster over to one of the loaded bookshelves, squinted over the top of his glasses for a moment and pulled out a thick title with a cracked black spine.

"Here, see." He pointed to a definition and pushed the page excitedly under Belle's nose. "*Praesentia Pretego* is advanced, wondrous magic. It is a pure presence, carried in a physical object, to act as a shield whenever it senses a need to guide you or to aid. Witches, those who are up to such complex magic, that is, will sometimes elect to leave a little of themselves behind before they pass to protect another who they love."

"My grandmother's . . . in this brooch?" Belle looked sceptical.

"More of an essence, so to speak. A whisper, a soul that once was. While the majority of her magic is returned to her coven on passing, the witch requests that a small trace be permitted to linger. To provide guidance, reminders of love. The feeling that one is not alone."

Belle thought back to the moments that the stone had shown itself in small ways to be a conscious thing. To guide her to Hecate House. To encourage her decision to meet Artorius. Now to assist in keeping her protected. It did seem to come alive in the moments that she needed a little extra reassurance. Her head swam, overwhelmed.

"Of course, while sooth stones themselves are common enough—most witches and warlocks have their own—it is remarkably rare that permission is granted by the magic system for *Praesentia Pretego* to occur. There has to be real purpose for it."

"So when it glows, when it seems to come alive . . . That's her?"

"Her soul presence, at least. I would say so, yes." Artorius smiled, thrilled at their discovery. "Utterly astonishing. Very special magic indeed."

He handed the stone back to Belle with an encouraging expression. Feeling the warmth of the glass against her palm in her pocket, she blew out a deep breath. Greater than magic, it was a deeper kind of witchcraft that couldn't be judged or taken away from her by the coven. It felt like a hand on the small of her back, gently guiding her forward in the right direction.

She swallowed hard and quickly wiped her eyes. Artorius handed her a slightly crumpled white hankie from the sleeve of his jacket, which she accepted gratefully.

"Sorry. I don't know why I'm crying. It's just kind of wonderful." Her voice was more of an embarrassing squeak than actual words.

"All kinds of wonderful. And now that we have a protection circle in place, perhaps we . . ." Artorius stopped, caught off guard. Without warning, the beaming gold around Belle had suddenly faltered. Its goodness faded, a pale yellow turned silver, then to grey. Then it dissolved altogether in smoke.

"We lost concentration. Knit another spell and we'll try that again."

Belle closed her eyes and summoned the feeling once more,

pre-empting the arrival of the gold around her. It came, but just a second later, the same thing happened. As quickly as it had appeared, the protection circle disappeared to smoke.

"Clear your mind again. You're not thinking properly."

"I *am* thinking properly."

"Try and keep hold of the feeling. Focus on retaining the presence of protection."

"I *am* focusing," she snapped back.

The same thing happened again. And again. The circle snuffed out, leaving Belle with an unpleasant cold plunging sensation every time.

"I'm sure it's nothing. Although it is an unusual sort of nothing," Artorius admitted. "Any witch should be able to conjure a protection incantation for herself and have it hold steadfast until she chooses to unravel her own spell. It's almost as though . . . Well, I don't wish to make a fiasco out of a fish pie, but . . . as though something is blocking your protection."

"Why would something . . . I mean, why would I not be able to protect myself?" She was too tired to consider the idea properly but couldn't help but feel a niggling sense of worry.

"Perhaps things are just a little off-kilter. It is no huge matter anyhow as, by a stroke of luck, your sooth stone seems to be acting in a protective capacity of its own accord, thanks to your grandmother. We shan't trouble ourselves too much while that's the case."

18

Extra Warmth

NINE LONG, ONEROUS moons already sailing away, Belle closed the door of 8 Quill Lane on the night's lesson, which had been altogether more studious than practical. It proved challenging in a different way to physical magic practice, it having been a while since her brain had been faced with any kind of academia. She was sure that her brain cell count had dwindled at rapid fire since university. The last few days of dense ancient texts on astrological patterns and their recognisable qualities all but proved it.

Days of being run off her feet to keep Lunar afloat, largely spent mopping up damage done by Christopher, were followed by nights of endless study. Writing, cross-referencing, note-taking. They pored over the many, many books in Artorius's collection, her eager teacher adamant that astrological learning was a worthwhile focus in their Earth Sorcery studies. Belle argued that, surely, Earth Sorcery should be largely based on Earth. Artorius insisted that the branch encompassed all things that could be viewed from Earth, too, which seemed a tenuous link, but who was she to argue?

The grimoire's challenge for Earth Sorcery unfortunately turned out to be equally, if not more so, un-illuminating than its Incantation offering. Belle had read the new allegory aloud so many times in an attempt to decipher its request that she had now committed it to memory.

> Beneath the ground, a warmth of riches,
> Hotter than the flames of witches.
> A blaze that stills the breath to naught,
> Drowning lest the mind is taught.
> Fire to earth, earth to fire,
> Create that which thy most admire.
> Water to air, air to water,
> Powers for the firstborn daughter.

"Word salad," Belle grumpily decided.

Her mind swam with a sea of stars. They had calculated constellation calendars and pondered planetary predictions, mulled over meteoric methods and hashed out hasty horoscopes. The golden orrery played a starring role in Belle's learning. With his palms outstretched, Artorius cast the wonderful thing in motion as he taught Belle everything he knew. With it, the old man created stars and moons from nothing, while mini constellations flew by in a palette of navy and periwinkle. They danced from one formation to the next across the darkened attic, enveloping Belle in her own night sky to learn from. Beautiful, albeit tough to commit to memory. She was getting there, though: over pie and copious amounts of velvety mashed potato that Artorius whipped up for the two of them, Belle had impressed even herself by casually pointing out through a mouthful of pie that Andromeda was in the window, foiled in gold leaf against the sky.

She'd learned more about her magic in a week than she had done in fifteen years, and her brain was aching like an overworked muscle. (Along with her back, but what else was new?) She was ready to collapse face-first into bed, dreaming of stardust.

Belle had left Artorius dozing in a chintz armchair underneath one of his hand-knitted blankets with his feet propped up on a pouffe. She wasn't the only one who was finding the mentorship exhausting. The old man was incorrigible. No matter how long and late the hours stretched, he bubbled over with enthusiasm. He brought her mind back to focus and encouraged her concentration until both she and he were confident that she'd as good as mastered the basics. They'd faltered ever so slightly in tonight's lesson when Artorius observed one particularly bright Venus hanging so closely to the moon's horned tip that they almost turned one and the same within the telescope glass. He'd seemed perturbed by the unusual view, pointing out the strangeness, a combination associated with trouble ahead. Belle herself was not convinced that the sky was dedicated to dishing out personally designed warnings.

Clicking the lock of Artorius's front door behind her, Belle headed out into the early morning, as crisp and sharp as the bite of an apple.

It was a clear sky (Alpheratz, Mirach and Almach all visible over the house, she surprised herself by noticing) but chillingly cold. She took the short cut home that she'd discovered the previous morning, a quiet alley that she'd found peaceful yesterday, but this morning held an ominous edge. The shadows of trees took on bigger shapes, throwing themselves just out of her sight-line. The corners of each turn made her a little more uneasy. It was only tiredness, she reasoned.

A rustle sent Belle's glance darting to check behind her.

Just a fox, face-first in the neighbour's bin bags, although not Artorius's faithful friend. The leaves of the trees ruffled as a strong breeze pushed itself down the alley, sending her hair trailing back. Belle wrapped her arms around herself tighter, making small clouds of breath as she trod down the path, the click of her footsteps the only sound to break through the silence.

She picked up her pace, trying to calm herself. But she was unable to shake the uneasy feeling. She knew it, could feel it. She wasn't alone. Another shuffle, barely audible this time, but she heard it. Someone. She went rigid, spun around.

No one. The lack of sleep was getting to her. She rubbed at bleary eyes, chastised herself for letting the sense of unease become silly paranoia.

"Should I be afraid of those powers yet?"

Belle jumped twenty feet out of her own skin, feeling her soul leave her body.

Lit by a small beam of torchlight emitting from his palm, Rune stepped out from the shadow of an oak tree, barely visible in his long black coat. Belle clutched at the spot where her heart used to be as she shot him a look of pure daggers.

"What is wrong with you? You're lucky I didn't kick you in the throat."

Rune looked taken aback. "My apologies."

"Throat kick, knee to the crotch, elbow to the face. Maybe all three. You are the worst watchman in the world. Why do you insist on being creepy every single time?"

"I was just waiting for—"

"Did we not learn from the last time you pulled this 'mysterious in the shadows' move?"

"I don't have moves," he said sulkily.

"Wait, why are you here?" Belle asked, still annoyed.

He stepped towards her, judging it safe now that her anger was subsiding. "It seemed a little too 'love interest in a teen rom-com' to come knocking on the door to ask if I could walk you home."

"So you thought you'd just lurk around the empty streets until I happened upon you, prowling underneath a tree?"

Rune looked at his hands, twiddling the ring on his thumb. "Looks that way."

"For future reference, I'd rather the teen rom-com moment than the homicidal 'slasher in the darkness' moment."

"Noted. I was just trying not to intrude, you made it clear you want your space," he replied, glancing up. "But the offer for a walk home still stands. If you want." He shrugged.

Belle looked at him sceptically.

"C'mon, don't turn me down," he said, one side of his mouth twitching upwards in a smile. "I'll conjure you some chips on the way."

Her stomach rumbled at the mention.

She nodded. "For chips."

Belle gestured to the right with her shoulder, and he gave her a quick nod as they set off side by side. With a click, Rune conjured a hot carton of chips to share. Ignoring the billows of steam, Belle impatiently popped a couple into her mouth, immediately burning her tongue. She winced.

"Hot . . ." she said, embarrassed as he watched her.

"This is already the best date I've ever been on," he said dryly.

"Needs more vinegar, though," she quipped.

He rolled his eyes and cast his fingers again. "I'm so glad that the centuries of magic under my belt can be put to expert use."

"Ketchup too." With a furtive side glance, Belle noted that he bit down on his lip to stop himself from laughing. "And this is absolutely not a date."

"A romantic moonlit walk, side by side, with dinner included? Sounds like a date to me."

They walked in pleasant silence, enjoying the hot food and the extra warmth of each other's company.

"If you're going to walk me home in the dark, then I should probably know a little more about you, Rune Dunstan. Aside from the fact you're a man who can't pull off a dramatic entrance to save his life."

"What exactly would you like to know?"

"Maybe we could start with the 'centuries of magic' part." He was quiet for a fraction too long.

"Slip of the tongue."

She blew on a chip, smiling smugly. "Really."

"Don't you know it's rude to ask a warlock how old he is?"

"I think those airs and graces go out the window as soon as you take the cauldron pledge."

Rune sniffed. "No need to say it with such disapproval."

"I don't mean to judge." Her feet scuffed satisfyingly on crunching leaves. "Each to their own when it comes to unnaturally enchanting a lifetime to span several centuries."

"Not something that's on your horizon, I take it?" Rune took a chip for himself. "Assuming the opportunity remains, post Equi-Witch."

Belle shook her head, scoffing. "Hard no. There's a lot about Selcouth that I don't understand, but the pledge is maybe top of the list. I can't believe anyone takes it."

"Maybe that's because you haven't yet delved into the true potential of your magic," Rune said.

"Even if I discover that, by some miracle, my magic is in fact a force to be reckoned with, the world does not need several hundred years of Belle Blackthorn." She laughed. "What made you take it?"

"Hard to explain. As soon as I came of age for my powers, they were the most intoxicating, inspiring drive for me. Everything else sort of paled in comparison. When the time came to decide, I knew I would always want more time with them to see what I could achieve."

Belle nodded in silence, contemplating the weight of the choice this man had made. "And what's the best thing you've done with it so far?"

"I'm sure you wouldn't be impressed."

"Try me."

He shrugged, giving Belle the impression he was absolutely playing down the work he did. "Made some discoveries along the way, a lot of focus on the brink between what can be considered good and bad magic. Key factors and ingredients that differentiate the two. It's a fine line that I like to look at more closely, trying to find the snap point from one to the other."

"Well, that sounds . . . very noble."

"I don't know about that."

"So it really is magic above all else for you? You've outlived friends, loved ones, watched the world change for longer than a human ever should. All for magic?"

"You make it sound like a hollow choice."

"Isn't it?"

"The opposite," he said, defensive. "Someone has to take the pledge, be willing to take one for the coven. After a while, you simply learn to live a more solitary life. It's easier that way."

There was only one question she really wanted to ask. "How long is a while?"

He didn't answer for a moment, thumbing his brow as he thought. "Lost count, to be honest. Somewhere near a couple of centuries at this point. I think."

Belle choked on a chip. "Two hundred?"

"I don't look a day over it, right?" He laughed grimly.

Silence passed between them for a moment. "And has it been worth it?"

He breathed a laugh, as though she were painfully naive. "It's not the great sacrifice you're making it out to be. You're only used to the primitive pattern of time that non-wicchefolk operate in."

"Did you really just call me primitive?" she asked, getting a laugh in return.

"I just mean that you forget that things are different in the magic realm. I spend my life surrounded by wicchefolk, many people around me have also taken the pledge at one time or another. It's what we do." He shrugged. "You're the strange one, in their eyes, for not seizing the chance to unfurl your years properly."

"I can't say I know my whole family tree, there's probably *someone* back there who took the pledge. But my mum hasn't, neither did my grandmother. They both fell in love with non-wicche folk, had children, loved non-wicche friends dearly."

He glanced sideways at her. "And that's the case for you?"

"Minus the true love and the kids. So far. Still, call me crazy, but when there's other lives and loves to match yours up against, you don't want to imagine your own unfurling for longer than theirs would last."

Rune shifted. "Like I said, I knew from the moment my powers came in. It's what I'm supposed to do."

"Have you ever thought about relinquishing?" she asked, knowing it was possible but not common for witches to go back on their decision.

Rune was quiet for a moment. "Once."

She was surprised. "For someone else?"

He nodded, clearly not willing to expand on the point.

"What changed your mind?"

Another silence. "I just reminded myself what needs to matter most."

Belle was struck by his quiet reply. "And what's that?"

"The coven. Making sure magic is going where it needs to and not being mistreated. Keeping hold of the balance of magic and non-wicche worlds for the good of everyone in both. That's something bigger than me, or any of the people I might be fond of."

Belle pulled a face. "Whatever that means."

"It means that magic in the wrong hands would spell disaster for every single aspect of this earthly plane, Belle. If it wasn't for those who dedicate themselves to witchery, who knows what the world would look like."

"All right." She rolled her eyes. "I just think if everyone collectively agreed to relinquish the cauldron pledge, then—"

He shook his head. "You're dreaming."

She faltered. "Don't talk to me like that."

"Sorry," Rune said, sounding like he genuinely meant it. "I didn't mean to offend you."

Belle's mind returned to the pews in the courtroom, witches and warlocks seated side by side. How many of them were several centuries old?

"Morena and Bronwyn are with you, I assume?" she asked. "There's no way Morena looks that good without a little help."

Rune nodded, pushing back the hair that fell into his eyes. "Plus a handful of coven elders. I'm the youngest by a fair shot to have made the pledge. They tried to encourage your mum to take it a few years back, and Caspar, too. They would be good assets to the future of Selcouth."

"Good assets." Belle mocked his formality. "Maybe the good assets are the ones who aren't willing to take on supernatural lifespans to keep hold of their powers. Maybe relinquishing them, letting old age and death come naturally, letting powers pass down a family tree sooner, would actually be the more beneficial option for the coven. Maybe things wouldn't be quite so archaic and outdated that way."

"You sure have a lot to say for someone who doesn't really know what they're talking about." He stared straight ahead, his jaw clenched.

Belle bristled. "I know that it's a weird power trip to choose to live for hundreds of years and keep your mitts on your magic rather than, heaven forbid, let it go back into the ether for the next warlock. There's no need to be quite so frightened of what comes next," she said with mock gentleness and a hand on his arm.

"Says the witch who's been too frightened to change anything about her own future," he said with the same mocking, overly bright tone.

Belle stopped in her tracks. He turned to face her.

"Don't give me that look. You said it yourself at your trial."

Okay, maybe she did say that. "At least I'm doing something about it now, though, aren't I? And I've got a guy who dresses like a retro vampire hiding in the dark and following me around for the pleasure of it."

The pair walked on in silence, both angrily picking chips off the top of the pile as they went.

"Not that you'll care, seeing as I'm too afraid and a waste of time and magic—"

"I did not say that." He rolled his eyes.

"But I should probably let you know about a weird thing that happened with protection circles. Seeing as you're supposed to be keeping an eye on things."

"Any more specific information than that?" he asked with a gesture for her to continue.

She felt reluctant to tell him something that probably just revealed her lack of talent yet again. "Artorius had me practicing protection circles in our Incantation lesson, and they wouldn't stick. Probably nothing, but—"

"What do you mean 'they wouldn't stick'?" Rune had stopped walking now, tugging Belle's sleeve to bring her to a standstill.

She raised her gaze to meet his, which had turned intent and concerned. "They wouldn't stick. The protection circles. I could conjure them for a moment, but they kept cutting out. Like something was preventing me from being protected."

"And you're only telling me this now? Belle, I'm your bloody watchman. Why didn't you tell me this the moment we started talking?"

"Because I was busy returning my heart rate to a normal level after you emerged from the shadows like a sewer rat. And then you conjured chips, and we've been arguing ever since."

"We're not arguing."

"Well, I certainly am. That means you are, too."

He growled with exasperation. "You are impossible. Just for future reference, any signs of mortal danger—even mild PG-certified peril, come to think of it—should be discussed first in our conversations."

"Mortal danger? That seems a bit much. It's just a spell glitch, probably my lack of ability more than anything," she said uncertainly.

"Maybe but maybe not. And I'm not risking your safety. Belle, normally I would have sensed something like that in a heartbeat. Broken protection spells? Rudimentary stuff, I can sense threats like that in my sleep. But I didn't feel a thing . . . Something isn't right here." He was rambling crossly, almost to himself. "Let me check the reports more thoroughly, ask around at Hecate House, see if anyone has any prior experience of failed protection."

"Don't go shouting it from the rooftops, okay? I don't want everyone thinking I'm failing. I'm doing fine."

"Will you give me some credit, Belle, please? I'm only in this for you."

She frowned.

He coughed, noting his wording. "Only here to help you, I mean."

Belle nodded reluctantly, shooting him a sly glance and finding that his eyes were still firmly fixed on her. They returned to walking quietly side by side, the early light leaking over them in silver and pink. She contemplated reassuring him with the news of the *Praesentia Pretego* enchantment from her grandmother, but it felt too private, too intimate for now.

"Nothing like the mention of mortal peril to make the conversation die," Belle said instead.

"Mortal peril aside, it's less than three weeks till Halloween," Rune noted, nodding his chin up towards the waxing moon that hung alongside the rising sun. "Do you feel as though you're seeing progress?"

"Sure. I mean, I think so. I've surprised myself so far."

"You shouldn't be surprised. You're gifted," Rune said matter-of-factly.

Belle's eyebrows shot up, taken aback. "Thanks, although I think that's pushing it."

"You don't need to thank me. It's not so much a compliment as a fact. I liked your manifests, most of them . . . Some questionable decisions, but the base magic was strong. You're capable of anything you want to do."

Their shadows stretched out long and thin under the burning of the golden streetlights, scattered leaves dappling the picture. They both wrapped their coats tighter in unison.

"Also," he eventually spoke again, as though daring himself to continue, "not that you care about my opinion, as you've made crystal clear, but . . . you're not a disappointment. Or unworthy of anything," he said, his usual confidence cracking to something altogether more interesting. His eyes stayed firmly locked straight ahead.

Something alarmingly close to chemistry flickered like a bolt between them. It had been a while, but she couldn't mistake that feeling.

"How did you find the astrological work?" Rune asked, jumping at the chance to restart the conversation.

She smiled at him. "Why do I get the feeling this question is a little redundant when you've obviously been keeping a close eye anyway, watchman?"

"Kind of true, but I'm only alerted if anything goes particularly wrong or danger presents itself to you," he said. "The grimoire is already detailing significant improvement, according to Bronwyn. I just wanted to hear it from you. Part of my job is to make sure you're feeling okay."

"That's handy, therapy is expensive."

Rune stifled a laugh. "I'm not sure I'm qualified to go that far, but I'm serious about this potential threat, bearing in mind the warlock who's involved in proceedings."

"Ah, that." She clasped her hands behind her back and kicked a few leaves.

"We have to assume he has some role to play in what happened to your protection circles . . ." Rune said, thoughtful concern audible in his voice.

"That wasn't him."

"You don't know that, Belle."

"I do."

She couldn't shake it. In their first week together, she'd almost entirely forgotten the clanging alarm bells and red flags that were originally attached to Artorius. When the reminder did occasionally appear at the front of her mind, it felt impossible to associate the man that she'd met with those nightmarish past actions.

Belle tried to explain. "This whole time, everyone's been banging on about the importance of instincts, and something's not adding up. The way Bronwyn spoke of him, I was expecting a monster. I thought he'd be awful and cruel and reluctant to share any knowledge at all. I thought he would be—"

"Belle, you cannot be naive about this man," Rune interrupted firmly, stopping in his tracks again.

"I am aware," Belle snapped, turning directly to Rune to stand her ground. "Obviously. And I'm not ignoring it, I'm not an idiot. But he has treated me with kindness and generosity and nothing else. I have to take him as I find him for now."

"You can't seriously like him, with the knowledge that you have, with everything that he did," Rune scoffed.

"I'm not saying I do or don't like him. I'm telling you that I am fully aware of the situation I have willingly put myself into."

Rune held his tongue, but she could have sworn she heard the word "impossible" muttered under his breath. They continued their walk in frosty silence.

"Is it much farther?" Rune asked curtly.

"Thankfully, no," Belle retorted.

After what felt like forever in the stilted silence, they reached the row of shops below Belle and Ariadne's maisonette. Commuters were filling the streets now, scuttling by with heads down and headphones on. The café below was dimly lit, with Mr. Ricci setting out the trays of freshly made pastries. The familiar smell of coffee and warm baked goods plumed outwards.

"I have something for you," Rune said shortly, avoiding eye contact. He held out his palm, and with a quick click, a small green bottle materialised with a flurry of sparks. "Thought you might be tired, so I've been working on it for a couple of nights." He offered it to Belle, who took it suspiciously. "A revitalising potion. Should help with the lack of sleep, and it'll mean you can lay off the caffeine a bit. Although I now see that you literally live inside a coffee shop, which makes a lot of sense."

"Above one. But . . . That's very thoughtful. Thank you."

"I'll see what I can find out about the protection circles."

"Look, I . . ."

"Belle! Hey! God, something in here stinks, I bet it's that cat food," Ariadne called. She was tossing a heavy black bag into the communal bins. Squinting closer, she froze. "Oh, sorry . . . I didn't realise you had company."

Belle willed herself to think on the spot. This was the first time that Ariadne had ever seen her with someone magical, apart from Bonnie and Alvina, who were both well versed in keeping the secret.

"It's . . . This is . . ."

"I'm Rune," he introduced himself smoothly over Belle's stammering, extending his hand out warmly to Ari. Knowing her friend like the back of her hand, Belle could tell that Ari was trying to remain collected but was in fact bursting with delight on the inside.

"It's *such* a pleasure to meet you." She grinned, overly cheery. "I'm Ariadne, I live with Belle. Are you guys coming in? I just brewed a fresh pot of coffee."

"Rune was just leaving," Belle immediately responded. There was no way that this could end well. She shot Rune what she hoped was a loaded look.

Luckily, he seemed to get the message. "That's very kind." He smiled. "But unfortunately I have to get going, business calls. I'll see you, Belle. Thanks for sharing my chips."

"Great. Brilliant. Cheerio."

Cheerio? Giving her a final, unfathomable smile, Rune turned on his heel and headed back the way they'd walked and into the commuter crowds. Only Belle's eyes were tuned to notice the transference, a faint glimmer of gold trailing on the pavement, wisps of magic left in his wake as he headed to . . . wherever it was that he went. Strange, really, that he'd chosen to spend time walking her home when he could have transferred them in a fraction of a moment.

Belle turned back to Ariadne with her eyes screwed shut in anticipating dread.

Ari wore an expression of complete and utter glee. She turned towards the flat and called back to her friend. "I shall prepare the torture devices to extract the details."

19

Bonnie Come Back

"YOU'RE NOT GETTING away with it that easily," Ariadne nudged as they both clutched coffee mugs in the kitchen. Jinx wove her way through their legs, pleased to have everybody convening at home. "I need a hot love story to live vicariously through."

"I'm caught bickering with a guy outside and it's big news, while your calendar is constantly filled with gorgeous people taking you out for delicious meals and them being grateful for the chance. I think you're still winning."

"Are you joking? You know better than anyone that I attract lunatics. Last week I spent an entire evening hearing about a woman's lifelong dream to live on her grandfather's DIY barge."

"That sounds like a pretty appealing plan. Maybe *we* should live on a barge. Sail far, far away and live off the land. A diet of only potatoes."

"Not sure the cat would love a life on the seven seas."

Jinx let out a loud, disapproving meow as if to agree.

"There's still nothing to tell," Belle tried to assure her best friend once again.

Ariadne raised an eyebrow. "At least tell me he's being good to you."

"He is. He's . . . protective."

"Sounds like delicate code for 'psycho.'"

"Not in that way. He's . . . looking out for me?"

"I don't like how secretive you're being about it. It's weird for us. You're making it weird."

"It's not that I'm being secretive. I'm trying to give it some time, see where it goes. I owe it to myself to give it a proper try and put my all into something for once." Ariadne didn't need to know that Belle wasn't strictly referring to a relationship.

"Fair enough," Ariadne replied a little shirtily, staring down into the bottom of her mug.

"I promise, by the moon and the stars and the sun, that I still love you the most forever and ever, amen."

Ariadne seemed appeased. "He did seem nice. Sensational hair, if nothing else."

Belle nodded, conceding that perhaps he did have good hair. "Yeah. He is nice. A little big for his boots sometimes, maybe."

Ariadne scoffed. "He's massive. The boots must be enormous."

✦ ⁕ ⁂ ✦

ALMOST TWO WEEKS down and still all six of the grimoire's allegories remained unlit. The lack of sleep was beginning to take its toll, so Belle had indulged in Rune's expertly brewed revitalising potion. She had to hand it to him, he was a talented alchemist. Maybe not *entirely* beauty over brains after all. The generous gift brought her back from the brink of burn-out and gave her a renewed determination to build momentum. She was resolute that she would see some strides in her magic before the next moon rose.

On the night of the thirteenth moon, Artorius insisted on whipping up an enormous midnight "snack" to build her strength. It was becoming clear that the old man believed in the restorative power of food as a separate kind of magic, and to be fair, it usually worked.

That night, he'd guided her through to the kitchen on his arm as though presenting her to a ballroom, and with a small flourish of cookery spells, a perfect feast had appeared. She'd practically dove head first into the steaming porridge drizzled with honey and the towering bowls of fresh fruit before downing what could only be described as a vat of hot chocolate.

"We shall return to Incantation work for tonight's lesson. Improvement in Earth Sorcery and Clairvoyancy feels satisfactory for the moment, to revisit as our deadline approaches. For now, we shall . . . mix it up, as you say." He grinned.

"Let's go back to transference, Arty," Belle said, reaching for a pain au raisin. The old warlock had been insisting that she use the less formal nickname. She was pleasantly surprised to find that the friendliness felt right, and he was pleased that it made him sound "rather hip."

Artorius seemed surprised, glancing up from the enormous newspaper which he held out in front of him, one leg neatly crossed over the other. He peered above the top of his glasses at her words. "You're sure? I was going to suggest something less taxing."

Belle nodded, decisively brushing pastry crumbs from her jumper. "I'm experimenting with this new thing where I try to believe in myself a little. I was almost there with transference last week. Sort of."

Reaching the sports pages, Artorius carefully folded his paper.

"Very well. But first, a little warm-up to start us off tonight, Miss Blackthorn. Some manifestive magic, perhaps. Pansies, pancakes, a polar bear . . . although I would perhaps advise against the latter. Selcouth's health and safety regulations towards me may struggle to approve any large mammals. Stick to ferret or smaller. Shall we adjourn to the attic?"

The old man was fully settled into his mentor role and was taking to it like an owl to the night sky. No longer did he politely suggest they try something. He was in fact rather bossy at times and apologised on a number of occasions when he found himself getting carried away enough to earn a scowl from Belle.

When her magic was warmed up, pleasantly balmy under her skin, Artorius gave her the nod that it was time to tackle transference. They had agreed to start with summoning by transference, inviting someone to join them before Belle gave it another go for herself. Pen lid between her teeth and notebook propped on her thigh, she scribbled the incantation quickly. Artorius watched in interest and admiration, rocking back and forth on his heels with his hands clasped behind his back. She tucked the pen behind her ear and examined her handiwork.

"We await with bated breath," Artorius encouraged.

Belle closed her eyes and sought out calm. Magic rose once again like mercury in a thermometer.

> Mother of mine, I call to join here,
> Wherever you stand, journey to near.
> Company precious, enduring love strong,
> Come to me now, this is where you belong.

Belle felt the rush of power course through her veins, molten and flowing. She flicked her pointing finger. In a fraction of a moment, Bonnie Blackthorn appeared before her, solid and real. An older version of Belle, everyone always said, although shorter, her hair a little fairer and much curlier. The curls were usually kept at bay with a brightly coloured scarf or a headband, and inevitably featured some form of greenery plucked from her garden—sometimes intentional, more often not. But the same dark eyes as her daughter, and the same kind but ever so slightly worried expression behind them. Plus, of course, the enormous Irish wolf-hound who was perpetually by her side. On arrival, Wolfie lolloped over to Artorius for an immediate sniff, followed by an approving hand lick.

Bonnie rushed to her daughter and grabbed her hands desperately. "What's wrong? What's happened? Belle, are you hurt?"

"What? Nothing, nothing. Mum, I'm fine."

"You are? You're fine? Why did you summon me?" The panic didn't leave Bonnie's face.

"Mum, take a breath. I'm okay, look. Everything's fine."

Appeased, Bonnie sighed with tangible relief. "I thought something awful had happened. You've never transferred me before. I thought you needed me, I thought—"

"I was practicing transference incantations. I needed to make someone appear, and who else would I have brought?"

Bonnie, still clasping her daughter's upper arms in fear, closed her eyes and steadied herself, loosening her grasp a tad. "Gosh, love. You gave me such a fright."

"Sorry. But hey, successful magic," Belle offered as compensation.

Bonnie pulled her into a tight hug. "Now that I know you're not in imminent danger, yes, I'm proud of you," she said as she kissed her daughter on the head. "Now, where are we, exactly?"

"Ms. Blackthorn. It's a great honour to have you here. I've read so much about you, your abilities in herbal magic are the stuff of legend," Artorius said, taking a soft step forward.

Bonnie's eyebrows jumped, chin shooting back as she realised who was introducing himself. "Mr. Day." She took a measure of the room around her and darted her eyes back to the man who lived there.

"This is Artorius, Mum. Everything's been going well."

"Well, I'm glad to hear it," Bonnie said with a polite smile, her tone unusually clipped. It was clear to Belle now that her mother had reservations about her daughter's mentor and had simply been keeping them private thus far. They were written all over her face. "I appreciate everything you're doing for my daughter."

"No trouble at all, my dear. I am of course delighted to be in her company. Such a bright witch, I can see it already. A flawless summoning transference tonight . . . It's promising, very promising. I'm thrilled to witness her progress," Artorius said with his usual wholesome enthusiasm.

Belle noticed a subtle shift in her mother's posture that echoed her own when she had first met the man. It changed from defensive and questioning to etched with pleasant surprise. She gave her mother the smallest, almost indistinguishable nod that she hoped meant *Trust me, he's very strange but kind of great.*

"Sorry again to pull you from . . . whatever you were doing with no warning. What does that even feel like?" Belle asked, wrinkling her nose at Bonnie.

"Summoned transference? The same, a little like you'd imagine being sucked up through a hoover would feel."

"Does it give you a warning?" Belle asked.

"Of course, it requires consent." Bonnie laughed. "Like getting a collect call from someone at the other end and accepting the charges. Otherwise, you'd have wicchefolk zipping and zapping unexpectedly all over the shop. Obviously, I wanted to find out what you needed from me; it's no trouble, love."

As Belle opened her mouth to encourage her mum to stay for tea, the attic lights overhead flickered. A moment later, they cut out entirely, plunging the loft into cloudy, violet darkness.

"I'll be darned. That blasted electricity board," Artorius muttered.

Bonnie flickered in front of her daughter's eyes, which were still adjusting to the darkness. Belle shook her head, assuming her contact lenses had slipped.

But it happened again, just then. Like watching a bad television signal fall over her own mother. Bonnie dipped in and out of sight like a camera flash.

"Mum, are you all right?"

But Bonnie was gone.

Silence fell abruptly across the attic, so sudden and blanketing that even the ambient sounds, the whirring and buzzing of the attic, paused in surprise.

"Did . . . did my spell unravel?" she asked Artorius, clueless as to what had happened.

Just like that, Bonnie reappeared. She was back as though nothing had happened at all.

But something was wrong. As soon as her feet landed back on the floorboards, Bonnie stumbled. She was gasping for breath, ghostly pale in the pitch-black attic.

"Mum. Mum? What's happening?" Belle cried, her voice snapping. She reached out to hold her mother, to keep her close.

Before she could take hold of the sleeve of Bonnie's dress, her mother vanished again. Belle's hand closed around darkness.

Belle's heart sped up, thumping against her ribs. She lunged forward over and over, grabbed out to try and hold on to her mother. But Bonnie continued to vanish into the black, then materialise again for one desperate, helpless moment.

"Belle." Bonnie choked out the word each time.

"What's happening? Arty? What's happening?" Belle's voice grew louder, more frantic. Wolfie barked, bewildered.

"I don't know! I don't know, Belle!" The old man, like Belle, lurched towards Bonnie in the fraction of a second she showed herself.

Bonnie reached out with a desperate, terror-stricken expression, grasping onto her daughter's wrist for only an instant each time. She pulled with so much force that it was as though she was being tugged away, something snatching her backwards, relentless. Belle fought to hold on to her mother's arm, wincing as the pull of skin on skin burnt all the way down her forearm.

"Please, Mum. Hold on."

Belle was crying now. Hot tears soaked her face, blurring her vision. The old man strained as he fired up his limited strength to support Belle's attempts, the pair yelling in frustration, fuelled by adrenaline as they tried to seize Bonnie firmly back to them.

For a moment, it felt as though they had her. But losing the strength of the opposite pulling force, Belle was sent flying backwards, stumbling over her own feet and crashing into one of the overloaded shelves. Heavy books thudded downwards all around her. An iron cauldron fell with force onto her shoulder. Her whole body thumped against the wooden eaves. But it didn't matter.

Ignoring the pain, Belle hurried to her feet and hurtled back towards where her mother had been. She fiercely cleared her wet eyes with the back of her hand, steeling herself to continue the fight.

But now there was nothing. No more flickers came. Bonnie had gone.

20

Entangled

BELLE SPENT A lot of her time afraid, but she had never known true fear before. Not really. Not like this.

"Where is she?" Her voice, startlingly loud in the sudden quiet.

There was no reply. Only Wolfie, giving a low whimper as she looked back and forth between Belle and the empty spot that had previously been Bonnie. Belle realised the moment of release that sent her flying backwards had taken Artorius with it, too.

The old man lay surrounded by broken bottles, emptied jars and fallen books, his wire glasses at an unnatural angle across his baffled face. He winced as he adjusted his brittle body, trying to right himself. Belle rushed to his side, throwing aside a lampshade, a rolled-up moth-eaten rug and an empty hamster cage which had toppled in the chaos.

"Artorius, are you all right? Where's my mum? I've got to help her." He coughed deeply from his chest, recoiling at the effort on his old bones.

"Belle, are you hurt?"

"I'm fine, I'm fine. But where's my mum? Where's Bonnie?" she asked hurriedly.

He spluttered over his words, trying and failing to make sense of what they'd witnessed. "I can't say for sure, I wish I could. It's almost as though—"

"Did my spell unravel? Where is she?"

"But it's impossible. It would be against every . . ." Artorius was muttering to himself, calculating possibilities only he could see.

"How do I get her back? Where is she, Arty?" Belle asked again, more desperate by the second as she wrung her hands.

Artorius turned clouded eyes to Belle. "*Subfuror Incantare.*"

"I don't need Latin definitions, Artorius. I need to find my mother."

"Of course, of course, Belle. Help me up, will you?"

The pair staggered to their feet together. Belle took a deep breath to steady herself and encouraged Artorius to do the same. The old man looked confused, dazed. She placed a reassuring hand on his shoulder, which seemed to help.

"*Subfuror Incantare* . . . it is a rare phenomenon, rare indeed," he began. "And for good reason. It goes against every law that exists within the magic system. With *Subfuror Incantare* at play, all balance is lost, all fairness gone. Power gains more power . . ." he rambled, tracing his own steps in circles as his thoughts tumbled out.

"Artorius, I have no idea what you're talking about." Belle rubbed her face.

"It is the art—'art' is the wrong word for something so unconscionable—the act of overthrowing another witch's powers for one's own means, snatching a spell from them without their knowledge or consent. A manipulation of magic."

Belle blinked, desperately trying to understand. "My spell? Someone warped it?"

"I suspect that, under *Subfuror Incantare*, someone was manipulating your spellwork. Someone was trying to overpower it, take over the intention behind it and make it their own."

"But what would anyone want with my magic? I'm pretty sure I've proved that it's not particularly worth having."

"On the contrary, young lady. Magic in every form is envied by those who don't consider themselves to have enough. You may think you are nothing special, but everything I have witnessed so far suggests otherwise. And it would seem that somebody else is aware of that, too. Somebody wants to take your magic from you."

"They can do that? Just . . . take it?"

"Unfortunately, it is indeed possible. It's not until the Equi-Witch trial is completed that your magic falls fully under the coven's protection. Until then, it is vulnerable."

"Even if that's true, the *Subfu* . . . whatever. What's it got to do with my mum?"

"Belle, we both know your mother is a brilliant witch. Perhaps fearing the two of you practicing together, the potential of what that could create if nurtured properly? Whatever the reason, they did not want Bonnie here with you."

"We have to find her."

Artorius looked racked with guilt. "I am dreadfully sorry to say there is nothing we can do at present. A witch entangled in *Subfuror Incantare* can only resist the control by summoning her own abilities, her own presence of mind to fight against it. It's down to your mother to escape this by herself."

Registering Belle's newly horrified expression, Artorius continued hurriedly. "But we both know there is no witch more capable than your mother, Belle," he said with emphasis. "She is renowned for the prowess of her powers. Her magic rivals that of the Gowden sisters. She is the very best of wicchefolk."

"But . . . I can't just sit here and wait to see what happens! I have to help her."

"Belle, as your mentor, I must insist that is exactly what you do.

If you value your magic or, more importantly, your mother's well-being. We have no idea how your own magic could be used against you or her at this moment. I implore you, it is not safe."

Belle stood aghast.

"Your mother would prioritise your safety above all else."

She raked her fingers across her scalp. Doing nothing went against every instinct. But the logical side of her brain said that Artorius had never yet steered her wrong. She reached for the one other thing she knew might guide her.

The sooth stone was aglow, fiercely golden and brilliant. In all her other recent times of need and doubt, the stone had come to life. Not only reassuring her but, as she knew now, protecting her. She found that it was clearing her mind, quieting it, providing answers to decisions that she didn't fully trust herself to make. The sight of its radiance was pacifying, calm amidst the chaos.

"So we wait."

Artorius gave a single relieved nod. "We wait."

* ✳ · ✦ ★

BELLE REFUSED TO leave the attic. According to Artorius, it made the most sense that *when* (carefully selected rather than "if") Bonnie managed to break free from the bind, she would escape to the same spot from which she had vanished. Remaining loyally by her side into the wee hours of the morning, Wolfie lay with her head on her front paws, stretched out alongside Belle, occasionally sharing her distress with a strained mournful howl at the moon in the window. Artorius ventured downstairs only once—to make a pot of tea and to collect his knitting to pass the stretch of time.

Belle sat cross-legged on the floor. Her back ached and her eyes were strained from staring at the same spot. But she wouldn't move. Instead she sat, rubbing at her face, biting at the inside of her cheeks, digging her thumbnail into the grooves of the floorboards. As another hour came and went, she picked at a loose thread on the hem of her jumper.

Pearly moonlight leaked through the round window in the attic eaves. Belle adjusted her shoulders. The weight of the day was dragging her whole body down like an iron anchor. Just as her eyes began to close, the creaking grandfather clock hidden under a dust-sheet suddenly chimed three times, stirring her.

"Witching hour," Artorius muttered under his breath, the first thing either of them had spoken aloud for hours.

A flicker against the floorboards.

A dash of light.

Another.

"Mum," Belle whispered, hardly daring to breathe.

Bonnie. Finally, she reappeared with a gasp and collapsed in a heap on the floorboards, the fabric of her dress billowing in a plume. It felt like slow motion in Belle's eyes. Wolfie hurtled towards her. Artorius rushed to rise from his armchair, dropping his knitting to the floor in a clatter of needles. Belle, swallowing a sob, scrambled to her mother's side.

Belle dragged her mother to Artorius's armchair while he provided blankets, chocolate biscuits and frilly pillows for propping. Eventually, by the time the sun came up in a rosy glow, a faint colour had returned to Bonnie's cheeks. Initially careful to avoid overwhelming her, Belle was now full of questions that wouldn't keep.

Bonnie shook her head, wincing at the movement.

"I couldn't see anything or anyone, love. Just darkness. Pitch black. Blacker than darkness. I knew that it was magic dragging me away from you, and . . . it's so hard to describe. As though it were tearing me from where I wanted to be. They kept ripping me away. Away from you."

She took a careful sip of tea. "I could barely breathe, like a hand was pushing me underwater and holding me there. And the

sound . . . someone screaming with rage inside my own head. Whoever it was, they were furious that I fought against whatever they
were trying to do."

Artorius was pottering around in his scuffed slippers, attempting
to build the attic back together again with swift motions of magic.
"*Subfuror Incantare*," he muttered, before turning to the witches.
"It is incontrovertible. Darkness, fear, emptiness . . . the theft of joy
and hope. All signs point to stolen, manipulated magic."

Belle felt as though her brain were spinning on its axis. She held
her head in both hands to steady herself. "This cannot be happening. Are we wrapped up with some kind of . . . of villain?"

Artorius gently cleared his throat to interrupt. "Belle, I must
confess . . ."

Her stomach plummeted. It couldn't be.

"I was trying to ignore it," he went on. "I thought I was being
overzealous with my concerns. The failed protection circles . . ."

"The what?" Bonnie interrupted with concern.

"It's just a thing, Mum." Belle waved a dismissive hand.

"The signs in the sky, I dismissed it all as coincidence. But magic
doesn't lie. It seems beyond doubt . . ."

"Please don't say it."

"You may indeed be in danger."

Belle tried to force a laugh. "Oh, so I have my own personal
baddy to fight now?"

"Ms. Blackthorn, I do not jest. And I am reluctant to add," Artorius continued, worry etched into his wrinkles, "we are evidently
dallying with something or someone who wishes you and your
mother not be on this path together. It is most strange indeed."

Belle chewed at the inside of her cheek, thinking. "It's someone
in the coven, then?"

"Possibly." Artorius considered. "Although at this point, someone outside of Selcouth is equally as likely. Perhaps another coven,

farther afield. Or independent wicchefolk, for that matter. It could be anyone."

"Brilliant. That narrows it down."

"We can only hope their spell strength is exhausted, at least for a time, from your mother putting up such a brave fight."

Bonnie gave him a weak but proud smile. It didn't linger. "Here I am, causing more problems for you when you've already got enough on your plate."

"It's fine, Mum. Stop flapping," Belle said as she adjusted the cushion behind Bonnie's head.

"Don't make a fuss, love. I just need to get home, get back to my stores so I can start thinking about the best way to look after you." Bonnie attempted to raise herself out of the chair.

Belle gave her mum an incredulous look. "Are you mad, woman? You're not going anywhere, you must be joking. You can barely hold yourself up."

"I'll be all right."

"Will you sit down? Transference is out of the question. There is no way."

Artorius interrupted their gentle bickering. "I should be delighted to play host to you until you are satisfactorily recovered, Ms. Blackthorn. And dear Wolfie, of course."

Bonnie nodded in reluctant acceptance.

"There are plenty of rooms," he went on. "You are welcome to stay as long as is required. There is safety in numbers, after all."

"Thank you, Mr. Day."

"Nonsense, it will be the honour of my life."

Monica was perfectly understanding when Belle called Lunar to let them know that her mother had taken ill and that she would be absent for a few days.

Christopher was less patient. "Is there no one else who can step in, though? She'd be best in hospital, then you can come to the shop.

You drive me bloody mad, Blackthorn, but things will go to pot without you here."

It felt good to say no to him.

✦ ✦ ✦ ✦ ✦

THE SMALL POSITIVE of the whole "Mum nearly drowning in a dark abyss of *Subfuror Incantare*" incident was that Belle and Artorius found themselves diving into a whole new branch of magic earlier than anticipated. With her main goal now to see Bonnie restored to health, a healing potion was first on Belle's list to conquer.

The Alchemy title page of the grimoire was illustrated with plump cauldrons in silver and oyster grey, laced with ivy and a million different bottles shaped like jewels on the page. Belle noted that Artorius's own ancient Alchemy books were all covered in smatterings of potions in every shade, like a particularly messy chef and their favourite recipe books. He explained that the measuring and accuracy of potion making had been something he had practiced in the name of science over the years, even without his magic.

> Boil and blend, stoke flame and cinder,
> A timid choice would merely hinder.
> Grab for new and grasp it tightly,
> Consider what leaves trace brightly.
> It shall not do to shrink nor settle,
> Thistle, milkweed, purslane, nettle.
> Chase with valour that which calls,
> Thrice brew, benevolence in all.

"Three benevolent potions, that seems plain enough," Artorius read, as though it were blindingly obvious. "We shall of course begin with a draught to encourage your mother's healing, aid in speeding up the process as best we can. Of course, magic cannot work miracles or fully heal any ailment. Such magic only displaces misfortune to another. But perhaps some ginger root powder, a sugar cube or two . . ."

He wandered off to peruse his shelves of endlessly packed ingredients, reaching for a vial whenever it caught his eye, while simultaneously referring to a copy of *Brewing and Stewing* with an extremely glamorous witch brandishing a ladle on the cover.

"The practice of potion brewing is one of finesse and concentration. Although a flair for creativity is also welcome to the science," Artorius said, pacing busily back and forth. "Healing, healing . . ." he muttered, adjusting his repaired glasses.

Belle shot him an unimpressed side-eye and grabbed a toffee from the bowl of sweets that Artorius had provided for class. He'd learned early on that her brain seemed to function better when it was given a little treat every once in a while. The ruby red wrapper rustled with static between her fingers.

"Is there not just an exact recipe we can follow? To make it as efficient as possible?" Belle surged forwards to catch a glass mason jar that was teetering on the edge of a shelf while Artorius haphazardly handed her container after container, each packed with something more unappealing-looking than the last.

"This isn't a ratatouille we're whipping up," he scolded.

"So I can chuck anything in as long as I mean well?"

He gave her a look. "Not exactly. We require ingredients, but their specifics are down to the witch at the cauldron. If your mother usually turns to the world of nature for healing, we'll start there. The familiar and the comforting will lead to healing."

"We'll need Earl Grey, then. Tea leaves."

"What else?" he encouraged. "Anything your mother always gave you when you were poorly as a child, maybe?"

Belle thought back to mornings against stacks of pillows, towels over the duvet, a washing-up bowl at the side of the bed.

"Black currants? She'd always give me glasses of warm squash. Malt for the warm milk. Bread and butter, if that counts as nature."

"Throw in a little honey to soothe. Willow bark for the pain. This is certainly starting to sound like a potion to me."

"Either a potion or the world's worst hangover cure."

A few hours later, there were flames licking at the bottom of the large cauldron in the centre of the attic, and the contents were turning a rich shade of brown roux, simmering gently with a nutty scent that seemed both medicinal and soothing. Strangely, it carried the smell of Bonnie's house by the time it came to a boil, which felt to Belle like a sign that it must be a half-decent spell.

She was vindicated when the grimoire glowed with a balmy amber light, indicating their success at the first benevolent potion, *Salutaris Medella*. Sagging with relief at the sight, Belle spooned a portion into a little china bowl.

She gave a small knock on the bedroom door, found her mum sleeping and crept in, trying not to upset the floorboards beneath her feet. Just as she reached the bedside table to tenderly lay down the potion, a jutting nail sunk against her small toe, and she let out a violent expletive.

Bonnie stirred and Belle apologised. "Sorry, sorry, sorry, didn't mean to wake you. My toe . . . Sorry."

"It's okay, love. What have you got there?"

"It's a healing potion. Don't worry, the grimoire approved it, so I don't think it'll poison you."

Bonnie wriggled under the duvet with an uncomfortable grimace, manoeuvring sore limbs to sit up against the striped headboard. She took the bowl from Belle and gratefully took a miniature sip.

"Down the hatch, Mum. I'm sure the combination of actual tree bark and curdled malted milk is a taste sensation."

"I never thought I'd see the day when you were the one sitting at the bedside looking after me," Bonnie said, offering a weak smile.

"It's the perfect Alchemy lesson. Actually very considerate of you to go and get attacked by some kind of dark forces."

Draining the bowl, Bonnie put it back on the bedside table and reached for Belle's hands, placing both between her own.

"I was so worried," Belle said quietly. "I didn't know where you'd . . ." She tried to say it boldly but couldn't make the words any louder than a whisper. Belle had only recently begun to notice a certain feeling that bloomed when it came to her mother's well-being. One unremarkable day, her mother had somehow stopped being something untouchable. Her mother was something that could break. Belle inwardly smarted at the realisation.

"I know, darling." Bonnie wrapped her arms around her daughter, stroking her hair from the crown of her head to the ends.

"I thought I'd lost you." Belle had her eyes closed now but felt her mother's hands on both her shoulders. She bit down on her bottom lip to steady the waver in her voice.

"Look at me, Belle. You listen to this, please. It'll take more than whatever that was to separate me and you. I would fight with every fibre of my being for you." She held her daughter's face. "Oh, darling, I'm not sure this is all worth it. I'm not sure it's safe. I was trying to give Artorius the benefit of the doubt, but—"

"Mum, don't start."

"I'm serious, sweetheart. Maybe this wasn't such a good idea. Bronwyn is occasionally wrong, and Morena is occasionally right. This can't be a coincidence. Under his roof."

Belle faltered for a fraction of a second, but her mind instantly returned to the moment of Bonnie's disappearance. Of the look on Artorius's face. The panic, the dismay, the distress that was only matched by her own.

"I know how it looks," she said slowly. "But this isn't down to him. He's a good man."

Bonnie stared at her with pinched eyes, then gave a sigh. "I do trust your judgement of character, love. But I trust my own, too, and I know that there's something not right in all of this."

"That could be the willow bark."

"I'm serious, Belle. I would give up every drop of magic in my bones if it meant that I could keep you safe."

"Mum, stop. Things have been knocked off-kilter since I set foot in Hecate House, so maybe the magic system is just a little unbalanced for me right now. It might not be anyone behind it."

Bonnie nodded hesitantly. "Perhaps . . . Why hasn't that watchman of yours been in touch? He's an impressive warlock. I'd feel better knowing that he was on the case, at least."

Belle shifted on the edge of the mattress, kicking one foot against the other.

"I haven't exactly told him what's been going on yet. In fact, I told him to back off."

"Oh, Belle. You need to—"

"I don't need him to protect or watch anything. I can look after myself." Belle shrugged. "Whatever it is, I can deal with it."

Bonnie rolled her eyes. "Belle Blackthorn, you are the most stubborn girl I have ever . . ."

"Fine, fine. I'll tell him. Not that he'll do anything. He'll just run a hand through his hair and thumb his jawline and brood."

Bonnie lay back against the cushions with her eyes closed, her energy levels depleted again.

"Get some sleep, Mum. I'm not saying that I'm the untapped genius of my witching generation or some kind of potions master, but I think there might be some colour coming back to your cheeks already."

21

Truth Time

BELLE WASN'T ENTIRELY sure how a summoning even worked between witch and watchman, but she thought of him. Tried to make it a clean line of communication, tried even harder not to dwell on his piercing dark eyes, the way his hair constantly fell into his face, that smirk. She hoped it was some kind of telepathic phone system, one that wouldn't pick up on the unsubtle pounding of her heart at the thought of his arrival.

"You rang?" Rune shook out his head a little before dusting down the collar of his shirt, unbuttoned just below his collarbone.

"Hi."

"To what do I owe the pleasure?" Rune asked, glancing around Artorius's living room to take in his new surroundings. He shrugged off his coat and threw it onto the back of a floral armchair. "You know, it's funny. I was just getting ready to pay you a visit myself."

"You were?"

"The watchman spell has been highlighting a feeling that I wasn't entirely comfortable with." He gestured to somewhere amongst his ribs underneath his shirt. "Right here. I've been feeling this real, tangible dread when I thought of you."

Belle shot him a look across the living room. "Charming."

"Not like that. Like something was wrong. I needed to check you were okay days ago, but I've been torn as to whether I should step in. I know you don't like me being around."

"I never said—" She stopped herself. Another time. "Well, you were on to something. Against my better judgement, I've been told I need to tell you if anything weird is going on, so . . ."

His face darkened. "I was right, wasn't I?" He took a step towards her, closing the space between them as though it were instinctive. "Something *is* wrong. What is it?"

"It's a long story." Belle hesitated. "Can I get you a drink? While we talk?"

"Later. Like I said, imminent danger first, please."

Belle sighed, brushing her hair out of her eyes. "Okay, truth time. You're not going to like it. In fact, you're going to freak out."

"And putting off the subject for as long as possible is really going to help with that."

"*Subfuror Incantare,*" Belle blurted.

Rune's brow raised. "What about it?"

"It happened."

He took another step towards her, close enough now that she noticed his scent again, the burnt caramel and earthy tobacco. "What do you mean, 'it happened'?"

"*Sub* . . . don't make me say it again. Whatever it is, it happened to my mum."

A look of deep concern etched itself across his forehead, eyes pinching into fine lines at the edges. "You're not serious?"

"Yes, I love making jokes about things I can neither say nor understand."

"Belle, will you just talk seriously for once in your life? Your mother experienced *Subfuror Incantare*? When?"

Belle fiddled with the tassel of a cushion on the sofa, buckling under the intensity of his furious stare. "I guess technically I experienced it, too. It was my magic, my spell that was under control of something or someone. I managed to summon my mum to Artorius's attic, finally managed successful transference of another person, and it all went catastrophically wrong."

"Are you okay? Is she okay?"

"We're both fine. She's tucked up in bed." Belle gestured upstairs. "Recovering well now."

"When did this happen?"

Belle grimaced. "Two nights ago." She tried to ignore how silly she now felt for delaying as he turned exasperatedly and paced away.

"Two nights! How many times, Belle?" He looped back towards her. "I'm supposed to be protecting you. Looking out for dark magic, helping you stay safe. Why are you so adamantly against asking for help with anything?"

She could see his chest heaving, the rhythm of his shoulders as he ranted.

"Will you keep your voice down? Mum and Arty are both napping. And I'm sorry, I've been a little preoccupied nursing my mother back from the brink to worry about what my own resident heavy might think of the matter."

"You are absolutely infuriating." His nostrils flared as he stared down at her, their eyes defensively locked on each other's. A fraction of a moment too long passed by in silence. His gaze darted to her lips almost imperceptibly.

She took a step back and turned away, breaking the spell. "Anyway, we're both fine, thank you for your concern. We need to work on your bedside manner, by the way. I'm just, you know . . ." She hesitated. "Slightly concerned as to what it means that someone might be trying to stop my endarkenment. So it felt like something I should probably tell you."

He took a calming breath. "You should tell me everything."

"Fine."

"Good."

A silence hung between them, and Belle dared herself to ask the next question. "So what does it mean?" She glanced back over her shoulder.

"It means exactly what you said. The protection circle I could dismiss as some kind of coincidence, a glitch or an accident. But *Subfuror Incantare* is no accident. The two combined is bad news. Someone is trying to take your magic before it's yours to keep."

"Why would anyone want to do that?"

"I don't know, Belle. I haven't quite had time to process this just yet. Off the top of my head, I'd wager they're feeling threatened. By what you could mean for Selcouth? I . . . I don't know."

"Aren't you supposed to be the one with the answers to all of my problems?"

"Normally, yes. But this is slightly beyond the remit I expected. *Subfuror Incantare* is really dark magic, Belle."

"So I've heard." She laughed bitterly.

"Of course, we need to consider the possibility that Artorius is—"

"How many times? It's not him." She raised her voice definitively, prodding the top of the couch emphatically. "I know it for a fact."

"Actually, you don't." Rune's temper flared again to match.

"You didn't see him when my mum was . . . breaking, literally breaking in front of us. It was . . . It was the single most terrifying moment of my life. He didn't know what was happening, either. I was . . ." She swallowed hard. "I was so scared."

She couldn't stop it. She burst into tears. Big little-kid crying. Heavy sobs that shook her whole chest. She buried her face in her hands to hide. And before she knew what was happening, two arms wrapped around her. Warm and entirely enveloping, a shoulder to press her face into that smelled like an autumnal dream, woody and spicy, clean and smoky. A chin resting on the top of her head. She let herself be swallowed up, a little sorry creature swept up in a blanket from the cold rain. She let her guard down just for a moment. It had been a long time since anyone had held her like this, like someone was around every part of her, a wall of safety between her and the world.

He breathed a rough, quieting shush into her hair. The soft sound was soothing, mollifying in its deepness.

A creak on the floorboards upstairs snapped her out of it, like a hammer to glass. She went rigid. He evidently sensed her change in comfort, dropping his arms instantly.

"I don't . . . This is weird."

"Right." He nodded. "Unprofessional. Sorry, I—"

"No, I'm sorry. That was really nice of you. Thank you. Sorry. I don't know why I cried like that. I'm just really, really tired."

"Because you've been through something awful." Rune sighed, looking at her as though trying to read her. "No one should have to witness a loved one caught up in dark magic. That kind of thing . . . It stays with you."

Belle glanced up at him through wet lashes.

"And will you stop apologising all the time?" he carried on. "Especially for crying. I know I'm pretty terrible, but I'm not that much of a monster."

Belle shook herself down, brushing the traitorous tears off with her wrists.

He lifted her chin with a finger to examine her face and find her eyes. "I'm sorry I wasn't there for you when your mother was in danger, Belle. I think . . . and I know you're not going to like this, but just hear me out."

She started to shake her head and brush him off, but he carried on regardless.

"You're exhausted, let me pick up the slack. I'll stick around a little more, swing by Quill Lane again. I've been operating the watchman spell at its lowest grade because you didn't want me around, but now I need to do my job properly."

"But—"

"C'mon, Belle, let me do this. I want . . . I need," he corrected himself, "to make sure you're safe."

She thought for a moment, then conceded. "Okay. But no watching my spellwork during lessons, because I know you'll laugh at me. No interfering with Artorius. Absolutely no pointing out my mistakes, because I'll simply have to kill you. And none of—"

"Deal." He smiled as her list of stipulations continued.

22

Fight or Flight

WITH BONNIE'S RECOVERY slowly but surely underway, Belle returned to work at Lunar sooner than planned. She had wanted more time, but the decision was mostly made in response to a carefully worded phone call from Jim, alerting her to the fact that Christopher was using her absence as the perfect excuse to ruin any and all of the shop's remaining charm. As a result, splitting her waking hours (and some of her sleeping ones) between two separate lives, the magical and the non-magical, proved immediately taxing all over again.

Belle knew she was behaving like a hag to everyone in her vicinity, could feel people treading on eggshells around her. But over two weeks into her mentorship, she was utterly exhausted, physically and mentally. Her hair was limp and unwashed, scraped back into a ponytail every day. Her skin was pallid, spotty and dry. Having moaned about the state of her appearance to her mother, Bonnie explained that it wasn't down merely to the lack of sleep. Draining her body of magic night in, night out would be taking its toll on every part of Belle's system, her powers strained and overburdened, like overworked, dehydrated muscles completing marathons on empty. Rune's revitalising potion had long since worn off, and she was too proud to ask for another batch. Her whole body felt bruised, tender to the touch. It would seem that compressing fifteen years of magical education into a few weeks was not the wisest choice a witch could make.

Ariadne had noticed, too.

"I mean this in the nicest possible way, but are you coming down with something? You look dreadful, babe."

"What?" Belle replied irritably. The night before's sixteenth moon had ended on a sour note with Artorius, his incessant encouragement rubbing her exhaustion the wrong way while she tried and failed to memorise omens of the tarot deck.

"Don't snap at me. As your friend, I'm just saying you look slightly like you've been dug up from the grave." Ariadne spoke with genuine concern, offering half of her banana as they put their coats on to go to work.

"I wish I had been. At least I'd get a decent sleep if I were dead."

"Let's do some face masks tonight. Drink some water. Maybe eat some vegetables."

"I don't want to do face masks," Belle snarled. "I'm knackered. It's taking all of my brain power to stop my eyeballs from falling out of their sockets."

"You should take a day off."

"I *can't* take a day off. Every time I'm not at Lunar, I come back to find Christopher has thought of all new wonderful ways to ruin something. Yesterday I discovered he's sacked the kids' entertainer, thrown away all of the arts and crafts supplies *and* swapped the entire Women's Fiction display for male CEO autobiographies," Belle ranted.

"All right. Jeez." Ariadne screwed up her face, looking at Belle with the expression of being stuck on a particularly difficult crossword. "I just feel like you're shutting me out. I barely see you as it is, and when we're both here, I can't do anything right."

Belle could hear herself being a terrible person, instantly regretting it, pleading with her mouth to stay shut. But she couldn't quell the sharpness. "*You* can't do anything right? My mum is still ill, and I'm worrying myself sick about her. Lunar is falling apart, and I can't figure out how to fix it. Rune is . . . well, Rune is Rune. Your guess is as good as mine what's going on there. As you just so kindly pointed out, I look a complete state and . . ." Belle flared with embarrassment, which only fuelled her flaming temper further. "And am I not allowed to keep some things to myself every now and again?"

Ariadne blinked at her. "Since when?"

"Since forever, probably," Belle said, unreasonably. "Maybe I don't need to tell you anything and everything that's going on."

"I never said you did. But it's kind of a given, at this point. Or so I thought."

"I've just been feeling differently recently. Is that okay?"

"Yeah." Ariadne swallowed, her voice very small. "Of course."

"Thank you. Okay. Have a good day." Belle grabbed her bag from the back of the door and shut it behind her, leaving Ariadne standing alone in the flat.

Of course, Belle felt like she might vomit at any moment for the rest of the day.

There was a tremor in her hands and no inclination to eat. She had achieved approximately nothing useful at Lunar all day because she'd spent the whole time hating herself and worrying that Ariadne would never forgive her. She felt terrible. She would buy a bottle of wine on the way home, some of those honeycomb things that Ari liked, a bunch of flowers to help her grovel for being such an arse.

And then there was the Rune thing. She'd assumed at first that not being able to stop thinking about the man was down to how much he'd infuriated her when they first met. Or the simple fact that he was her first real magical encounter. But there'd been plenty since, and still . . . Now was not a good time to be falling for somebody, let alone somebody like him. She could not have chosen a worse time or a more incompatible person. Not that *that* was what was happening here. Absolutely not. She could not and should not even be thinking about *that* with everything else going on.

Belle leaned heavily on her right hand, pushing up her face into her eye socket with an elbow propped against the till. The day's biggest challenge should have been ensuring that the paper Jack-o'-lanterns were matched up properly with the fairy lights beneath them, strung across the ceiling in a pretty sweep. In actual fact, staying awake was proving the much larger problem. It had taken her third cup of coffee to bring the realisation that she was wearing her jumper back to front.

"One too many last night, Belle? Right there with you, darlin'." Christopher's voice felt like a sledgehammer to the brain, snapping Belle out of her unsubtle nap. Worse still, he placed both his hands on her shoulders and squeezed them tightly.

Monica did a terrible job at hiding her disgust across the shop floor.

Belle grimaced a polite, tight smile, shrugging him off. "Just not sleeping too well," she said.

"Not pregnant, are you?" Christopher said, momentarily looking genuinely concerned. "Let me know before we get sucked into maternity pay. I'd get pregnant for that." He guffawed, glancing at Jim for camaraderie.

Jim looked baffled.

"Do you need something, Christopher?" Belle looked at him through pinched eyes, retying the bow around her apron to resist the urge to strangle him. Her tiredness had led her to bite even Ariadne's head off that morning, so she couldn't be held responsible for what might happen to Christopher. Her finger itched to send out some form of receding hairline spell.

"Just a catch-up with my diamond girl. I can't resist those jeans."
He winked, making her skin crawl.

"I don't have the time or energy for pretending you're not grossly
offensive today," Belle replied before she could catch herself.

Taken aback, Christopher's expression changed. He could normally rely on her to take it on the chin, to laugh along, to roll her eyes
in an "oh you" polite kind of way. He mopped his forehead on his
forearm, ran his tongue over his teeth, pushed back his oiled hair.
"My office in ten." He clicked his fingers at the rest of the team. "I
want to see everyone in there. Put a Closed sign up. Anyone who
doesn't come armed with how they're pushing sales is going to need
to explain in extraneous detail to me why they're so useless and why
I shouldn't fire them on the spot." He stormed off without so much
as a backwards look. Belle rocked back on her heels and stared
fixedly at the spiral staircase while counting to ten.

"Belle . . ."

"Don't." She held up a hand to Monica. "I'm too tired for his
shit." Then she instantly felt guilty, seeing the expression on her
junior's face. "Sorry, sorry, sorry. It's been a long week."

"He gets more repugnant by the day," Monica said sympathetically, offering out the biscuit tin to Belle across the till. Belle nodded, stifling a yawn as she took a chocolate chip cookie. "Do you
both have something you can bring to him?" she asked Monica and
Jim. "It doesn't have to be great, he'll hate everything we say,
anyway."

"We have a ton of ideas." Jim nodded, chewing on his pen. "But
he's not going to like them. They're all lovely and charming, for one
thing."

"Today's not the day for creative joy. Just lay down and let him
bulldoze over us so we can get back to doing what actually needs
doing. I've got this. Maybe."

⋆ ˙ ✳ ˳ ✦ ˚ ✦

IT WAS NO real surprise that Christopher gave less than zero concerns to everyone's overly long to-do lists, arriving late to the meeting that he'd demanded before launching into a miserable tirade about performance reviews and verdicts on Lunar being a directionless mess, with a need for corporate thinking. He visibly enjoyed dismissing each and every new idea that was brought to the table, grinning with untouchable arrogance as he did.

"What have you lot even been doing lately? Not working hard, that's for sure. All I'm seeing is a load of hipster guff. We're trying to make money here." He sliced one side of his hand onto the other palm for effect.

"I don't know how many times I need to tell you," Belle said, trying to stay calm, "the reason Lunar has been a community favourite for so long is the . . . the magic of it. And you're stripping every last bit of that away. The value is in the details that we've created, the special feeling when you walk through that door. Everything that you're dismissing."

"The only value we need to worry ourselves with is financial. You're already on thin ice, Blackthorn. Do not push me." Christopher pointed at her.

"Christopher, these are beautiful ideas and good investments," she argued back. "Violet would love them."

"My mother is not in charge anymore. I am."

"We're adding to the wonderful experience of getting lost in Lunar. It's supposed to make you feel something. It's supposed to take you somewhere when you step inside. They're supposed to feel—"

"Blackthorn, this is your last warning."

"But if you'll just think about—"

"Enough!" he roared, adjusting the cuffs of his stretched shirt. "I don't know who you think you are today, Belle, but I would like to remind you that I am your boss, and you need to learn to shut up when I tell you to."

The room fell silent. Belle pressed her lips together firmly. Hot tears prickled at her eyelids, threatening to show themselves in front of everybody. She picked at a cuticle mercilessly to distract herself and avoided glancing at Monica and Jim, who were both determinedly trying to catch her eye for some silent reassurance.

After wasting their precious time for almost an hour, Christopher left the room with a sniff and a "Back to it." He flipped open a pack of cigarettes as he shoved open the front door.

Belle speed-walked to the toilet before she finally let herself buckle. She angry-cried into her sleeve, digging the heels of her hands into her eyes to try and curb the onslaught. She'd be okay. Just a quick meltdown. Then she'd be fine.

She leaned her head on the toilet roll and let out a tiny exhausted roar of frustration. At Christopher, of course, but also at herself, her fight with Ari, this entirely terrible day. She was just so tired, and she didn't know how to cope with everything going wrong around her, whether magical or mundane. A shiver travelled down her back, fingertips tingling from picking at them insistently during the meeting.

There was a knock on the door.

"Mon, I need a minute. I'll be out in a sec."

She'd steal back her moment of solitude when she got home. Except she wouldn't be home for hours because she was heading straight to Quill Lane for Clairvoyancy study. Relentless. She wiped hastily at inevitable mascara trails, although they were probably the same colour as the dark half moons under her eyes, anyway.

"What happened?" Rune was sitting on the sink when she emerged. He sprang to his feet and came closer when she looked up, revealing tear-stained cheeks and puffy eyes. She noticed him flare, as though to control himself.

Belle was too tired to wonder why on earth Rune was in the

toilets at work. She didn't even have a snarky comment to offer about it. She sighed with acceptance that, of course, a warlock watchman was hanging out in the loo.

"What are you doing here?" she asked emotionlessly. Despite herself, she was pleased to see him.

"I told you I was upgrading the connection after what happened to your mother, keeping a closer eye. I knew something wasn't right."

Belle nodded with flat acceptance. She rubbed at her damp face.

"Why are you crying?" he asked gently.

"It's not a magic thing."

"Doesn't matter. What is it?"

"I've made a mess. Of literally everything."

"You're doing just fine." He reached out and wiped a tear from her wet cheek with his thumb. Both of them froze, taken aback by the gesture. He cleared his throat awkwardly.

"Sorry. Don't know why I did that."

Belle shook it off. "It's my arse of a boss. He's generally quite awful."

Rune flared another breath. "This is who made you cry?"

"Yes. It doesn't matter. It's a regular occurrence."

"What did he say?"

"The usual. He hates everything that Lunar is supposed to be. Despises everything that would add to the magic of it. Thinks I'm an idiot but also happens to call on me for anything and everything that ever needs doing to cover his own back. I don't think I've ever met anyone who disrespects women like he does, but he seems to hold a particularly special place in his heart for me. Anyway, do you need something? I've got a lot to do before I can go back to Arty's place." She couldn't have sounded more done with everything, resigned to being miserable for the rest of time.

"Where is he?"

"Arty?"

"Your boss. The guy who made you cry. Where is he?"

Belle looked at him blankly. "I think he's outside smoking. Why?"

Rune held her gaze for a moment longer. His expression stayed a picture of composure, but Belle noticed his jaw muscle tighten the tiniest amount. His fingers flexed, and a dusting of sparks fell from the tip of his thumb before he turned and exited.

"Rune?"

He didn't respond, simply carried on walking at a fast pace through the back of the shop and out onto the floor, the tail of his coat flying out behind him as he swept past the cookery section and down the spiral staircase at breakneck speed.

"Rune. What are you doing? Wait, hang on a second." Belle tried to keep up, grabbing her jacket frantically from underneath the till on the way through. This could not be good. Monica and Jim watched their boss sprint, with no explanation, hectically after an extraordinarily handsome, furious-looking man in a long leather coat.

Rune smacked the front door open with the palm of his hand before he took a moment to find what he was looking for. It didn't take long. Christopher was on the phone roaring with laughter, plainly and loudly discussing a woman standing only a foot away on her own break, who looked distinctly uncomfortable. He momentarily paused laughing, bemused as Rune approached.

"Nice coat, mate. You on your way to a séance? Bit of grave-digging, is it?"

Rune offered him a dry smile. "Christopher?"

Belle, catching up, reeled backwards from the scene and darted into the second-hand clothes shop to hide behind a display of fluffy Afghan coats and watched through the window, not daring to follow in case Christopher spotted her and connected her to Rune.

Christopher sneered. "Maybe. Who are you, mate?"

A second passed in what felt like slow motion. Before Belle

could take a single step to stop him, Rune threw a clean, solid punch effusively into Christopher's left cheek, smacking the cigarette from his mouth and colliding directly with the bridge of his nose. There was a crunching sound as it connected. Bystanders gasped, pointing at the scene while keeping a safe distance. Christopher whimpered, cradling his broken nose, hunched over in two to cower away. Rune, shaking out the hand that had thrown the punch, shook back the hair that had fallen in his face to regather his composure.

"If you ever make her cry again," he said simply and slowly, "if you dare to even darken her day in any way . . ." He swallowed the end of his sentence.

Christopher nodded frantically, clearly clueless as to who Rune was talking about. Holding his bloodied knuckles, Rune calmly walked away.

"Haven't got a clue, have I?" Belle heard Christopher roar down the phone to his friend. "Some madman. Could be anyone." He gulped, dabbing at his mouth and leaving a bloody smear across his expensive shirtsleeve. "Could be a few birds. That one from last night, maybe."

Belle waited for Christopher to turn away before she made a swift exit, crossing the road into the lunchtime crowds and sprinting after Rune. She finally caught up with him, grabbing the back of his coat to spin him around.

"What is *wrong* with you? Are you completely and categorically insane? You just punched my boss."

"He made you cry," Rune replied, as if it were the most obvious thing in the world.

"Lots of people make me cry. I cry all the time! I cried at a donkey sanctuary advert this morning, are you going to punch everyone who mistreats donkeys?"

Rune raised a confused eyebrow. "I'd love to. And he deserved it."

"That's not . . ." Belle shook her head. "That's not the point."

"I could have done a lot worse."

It was true. It was a lucky turn of events that Rune hadn't decided to unleash any kind of vicious hex or nefarious curse instead of a swift punch.

"And am I supposed to thank you for that?" she shouted, disbelieving. "You can't just go around punching people who make me cry. Why do you care so much?"

"I'm supposed to be protecting you."

"From dark magic! Not from my boss when he embarrasses me in front of my colleagues. That one is for me to deal with and me only." She flared. "My non-wicche life absolutely does not need a watchman."

Rune looked taken aback for just a fraction of a second. "I see. Of course it doesn't." He was about to say something more, then thought better of it. His expression darkened. "Won't happen again."

"Right. It won't." She nodded. "Now I have to go in there, get back to work, act like everything is normal. Oh god . . ." Realisation dawned on Belle's face. "I bet Monica and Jim saw me legging it after you."

Rune didn't reply, busy examining her face with his gaze.

"You look exhausted. I'll make you something again to help."

"Why does everyone feel the need to keep telling me I look like garbage? I don't think I need any more of your help, especially if this is what it looks like." She gestured to Christopher, now on the inside of the shop window with two pieces of tissue stuffed up his nostrils.

Rune swallowed, then nodded slowly in defeat. "Fine."

"I'm sorry that all I seem to do is ask you to leave me alone, but once again, please, can you leave me alone? I'll summon you if I need you."

"But we agreed . . . You're not safe."

Belle turned to leave. "Oversee my lessons with Artorius, if you must. But that's it, no more involvement in my life." She had a final cross thought. "And don't use magic to transfer away, there are too many people around."

Rune shoved his hands deep into his pockets and gave her a quick, sullen nod. "You got it." He walked away with his head bowed.

23

Earth Sorcery

SLEEP HAD MADE things feel a little brighter, but the constant coat of worry that Belle wore across her shoulders still felt too big, uncomfortable to carry. Falling out with Ariadne made everything feel entirely wrong. It hadn't happened for years. The wine and snacks had tentatively repaired things, but an uncharacteristic awkwardness lingered between them and refused to be batted away. The feeling that yes, they'd both said they were sorry, but neither side entirely took back what they'd said. Something had changed—and stuck.

At work, Christopher wound his neck in a little more than usual but played the sickly sweet victim who insisted on buying sandwich platters to thank everyone for their kindness after his unprovoked attack. Meanwhile, she managed to cobble together excuses with Monica and Jim, explaining that the man she was sprinting after across the shop was a supplier who'd brought the wrong cover design for an upcoming launch party. Monica asked whether she had a number for him because she might ask him to after-work drinks next week.

It was her mentorship that pulled focus above all else, however, as the nineteenth moon dawned mild and milky, nestling itself snugly into a pocket of the sky for a long night of guarding everything below. Belle, tiredness now a fundamental feature of her personality, rested both hands on top of her head and took a deep, drained breath of frustration. The attic floorboards creaked beneath her feet as she rocked back onto her heels.

"It's literally impossible, there's no point. I can't do it," she whined.

"Stop that at once. You absolutely can," said Artorius, brushing off her defeatist attitude, as he did every time she expressed doubt in herself. They'd grown so used to each other's company by now that any need for politeness was long faded.

Tonight they had begun fresh work on Alchemy. It had been about as productive as a chocolate cauldron and considerably less delicious.

"We've tried. Over and over. And look." Belle gestured with indignant desperation at the individual-sized cauldron. "It's still a bowl of what is effectively soup with added crap chucked in. If this is magic, then my gutters are, too."

Belle peered back into the cauldron with a smidge of hope that it might have started doing something promising. "Minestrone." She grimaced. "Maybe we could try a different potion. How about a reviving brew, something for the tiredness?"

Artorius shook his head. "Perhaps not one for your current skill set. Revival potions are some of the most demanding brews and require immense concentration, real care and effort for prolonged periods. One has to be most dedicated to the potion to produce something successful."

Belle had no idea Rune had gone to so much effort for her. She was still furious with him but couldn't hold back a small secret smile at this revelation.

"Look at what you have managed to achieve already," Artorius reassured her, patting her arm cheerily. The warlock pointed eagerly to a piece of lined paper that he had pinned to the wall. He had carefully written out the six branches of magic and had triumphantly crossed out, in glowing ink, their first completed challenge.

With some help from Jinx, the pair had crossed off Animal Affinity from their lesson list in a matter of seconds, which almost made up for the lack of progress everywhere else. The grimoire had revealed the challenge the night before.

> Soul always borne to find its pair,
> Connections tied in knots of care.
> Through years of life, some pillars stand,
> Unyielding trust and love in hand.
> Familiar of thine greatest heart,
> N'er to unravel nor fall apart.
> Mammal, amphibian, reptile, bird,
> This magic beyond spoken word.

It was plain to see that she and Jinx were a natural witch-familiar pairing. The fact that the cat was never far away during Belle's practical magic was a sure sign. Jinx, who had been summoned to Quill Lane for the occasion, entirely refused to leave them alone to their work, and Belle had been close to several heart attacks just watching Jinx weave her way in and out of Artorius's elderly ankles— particularly alarming when he was stood near the attic stairs. Belle had managed some impressively speedy incantation work to change the wooden stairs into a bouncy castle, saving him from tumbling to his doom at the paws of her needy familiar.

While they tucked into boiled eggs with golden yolks and crisp buttery soldiers, she had shared stories of the cat headbutting her affectionately while she cried over heartbreak, how sinking her fingers into Jinx's fur always grounded her. She'd explained, aware that she sounded completely mad, that they understood one another.

Not that Jinx could talk or anything—that would be ridiculous. But her familiar was part of her. If soulmates existed, they were that. She knew they'd meet again next time around, every time around. They'd always find each other. There was no doubt about it, this witch and her familiar were kindred spirits.

"The reason that endarkenment occurs on one's thirtieth birthday is tradition, of course. But it's also more than that," Artorius explained to Belle. "After three whole decades of time, one begins to discover the pillar relationships that life has delivered for the long haul. Those precious folk who remain through all weathers, through all tempers. Those to be cherished, who make us feel more ourselves with them than when we are alone. Your mother is one. Ariadne, too, from what I have heard. And Jinx here is undoubtedly such a spirit."

The allegory had lit up as soon as Belle lifted Jinx to place a padded paw upon the page, and the sheer relief was a happy respite. It was when Artorius suggested they dip their toes back into Alchemy, with the second of the benevolent potions, that things had taken a turn for the worse.

"Maybe it makes more sense to cover more Earth Sorcery theory first and understand what I'm actually chucking in the pot before I start trying to combine all of this lot," Belle said in compromise while turning back to stir the soupy sludge.

"Very well. I'm sure your mother will be delighted that we are venturing into her specialist subject while she's here with us. I dare say it's time we checked on her, anyway," Artorius added, glancing at the face of the dusty grandfather clock.

Bonnie had slept in the guest room almost continuously since her vanishing a week ago, Wolfie guarding her bedside loyally and Jinx joining them when it suited her. The animals were surprisingly amicable with one another, Wolfie only occasionally accepting a perfunctory swipe to the snout if she acted in any way that Jinx did not approve of.

Bonnie promised Belle that she was now well enough to emerge, joining them as they convened in the living room. Under her arm, the elder witch gripped her own grimoire, the threadbare spine clinging on for dear life. Pages stuck out at every possible angle like a beloved family scrapbook, decades of learning gathered and celebrated, along with several ringed tea stains on the front cover.

"I haven't been this well rested in . . . well, probably thirty years, actually," Bonnie said.

Artorius slid himself from the plump armchair, patting Belle fondly on the shoulder. "I'll get the kettle on." He shuffled out of the living room, leaning on Wolfie as he went, who followed alongside for a guaranteed biscuit. As soon as he was out of earshot, Bonnie grabbed Belle by both arms and forced her to sit down on the sofa.

"I'm sure there's a million things you've been keeping from me." She spoke quickly and a little fretfully, scanning her daughter's face for any signs that something might not be quite right. "How are you getting on? Are you okay?"

"Still no luck with Alchemy. I feel like my magic is . . . holding back on me?"

"If part of you is unsure of what could lie ahead with this, then it's bound to affect your craft," Bonnie said thoughtfully.

"But it's almost the other way around. My instinct truly believes that I'm safe. You probably think I'm mad for it, but I know I'm not at risk from Artorius and his magic."

Bonnie hesitated, then gave a small smile. "I happen to agree."

"You do?" Belle glanced up from picking at her fingers.

"Funnily enough, yes. I worry about you incessantly. It's my job and has been for three decades. But it only took a moment of being in this house to feel that you're . . . meant to be here. The care, the loyalty . . . it is palpable. That man is not the monster that Selcouth has believed him to be, which is confusing . . . but reassuring."

Belle felt instantly soothed. "I mean, how could anyone be scared of that?" She jerked her head towards the kitchen, which was currently echoing with the dulcet tones of a warbling old man singing a power ballad and harmonising with Wolfie's howl.

"This whole situation continues to grow stranger by the day, darling. But we know that Selcouth is overseeing. I know Cas wouldn't let anything that didn't follow the rules go ignored, for one. And there's that watchman of yours."

Belle instantly felt her face flush and tried to play off her embarrassment. "It's reassuring, I guess, to know that he's around."

"Rune Dunstan. Nice lad, handsome." Bonnie pursed her lips tightly, attempting to keep a straight face. There was that frustrating, knowing glint in her eye which appeared whenever Belle so much as mentioned someone of the opposite sex.

"Stop. If you utter one more word, I fear I may die right here on this couch."

"I won't say a thing!" her mother replied indignantly, hands to her chest in surrender. A rattling tea tray emerged from behind the door.

"Ladies, I apologise profusely for the interruption." Artorius, pink bobble hat first, poked his head into the room. "I will adjourn to the attic and meet you there. I've also whipped up some rather good eclairs, if that bribes you at all . . ."

"I have never known someone to have such a constant supply of cakes in my entire life. It's impressive, Arty."

"We'll be right there," Bonnie told him kindly as he began ascending the stairs with a full orchestral soundtrack of groaning floorboards, rattling teacups and his own vocals.

"Allow your magic to lead the way, Belle," Bonnie said, turning back to her daughter with eyes radiating her signature soft kindness.

"I know that may feel like an unnatural, confusing challenge when you're so used to letting your logical non-wicche side take over all the time. But just this once, try surrendering to it."

✦ ˙ ✳ ˙ ✦ ˙ ✦

"EARTH SORCERY: TO be at one with nature itself."

Belle and Artorius were seated in what had become their designated chairs while Bonnie took centre stage in the attic. Rune, much to Belle's mortification, had joined the lesson as planned. She'd assumed that their argument would have left him sulking, but he'd transferred just as he said he would. They said a curt hello, Belle immediately busying herself elsewhere, and he parked himself in the bay window after a formal introduction with Artorius, both men equally wary of the other. Belle was surprised that Artorius perhaps seemed the more antagonistic of the two, eyeing up his new acquaintance with the look of an untrusting, overprotective father. Even if he was almost a foot shorter.

"Watchman, eh?" He peered over his glasses. "A fine job you seem to have been doing, young man, looking after our girl."

"With respect, we have no idea what we're up against. There's only so much protection I can . . ."

Belle rolled her eyes. "Ignore him," she told Rune.

Artorius shot her a mischievous wink and hissed a laugh.

"To understand the power that it holds in a curled-up fist." Bonnie spoke loudly, reclaiming their attention. "And more importantly, remaining grounded in 'what will be, will be' and trusting that said ground carries us forwards. Remembering what really matters."

She picked at invisible lint on the sleeves of her top and cleared her throat nervously.

"Did you make a presentation for this?" Belle asked, amused by her mother adopting such uncharacteristic formality.

Bonnie shot her daughter a look. "As you know, because you are . . . well, my daughter"—she coughed nervously—"I specialise and always have specialised in herbalist magic. If you ask me, there is no greater power than that of the earth beneath us. The changing of seasons, volcanos, tsunamis, vast oak trees, the way the sky holds the weather in the palm of its hand . . . Nothing compares."

It was reassuring to be in the hands of someone so passionate as well as familiar. And now she had two of these figures in her life, the other one sitting next to her, listening in rapture like a proud grandfather. Gratitude sung loudly inside Belle.

"It's been a while, love, since we practiced the craft together. These days I'm more solitary than ever, got used to my own company when it comes to casting. So I'm sorry in advance if I'm a bit set in my ways," Bonnie rambled nervously.

Belle nodded over to the dregs within her cauldron reluctantly, and her mum edged over towards it. "Don't worry. Have you seen what I attempted earlier?"

"Heck." Bonnie glanced inside with a look of concern. "What on earth is that?"

"Not sure anymore. I think drinking from the Thames would be more appealing than this," Belle admitted glumly.

With a quick flourish of her hand, Bonnie vanished the remaining dregs. "Sweetheart, we can't all be good at everything the first time. Potion making is all about practice, practice, practice, which will probably make it *your* least favourite branch. But Earth Sorcery is the keystone to it, understanding your ingredients first and foremost. You wouldn't make lemonade without checking your lemons were all right. And this is your standard-issue individual cauldron, as you know. Tell me what you notice about the shape of it," Bonnie asked her daughter.

Belle looked at her blankly. "What do you mean?"

"What do you mean, what do I mean?"

"What *about* the shape of it? It's cauldron-shaped, isn't it?"

Both witches turned to shoot daggers as Rune snorted from across the room. He was listening in while investigating a selection of the jars in Artorius's collection. "Sorry," he muttered.

"If you're going to be like this, Belle . . ."

"I'm not being like anything! You're asking me stupid questions, Mum. It's the shape of a cauldron."

"It's round, Belle! Round, feminine, womb-like . . ."

"Womb-like? What are you on about?"

"Will you listen, please? Its curves and roundness are astutely feminine. It's symbolic of the vessel where life itself begins," Bonnie enthused.

"That is . . . actually very cool," Belle admitted, picking up a smaller cauldron in her hands from a cardboard box on the floor. The nicks and scrapes, the imperfections in the metal, the marks of the past, telling a story. She tried not to think about her own neglected cauldron back at the flat, currently holding the fittings for her juicer. "Message received. Respect the cauldron. But if I'm ever caught short, if I want to whip up a quick potion, and I haven't got access to an actual cauldron, can I use anything? A saucepan, a colander . . ."

"A colander? Really? A cauldron full of holes is just what you need," Rune scoffed.

Belle shrugged indignantly.

"Belle, will you please be serious?"

"I am! That was a serious question. Living with Ari makes it tricky to have bloody cauldrons lying around the flat. I'm not sure I can convince her again that they're candle holders."

"Actually, saucepans are fine," Bonnie relented. "A lot of witches favour them, in all honesty, for kitchen magic at least. No washing-up bowls, though. There's been some melting-based disasters that have not been pretty."

Bonnie emptied the contents of her handbag onto a nearby table. Mary Poppins sprang to mind as everything toppled out of the lining in a jumble. Among the chaotic debris, Belle saw a bunch of basil tied up with brown twine. A small jar of what looked like elderflower beside brittle stems of dried lavender, a scattering of squashed juniper berries, and a slightly droopy selection of rosemary, hellebore and gardenias. All of these, of course, were alongside endless receipts, two glasses cases without any glasses in them, some mints mixed in with a handful of loose dog treats and a couple of emergency poo bags.

"If they cart you off to an asylum one day after seeing what you carry around inside your handbag, I can't say I'll blame them," Belle said.

"This is just what I like to keep on me. You never know when the time might strike to put something together while you're on the move, so keep a stash of your favourites close to hand for emergencies. I've been known to brew up a potion in a department shop loo when needed," Bonnie said proudly.

"What? In the actual loo? Like the—"

"No, in the sink, you daft . . . Look, tell me what you recognise. Group them together by their qualities, we can begin to identify some purposes."

Artorius and Rune both wandered over in unison, quietly observing the two witches at work. Belle turned her attention back to the table for a proper look at everything that had cascaded unceremoniously from her mother's bag. Her rummaging noises made Jinx's ears scoot backwards horizontally in alarm.

"Mum, I mean this in the nicest possible way. I know it's important and special to you, but . . . you can't seriously tell me that these things all lead to healing or . . . well, anything at all. Other than compost."

"Of course they bloody do. What could possibly be more powerful than nature? Say you're out walking, and you're wearing those silly cropped jeans of yours. Why you're paying more for less denim,

I'll never know. But a stinging nettle catches your ankles. It's itchy, it's sore, it feels like it's burning. What do you do?"

"Look for a dock leaf."

Bonnie gave her daughter a smug, satisfied look. "Exactly. Nature heals."

To her surprise, Belle found that she recognised most of the chaos covering the table, with knowledge that had been long dormant and neglected. She began separating it into a selection of different small piles.

"Basil, gardenia, lavender . . . easy enough, they all pull towards love." Belle racked her brain for the dregs of past schooling in Bonnie's greenhouse. "Cedar and elderflower, healing. Juniper . . . cleansing, right?" She shot a look at her mum, who gave her a quick nod of encouragement.

A few moments later, everything had been arranged neatly.

"Not bad, darling. You're almost spot on with everything. There tends to be a lot of overlap with certain ingredients, anyway, different types of spells for different souls."

Belle beamed at the praise and noticed how good it felt to have these three encouraging presences around her.

"Now, how about we get the next of those blasted challenges lit up like bloody Blackpool, shall we, love?"

⋆ ˚ ✦ ⋆ ✦ ˚ ★

THREE MORE MOONS had passed with Bonnie nearby and still no satisfactory glow from the book. "Remind me what the grimoire says again?" she asked her daughter patiently.

Belle let out an exasperated sound like some kind of flattened frog. She knew the Earth Sorcery ballad entirely by heart:

> Beneath the ground, a warmth of riches,
> Hotter than the flames of witches.

A blaze that stills the breath to naught,
Drowning lest the mind is taught.
Fire to earth, earth to fire,
Create that which thy most admire.
Water to air, air to water,
Powers for the firstborn daughter.

Sitting on an old crate in the attic, she bent over to touch her toes, letting her head flop between her knees. Bonnie was walking continuous laps around the room, driving Belle slowly insane with the repetitive movement. Artorius was poring over a purple-bound book entitled *The Nature of Nature*. Rune was downstairs on the sofa watching late-night television after Belle stropped that his observation was off-putting and temporarily banished him from the attic.

"We are still no closer to figuring this one out. And will you please stop pacing before I rugby tackle you to the floor?"

"Sorry, sorry. It's the nerves, I'm a dither," Bonnie said, flapping. "We've addressed about every single possible plant, weed, tree, shrub, potted plant, cactus . . . Flora and fauna has provided nothing. I'm at a dead end."

"We have concluded that we must think bigger than the average spell jar," Artorius spoke up. "For one reason or another—likely the heritage of Earth Sorcery talent—the grimoire has decided that this particular challenge must be more . . . challenging."

"If I have to conjure one more ray of sunlight or emit one more rainstorm from my fingertips, I think I will probably surrender to madness," Belle whined. They had been attempting small-scale spellwork with sunshine, wind and water to grow plants more quickly, and she struggled with them all. It was soggy, muddy, grubby work.

Artorius suddenly exclaimed, looking up at the Blackthorns with an expression that indicated he had made an important discovery. "Look." He pointed to a particular page in his research, beckoning the mother and daughter to his side.

Calling for the elements relies on a steadfast belief that a witch is worthy of such potent magic. The dynamics of the elements being brought to hand, a power bestowed only upon a firstborn daughter, is almost entirely reliant on a potent confidence in her own deserving.

"That's it. That's what the grimoire is asking for. Earth, wind, water, fire, firstborn daughter . . . all there in the allegory," Bonnie said, referring back to the words of the challenge.

No one said anything for a moment.

"Well, how the bloody hell am I meant to do that, then? That's nuts."

"Now, Belle . . ."

"No, I'm sorry, Arty. But hanging out with the cat, fine. Done. Transference, I'll get there. Three benevolent potions, challenging but manageable. And now, suddenly I'm supposed to be harnessing all the elements at once? This bloody book is off its rocker."

"I don't know why your first instinct is always to assume that you can't do something," Artorius said, distinctly unimpressed.

Belle frowned back.

"I just . . . I just don't think I'm ready for that."

Bonnie and Artorius glanced at each other across the table and sighed in unison. "We'll return to Alchemy on a later occasion," Artorius said, sounding forlorn.

The morning's orange October light was splitting the sky like golden repairs for broken pottery. Another moon shrank back shyly, leaving Belle with only eight remaining before her return to Hecate House.

24

An Element of Chaos

IN A STRANGE and entirely unexpected turn of events, the twenty-fourth moon of October ended with her second glowing grimoire page.

Bonnie had finally decided that she needed to return home. Since there had been no further signs of danger, and now that she was back to full health, her little house filled with charmed treasures and trinkets was calling to her (although she confessed that Artorius's apple crumble and velvety custard may have been enough for her to move in permanently).

Having reluctantly said goodbye to her mother and Wolfie as they vanished into the night, Belle took a quick snack break with Artorius, each armed with a bowl of chocolate cereal. Belle had almost choked at the sight when the grimoire page lit up before them, mid-mouthful. Evidently, the batch of flourish potion that she had spent the previous night bringing to a perfect simmer, along with a concoction of simple infatuation and the healing potion she had crafted for Bonnie, had scraped through the boundaries of acceptable as a trio of benevolent Alchemy work. The grimoire radiated the welcome warm light that she'd forgotten she was even waiting for. She and Artorius seized each other in a ridiculous hug, throwing cereal across the kitchen, and jumped up and down on the spot in a circle, clutching each other and whooping.

Artorius had sent Belle home a little early, deciding that a few precious hours off were well earned. A late evening at home, the rarest of treats, was so welcome that she almost cried when she shut the front door on the world and spent the hours with only Jinx and an enormous bowl of pasta for company. The one bittersweet note was the lack of Ariadne, who had packed her social calendar to stay busy. They were still avoiding spending their usual time together, each side overtly aware that things hadn't fixed themselves just yet. Thinking of the current gulf between them sparked a deep-seated pang of sadness in her chest that Belle tried to squash down.

There was a knock at the front door. In her last resort Christmas-print pyjamas, Belle shuffled to answer it in her slippers, with the cat balanced on her shoulder like a parrot.

"I went to Artorius's place, but he said you . . . Oh wow. Truly your best look yet."

Belle felt her face heat and the not-unwelcome pull of something at the pit of her stomach as Rune's dark eyes took her in from head to toe. She placed Jinx on the ground. The cat collected her head scratch dutifully from Rune and went on her way.

"Yeah, well, I felt festive."

"As is your right," he said with his usual tone of faint amusement.

"It's not like you to knock and wait patiently on a doorstep. Are you sure you don't want to launch through my window in the dead of night or appear at the foot of my bed without announcing yourself?"

"If that's what you've been waiting for, you should have only said."

She rolled her eyes, hand still gripping the door handle. "What do you want, Rune?"

"Well, I was going to give you these." A quick snap of his thumb and forefinger, and he pulled a bouquet of enormous butter yellow sunflowers from nowhere, a trail of golden sparks hanging at their stems like a ribbon. "Heard you passed your Alchemy challenge and wanted to congratulate the EquiWitch. But with a welcome like that, a man should probably take his congratulations elsewhere."

"Oh . . ." That was not the answer she was expecting.

"It was a stupid idea. Forget about it. I'll just see you—"

"Do you want to come in?"

Rune turned back, eyebrows raised, as surprised as she was that she'd blurted out the invitation. "Do you want me to come in?"

The silence crackled between them for a moment. Belle gave a quick nod, which earned a subtle but definite ghost of a smile as he headed inside. He offered the flowers to Belle.

"They're beautiful. Thank you. Wow, they smell like . . ."

He shrugged casually, returning his hands to his pockets as he followed her into the living room. "Toffee apples. It's nothing. Just a little incantation while I was on my way over. Not sure why I did that." He scratched at the back of his head awkwardly, letting out an uncharacteristically self-conscious laugh. "Where's Ariadne?"

"She's not home. We . . . had a weird argument."

"Sorry to hear that."

"Yeah. We'll fix it. It's next on my list of destruction to mend."

"So . . ." He looked everywhere but at Belle, then found her eyes. "It's only us."

"Well, apart from the cat. Yes. It's only us."

With the confirmation hovering in the air, Belle was acutely aware of the fragile inches of space between them. It would be easy to close the gap.

She couldn't.

"Can I get you a drink? I think we have wine or beer or tea or . . . A glass of . . . cold milk? Or warm, I guess." She swallowed hard, cursing herself for being entirely the most embarrassing person who'd probably ever existed. Catching sight of the embroidered elves on her sleeves didn't help. She tugged at the fabric, wondering why on earth she'd chosen to make today of all days laundry day.

Rune wandered towards the coffee table and picked up the small bottle of the palest pink liquid that Belle had set down when she arrived back from Quill Lane. A film of tiny iridescent bubbles coated the surface and fizzed expectantly.

"You're home-brewing now?"

"Oh, I should have put that away. It's nothing, it's from the trio of benevolent potions that finally led to some more grimoire success."

Rune held it up to examine closer, and it sparkled in an inviting way against the candlelight. "Looks like quality stuff. Where are the others?"

"Mum finished off the healing potion before she left, and the flourish potion is over there. I'm saving that for a rainy day," Belle said, her heart feeling a little jittery at the sight of him in her living room for the first time, like he belonged there. As though it could be so easy for both elements of her life to blend together like that.

She distracted herself by heading into the kitchen and making a cafetière, placing two cups on a tray. She hesitated, then topped up a little glass bottle with milk, pushed in the mini cork stopper and chucked some sugar into a bowl. Maybe an artfully draped tea towel for sophistication? Too much. Did he want a biscuit? She added three to a plate. At what point exactly she'd turned into her mother, she wasn't sure.

"Thanks," Rune said, giving her a half-smile. He was standing by the fireplace, examining the collection of photos in mismatched frames of Belle, Ariadne and their wider group of friends.

"Do you want to . . . sit?" Belle asked clumsily, gesturing to the sofa as she placed the drinks on the table.

They took a strangely formal, rather rigid seat next to one another.

"Coffee. Sorry. We didn't actually have any wine. Or beer. Or tea. But we always have coffee." Belle laughed breathily.

"No, no. Coffee is good." Rune nodded over-enthusiastically, the pair of them pretending that this was an entirely normal situation to have found themselves in. The cosy air of the room, lit warmly by the candles that Belle had been burning, seemed to crackle between them. "It's a nice place you guys have. I like the . . . furnishings."

Belle reached for the cups, pressed the coffee, and distractedly added half the milk to each. "Right. Who doesn't love furnishings? We're big on blankets," she mumbled.

Their eye contact caught, an almost magnetic feeling locking into place. Rune tore his gaze away, immediately looking anywhere and everywhere else in the room. They sipped politely, Belle desperately ensuring that no silence fell between them by rambling about the sandwich she'd had for lunch in extraneous detail.

"God, that tastes good. Ridiculously good. What is that?" Rune asked, after draining the last dregs of his mug.

"Just coffee. But you're right. It was *ridiculously* good. I didn't do anything different, I just . . ."

She glanced at their two empty mugs together, trying not to enjoy how normal and domestic the scene was, the two of them sharing cups of coffee. The sugar she'd brought through for them and the leftover biscuit. The little bottle of milk just to the right.

But she'd used the milk a minute ago, she'd emptied it into their cups. So why . . . ? Her hands flew to her mouth. "Oh no."

While the milk bottle remained full to the brim, she realised with abject horror that another little bottle just to the left of the mugs stood empty. Only droplets of candyfloss-coloured liquid, barely distinguishable from white in the low light, still clung inside the glass vial.

"What is it?" Rune paused, then swallowed, noticing the twin bottles for himself. "Oh no."

Belle swallowed. "Infatuation."

Rune's dark eyes widened comically. He glanced at the empty bottle, then back to Belle. "You have got to be . . . Why are you brewing infatuation?" He sprung to his feet, and she mirrored his move at the other end of the couch.

"Artorius said it was one of the easiest recipes for my challenge! Anyone can make infatuation for themselves, you can conjure it practically from nothing."

"I thought it was just light-heartedness or a good luck charm!"

She flared back. "Oh, forgive me for not baby-proofing the place. If you couldn't tell from the outfit, I wasn't expecting visitors!"

"Do you know how powerful infatuation is? And you just place it next to the bloody chocolate biscuits?"

"I was distracted! You being all large and overwhelming in my living room, turning up unannounced with big yellow flowers that smell all . . . nice. Maybe if you—"

"You're telling me we've both just sunk an infatuation potion?"

"Looks that way!"

"For someone who overthinks every possible element of life into oblivion—"

"You don't know anything about me!"

"I know enough!"

They had been taking unconscious steps towards each other. Their shoulders rose and fell in unison, both breathing heavily. The fire in the hearth crackled and popped against the silence, the energy between them echoing the sound. Suddenly, Rune's hand found Belle's waist, closing the already shrinking space between them. He tugged her sharply towards him as though it were instinct, as though he had to, as though he couldn't possibly contemplate her body not being pressed against him for a second longer.

His lips found hers, and Belle felt as though she would melt as her stomach flipped in an intense, tugging somersault. The kiss was all-consuming, the frenzied feeling of a forest fire ravaging everything in its wake. His hips fit perfectly flush against hers, he rolled against her as though to prove it, and a throaty, gravelly sound came from the base of his throat.

"It's the potion . . ." she whispered. She knew it, grappling for an ounce of reason or control but only finding need when his arms wrapped around her and his hands followed the base of her back.

"Just go with it. Do you want to go with it?"

"Yes. Definitely yes. Do you?"

"I've never wanted anything more."

Belle's hands moved to tangle in his hair as the kiss slipped deeper, Rune taking stumbling steps backwards towards the sofa as they collapsed onto it together without separating.

"I was wrong, by the way."

"About what?" Belle said breathily, leaning in against him as her fingers fumbled at the hem of his T-shirt, tugging it over his head as quickly as humanly possible.

"I don't know enough," he breathed back. "I could never know enough about you," he said, leaving behind slow, hungry kisses on her throat to linger and burn on her skin. "You're fascinating. And a wonder. And weird. And beautiful. And impossible. In the best ways I've ever known anybody to be. I want to know all of you. Everything."

His words buoyed her confidence beyond its usual remit. She threw a leg across his lap and his body responded, hitching her to sit just right as she straddled the thighs of his jeans. Belle felt out of control in her own body, like her instinct had been heightened to a level she'd never found before.

"Look at you."

The words caught in his throat in a growl as his gaze flipped between exquisitely soft admiration and a liquid, languid desire that she thought might just kill her. He held her steady on his lap, a burning friction palpable between them, thumbs brushing over the curves of her as his grip just below her ribs tightened possessively. Whatever magic was passing between them was a force to be reckoned with.

The tinkle of glass snapped their senses like an elastic band. As a cushion toppled from the couch, the small vial that had held the infatuation potion was knocked off the coffee table and smashed into an array of tiny pieces on the wooden floor. They both turned their heads to look at it, and it was as though they had awoken from a dream, reality barging into the scene. A spell broken.

What was she doing? If this was going to happen, she didn't want it to be because of a spell. She swung herself off his lap. Rune gave a sniffed half-laugh.

"That was some potion," Belle said, her voice sounding hoarse as her shoulders heaved and she caught her breath.

"Right. The potion," he said quietly.

"Amazing what some blood orange, rose quartz, ginger and vanilla extract can do together . . . Smelled like cake mix by the time it finished brewing. Good to know it works. I can't . . . I can't believe that just happened. Can you believe that? That's the worst possible thing we could have let happen." She gave a strained fake laugh and chanced a glance over at him still sprawled on the sofa.

His smile had fallen, the usual look of composure returned as he stared fixedly into the flames of the fireplace. He tugged his T-shirt back over his head. "The worst possible thing," he agreed quietly.

"Not our finest hour," she rambled, replacing the sofa cushions that had tumbled to the floor.

Rune studied her face for a moment. He shook his head, as though clearing his thoughts. "Totally. My bad. I shouldn't have . . ."

"No, I should have paid more attention. Whatever, let's not let this make things awkward, right? We're adults, it's fine. Let's just go back to—"

"Like it was before. You got it."

Neither of them moved, Belle standing with her hands on the hips of her Christmas pyjamas, Rune decidedly focused on spinning the ring on his thumb. He went to speak. "Belle, I . . ."

The house phone rang. "I'll get that," Belle said, overly shrill and smiley. "Hello? Belle and Ariadne." She shot a polite, strained smile over to Rune as he rose to gather his jacket.

"Belle, my dear. Glad I caught you before bed. I was just tidying up the ingredients that we'd left lying around the attic. Nothing to worry about, but I thought I had better let you know."

"What is it, Arty?"

"The vanilla that you included in the recipe for your infatuation potion. Please do pardon my mistake, but it transpires that the blasted stuff expired a good eighteen years ago. Luckily, the grimoire doesn't seem to have noted our error and your challenge remains successful, I suspect because it's no fault of your own, merely the supplies. But it would render the potion entirely a dud, with no effect whatsoever. Not that you'll necessarily be using it, but I just thought I'd better warn you. I'd stick to sampling your flourish potion, which will remain effective still."

Belle's face blanched as she shot a covert glance at Rune. She caught his eye and he immediately looked away, thumbing the side of his jaw. "Great, thanks for letting me know, Artorius. Good night." She hung up the phone.

"What was that about?" Rune asked dryly, hands buried back in his pockets.

She remembered where they'd been, how they'd travelled across her body. So it wasn't the potion. There was no spell at play, no magic to blame for the way they'd just collided—not that kind of magic, anyway. The feeling of being drawn to someone so acutely, so undeniably, was something that she had forgotten could exist. She had been purposefully pretending, convincing herself she was mad to think there could be something between them, but only because she had been afraid that she was wrong. Their connection had been something else that she was afraid of ruining, making imperfect.

She hadn't been imagining it.

That meant there was a conversation to face, one that she wasn't sure she was ready for, with everything else currently fighting for space in her brain. Worse still, what if he'd changed his mind now that she'd dropped the curtain, let herself be vulnerable enough to let him in a little more. He'd just admitted it, he didn't tell her she was wrong. The worst thing possible, he'd agreed.

Best to drop it, best to forget about it. She had to protect herself.

"Oh. Crossword answer," she replied.

25

Trusting Memory

BELLE AND RUNE had been sitting together in a cosy corner of Lunar Books for a while, just talking, tucked between the science fiction and the current charts, watching the sun come up through the shutters and in between the window pumpkins, lighting the pulpy carved faces.

They'd met outside her flat, the world wrapped in a scarf of October mist. He was leaning against a lamp-post when she returned home from Quill Lane bleary-eyed, reading a book she'd mentioned in passing a few mornings ago, she noted. It had felt a little too intimate to invite him upstairs after what had happened last time. Both were pretending it had never happened, and it felt a little maddening. She didn't like to consider whether the decision not to tell him the truth was the right one and equally didn't like to admit that she was growing far too fond of his company.

"There's not many people I'd sit in a beanbag for," Rune said grumpily.

"It's either these or the kids' chairs, and one of those is ice cream—shaped, so this is for your own dignity," Belle told him. She privately thought he looked adorable, his long legs bunched so that his knees were almost by his ears as he slumped against the yellow beanbag.

"I've been wanting to ask you, but I knew you wouldn't tell me the truth . . . How are you doing? You know, evidently being the target of dark forces and all," Rune said, concern clear behind his eyes as his brow furrowed.

"I'm doing okay, especially when you word it like that," she replied uncertainly, clutching the takeaway cup that he'd been waiting for her with. It contained good coffee laced with another batch of his reviving concoction, which had stopped her from feeling like quite such a creature from the depths and returned her to something that resembled a human being.

"Yes, it looks it," he replied with a raised eyebrow, gesturing to her fingers, which had been bitten to shreds over the past weeks, three currently wrapped in plasters and one bleeding onto her cardigan.

"Honestly, I'm fine. If we ignore the small matter of *four* grimoire challenges that still haven't lit, of course."

"Never mind the damn book," Rune dismissed.

"Easy for you to say. I'm not going through all of this for nothing. I've lost my best friend. I've all but lost this place." She jerked her head towards their serene surroundings. "I nearly lost my mum. I've definitely lost my mind, we can all agree on that. And I'm on track to lose my magic in a matter of days."

The admission brought out a hidden queasiness in Belle's throat, all the way down to the pit of her gut. She smiled weakly. "Did you speak to Bronwyn?"

"I did. She's furious. Mostly with me for letting you continue after the *Subfuror Incantare*," Rune said. "I have to tell you, she wants to pull you out of the mentorship—"

"Surely no one can make that call apart from me," Belle interrupted.

"If you'll let me finish," he said. "But I assured her that it was out of the question, that you weren't normally one to listen to anything as insignificant as logic or reason. And that you absolutely wouldn't quit the habit now."

Belle bit down on her lip to stop a grin. "Thanks for standing up for me."

"Anytime." Rune mirrored her smile. "She blames herself, I think."

"She just wanted the best for me. She couldn't have known whatever this is was waiting in the wings."

"Well, that's just it. The coven *should* know. The fact that Bronwyn and Morena are just as in the dark as we are is the most concerning part to me."

Belle glanced at him, unable to keep hold of the question. "What exactly do you think I'm up against?"

He sighed. "I'm looking into the possibility that it's an unknown. When things like this have happened in the past—it's rare, but it's happened—it's been a witch who hasn't disclosed themselves, looking to make themselves known. Living alone with magic, and without the support of Selcouth, must be overwhelming and terrifying at times. Makes people do strange things."

"How do we find them?"

"It's a big task," he admitted reluctantly. "But it's my main priority, my only priority. I've been working on tracing the source. It's how we trace the emergence of new witches who don't come through a family tree. There are systems at headquarters which allow for this kind of thing, but so far, I can't seem to make the spells extend their focus farther than Hecate House."

"I hope they're paying you handsomely for all this extra research to make sure I'm not hexed into oblivion. Unless oblivion happens to be all-inclusive? I could use a holiday." She smiled. "I'm sure you have plenty more important things to do."

He laughed under his breath, a look of sincerity falling across his face. "Belle, I don't know how many times I have to tell you. There is nothing more important to me than you."

She felt her cheeks flush and saw his do the same.

"For the remaining moons, I mean. While I'm on duty for you."

Her heart started beating again. "Right."

"It's my top priority to get you safely through this mentorship," he went on, nudging her foot softly with his own. "But there's still something we need to discuss in more detail. Artorius. You need to ask him about his past. Confront him."

Belle instantly prickled. "Confront him about what, exactly?"

"About all of this. Yes, as far as I can tell, there's no dark magic being *created* at his home, so I have to give him that. But evidently, it's drawn there. That can't be a coincidence."

"Even if it does turn out to be him, which it won't"—she interjected with a pointed finger—"what are you expecting from a conversation like that? 'Oh, silly me. You're right! I *was* trying to kill you! Caught in the act.'"

"I'm not expecting a confession, but it might make him stumble. It's arduous, knotty magic. We should be doing whatever we can to impede his . . . *their* efforts."

Belle sighed. "If I lose out on his apple crumble as a result, you owe me."

✦ ⁎ ⁎ ✦ ✦

ARTORIUS SPUN ON the spot and began rummaging through a packed set of drawers, lively contents bursting out the moment he opened them. "Now, *where* the cursed cat whiskers did I . . ." A silk scarf flew in one direction, a broken badminton racket went careering in the other. "Bingo!"

With a quick gesture of his palm, the old man tossed a pinch of deep purple powder into the sooty grate to prepare their Clairvoyancy lesson: the basics of flickering magic, pyromancy and candle reading.

Belle felt her stomach knot with dread. It had to be done. She steeled herself for her next words, grasping her own fists with white knuckles. "I need to ask you something, Arty."

It felt surreal, knowing she was about to confront it all. Artorius took a seat in the usual tattered armchair and cast out his palm, bringing forth an old wooden crate for her, which was stacked up in the cobwebbed corner. With another small flourish, he produced a cushion to place on top. The old man looked at her with expectant eyebrows, gesturing for her to take a seat.

"By all means, Belle. Questions lead to the most fascinating lessons."

Now that she'd started, she didn't even know what she wanted to ask. What was the next part of this conversation? "Firstly, I am so grateful that you have given me this opportunity. That you've opened your home up to me this way. But I have some questions about, well . . . about your past. The things that I was told by Selcouth about you."

Instantly, Artorius's face dropped. "Oh. Yes. Of course you do." He sighed deeply, removing his pink hat for the moment. Between his gnarled fingers, he began twisting the fabric, pulling at a loose thread. "And I shall explain everything, answer every question you may have. I regret bitterly that you have probably been fretting for so long now. We should have addressed this immediately, but I have shied away from it, too. I apologise for not being bold enough to confront the subject myself. Sleep has evaded me often this past month for regret that I had invited someone into my home without explaining myself."

Artorius looked even frailer and smaller than usual. His shoulders curled over like the edges of worn paper. He folded in on himself before finding Belle's gaze with a determined expression. "I am sure the coven spoke to you of why I have been banished from their world for so very long now."

"Yes, they did. Bronwyn insisted that I know the full history behind your banishment."

Artorius nodded. "She was right to do so. Without question. Knowledge is protection."

He turned his head with haste but wasn't quick enough to hide the tears that were gathering in his eyes. With laboured difficulty, he rose from the armchair and shuffled towards the round window, clearing the condensation with his jacket sleeve.

"My deepest shame. How you must fear me."

"I don't fear you, Arty."

It was true. She didn't fear the man in front of her, she never had done. But she did fear the things that Bronwyn had told her. She feared the magic that he'd once made, and the revenge, the jealousy that had fuelled his impulsive decision. Belle considered which truth it was that she wanted or needed to know.

"I'd like to hear your story straight from you. If you'd like to tell it to me."

Artorius nodded while staring at his slippers. He chuckled softly. "How I wish I could, my dear. I would love nothing more than to be an open book. But I'm afraid my version of events is a hazy one, to say the very least."

He gingerly returned to the chair opposite Belle and balanced his hands on the knees of his trousers. "Where to even begin?" His gaze was fixed on the purple fire as though it were showing him things, flames reflecting patterns of kaleidoscope amethyst in his eyes.

"As I'm sure you know, after my brother's death, I was held for questioning at Hecate House for some time. The days became weeks, the weeks turned to months, soon it was years . . ."

"Years?" Belle balked. She hadn't known he had been held at Hecate House for so long.

"A bleak time. The coven didn't know what to do with me. I was just a boy, really. I had lost the most important person in my life to terrible circumstances, and it seemed I was responsible for his death." His voice was soft and hoarse, catching in his throat. The old man's cautious choice of words struck her.

"'It seemed'? Do you mean you disagree that you killed your brother?"

"They told me I had murdered Savaric. And when I think back to that fateful night, I do indeed see myself creating the potion that killed him. Every night, even now, I see in my memory my own young hands reaching out and adding the cursed ingredients that would lead to his demise."

Artorius's voice was barely above a whisper. "But, it's strange . . ." His hands stopped fidgeting with the pink hat. He looked directly at Belle. "I have no recollection of performing the action itself, Belle. Never have done. That is to say"—he closed his eyes in confusion—"I could see the action taking place in my mind's eye, I still can see it happening. But I could never, and still do not, *remember* it happening. There is a dissonance between the two."

"A dissonance?" Belle leaned forwards. "As though the memory isn't right?"

"But they all told me that it was me who had killed my brother." The old man hesitated, confused. "So I believed them. I *must* have killed him. I could see the very moment that I did it playing out in my mind."

"I don't understand," Belle admitted.

Even Artorius was stumbling over his own explanation. He shook his head, trying to clear cobwebs of age. "I'm not explaining this too well, am I? It's as though . . . How do I . . . ? Ahh!" The old man snapped his fingers. "Those newfangled video cameras. I imagine your mother may have one, and so perhaps you've watched on film moments of your own childhood play out on-screen. You don't remember them happening yourself, but you see them on a television. You see them played out, and later it feels as though you *can* remember living them. They imprint on your memory. But really, you just see the image that was captured on your behalf. What you actually remember is the last time you remembered it. It is a trick."

Belle, with hesitant surprise, found she understood. "There's footage from my childhood that I've seen so many times, it feels like I remember it happening. But I've just watched the recording. I don't actually remember it."

Artorius nodded. "The truth of your past and constructed memories become blurred. What did you truly experience, and what do you merely recall seeing occur?"

She pressed on. "Do you think that maybe the memory is just confused after so long? Or are you telling me that you think Savaric's death was caused by . . . something else?"

Artorius sighed, staring deep into the fire. Belle knew that he was remembering his brother.

"I cannot say for certain. And I certainly didn't help myself back then."

"What do you mean?"

"Those dungeons were my home for years. I couldn't stand to be alone with my own thoughts anymore. One night, I broke out of the dungeons. And I . . . I cursed myself."

Belle's stomach shot up to her throat, then dropped to a plummet.

"I simply couldn't bear it anymore. Any wicchefolk who finds themselves in true despair can summon a different type of power from within their soul. They probably won't even know they're capable of such a caliginous force until it happens. It's known as *Tenebrae Obscurum*. And on my escape, I hexed myself. I wiped all recollection of losing Savaric from my own mind, too painful to keep reliving over and over."

Belle was frozen with horror, hanging on his every word.

"At least, that's what I tried to do. The hex went wrong, of course." His usual chuckle was laced with melancholy.

"I was young. Much younger than you, Belle. So unskilled with magic, it was entirely unrefined. My curse merely blurred the memories rather than removing them entirely. So now, I remember the feelings and the pain as if it were just yesterday. I remember the loss and the grief and the sorrow. But not the true recollection of the action in the moment."

There was nothing that she could say. Belle found that she believed him entirely. "Artorius, I'm so . . . But if you even *suspected* that it wasn't you who killed Savaric, why didn't you stand up for yourself? There must have been another explanation. You were so young, and they just accepted it, closed the book on you. Where were your parents?"

"My father was already gone; my mother quickly followed Savaric, unable to cope. No one at the coven wanted alternative possibilities. Savaric was the answer to everybody's prayers for Selcouth. He was the future of the coven, the warlock with the talent and charm everybody was seeking after years of turmoil. Bitter grief makes rash decisions. It also sealed my fate."

The fire crackled and spat out a rain of angry violet ashes, scorching the floorboards before they extinguished themselves.

"Grief made my own decisions, too, it is a powerful guide. If it meant that my brother could rest peacefully, I was willing to accept the blame. And besides, I could not confidently say that I hadn't killed him, either. Truth potions and revelation spells to reveal my mind's eye . . . I can see the memory itself, so they all showed the fateful moment during questioning."

Artorius's voice trailed off as he got lost in thought, remembering and remembering.

"Arty, we have to tell the coven," she urged. "We should tell

Bronwyn, she'll listen." Belle stood up, ready to travel straight to Hecate House with him in that moment.

Artorius extended a grateful smile but shook his head. "Too much time has passed and, I would wager, only fed the growing legend of my actions over the years. Besides, my memory curse still hangs over me, even now. It was a dark, messy curse. I still can't tell the truth of it."

"We could reverse the curse?" Belle said hesitantly, not having a clue what she was suggesting. "If we used both of our magics together, and I could bring in my mum, too, for—"

Artorius held up his hands to stop her, grateful but decided. "I am afraid to lift it, if the truth be told. Afraid of what I might uncover, and now afraid of what it would do to my body in my old age. My dance moves may suggest otherwise, but I am in fact a rather old man," he said with a smile. "Besides, I am content with my quiet life. I've long let go of the need for answers. I keep to myself, I note the birdsong in the mornings, and I wait for a quiet death with the open arms of a friend. When the time comes, I'll see Savaric again, and the truth will be known to both of us."

A silence fell across the attic, billowing between them like soft fabric. Artorius's gaze remained on the flames in the fireplace, dancing as a gentle night breeze carried in between the roof tiles.

"I must make another confession to you, Belle."

She stiffened, steeling herself for what else he could possibly have to share.

"My magic never left me."

Her brow furrowed. "What do you mean?"

"My banishment from the coven didn't entirely work as they planned. In my research since, I have uncovered that it may have been a result of incomplete endarkenment. As my powers weren't fully instated in the first place, the coven's attempts to strip me of them didn't work. It's why I have been so eager to remind you that your magic is yours and yours alone, no matter what the judgement of others may declare, even if you did neglect it somewhat prior to our adventures together. I have retained my magic this whole time and have quietly practiced my craft ever since."

She'd known it deep down, really. That such skill and knowledge couldn't be from tomes and scrolls alone. He'd shown her so much first-hand experience of real magic, and now it made sense. It plagued her with sadness to think how he had kept it to himself for such a long time.

"Not entirely a surprise, honestly, Arty. I saw the spatters on your Alchemy pages and knew they weren't Bolognese." She laughed weakly. "I do believe you. Just so you know."

"You may be the first, Belle."

"But please hear me out. I still think we should speak to Bronwyn. She was so patient and understanding with me. I can't believe she wouldn't be willing to at least listen to you after all of these years."

"Nonsense. The sage witch of the United Kingdom's esteemed coven? She has better things to worry about than a disgraced old man who doesn't deserve the chance. I wouldn't trouble her for it. I appreciate your kindness more than words can say, but my day has long passed, Belle. Now, we must turn our focus to you, for this is your time to shine."

He hesitated a moment, then spoke again.

"Admittedly, when I received the letter from Selcouth informing me of my selection for mentorship, a part of me did dare to think that perhaps . . . Perhaps if we were to succeed in your endarkenment, they may take a new moment to consider my fate."

This was not just about her own future, her own second chance. It was his, too.

26
The Flourish of Fate

HAVING A SECOND completed challenge in her grimoire had proved a temporary joy for Belle. Rather than victory, it now felt as though it only served to highlight the fact that four remained unlit, and only a handful of moons remained. There was still so much to do, to resolve. And she still felt a constant tickle of uncertainty that something else was distinctly and absolutely not right. While she tried to rationalise her situation—Rune was on guard at all hours, Bonnie and Artorius were both highly vigilant to her welfare—it felt as though she were subconsciously picking at a cut that would heal over during the day while she was preoccupied with other stresses but then split open again as she peeled away the worries each night. The most pressing of these being the very real possibility that she was in great, far-reaching danger and therefore bringing everyone close to her into harm's way, too.

Ariadne remained her chief concern. Although standing outside her office with a boom box wasn't entirely out of the question, it should probably be a last resort. While they were technically friends again, the smiles were too polite, the conversation stiff and entirely unlike them. They'd barely said a comfortable word to one another since their fight, their usual secret language swapped for perfunctory comments about heating bills and a leaking tap. Belle had knitted a quick *Exsarcio Lavatio* fix for the latter to try to do something nice for Ari, even if it was only grout-related. Her determination to try again with another apology was brought to a halt when Ari left a curt note on the fridge (no smiley faces or kisses, which said it all) to inform her that she had headed up north to see her sister. Belle hadn't called, considering that it was perhaps for the best that Ariadne *was* away for now, kept far from the danger that Belle seemed to be inextricably linked with.

Ariadne being absent, although gut-wrenching, did make things a little smoother for Belle. She could let her magic wander freely, sweet starry flickers of it wafting through the flat at any given moment. Non-wicchefolk barely ever noticed the visible traces of magic, almost always too distracted. Ari had only ever spotted it once or twice over the years, blaming it on standing up too quickly, sunlight reflecting or having something in her eye. But it certainly made life easier for Belle to not have to second-guess her instincts. Alone, it bounced from the lamps, circled the doorways, gathered in the corners. It clung to her in wisps and radiated from each nerve, and it felt freeing to allow it that liberty, a state she had never existed in before. After three weeks of mentorship, dedicated to herself and her potential alone, Belle noticed that, although faint, she had begun to develop the same glimmer of warm gold around herself that she always admired around Bonnie. Rune wore it, too, so had Bronwyn and Morena and every member of Selcouth. Belle's magic was beginning to come alive again.

On her way out the door, the windows aglow with a hazy orange, Belle was wrapping a thick striped scarf around her shoulders when she stopped short. Her flourish potion. She'd forgotten all about it, but the small flask of iridescent treacly mix seemed to wink at her in the light: a brew specifically to bring temporary extra sparkle to one's life, the kind that makes everyone around you simply have to comment on how there's a glow about you. To drag boldness and braveness to the forefront, for confidence and contentment to shine through. A luxurious, indulgent spell for shining and star quality, if only for a little while. Artorius had encouraged her to take it as a celebration when the Alchemy page declared her success, ignoring Belle's suggestion that he keep it instead.

"Absolutely not, my dear. I have been feeling enough of a flourish to my life of late. Two new friends to my name, three if you count the lad, although I'm not sure he'd admit to being my pal," Artorius had told her. "Your sparkling company to look forward to each day, the pleasure of watching your magic blossom so confidently. My luck is already redeemed thrice over."

Not waiting to second-guess herself, Belle unstoppered the bottle, savouring the zingy, sunny flavours of citrus fruits, rhubarb and custard, a fine dusting of aventurine. It fizzed ferociously as she drank. She hoped that it would kick in full throttle before she headed back to Quill Lane and boost her chances of a third glowing grimoire allegory that evening, but maybe it would come in useful before then, too.

✦ ˙ ✳ ˳ ✦ ˙ ✦

LATER, BELLE BEGAN to question whether the ingredients for this one had also been a couple of decades past their best when her shift at Lunar took a turn for the worse. Christopher, ignoring the fact that she was mid-recommendation with a customer, had summoned her to his office.

"You're pushing your luck at the moment, darlin'. Now, I don't want to have to report it to Violet, my suspicions and all." Christopher tapped his pen impatiently against the Filofax on his desk, one leg resting on the other thigh. "But it was out of order to take time off. I'd expect it from the weekend kids, but I thought you knew better than to try and pull one over on me. You left me high and dry. All for some guff story about your mum, who's suddenly, miraculously, fine now, is she? Funny that."

Belle blinked. The man was not normal. "Sorry, can you say that again? I thought for a second you were accusing me of lying about my mum nearly dying."

"I'm not saying that, I'm not, I feel for her, I really do." Christopher threw up his hands in feigned innocence. "I just think it's very convenient that it all kicks off on the days that you knew would leave me stuck here. I break my back doing everything around here while you lot swan in and out as you please. It's like you don't even care about the place."

She was squeezing her fists so tightly that her fingernails stung against the skin of her palms. She could feel the prickles of magic ready to burst, settling into the lines of her hands.

> Conviction in thy words must hold,
> Speak a truth that's brave and bold.

Something went off like a firework in her mind. Something flourished, a fizz in her chest. Without allowing her brain to connect too many pathways together, to contemplate what she was about to say and what the reality of it all would mean for anything else, a decision fell into place. It took hold, brave and bold.

"You know what, Christopher?" Belle stared him down, even dared a little airy laugh as she looked at him with pure contempt. "It's been a joy and a pleasure getting to know you, and as always your company leaves me feeling as though I might profusely vomit at any moment."

That made him look up from his pager.

"But I quit. That's it. I quit."

A look of utter confusion dawned on his sweaty face. "You what?"

"We are done here," she said, perfectly calmly. "I have officially had enough of being treated like I am some insignificant child who is lucky to be running around after you, picking up all of the slack that you drop, when in fact I am far more capable and skilled than you could ever possibly dream of being."

Christopher snarled. "Is that right?"

"It is. I've got . . . conviction in thy words—I mean, my words. I deserve better, I deserve more. You can expect my resignation letter tomorrow."

"You can't . . ." He barked a laugh. "You can't quit."

"Yep. I can. I absolutely can," Belle said, surprised to find that it was, in fact, true. Of course she could. She'd figure it out. She always did.

> Be thy assured all shall be well,
> A fortune magic cannot tell.

"It's either leave this place of my own free will, right this moment, or launch myself into space if I have to stay here under your revolting, beastly presence for even one more hour. So I quit being any part of your soul-destroying plan to turn this beautiful gem into a despondent hell-hole with immediate effect and wish you all the luck in your future endeavours at being the most first-class, unpleasant maggot to ever walk the planet."

Christopher spat as he spoke. "You haven't got another job lined up, so you can't quit. You can't go anywhere. And I won't be giving you a recommendation after this little tantrum display, you can be sure of that."

"Actually, I don't need anything from you. In fact, I'd worry about your own job, if I were you. But while we're on the subject, should I ever need a reference, you'll be giving me the most radiantly glowing recommendation that the book world has ever seen, having done your job for you for the past three years. Otherwise, everyone you've ever worked alongside will be hearing in great detail about the abysmal way you treat every single woman you encounter, all of them with more talent in their little finger than your entire loathsome being."

Christopher's face turned such an alarming shade of cardinal red that Belle faltered for a second, wondering if her words were causing serious health problems. "Belle Blackthorn, if you walk out of here, you will never set foot through that door again, not if I've got anything to do with it."

"Luckily, I wouldn't count on you having anything to do with it for much longer. Toodle-oo!"

It was only once she crossed the threshold of his office and stepped back onto the floor of Lunar Books that Belle sunk under the weight of what she'd just done.

"Belle, are you all right? Maybe you should sit down . . ." Monica gulped, craning her neck around the Stellar Reads to see her boss sway on the spot, clutching her suddenly very sweaty forehead.

"I think I might be sick," Belle said.

The thought of leaving Lunar behind, of feeling it fade away from her like the last moments of a firefly, was too much to bear. But there was another way, if she could just hang on to this new-found bravery. She could keep the firefly safely in her pocket, bring it back to life, if only she'd allow herself to try.

✦ ✦ ✦ ✦ ✦

"VI, IT'S ME. I think it's time. I mean, I know it's time. I want to buy Lunar Books, like you've always said I should. You were right. We're supposed to do this, I'm supposed to do this. I have so many ideas . . . It's going to be . . . Well, call me when you get this. Okay, bye. I'm excited. Bye. Bye bye bye."

Belle left her convoluted, chaotic message on Violet's answering machine and promptly bit down on the phone cord like a feral dog, the pumping adrenaline still coursing through her. Along with the flourish potion, which must still be streaming through her veins; otherwise, she'd never have been able to take the leap of faith she had today.

But . . . Belle tapped the phone against her chin as a confusing thought popped into her mind. She'd tried magic for bravery and boldness before, every version of it under the sun when she was younger. Those times had even showed up in her manifests for Selcouth—how she'd left herself bruised and battered with desperate attempts to change who she was, trying to rush something that wouldn't come. And they'd never, ever worked. Only reminded her of everything she felt she should but could and never would be. So what made this spell different?

Of course, she'd learned a lot more magical theory since then, and this brewing had been under Artorius's expert guidance. But she supposed potions couldn't work to change a person fundamentally. Magic couldn't manipulate a person's make-up or change who somebody really was. That was impossible.

The difference was that this time, she was ready. She was ready to receive it, to be bold and brave, and to flourish by herself. In fact, she already was. She just had to keep going, full speed and pedal to the metal, and in four moons, she'd have her decision from Selcouth.

Whichever way it swung.

27

Solanaceae

SOMEWHERE IN THE timeline of the night, when the sky was at its richest shade of inky black, Jinx leapt from Belle's chest with such a start that it broke her deep sleep. Belle slid her bedcovers back up to her nose. Her heavy lids shuttered closed, but she was woken again when the cat let out a low, yowling growl of unease. Belle growled similarly in annoyance, leaning up onto her elbows to see what all the fuss was about. Zoomies, probably. It was so pitch-black outside, a thick blanket of night laid down across London, that she had to squint to even make out Jinx's fur in the darkness. Her annoyance became dismay when she saw the cat's drastically arched back, the fully fluffed tail that showed high alert.

"Jinx? What have you got there?" Belle asked in a voice thick with sleep. "Please, not another mouse. I can't do that again." She'd given up on trying to catch the last one somewhere behind the dishwasher and the washing machine.

She clicked on the bedside lamp and jumped as the light threw a jagged shadow against the wall. Just a trick of the light. Nothing was there, but Jinx remained in a fearful, sharp arch. Belle rubbed at her eyes.

"Jinxy?" she beckoned.

The cat continued letting out a low hiss, her stare transfixed on nothing at all, staring at the wall. Sometimes it felt as though she could feel things that Belle couldn't, and it always gave her the creeps. Belle rolled her eyes in drowsy discontent, flicked the light back off and yanked the covers with her as she turned away. But seconds later, Jinx was growling again, her tiny voice more and more high-pitched, sounding strained and defensive against the silence. Belle let out an exasperated sound, on the edge of irreparably waking when what she needed most was a good night's sleep.

"Jinx. Shut. Up." She yanked the light back on again.

A sparking of pinpricks slithered up the back of her neck. She threw a hand towards it to scratch, but the sensation spread like wintry running water across the wings of her back. The feeling travelled down her arms and her chest, icy cold and burning at once. She kicked at the suddenly unbearable covers and reached across the bed to turn the light on but realised she'd only just done that very same thing. The power had cut out. She heard Jinx's claws skitter on the floor as she bolted from the bedroom.

Belle's stomach gurgled angrily, a flash of knotted pain. Hot prickles covered her entire body, her breath quickening as she touched the back of her hand to her forehead, to find beaded sweat beginning to trickle at her temples. She tried to bring herself out of the lull, to drag herself to the bathroom to splash her face, but a deadening pull towards sleep wrapped a tight fist around her.

She eased herself back down against the pillows, trying not to panic as her breathing became more and more shallow. And then a sudden pressure. Against her sternum and her collarbones. She willed her legs to kick, her arms to push, but she couldn't make her body obey her thoughts. Something pushed down firmly on her chest, feeling so heavy that she thought her ribs would crack.

A figure, somehow darker than the darkness. A faceless, shapeless figure, who was at one with the shadows themselves, outlined only in the faintest touch of moonlight, watching from the foot of the bed. The blur of shadows pinned Belle down into the mattress, crushing her, enforced control on every part of her body other than her mind. Her mouth filled up, tasting of darkness and dirt and clogging earth, choking as she chewed on shadows. She felt it make a nest in her ribcage, settle itself as though it would never leave, and she heaved a final, fighting breath to surrender to it.

A burst of sparks so blinding that Belle felt as though it scarred her eyes.

The pressure relinquished. It flowed away, slow, controlled, the darkness pooling down her body and slinking away from her. The light beside her snapped back on as the power returned.

She gasped for air, convulsing upwards in a jolt. Her eyes were watering, tears carving their way down her face.

She began to focus and readjust, to register reality again.

Rune was there. He stood over her, chest heaving, one fist clenched tightly around a mason jar. Inside it, the lid firmly bolted shut, a pitch-black substance churned and roiled like a storm cloud and molasses, which seemed to be fighting against the glass to break out.

After a moment, allowing her to find control of herself again, wipe her face on the duvet, swing her legs over the side of the bed to bring herself upright, he spoke calmly.

"You're okay. Easy, don't get up."

"What was that?" she spluttered, her voice full of fear.

"Night terror," he replied softly but matter-of-factly, only seating himself in the armchair just across from her bed when she seemed to steady a little.

"No. No, that wasn't just a nightmare," she said. "That was real."

"I never said it wasn't real." Rune had just about caught his breath back, slumping against the chair himself. He seemed shaken. "I came as soon as I sensed it. I thought I wasn't fast enough. I saw this vision hanging over you, a black cloud, an ink stain, a . . . I thought for a moment I hadn't been quick enough." He exhaled to steady the slightly frantic panic in his voice. He frowned as he glanced inside the dream behind the glass, evidently disappointed in himself that he hadn't unravelled the strange spell sooner. He stowed the dark jar away in the inner pocket of his coat. It vanished swiftly.

"I could feel it, I could feel them, sitting on my chest. Jinx knew, she—"

"I know, I know. I was here the moment I sensed it, I promise. It was so difficult to unravel . . . Taking dreams away should be child's play. Hey, calm down, all right? Take a moment."

Belle steadied herself, reaching for the glass of water that Rune conjured for her. She took a long, deep drink, feeling it soothe her rasping voice. As she placed it down on her bedside table, it clinked against an empty mug.

"Your coffee consumption is concerning," Rune said with a half-smile, nodding at the cup.

"I had a hot chocolate before bed, actually," Belle said indignantly, rubbing her fingers against her bruised throat as she swallowed. "Artorius had me reading auras all evening. I needed little marshmallows. And then . . ."

Rune eyed her. "And then?"

"I added the last dregs of the flourish potion."

Rune's eyes pinched. "May I take a look?" He stood to take a step closer, then hesitated for a second, wondering whether their proximity was okay.

"It's fine. You're fine." Belle gestured him closer. For the first time, she was truly grateful for their protective arrangement. He picked up the drink from her bedside table, holding it towards the lamp for a better look. He brought it to his nose and instantly recoiled.

"Well, that explains the night terror. Belle, what the hell is this?" He sounded baffled. "Are you for real? You could have killed yourself."

"What?" She snatched it from him. A faint smell, but once she'd noticed it, it sent her reeling. Overbearingly sweet, turned thickly rotten, a putrid, carrion combination. "Oh my . . . What *is* that?"

"Poison, sitting pretty on your nightstand. Enough to make you hallucinate to hell and back, to literally scare the life out of you."

Belle's eyes widened. "Poison?"

"Solanaceae, if I'm not mistaken. Deadly nightshade. Ironically, commonly known as belladonna . . . You seriously drank this? No wonder it took hold of you so deeply," he said incredulously.

"Yes, but . . . Rune, I swear, that wasn't the potion I brewed. It can't have been. I took most of it this morning and it was good. It worked. Even the grimoire said so."

"Then it's *Subfuror Incantare*. Interference with your magic from a distance again. This is worse than I thought. Count your lucky stars that you drank most of it before it had been tampered with." He sounded entirely disbelieving, as though it couldn't be real. "Your own brew tampered with extra ingredients added by transference. It's highly illegal, against every Selcouth rule imaginable, it's . . . Who did this?"

"Well, I don't know, do I? Maybe it was Christopher." She offered a watery smile.

"Will you stop turning everything into a joke to try and distract me from seeing that you're scared? As if that buffoon could have anything to do with this." Rune was growing visibly more frantic, beginning to pace the length of her bed as he tried to think.

"Oh, please don't start pushing your hair back *angrily* now."

"You've been poisoned, Belle! By your own magic, no less. Manipulated by someone else!"

A momentary silence hung between them. Once the quiet

allowed her mind to form its own real thoughts, she knew what she needed to say. "I don't think I can do this," Belle said in a small voice. Her shoulders were slumped, exhausted. "I thought I could, but I can't."

Rune sighed. "Sorry. Sorry. I just . . . I should be able to see exactly what this force is. Exactly who is hurting you. It's driving me insane that I can't stop it. I'm trying so hard to protect you. I'm not sleeping, I'm working around the clock, and nothing's working."

"It doesn't matter. Whoever it is, whatever it is, they can have what they so clearly want. It's done. I quit."

"Belle, you're so close."

"I'm not, though, am I? Arty and Mum keep saying things like that to try and make me feel better, but I'm not. I still have four challenges unlit in the grimoire. Four in four days. Even I'm not delusional enough to think that sounds doable. But that doesn't matter now. I can't keep putting myself through this."

"But your magic . . ."

"I love being a witch, I love my magic. The past few weeks have brought some of the greatest joys, seeing it come back to life. I thought things had changed today, I thought I'd turned a corner but . . . this isn't worth it. I'm losing it. Every day, something else seems to disappear from me."

"May I?" Rune gestured to the bed and took a seat on the mattress when she nodded.

"If Ariadne had been here tonight," she continued. "Imagine what could have happened. It's probably putting you in danger, it's probably putting Artorius in danger, my mum, even the coven itself . . ." She felt her bottom lip quiver; it made her feel like a child.

"The coven is not your responsibility."

"But it is, if I'm the one bringing danger to its doorstep." Belle pushed her hair out of her face, still clinging from the sweat that had beaded at her temples.

Rune reached out to gently tuck it behind her ear. She sighed, eyes closed.

"I've made up my mind."

Rune was thoughtful for a moment, searching her face. "The watchman side of me wants to tell you that, honestly, maybe it is the best decision. The most sensible one, at least." His dark eyes were locked on hers, trying to read her. "But as your . . . friend, who's been witnessing your magic bloom, despite all of this, I can't support you giving up. You're meant for this."

For a second, she faltered. But it didn't last. "I'm sorry, but I don't need your support. I choose to protect everyone. It's obvious. I'll go to Artorius in the morning and tell him, and then I guess I'll have to inform Hecate House to surrender my powers formally. This isn't meant for me."

Jinx peeped a head around the door-frame. Sensing that the coast was clear of all threatening shadow forms, she curled back up on the duvet, satisfied yet looking distinctly unimpressed that a large man seemed to be taking up her usual spot at the foot of the bed.

"What a fat lot of good you were, oh brave guard cat," Belle said.

A thought occurred to her. "My sooth stone. It seems to like letting me know whether my decisions are good ones or not. It always glows whenever it's trying to encourage me one way or the other. It can make the call for me. Maybe it was trying to protect me from . . ."

She reached into her bedside drawer and fumbled around the contents, sliding aside painkiller packets, bookmarks, a biscuit wrapper. Her brow furrowed. She summoned a light cast from her finger, guiding the torchlight around in the darkness, checking behind the table and underneath.

She glanced back at Rune. "It's gone."

28
Scrying Not Crying

BREAKING THE NEWS to Artorius that she intended to end her endarkenment was, categorically, one of the worst moments of Belle's life. The look on his face was one that would never leave her.

She and Rune had debated back and forth intently on the matter for the majority of the morning. With Belle unable to sleep again, Rune had insisted that he accompany her to Quill Lane. He made coffee the non-wicche way while she showered and dressed in an attempt to reset her mind, and she was slightly alarmed to discover that the calmness of his quiet, companionable presence was, in fact, extremely comforting. He had, however, refused to take the bus as she normally did, absolutely mortified by the idea. Instead, he reached for her hand for an instant transference to the doorstep of Quill Lane, only dropping it, Belle noticed, when Artorius opened the door.

"Belle, I implore you to reconsider. So far in our time together, your magic has shone in more ways than I care to remember," the old warlock lamented. "It is with the greatest regret that I think of your magic being relinquished to Selcouth—particularly when you have been unjustly backed into a corner by fear."

It was unfair. Belle agreed on that much, as did Rune. The mood quickly soured further with the news that her sooth stone had vanished, taking away the level of protection that it had guaranteed until then.

Artorius clasped Belle's hands between his own, pressing them together. "I beseech you, do not give up on yourself." She noticed that tears were springing in his brown eyes, and the sight made her own fill almost instantly. This man, whom she had grown so fond of in their time together, had an unwavering kind of faith in her that she'd known once before, from her grandmother. The feeling tugged at her, the closest she'd come to changing her mind.

"Artorius, I . . . I just can't. You saw what happened to my mum. I'm putting everyone I love in danger. And now that my stone is gone, there really is nothing standing between me and whatever force is at play."

"Your affinities, your incantations, your intuitions, your readings . . . more so, your nature. Belle, you are destined for magic," the old man insisted.

She wasn't, though. Not anymore. She was no longer all of the brilliant things they had once viewed her as. Remarkable was not for her. "I can't do it, Arty. I'm all burnt out. The magic isn't there anymore."

Artorius was silent. He patted her hands with the gentlest of touches, his thin, papery skin around hers. "The decision is yours, my dear. But allow me this. One more lesson, just one more." He continued before Belle could protest. "I was up all night deciphering the grimoire Clairvoyancy challenge, and I suspect I may have cracked it. Allow me this one final chance to teach you one more lesson before your magic leaves you."

"I don't—"

"Trust me," Artorius urged. "I think you will find an honest kind of magic in it."

After much persuasion from the old warlock and also from Rune, who partially encouraged and partially made things worse by reminding her that she had nothing left to lose, Belle agreed to one final lesson. She insisted that it was pointless, that it would be her worst yet. Artorius reassured her that it was always worth a try and simply to trust him. Of course, by now, she did.

He guided her to a small spare room, one that she'd only poked her head into for a curious glance, holding a single bed with an iron frame, a flowery cover and a handful of crocheted cushions. The only other furniture was a small dressing table, surprisingly ornate with carved drawers and small glass handles. Atop it sat a dusty tabletop mirror, framed in tarnished gold details that twisted into small roses.

Belle took a seat in front of the mirror as instructed. Artorius lay the grimoire down next to it and reopened the heavy book to the page revealing her Clairvoyancy challenge. The paper had a ghostly feel to it, unearthly illustrations of clocks and faces that seemed to blend into one another with their own haunting accord.

> That which lies behind must stay
> Forgotten, buried, earth decay.
> Though time be oft a fickle thing,
> The past a lighthouse for to cling.
> Refine thy senses for the task,
> Speak words of peace in thine contact.
> Sooth a babe with placid milk,
> For what's to come unfurls like silk.

"Scrying. A technique of mind-bending and meditating to alter consciousness. All you have to do is speak the incantation and focus your mind just beyond the surface of the mirror. All being well, you should slip somewhere else. It is nothing to be feared," Artorius told her, leaning over with a reassuring hand on her shoulder.

"Kind of a scrying-not-crying mentality?" she asked with a reluctant sigh.

"Good luck, Belle," he said quietly, backing out of the room and clicking the door shut behind him.

She read the allegory again, the cogs in her tired brain starting to whir. It wasn't until she reached the end of the page, flipped over to the next and back again, that she noticed a small pair of words which had been scribbled in haste by the old man's almost illegible scrawl.

Mihipte Solacium. My own solace.

He had left the incantation and translation for her. She spoke the words aloud.

Nothing happened. She leaned towards the scrying mirror, glimpsing herself through the thick dust that covered it. She wiped it quickly with the end of her sleeve, dust lacing together and falling onto the table like snow. Now she could see her face properly, blotched red with tears from the night before, shadowed with tiredness that hadn't lifted since her birthday. But past all of that, she just saw herself.

"Mihipte Solacium." A little louder and bolder this time, trying the pronunciation as best she could while her line of sight drifted to something farther, something deeper.

The mirror rippled, casting iridescent rainbows so bright that Belle had to shield her eyes against the glass. The moment she removed her hand, the picture changed. She still recognised the reflection, but it was a person who she hadn't seen for a very long time.

Belle locked eyes with her younger self. Not a day over sixteen, judging by the questionable haircut, the black eyeliner, the full freshness of her face. In fact, she recognised the moment to an exact pinpoint, because it was one that she'd seen only recently. One of the earliest of her manifests, from her trial at Hecate House all those weeks ago, when she'd first practiced light levitation with Jinx. A mirror had been opposite her as she sat cross-legged on the floor, and now here she was, watching from the other side of that glass. She thought back to the moment now and had hazy recollections of a short conversation breaking up her practice. The memory felt like shattered glass fragments; she couldn't remember who she had spoken to. But it had bolstered her at the time, she knew that much.

Her shy younger self shifted her gaze awkwardly, not one to start a conversation willingly. Belle knew she had to take the lead but could barely bring herself to say a word.

Speak words of peace in thine contact.

"Hi."

"Hello," her younger self replied shyly, untucking her hair from behind her ear to let it fall around her face, an extra layer of protection between her and the world. Belle's heart leapt. They could communicate.

"Wow, this is . . . This is very weird. Do you . . . know who I am?"

"You're me in, like, thirty years," the teenager replied matter-of-factly, shrugging as though it was the world's most obvious scenario.

Belle tried not to be offended. "More like fifteen years. But yeah, I am. And you're me."

"Right." Her reflection fiddled with the stack of bracelets on her arm.

"I . . ." Belle swallowed. "How are you?"

Her younger self frowned. "All right. Surely you know how I am?"

"I suppose I do. Although it feels like a long time ago. I remember, though." They glanced at each other nervously through the glass. Older Belle added, "I think I'm supposed to tell you what things are like for us now. You won't remember this later. Knowledge gained from time-bending spells doesn't stick to the past, but . . ."

"I don't think I want to know if it's bad. Is it bad?"

Belle shook her head. "It's not bad," she said gently.

Seeing her younger self look right at her, full of apprehension for the future, was overwhelming. She felt an all-consuming protective-ness towards the girl in front of her, a longing to make her believe that she really was okay. She wanted to tell her that she was every-thing, every single thing that she needed to be. Belle felt her voice break.

"You're so ready for the world," she whispered.

Her younger self frowned again. "You're not doing a very good job at reassuring me that everything is going to work out, if that's what you're here to do. I thought scrying would be all fun and mys-tical."

"Sorry, sorry. This isn't about me. This is about you," Belle said. "What do you want to know? You can ask me anything, I'll be honest."

"Um, what is it we do?"

"What do you mean?"

"Well, we ended up doing something cool for a living, right? That's all anyone ever talks to me about. What I want to do, what I'm going to be. So I'm hoping the plan worked out?"

Belle tried to remember what the plan was but couldn't remem-ber ever having one. There must have been one, at some point. "We own a bookshop. Almost. I hope. It's small but cosy, and covered in wisteria in the summer, and the leaves turn fiery orange in the au-tumn. And it's in London."

"We live in London?" Her younger self gasped, the first clear, pure excitement breaking through the façade of downplayed reactions.

"Right, I should have led with that." Belle laughed to herself. "Yes, maybe not quite as glamorous as it sounds to you right now, but yes. We did that part, with Ariadne."

"That's cool. And what about the rest?"

Belle opened her mouth to answer but realised she wasn't en-tirely sure what to share. Perhaps the majority of it was best left unsaid. Seeing the girl in front of her now, there was only one thing that she really wanted to make sure that she did say.

"I don't think I'm supposed to tell you everything that happens, it doesn't feel right. But what I will say, what I feel I need to say to you, is that I'm so sorry."

The girl looked back at her. "For what?"

"I let you down, I think. I'm so sorry I haven't done any of the things you wanted to do."

Her younger self looked taken aback. "Like what?"

"Well . . . I'm not married. I don't even have a boyfriend. I don't have any children. I'm not particularly successful, whatever that even means. I'm definitely not rich or famous."

Her reflection was quiet for a moment, chewing on the inside of her cheek, picking at a cuticle. "But . . . are we happy? I don't mean, like, now. Obviously you're not very happy right now. You're ugly-crying," she said, awkward again. "But are we . . . ? Are we happy? And are . . . Are we loved?"

Belle felt a heat inside her chest, swelling against her ribs. And she didn't even hesitate with the honest answer. She nodded. "We're so loved."

"We have people around us who we love, too?"

Belle nodded again.

"And Ariadne?"

"Still here. Still our best person," Belle said.

"Then everything will be okay?" her reflection asked.

Belle took a moment, blowing out a steadying breath. "Everything will be okay. I promise."

Her reflection gave a sheepish smile. "And how's the magic? What have we done with it?"

"Funny you should ask. It's a long story, but today is my last day as a witch."

"What? How could you? My magic is the only good thing about me."

"Are you . . . Are you kidding? Belle—wow this is weird—but Belle, listen to me. There are *so* many good things about you. You're trying your best literally all the time. You're always thinking about other people and trying to make everybody happy. That's so kind of you, do you know that? You're putting insurmountable pressure on yourself to constantly be perfect, to be impressive and amazing, and you're taking it all on the chin. You're such a good person."

"I'm not," her reflection replied quietly, back to picking at the skin on her fingers. "Nothing I do is good enough. Everyone is ahead of me, everyone is doing better things."

Belle sighed, her heart breaking as she realised that her younger voice was still so loud. She still felt the same things, even now. She wanted desperately to reach out and hug the girl, make her feel enough for anybody who really mattered.

"Listen to me. You've done so well, love," she went on. "You're doing so well. There will be things we can't do. There will be things we hope for that don't happen. We can't do all of the things, every time, all at once. But it always works out, and you're not a disappointment. Happiness is waiting for you, I promise."

Her younger self looked back at her doubtfully but nodded after a moment. "Can I ask you for one more thing?"

"Of course."

"Please try and keep hold of our magic?"

Belle swallowed hard, shoving down what felt like a rock in the middle of her throat.

"It's so beautiful." Her younger self laughed as kitten Jinx reached up from her lap to headbutt her chin. "I don't want to lose it."

She was right. How could she let this go, forever? "I'll try, for you. For me."

Her younger self nodded, satisfied with the answer.

Belle nodded back the very same way, and before she could say another word, the reflection turned back to dust-covered glass. Back to herself as she was now.

She hadn't left that version of herself behind. Her fears ran deep. But so did her magic.

She started. A sudden light from underneath her left wrist, leaning on the open grimoire page, beamed like a golden aura. The words of the allegory glowed underneath her arm, sunshine itself come to guide her the right way forwards. The grimoire declared her Clairvoyancy challenge to be her third success. She had gained what she needed from the spell—more than she could possibly have imagined that she'd need.

She opened the bedroom door to find Artorius and Rune both waiting on opposite ends of the landing, Artorius jolting backwards from very obviously having his ear pressed against the wood, a water glass still in his hand like an old-timey sleuth.

She eyed him suspiciously. "You knew that was going to happen, didn't you? That my younger self would persuade me."

Artorius shrugged, scuffing the toes of his slippers together. "Might have had an inkling."

She rolled her eyes and turned to Rune. "He told you all about his cunning plan?"

Rune smirked. "We both had a feeling that it was only ever yourself who would be stubborn enough to persuade you."

29

Just Us

ARTORIUS APPROACHED THEIR final branch of lessons with renewed levels of enthusiasm that even he seemed surprised by. Belle was reminded of a child who'd been left to their own devices with a bag full of trick-or-treat sweets. Three challenges remained, as did three moons, including Halloween. It was almost, but not entirely, impossible. While they were all too aware that the grimoire remained frustratingly unlit for the allegories of Earth Sorcery and Incantation, there was one branch of magic which they had yet to approach: Necromancy.

The art of communicating with the dead was the branch that Belle had, understandably, been most wary of. Rune had double-checked immediately that she wasn't confusing things with necrophilia, which would have been an entirely different issue altogether. She had made it clear that she simply couldn't shake the images that immediately sprung to mind: zombie eyeballs falling out of sockets, pirate hats crumbling on skull and crossbones, witches performing unspeakable acts in graveyards (too close to home). Artorius did his best to convince Belle that these assumptions were entirely Hollywood.

"You're being ridiculous, young lady. You know as well as I do that any form of reanimative Necromancy, resurrection, weaponising the dead, etcetera, was absolutely stricken from the code about a hundred generations ago."

"Weaponising the . . . I miss the bookshop," Belle said under her breath.

"No plans to raise an army of the deceased anytime soon?" Rune asked, busying himself with some form of Selcouth paperwork, which he had summoned to get on with while Belle and Artorius launched into their twenty-ninth moon of study.

"Maybe Wednesday," she replied.

"It's frustrating how popular culture tends to tar all Necromancy art with the same brush these days. It's always killer zombie this, contacting demonic presences that. Hell forbid it's ever considered astral art anymore, never sympathetic magic . . ." Rune said, muttering to himself.

"Go on, Grandpa, tell us more about the good old days," Belle replied.

"Pop down to the study and find my notes on death magic, will you, Belle?" Artorius asked. "They're in a small pile on my desk somewhere."

She headed downstairs to the study, knowing full well that the "small pile" he referred to was actually a chaotic spread of loose pages, jotted notes and half-filled notebooks covering the whole office, with little to no organisation system. She began rifling through the papers, looking for anything that might specifically reference chatting to summoned souls or catching up with the dead. Noticing the words "under the umbrella term of 'spirit,'" she lifted up a small paperweight on top of a large stack of files to reach for it.

She froze. In her hand, she held a small crystal pebble, like a shard of stained glass. The paperweight was full of inky colours, slowly moving and swirling inside, smoke behind glass like tiny storm clouds gathering.

For a moment, a feeling of dread leadened her insides. Why was her missing sooth stone in Artorius's study? She snatched it up, examining it so closely that she felt her eyes cross. No, it wasn't her sooth stone, something wasn't quite the same. It was almost identical in shape and style, but it was mirrored, the intricate carvings made in the opposite direction to her own. The colours, the nature of its movement behind the glass, was the very same but twinned.

"Did you get lost along the way?" Rune leaned around the door. "What have you got there?"

Belle spun on the spot to face him. "Is this what I think it is?"

Rune held out his hand to take the stone from her. He examined it closely, turning it over in his palm. "A sooth stone. I didn't know the old warlock had one. Funny, it looks—"

"Just like mine?"

Rune nodded, looking every bit as baffled as Belle. "It was just sitting there next to his pen pot, being used as a bloody paperweight. But there's no doubt about it, right? That's a sooth stone. Or have I crossed the bridge to full-on insanity?"

"If you're there, I am, too. And there's absolutely no question. This sooth stone is the other half of your own. There are some wicche family sooth stones that are all connected, chipped from the same larger piece of glass, for example, or carved in intertwined designs that fit when they're placed together. Often, you'd never notice the connection unless you examined them together very closely. It's a neat design choice."

Belle nodded. "I've noticed before that the patterns in mine are similar to Mum's. And now . . . Artorius has a third Blackthorn stone? What does that mean?"

"I can't be certain." Rune shook his head. "Unfortunately, I'd wager that the old man's backfired memory hex may get in the way of us finding out."

Belle raised her eyebrows in surprise. "You know about that?"

"We talked. Last night. While you were in the midst of the Clairvoyancy incantation. I pressed him on whether there was anything he knew, anything at all about the trouble that you've been facing. We started from the beginning."

Belle was taken aback by Artorius's honesty with Rune, then realised that he was willing to share his story whenever anyone cared to ask. Perhaps, up until recently, no one ever really had.

"He wanted me to know everything so that we can best help you together. Unfortunately, with his mind as it is now . . ."

Rune was right. There was no chance that Artorius, his memories in hexed heaps of ash and dust, would have any answers as to how a Blackthorn sooth stone had ended up on his desk.

"As his mind is now . . . Interesting . . ."

She sprinted towards the stairs, taking them two at a time. Rune chased after her, still clutching the stone.

"Artorius!" Belle shouted as she tried to catch her breath. *"Mihipte Solacium!"*

The old warlock didn't even glance up from his page. "Hmm?" he asked, pointing his chin towards Belle in the attic doorway but continuing to read.

"Mihipte Solacium! Solace for oneself! You need to make contact with your younger self. Before your curse took hold. Reaching out to young Artorius can give us the answers we need."

He reluctantly put down his reading. "Belle, I told you when we spoke of this. I have long relinquished the need for answers to my past. They are for me to find in the next life."

"Then what about *my* past?" she asked adamantly.

This caught his attention. His head turned to see Belle take the stone from Rune and hold it out towards him in the palm of her hand. With difficulty in his creaking bones, Artorius rose and scuffed his slippers towards them. "Whatever did you bring that old thing up here for?"

"Don't you see? Don't you see what this is? Artorius, this is a sooth stone almost identical to my own. It must have come from the same family collection as mine. Why do you have this? Where did you find it?"

Artorius gazed at it in wonder, reaching out to take it from Belle into his own hand. Instantly, it reacted to his touch, the smoke inside bending to new shapes. He gasped. "I haven't, I didn't, I . . ."

"Artorius, you have a Blackthorn family stone. Or maybe I have a Day family stone? Whatever. Whichever. We need to find out why. We need to ask your past. It's time we all got some answers."

⋆ ∗ ⋆ ∗ ⋆

WITH AN UNDERSTANDING that partaking in the Clairvoyancy enchantment would benefit Belle, Artorius swiftly obliged, but not before insisting he make them dinner first. Knowing him well by now, Belle could hear the undercurrent of fear in his voice, the cooking of roast potatoes a distraction to hide the slightest dulling of his bright cheeriness. "You're sure you don't mind us being here for this? It felt like quite a private experience for me yesterday," she asked, when he could no longer avoid the task at hand.

The old warlock tried to remain as enthusiastic about the situation as ever. "Belle, you know what my mind and my memory are like. If we are to discover anything under *Mihipte Solacium*, it's best that there are alternate witnesses. Of course, we can't be sure what the spell will actually show us. Scrying is an unpredictable art form. The words *Mihipte*, 'to myself,' and *Solacium*, 'comfort, relief, solace,' are not indicative of providing the same experience for every witch," Artorius explained.

"Like we said, Mr. Day, anything that you find too upsetting, too hard to see, just say the word, and I'll unravel the spell," Rune added, watching from a distance.

"When you're ready, Arty," Belle said encouragingly. She patted the old man on the shoulder, and he rested his hand on hers in return.

"*Mihipte Solacium.*"

Just as it had done for Belle, the mirror rippled and roiled with an incandescence, a force like a wave emitting over Belle and Artorius, who sat side by side at the dressing table. While one single silhouette had appeared in the mirror for Belle, this time they watched as a whole scene appeared, forming from undulating glass into slowly identifiable shapes. The reflects of light swirled in billows and finally settled into a picture.

*. *. .* *

TWO BOYS SAT opposite one another at a wooden dining table made crudely from splintered planks. The room was a modest family space: seven chairs around the table, the last of the embers in the fireplace, hand-sewn curtains hung, remnants of little lives together scattered around the room.

"You're so lucky, Sav."

"It's not luck, little brother. There's a divine reason that I was firstborn. My very soul was manifested for this purpose before I even arrived onto this earthly plane. It was destined to be."

Belle tore her gaze away to glance at the old man next to her, to check that he was okay.

Letting out a whispered "Oh!" he was enraptured by the scene inside the mirror, his eyes already pooling with tears that reflected back the rainbow light. His frail hand reached out a few inches, as if desperate to return to the scene that cradled his older brother alive and well.

"I think destiny made a mistake. Why not me? I could do it."

Savaric laughed. "Because, Arty, *you* were destined to be *my* little brother. And I am to lead the whole of Selcouth and continue father's great leadership. Maybe even improve on it, truth be told.

There's a place for you, too, of course. I have plenty of ideas for the coven. How we can improve our strength, how we can build our magic even further."

"Sounds boring."

"Boring?" The older brother rocked on his chair, balancing on the two back legs. "And what would you do with it?"

Artorius shrugged. "I don't know. Something wicked, something fun. Decree that our house has to be a castle with a moat and a draw-bridge. Make sure that everybody could conjure the perfect treacle tart before being accepted into Selcouth. Transform all wicchefolk into dragons."

"I'm not sure about the rest, but I rather like the dragon idea." The older boy leaned back farther, swinging his feet onto the top of the table and crossing his arms.

⋆ ˟ ⋆ ⋆

THE SCENE CHANGED, and Belle was surprised to find that it was one she had visited before, in words. The story that Bronwyn had told her; the Day brothers gathered around a cauldron, brewing the potion that would soon lead to Savaric's tragic demise. She heard a soft sob from the old man next to her and placed an arm gently around his bony shoulders to hold him.

"I cannot . . . I cannot watch."

"Artorius, look. It's okay." Belle encouraged him to look back to the mirror as Savaric and his younger self left the bubbling caul-dron, and the barn door clicked behind them.

"Mr. Day, remember, it's a benevolent spell. It won't show you the . . . the moment you lost your brother. Only comfort, or the an-swers you're seeking." Rune spoke softly as he watched from a polite distance.

Belle gave him a thankful look over her shoulder.

Artorius steadied his breath and nodded, glancing back up to the mirror just in time to see the colours swirl and change.

✦ ✳ ✦ ✦ ★

BELLE PREPARED HERSELF for the worst, prepared to see a young Artorius filled with rage and jealousy emptying spearmint, ash, fireflies, black salt, without care or consideration into the cauldron. She could have been wrong this whole time, been strung along yet again.

But it never came.

Instead, two girls appeared.

Belle gasped.

One was older, around twenty-five, pretty with her hair in a neat plait and scarf. The other was a little younger, awkward and slightly lanky, although with immaculate curls. The older girl was desperately attempting to comfort the younger, trying and failing to wrap her arms around her, but only soliciting greater fury in response.

"Get off me! Don't you see? Everything is broken, everything is ruined."

The older girl rushed forwards again. "We're still a family. You and I can rebuild for the others, we'll take care of them. We have to look out for each other now. Otherwise, we'll never get through this loss."

"You always say that, that we have to stick together and look after one another, but it never happens. Nobody ever looks after me. Father is dead. And now Sav, too. Mother is as good as gone. She will never, ever recover from this. None of us will."

"Which is why it's all the more important that we stick together."

"I hate you. I hate everybody. It's always left to you and me to sweep up the mess that everybody else has caused. This godforsaken magic, it's the reason that everything is ruined."

The fury stopped for a moment. The younger girl's fingers flexed at her side. Almost imperceptibly, a small flurry of golden sparks jolted from her palms.

"What are you . . . ? What are you doing?" The older witch faltered, noticing the magic building in a frightening electric current as though she could barely keep it under control. "Wait, no, darling. You can't."

"Tenebrae Obscurum."

A scream, and the scene changed again.

✦ ˟ ✦ ★

"I DON'T . . . I'M not sure I understand. I don't know who those girls were," Artorius stuttered. For a moment, neither Rune nor Belle said a word.

"I think I do," Belle whispered, her fists balled, trembling with anger. "That was my grandmother."

Artorius blanched. "Your . . ."

Belle nodded, slowly. "The older girl, that was my nan. Alvina Blackthorn. We have albums and albums of photos. I'd recognise her anywhere."

"But what does she have to do with Savaric?" Rune asked.

"Or with me, for that matter?" Artorius added.

Before she could speak any further, the mirror's picture came into focus. The younger girl from before returned in rippling rainbows. This time, she towered over a boy. Young Artorius again, shuffling backwards on his bottom into a corner as she prowled towards him, a cat relentlessly stalking her prey with hands outstretched, those threatening sparks of magic gathering at her palms.

"It was your idea! This is all your fault!"

"It wasn't, it wasn't my idea. It can't have been. Sav was—"

"You told him to try the spell! You encouraged him to do it!"

"I did, I did! But I didn't tell him to add more ingredients to the potion, I didn't tell him to make more fire. We were doing it right, we followed the book by the letter. It can't be my fault. It can't be." He was choking on sobs, spluttering on childlike fear.

"It's all your fault." The girl spat fury through tears. "If you'd never suggested the spell in the first place, then she never would have . . . She wouldn't be . . ."

"Please, Morena."

"No!"

"We have to look after each other now. We have to look after Mother and Alvina and . . ."

"*We* do not have to do anything," she said determinedly. "I'm sorry, Artorius. This is the only way."

"Please, please, no. Morena, stop!"

"*Tenebrae Obscurum.*"

Young Morena flipped out a hand, swirling a vortex of magic around the young boy. The spell encircled him completely, rushing his skinny body from every angle with such a force that he was knocked out cold as his head banged against the dirt floor of the barn.

"Artorius is to blame. So it shall be." Still sobbing, Morena spoke the words into the spell, and the glimmers of magic settled on the ground, sinking into the earth itself.

★ ˙ ✳ ˳ ✦ ˙ ★

BELLE SHOT UP from the seat beneath her, backing away slowly from the mirror.

"This cannot be happening." She couldn't breathe, pulling at the neck of her dress, cloying and tight.

Artorius looked back at her, bewildered.

"Morena. She's your sister," Rune said, his voice awed.

"But that was my nan. Morena hurt her. She did something to her."

"*Tenebrae Obscurum*," Artorius whispered. "The very same memory curse that I tried to inflict upon myself in the depths of Hecate House. No wonder the dark magic didn't work as I intended. It had already been used upon me years before by Morena. And she used it on your grandmother, too . . ."

"My grandmother . . . Your sister?" Belle's voice was barely audible.

"My brain is running at a faster rate than I can keep up with. But surely this also means that I had, in fact I have . . ."

"Three sisters," Rune finished.

"Bronwyn," Belle breathed.

As though reacting to the name, the mirror morphed again.

✦ ˙ ✳ ˳ ✦ ˚ ✦

BEYOND A SHADOW of a doubt, now that Belle knew it, the teenager was so clearly Morena. The same pinched, pained expression was instantly recognisable. The same sliced, high cheekbones.

And another girl. Small, no older than eleven. A freckled nose. Straw-coloured red hair. Bright green eyes.

As plain as day, the Gowden sisters.

"He deserved it. You said it yourself, Mor. He was far too big for his boots," young Bronwyn giggled.

"Yes, Bron! I did say that! But how could you possibly think that that was enough to *kill* him?"

"Well . . ." Bronwyn hesitated for the first time. "Let's say I didn't actually mean to . . . Maybe I got carried away. Perhaps I do regret it, at least a little. But what's done is done." She waved off her sister's reaction.

"He was our brother! He was a good man!" Morena wiped her nose with the end of her sleeve, coughing away a sob. She was throwing clothes into a bag, haphazardly scooping items out of wooden drawers, stuffing them inside.

Little Bronwyn rolled her eyes, swinging her legs off the end of the bed. "Everyone is always on about good and bad. Nobody is either. Everybody is a mix of both."

"He deserved to be—"

"He didn't deserve anything!" Bronwyn interrupted, shouting now. "He was a useless, arrogant warlock. He didn't deserve to be important or powerful. My magic could run rings around his, and I'm half his age. It's not fair. Just because—"

"You're insane!"

"Just because he was the oldest boy. It's nonsense. When I'm in charge, I'll—"

"You will never be in charge! Not now! Don't you see? We have to leave. We have to run away and never, ever come back. If we stay, they'll separate us and we'll never see each other again."

The little girl faltered. "What do you mean?"

"Bron, what realm are you in? You're not even supposed to have your magic for another four years. And now this? You're an anomaly, and Selcouth does not like anomalies. They'll have us all thrown into the dungeon for not telling them that your magic came in early."

"So where are we going?" For the first time, the little girl's confidence faltered.

"Away. I don't know, but away," Morena said matter-of-factly. She composed herself as she closed up the bag.

"Arty? And Vina? They can come with us."

"You are living in a dream world, sister. I've already fractured Vina's and Art's memories, and I spoke a forced truth into the earth. They'll blame him for Sav, but he's a boy and he already has his powers, so he'll be taken in by the coven and he'll be fine. They'll probably call it an accident. He'll probably take over leadership once he comes of age." Her voice wavered as though she were trying to convince herself of this.

"But that's not fair!" Bronwyn cried. "He's half the wicche that

I am! Mother and Father always said I'm exceptional. He's an idiot. He won't even be able to hide properly while they're looking for him."

Morena furiously grabbed her sister by the collar. "Do you want us to stay together or not?"

Bronwyn blinked in surprise but nodded hesitantly.

"Then forget the coven. Forget Selcouth. Forget Mother and Vina and Arty. It's just us now. We have to start again."

30

Starlight and Silver

"WE HAVE TO get to Hecate House. Immediately. Can you transfer us?" Belle was already halfway down the stairs, grabbing her jacket from the banister and yanking it onto her arms.

"Will you slow down for just one minute? Belle, for the love of . . ." Rune came careering behind her, grabbing her shoulder to spin her around.

"Are you kidding me? Did you just witness the same thing that I did?" She pulled her hair out from underneath her collar with one hand, struggled to keep her balance as she shoved on a shoe with the other.

"I saw it. But we can't just tear in, all powers blazing, and accuse the heads of the coven of—"

"Take your pick, Rune." She shook him off. "Of committing and covering up the murder of their own brother? Of blaming the whole awful thing on their other, entirely innocent brother? Of inflicting forbidden hexes on their third sister, my own grandmother, to change memories, to change the whole trajectory of the magic system? Am I missing anything? How about building the legacy of a coven on a selfish, vicious lie, and an obsession with tradition, all for their own gain?"

Rune placed a hand on each of her shoulders gently, grounding her. "Just think about what you're saying, for one second. You're talking about something that's about to shake the wicche world in Selcouth and beyond."

Belle's temper flared. "I don't care about them. Right now, all I care about is my family and Arty. You saw how broken he was, watching that play out. He's lived his whole life alone, plagued by guilt because of Morena's choices and Bronwyn's actions. And those two hags have somehow ended up on top after leaving a trail of nothing but brokenness behind them."

"Belle, please. Think about this. Think about your mentorship, the grimoire challenges, you still have . . ."

"I couldn't care less. I never want to see that book again. The whole of Selcouth is standing on the shoulders of two witches who will stop at absolutely nothing to snatch more power and cover their tracks."

Rune rubbed his face, scratched at the stubble across his jaw. "I know, I know. I'm just trying to think rationally."

"I'm afraid we are way past rational and straight into delusional levels of blind revenge."

Belle reached for the front door handle and slid the chain across to open the door. But it promptly relocked itself of its own accord. She turned to see Artorius at the top of the stairs, a hand outstretched, using his magic to fasten it shut.

"Rune is right, Belle. I will not allow you to put yourself in danger for me. You've been through enough, and that was only the surface of what the Gowden sisters are capable of."

He slowly made his way down the stairs, gripping onto the banister as he continued. "You are rushing to think of your grandmother and of myself, for which I am most grateful. But you are failing to consider other consequences of this new information," Artorius continued. "Think for a moment."

Realisation marked her face. "Morena and Bronwyn. It's them, isn't it? Sabotaging my lessons. They want me gone, by any means necessary."

"I suspect that explains why Morena was so reluctant to allow you to even have a chance at endarkenment in the first place," Artorius pointed out.

"But then, why did Bronwyn encourage the mentorship?" Rune asked.

"I really miss when I didn't have to consider dark magic traps and killer witches as part of my day-to-day contemplation," Belle said, more to herself than anybody else.

"Bronwyn evidently had ulterior motives up her cloak sleeve in pairing us. She may have assumed it would be easier to take us down together in one fell swoop. She knew that your failure would ensure mine, too. The coven would shut its doors to me forever if I failed to provide adequate mentorship to you. She underestimated us both in many ways. And of course, we've had a helping hand along the way."

He gingerly took a step to the bottom of the stairs and continued.

"Didn't you say it was your sooth stone that encouraged you to accept the offer of mentorship? That it seemed to be guiding you towards something this whole time?"

Belle faltered. "I did."

"I regret to side with him over you." Artorius rolled his eyes in Rune's direction, who muttered something about wondering why he bothered. "But I do think Mr. Dunstan is right. We should not rush to Hecate House just yet. We may have one final witch to speak to first. And one final challenge that we are yet to undertake."

Belle stared up at the ceiling and inhaled deeply. "If you're about to suggest that the next logical conclusion is communicating with my dead grandmother . . ."

"The grimoire couldn't be clearer," Artorius said, recalling the Necromancy allegory.

Eternal sleep, peaceful gift,
When death has come, soft and swift.
Another room across the way,
Ne'er far from those who have to stay.
Call with heart to gently rouse
Their bleary eyes, the hazy drowse.
Part of thine self, a splintered soul,
Unbroken since the bell did toll.

"It is asking you to communicate with someone who has passed, someone who was part of thine self, a splintered soul."

"It must be her, Belle," Rune agreed. "Your stone, her protection spell, the Gowdens, Artorius, everything we just watched in the mirror . . . Your grandmother is the missing link to all of this."

"But Morena's memory curse . . . She won't remember a thing."

"Outstanding magic washes away when death comes to take a witch. She will have returned to her true self when her eyes closed to rest," Artorius said softly.

⁎ ⁎ ⁎

AS THE THIRTIETH moon of October lay low and charmed in the charcoal sky, as though it were intrigued by their endeavours, Artorius offered an arm to Belle. Conjuring the spirit of Alvina Blackthorn was not something that had been on Belle's bingo card when October first arrived, but it strangely felt a perfectly fitting end to what had been a month of unabridged chaos across both her magic and non-wicche-related life.

"The fact that it happens to be Samhain morning will certainly work in our favour, I would wager. The veil between the living and the dead is at its thinnest for Halloween," Artorius explained, as the three unlikely friends moved the furniture aside to clear the living room floor. Once armchairs and clutter had been stacked at the walls, Belle, Rune and Artorius (just about) sat cross-legged together in a circle.

"This is new magic to you and me alike, Belle. I cannot bestow any prior experience. Rune, I suspect you've dabbled in the art of Necromancy once or twice? You look the sort."

"What's that supposed to mean?"

"I think it's the coat," Belle said, gesturing to his signature long leather jacket.

"Oh, stop it, you two," Arty shushed them while he placed an array of black, white and navy blue candles around them.

In Belle's lap lay a small pile of seemingly random items, but each held an important meaning. She'd cut a handful of pale pink roses from the garden, always her grandmother's favourites and always blooming through the trellises of her garden before she'd grown too old to take proper care of them anymore. A delicate china teacup that she'd been particularly picky over, never one to drink her tea from anything so clunky as a mug. Belle had summoned it from her mother's dresser at home, hoping that Bonnie wouldn't notice until she could explain properly. A gold lipstick tube that she'd saved when they cleaned out Alvina's house. And finally, her glasses, which Belle hadn't really known why she so desperately wanted to keep in the end. They just felt far too intrinsic a part of her grandmother to ever let go of.

"Any last-minute words of wisdom?" Belle asked, stretching out the sides of her neck and dropping her shoulders, adjusting her seated position.

"Keep it simple. This kind of magic relies on heart far more than head. Refer back to that previous summoning spell created in your Incantation lessons to avoid complication. It works under the same principles, especially while the veil is paper thin."

"Will I just be able to . . . talk to her, as if she were here?"

"All being well, yes. Of course, this does rely on the deceased wanting to be in attendance, but we can safely assume from your grandmother's dabbling with *Praesentia Pretego* that she will."

"How do we know that this isn't going to take some awful turn?" Rune asked sceptically. "Everything else significant that you've used your magic for recently, there's been . . . interference, to say the least."

Artorius shook his head. "This kind of magic comes with a certain amount of privacy around it. They—the sisters, that is—won't even know that this is taking place, they won't have the time or the foresight to affect it."

It was reassuring news. "In fact, I suspect you'll have more success if you undertake this one as a solo endeavour, my dear. Come along, young man."

"If it's all the same to you, I should probably oversee—"

"I have a little sherry in the cart." Artorius waved, dismissing Rune's retaliation as he rose unsteadily. "You can tell me all about your intentions towards Belladonna here while we indulge."

It worked like a charm.

"Intentions? Artorius, you have got some bloody nerve . . ." Rune shot up and quickly exited the room behind the old warlock to argue his corner, snicking the door shut after him.

She was alone. Belle held her breath as she cast a finger towards the selection of candles that Artorius had left, lighting them in a flash of small fires. She didn't allow herself to overthink, didn't allow herself to question the possibilities. She had never needed anything so much as she did in that moment.

Chanting in a low whisper, with only a few tweaks, the words of her previous transference came to her naturally. Supernaturally.

> Grandmother of mine, I call to join here,
> Wherever you are, journey to near.
> Company precious, spirit so strong,
> Appear to me now, a love everlong.

And before she could stop herself, against the quiet rippling breeze that plumed the curtains: "Please, please, Nan. I need you. Are you there?"

An air of spectral, silvery movement, as though breathing warmth into cold night air, swayed so faintly that Belle rubbed her eyelids. Airy glimmers, an apparition of barely there presence, crept into her surface of consciousness and sight. And there she was. Her grandmother, her silhouette made of a veil so delicate and impossibly fragile, it seemed an invisible, beautiful silk.

"Hello, my love."

She was just as Belle loved to remember her. When her childhood had woven them so preciously together by walking to the park, by baking flapjacks and by playing horses on a rolled-up duvet cover. Neatly curled hair no matter the time of day. A lilac cardigan that she'd knitted herself, a floral collared blouse smartly pressed underneath. Painted shell-pink nails and the scent. It was the first thing to hit Belle when Alvina's spirit appeared, before she could register even seeing her, being here with her. The scent of bluebells and clean laundry, faint flowers from always being in the garden. Belle clasped one hand over her mouth and the other on top of that. Her heart broke and mended a million times over, all at once.

"Oh, darling, don't cry. There's a good girl. Here, dry those eyes, petal."

Alvina's spirit reached out and offered a delicate scalloped handkerchief through the air for her tears. Belle held back, not wanting to find that touching her grandmother's hand brought coldness or emptiness. But as her fingers closed around it, it felt as real, as tangible and solid, as the items already clasped tightly in her hand.

"I can feel it . . . Does this mean I can hug you?"

Alvina laughed softly. There it was, the sound she remembered. "Of course, darling. How I've missed hugging my girl."

Belle flung her arms around her grandmother and felt herself held by her for the first time in so many years. The warmth, the texture of her hair against her face, the scent, the softness of her clothes. It was all the same. Just as it had been her whole life.

"I miss you. I miss you so much." She spoke as best she could, but her voice failed her. It was overwhelming, the raw combination of grief and gorgeous, intoxicating nostalgia holding her in loving arms.

"Oh, I miss you, too, Belle. I miss you and your mum. But I'm here, I'm always here."

"Are you okay?"

"What a funny question," Alvina chuckled. "Of course I'm okay. It's peaceful. Not so different but happier. And not far away. Like when you used to be playing in the garden while I watched from the kitchen window. Now I watch while you're busy building a little life for yourself, making wonderful things happen."

Something told Belle that she didn't need to know any more than that about what came next. The idea was comfort enough.

"Darling, we haven't much time. A spell like this, it won't hold for long, even on Halloween. But I'm so proud of you, Belle. Look at you, grabbing onto your magic with both hands."

Belle laughed through tears, grasping onto her grandmother's hands, feeling them soft in her own palms again. The knuckles, the ridges and the painted nails, the simple wedding band.

"I saw everything," Belle said. "I'm with your brother, Artorius, and we saw it all. We used the scrying mirror, and we saw what she did to you. What Morena did. And what Bronwyn did to Savaric."

"I know, love. I've been waiting for you to meet me at this moment. I was trying to guide you towards the truth, but there were so many steps to get here, towards the answers that you needed, and I'm so proud of you for finding them."

"Why did she do it? Why did Morena curse you and Arty like that?"

"It's complicated, darling." Alvina shook her head with soft pity. "Families always are. They say blood runs thicker than water, but magic runs thicker than blood. Morena always had a deep loyalty to Bronwyn. They were always closer than the rest of us."

"So she chose her over all of the rest of you? Even after what Bronwyn did to Savaric?"

"I think she always saw something in Bronwyn, could tell that her magic was perhaps the most potent of all of us. Oh, don't look at me like that, love. You know yourself that Bron is a force to be reckoned with. She always was. Even as a little girl. We all knew from the moment she arrived that she would grow up to have an extraordinary wealth of magic at her fingertips, and Morena knew it better than anybody. They shared a great deal of secrets while they grew up. Morena was more a guardian to Bron than our parents were, a protective-older-sister loyalty that's hard to understand. I often felt a little left out, truth be told." Alvina chuckled under a sigh. "Before she knew it, that fierce loyalty Morena always felt for the youngest of us had spiralled, grown into something that had her trapped in lies, too deeply involved with Bronwyn's mistakes to ever turn her back on her."

"What happened to them, between the day that they ran away and their rise to Selcouth? How did they manage it?"

Alvina sighed, shaking her head. "It's a story I've never quite known the full version of. I'm not sure anybody does, except for Morena and Bronwyn. As you saw in the mirror, both girls turned to complex, dark magic to cover their tracks. But I have since learned through whispers on the other side that their lies snowballed to a size greater than they ever expected. Morena spoke truths into the earth itself to shape what the coven knew about our family—a most manipulative spellwork that is highly forbidden. As a result, Selcouth lost the truth of the five Day siblings in its history, and they could flee as forgotten sisters. I was left on my own to begin everything again. They only existed in my mind as uncertain gaps that I couldn't fit together. But I met your grandfather, and I put my questions behind me."

"I'm so sorry, Nan. I wish I'd known everything you went through. I wish we'd talked about it."

"Even I didn't know, Belle! It wasn't until I passed over that the hexes Morena created were cleared and I could see what had truly happened. None of it really mattered then, anyway. And besides, I had a good life in the end. The very best. I made happiness for myself."

Alvina cradled the side of Belle's face.

"What am I going to do, Nan? How do I handle all of this?"

"That's up to you, love. All I want is for you to be happy and safe. I've seen everything that's happened recently."

"Can't you just tell me exactly what to do?" Belle asked pathetically. "You must have some kind of all-knowing, all-seeing wisdom that you can dish out."

"Of course. All you have to do, the precise instruction you have to follow . . . is trust your instincts." Alvina winked.

Belle rolled her eyes and laughed. "That's not helpful at all, Nan. My instincts feel as though they're made of crushed-up corn-flakes after the past month. I don't know what to think anymore."

"What I can tell you is that there are more secrets to Hecate House, Belle. What you saw in the mirror, it's not the end of this. In fact, it may only be the beginning."

Belle groaned. "I was afraid you'd say that." She suddenly remembered the confession that she had to make. "And I lost my stone, Nan. Or it was taken. My summoning spells can't find it."

Alvina gave her a soft smile. "Not to worry. Precious lost things will always turn up when we need them to." She paused for a moment and held Belle's face in her hand, stroking her thumb across her cheek. "Whatever you decide to do will be the right decision."

"If I'd just used my magic properly from the beginning, if I hadn't let it slip away from me, this whole thing would be—"

"Probably exactly the same," Alvina interrupted, chuckling. "Fate can't be twisted and turned as you like, Belle. What's meant for you is meant. No matter which turn you take or hurdle you stumble at, you'll always end up on the path that's meant for you. Love, let the dust settle on choices that you've made or that you didn't make. Leave all those different lives behind and make peace that this is the right one. Tell yourself, this is how my story is supposed to go, but I am the one who can write it as it's supposed to be."

Belle rested her head on her grandmother's iridescent shoulder, savouring the peace of being beside her again.

"And if that story just so happens to involve saving your magic and righting a few wrongs along the way for others, then all the better for it," Alvina added, turning to kiss her granddaughter on the forehead. "Tell Artorius I'm sorry, will you?"

"He won't want you to say that."

"Tell him, anyway," Alvina said softly. "I loved him dearly before it all." She smiled at Belle fondly. "You're doing so well, love."

Belle felt a swell in her chest that could only be described as a burst of sunbeams, of all-consuming, binding love. She revelled in it, like sunlight on her face. Then the feeling of a tangible, solid presence next to her slipped away like shadow in a changing light. The hands around hers faded away.

The spell unravelled, and the wisps of a delicate, cloudy figure, of starlight and silver, drifted across the candles, carried away on a breeze that took the flames along with it.

31
Loose Ends

I T WAS WITH great trepidation and an extensive phone call explaining that everything was fine, except not actually that fine, that Belle reluctantly agreed to bring her mother back to Quill Lane by transference.

She would have much preferred for Bonnie to drive for safety, but they had only a handful of hours to put a plan together before the moon of All Hallow's Eve. And, like most aspects of life, she couldn't settle on anything without her mum's verdict on the matter.

It had been a long conversation, a convoluted one. Belle attempted to explain what exactly the matter was in a roundabout way, wary of upsetting her mother with the shocking details—including the small matter of a visit from her long passed maternal grandmother. Bonnie, in her usual fashion, kept swinging the conversation off-kilter to something else entirely—dog updates, the restaurant she'd been to last week, gossip from her allotment. The phone was promptly passed to Artorius, who made slightly better progress. He only stumbled when Bonnie, still not having taken on the gravity of the situation, remembered that she'd meant to ask him for his scone recipe. When Belle heard mention of sultanas, she seized the phone and shoved it towards Rune as a last resort. Surprisingly, he did the best job of the three.

"So you see, Mrs. Blackthorn, that's why we could really do with you making your way down to London when you get a moment," Rune said, simultaneously trying to remain polite and attentive while Belle mouthed various other snippets of information for him to interpret as and when they popped into her head.

"Get her to come here as soon as possible," Belle stage-whispered. "Actually, no. There's something I have to do before we go and effectively unleash chaos on the magical structure of this country."

Rune pulled an indignant face and rolled his eyes but began to pass on the message.

"Actually, no," she began again, thinking out loud. "Could she meet us here, but tonight? So we can travel to Hecate House together? How are we going to know where it's incarnated for Halloween? We're more likely to run into problems if we're split up."

Rune took a deep breath but nodded again and mouthed "fair point" in response, suggesting the new plan in between Bonnie relaying something or other about needing to walk Wolfie. But yes, that would work.

"Hang on. New plan. Rune, as far as *they* know, *you* don't know anything that *we* know. You know?" Belle's eyes were so wide, it was as though the speed at which her brain was operating was causing some kind of inflating friction against her skull.

"What are you . . . Excuse me, Mrs. Blackthorn, one moment." He covered the end of the receiver with his palm. "Sorry, *what* are you talking about?"

"The Gowdens. They're none the wiser to the fact that you were with us for the scrying. And the Necromancy spell was private magic. What if you go to Hecate House, act like everything's peachy ahead of my retrial and get the new incarnate location for us to meet you there? Tonight, at sundown."

Rune rubbed a thumb over his forehead, trying his best to keep up. "I think I follow. But you won't be able to take the main entry into Hecate House, anyway. They'll know as soon as you walk through the door." He pondered for a moment. "Leave it to me."

He handed the phone to Belle to take over. His hands took hold of her upper arms as he navigated her out of the way, and she felt him give an almost imperceptible squeeze as he did so. He transferred himself away with the promise to be in touch with answers as soon as he could.

The plan—or as much of a plan as a highly unqualified witch, a banished elderly warlock and a witch dithering somewhere up north could have in place without entirely knowing what it was they were hoping to achieve—was vague. All that they knew was that Selcouth needed to know the truth and that the Gowden sisters had landed their positions of power through treacherous means. Not to mention, it was highly likely that they were behind the sabotage of Belle's mentorship, therefore controlling coven admissions for their own gain. They could have been manipulating prospective members of Selcouth, the future of magic itself, for decades.

But there was another crucial matter that she had to tackle first, before she could even consider the possibility of Hecate House.

She explained to Artorius that Rune or Bonnie would transfer with him to wherever it was they needed to be that night once Rune had gathered the facts. Artorius pointed out that it was a loose plan—barely a plan at all, in fact—to which Belle politely encouraged him to suggest his own if he had anything better.

"Well, it is something," he replied brightly. "And that is a start."

✦ · ✹ · ✦ · ✦

"ALL RIGHT?" ARIADNE grunted, picking at a plate of fish fingers while she flipped through a magazine, having returned from her sister's the previous night. Belle suspected she'd grabbed it hastily the moment she heard the door opening, because it was upside down while she read, and Ariadne didn't seem to have noticed.

"You're back. Good." Belle slammed the door behind her and marched towards her friend at the table.

"Seems that way," Ariadne said, peering determinedly at an upside-down page as though it were the most fascinating piece of journalism ever written.

"Look, I haven't got time for us to be shirty with one another anymore," Belle said, snatching the magazine away and chucking it over her shoulder. "I love you. I love you to death." She pulled the other chair from the table and sat herself directly in front of Ariadne. "I would play Scrabble with you every day in an old people's home in like fifty years' time, until we've lost the plot enough to think we're somewhere else. I would genuinely live on a DIY barge with you if you so wished. I would do anything for us to be okay again."

Ariadne snorted, then promptly rearranged her face back to lofty and disinterested.

Belle sighed. "I am a horrible, rotten crone for how I've treated you."

Ariadne stuck her nose in the air. "You are, actually."

"And it's no excuse, but I've just had more on my plate than an innocent teenager of thirty years old should ever have to handle by herself."

"You're not supposed to handle it by yourself, woman." Ariadne turned herself on the chair to face Belle. "That's the point. Our whole friendship is just taking it in turns to be insane. You're supposed to dump it on me, and I'm supposed to dump it on you, and eventually everything works out okay. You are so bad at asking for help, it's maddening."

"I know, I know," Belle said desperately. "And I will tell you everything, I promise, if I survive tonight."

Ariadne's eyebrows shot up. "Survive tonight? What's tonight?"

Belle waved her hands dismissively. "I just have to go and see a coven about potential overthrow because I suspect that two nefarious magical leaders of huge influence have possibly been trying to kill me. And my mum. So I just had to come back here and make sure that you're my friend again. I need you to be my friend, always. Otherwise, I'll have to come back as a ghost to haunt you until you forgive me, and I just can't be arsed to do it. It sounds like a lot of work."

"What are you on about? Ow."

Belle grabbed Ariadne's arms from where they were crossed over her body and forced her so tightly into a hug that she snatched the wind from both of them. "Say you forgive me."

"I'll never say it."

"Say it."

"I'll never . . ."

"Say it!"

"I forgive you, you deranged lunatic," Ariadne laughed, squeezing Belle equally as uncomfortably. "Hang on, I really can't breathe." They let go of each other. "For what it's worth, I am also sorry, for not giving you space when I could tell that you needed it. I should have just backed off and waited until you were ready to come to me about whatever is going on. Which I can only assume really is, of course, a coven? And some murder? And whatever else you just said?"

"I'm going to give you a moment to consider how I would come up with something like that if it wasn't actually true," Belle called back as she grabbed a towel and headed into the bathroom. "I have never needed a shower so much in my thirty years of existence."

On the bus back to the flat, leaning her head against the window, Belle had come to the realisation that her biggest mistake of all had been not confiding in Ariadne. Not telling her everything right from the beginning. Of course she should have shared it all that first night of her fifteenth birthday, mid–movie marathon, when everything felt too big and terrifying for one girl to hold on to. That berating, untrusting voice she'd heard in the entryway to Hecate House might have sounded like Ariadne, but it wasn't her, nor could it ever be.

So it was time to crack the secret open, break it apart with her bare hands and take away the power that it had held over her for so long. If she made it back home, she'd tell Ariadne everything.

"Oh, there were messages on the machine when I got back. Lots of them," Ariadne told her when Belle emerged from the shower. "I'm assuming you've been at Rune's place, because Violet has tried to call you like a hundred times."

"I'm on my way to see her right now. That reminds me, you don't know yet. I quit Lunar."

Ariadne stopped in her tracks to the kitchen. "You quit?"

"Spectacularly so," Belle replied, shouting from her room as she shoved her hair half up. "Bridges burned. Shots fired. Took the wagon, hitched up the horses, sped off into the distance."

"You finally lost it, hey?"

"I think I've actually found something. So I'm now going to go and beg for my little, insignificant life from Violet and tell her that I still want to buy the shop if she'll let me."

Ariadne blinked, baffled. "What exactly did I miss? I spend a week up north and you've gone mad. In a good way."

$$\star \cdot \maltese \cdot \maltese \cdot \star$$

AFTER THROWING ON clean tights, a velvet skirt and a top with large billowy sleeves that made her feel as though she had her life together, Belle power-walked straight to Lunar Books. Confronting all of this at a million miles an hour was the only way that she'd be able to stick by her guns without buckling.

"Vi?" She burst through the door of the bookshop, the dainty bell tinkling its familiar sound as she arrived.

"Out back," Monica called, reaching on her tiptoes to slide a couple of titles onto a high shelf. "She's got a right cob on with you. As have I."

Belle grimaced, shrugging off her coat, scuffing her boots against the book-shaped doormat. "Thanks, Mon. We'll talk, I promise. Don't hate me. There's a plan. Sort of."

She hurried across the shop floor, giving small waves and polite smiles as she shimmied through the regular customers. No sign of Christopher, she noted with relief. She slid open the stock-room door into the space where she'd come face-to-face with Rune what felt like such a long time ago. Violet, feeding a letter through the fax machine, turned on her stick towards Belle.

"Vi. I'm here. I'm so astronomically sorry for missing your calls."

"Ah, she's alive after all. Call off the searches, Jim." He was hunched over a comic book, munching on an apple in the wobbly corner chair reserved for break times. "Give us a minute, will you?" she added, waving her stick in the direction of the door.

He sighed and chucked his apple core into the bin as he stood up. "Can't a man enjoy Spider-Man in peace anymore?"

"Not when I've seen that he's got two entire boxes of delivery to fit onto the fiction shelves before he should be clocking off," Vi responded. She prodded him in the back with her stick as he left, and he pretended to stumble spectacularly to earn a cheap laugh. It always worked with Vi.

"To what do I owe this pleasure?" Violet asked, tapping the numbers on the fax machine to make it clear that she was far too busy and important for this conversation.

"You know I wouldn't have ignored your messages on purpose. I got called away and have had a week like you wouldn't believe." Belle sighed, tidying up a small stack of proof copies by instinct. "But that's no excuse. I'm so sorry. And I totally understand if the offer doesn't stand anymore."

Violet turned with a neat, smug smile. "There is no longer an offer, Belle."

Belle's face fell.

It was over. The dream had slipped away once and for all. How could she have dared to think that it wouldn't?

But there was a glint in Violet's pale eyes. "There's no offer because it's confirmed. Lunar Books is yours."

Belle's hand flew to her heart. "Seriously?"

"Seriously. This is instruction to my lawyer to begin the process, in fact." She gestured to the fax. "It'll take a while to deal with the legalities, but I'm ready to pass this place on to someone who I know truly loves and cares for it, who has the time and energy to keep hold of its charm in this mad modern world."

Belle's grin momentarily turned to a frown. "And . . . what about Christopher?"

"Thanks to your venerable colleagues out there, who finally decided after you walked out that honesty would indeed be the best policy, rather than your well-intentioned-but-ridiculous approach of trying to save me from the truth, I am now well aware that my son is *not* that someone. We have had words. I'm cutting him off, so it's up to him to support his own ridiculous lifestyle. And I can't believe he didn't like the fabulous window display. The fabulous window display stays."

Belle couldn't help but let out a disbelieving laugh. "I tried to tell you . . ."

"Well, you should have tried harder. But I was wrong to blindly believe that he knew what was best. I should have remembered that, as it always has, almost all of the magic of Lunar comes from you."

Belle grinned. "We're really doing this?"

"I've known you for long enough, Belle. I know by now that you wouldn't ignore me on purpose. I know this place is a part of you. I know your heart."

"I won't let you down, Vi."

"I know you won't, sweetheart."

Violet left Belle with a file of dense documents and insisted that she at least take a peek at them before she left. Violet herself couldn't stay. She had her monthly women's meeting, which Belle had never really known too much about, other than the fact that a selection of elderly wealthy women all seemed to enjoy getting together to moan about their elderly wealthy husbands, and it drove Violet up the wall because they were all so dull.

Now wasn't the time for important legal documents, hefty paragraphs about deeds and ownership and freeholds and leaseholds. But she jotted a pen across one or two, slid a highlighter over a couple of paragraphs so that Violet would see that she'd given it a try. Hopefully it would seem as though she'd been distracted by the shop floor instead. Her mind was entirely elsewhere. Although utterly relieved that she hadn't lost her chance of owning her own little bookshop, now all Belle could focus on was what lay ahead.

Halloween night was about to begin.

She pulled a pink highlighter across something or other about damp proofing that looked important, but her attention was snatched to the bottom of the page. A line appeared like a footnote, the letters forming by themselves, and soon turned into words handwritten in black ink. They glowed as she read before vanishing again like puffs of smoke.

Queens Wood oak circle. See you all at 6 p.m. Don't forget uniforms.

Rune.

Belle had seen pictures of Queens Wood before, with its otherworldly clearing of trees right at its centre, the space surrounded by oaks in an almost perfect circle that mirrored the Hecate House atrium.

Belle glanced at the clock on the back wall. Twenty minutes to six. Typical Rune to give a moment's notice. She'd have to sprint home, grab her cloak and hat, jump on a train almost immediately . . .

Unless she risked it. Unless she believed in herself enough to knit a successful transference spell for the first time. Daring to believe it set off an unconscious flare of sparks at the end of her finger. As Artorius had reminded her numerous times, what was the *best* that could happen?

Belle headed out of Lunar, giving the front door a tap for luck as she left, as though reassuring the shop—her shop—that she'd be back soon.

The high street buzzed in the evening glow with throngs of parents and children dressed up in handmade Halloween costumes. She spotted adorably hilarious vampire collars sticking out at all angles, a trail of toilet paper spilling from a miniature mummy and, best of all, throngs of witches in the early stages of girlhood, all in their best capes and hats, celebrating their own pull towards the magical. They clutched at small brooms, carried little cauldrons and beamed sticky smiles as they skipped along hand in hand.

Belle slipped around the same corner that she'd dragged Bronwyn to all those moons ago when she'd arrived to share the news about the mentorship. Bronwyn, who had seemed so kind thirty moons back, with the best, most selfless of intentions. Belle prickled, trying to grant herself grace for falling for it. She could never have known what was to come. She shuffled back between two large bins and tried to ignore the smell. The air was cold and fresh, coated with the last of the apricot light from the row of shops. She flexed her finger, feeling the rush of that remedying glow, her magic coming to life.

"Take me home," she whispered.

✦ ˙ ✹ ˳ ✦˚ ✶

HER STOMACH LURCHED, dropping into the balls of her feet and falling through her heels. It was the sensation of tipping over the edge of a rollercoaster, free-falling at a speed so extreme that she felt her skin shrink back to wrap every nerve ending within her. Her tongue pressed against the roof of her mouth from the force, her hair flew upwards, caught in a current. And then it was done. She felt a firmness beneath her toes. The scent of Ariadne's favourite candles was the first thing that she noticed. She opened one eye. The living room.

"What in the ever-loving fuck?"

The slight, now very apparent issue was that she had transferred herself to the very room where Ariadne was currently sitting sprawled out across the sofa. Belle had never seen her move so fast. She jolted upright with such a fervour that it looked like an electric shock.

Belle cringed. She was going to tell Ariadne everything, but this was perhaps not the gentle approach she should have taken in introducing her non-wicche friend to the phenomenon of real-life magic.

And she had to get to Queens Wood.

"I'm so sorry. Ignore me. I'm not here," Belle chimed, heading straight into her room to pull the Selcouth cloak and hat from the pile of clothes on her armchair.

Ariadne, verging on hysteria, scrambled up from the sofa. "Did I miss something? Where did you come from? You left. I thought . . . What are you wearing?"

"I know, the hat is terrible," Belle said, pulling the point into place.

"Either you're having a breakdown or I am. We can't both have one at the same time."

"It's not a breakdown. This is happening. I have handled this terribly, but now you're in the deep end, and I'm going to need you to keep swimming just for a couple more hours while I go and fix a few things." Belle was rambling at a speed she didn't even know was possible as she gripped her friends' forearms. "Please don't entirely lose the plot until I'm home again. I know this kind of thing has sent people into madness before, but we're strong modern women. We've seen weirder stuff than this. It's just the supernatural. Some people believe in the stock market, in the internet, in aliens . . . I'm going to need you to believe in this. You can handle this, right?"

Ari made a noise that was somewhere between a confused huff and a scoffing honk.

"Great. I'll be back," Belle said hastily before casting out her finger and transferring straight to what she hoped her magic would know to be the oak circle.

32

The Final Challenge

"YOU TOOK YOUR time," said Rune.

"It is literally three minutes past six," said Belle, finding him waiting impatiently next to her mother.

"Exactly. I told you to be on time," Rune said firmly, pulling down the sleeves of his jacket as she landed on the ground of Queens Wood.

"I've just left my non-wicche friend questioning whether she belongs in an asylum after self-transferring directly in front of her. I think you can spare me three minutes," Belle snapped at him.

"Ariadne witnessed magic?" Bonnie gasped, clutching her necklace.

"I'm just saying," Rune interjected, "that funnily enough I'm on quite high alert when it comes to your safety. I was starting to think that you might have run into some trouble."

Belle took a moment. "Fine," she said reluctantly. "That is actually quite thoughtful."

"Successful self-transference, though," he pointed out, looking impressed.

"Belle, what about Ariadne?"

"It's fine, Mum. Just the cherry on top of the cauldron." Belle forced herself to relax. "It's going to be fine. Hi, by the way." She gave her mum a hug. "We have so much that we need to talk about."

"No time for that now. Rune has filled me in, I know the dot-to-dots. Rune, would you like to do the honours with Mr. Day, or shall I? He was a little anxious to make the journey himself."

"I'll fetch him," Rune replied, disappearing for what must only have been a handful of seconds before reappearing again with Artorius hanging on to his forearm, looking impossibly small and frail next to Rune's towering height. They touched down onto the dry earthy floor of the bare circle in the woods with a whirlwind of sparks, kicking up brown dust as they materialised.

"My, that hasn't gotten any more pleasant over the years, has it? You'd think in this day and age we might have refined the process slightly," Artorius said, looking a little green around the gills. He gripped his thighs for a moment, head down to steady himself, then glanced up. "And where might we be, exactly?"

"This is a perpetual gate to and from Hecate House, no matter where it incarnates. Leaving the quad via the stone statues always brings you out to the oak circle here. Nonetheless, I spent most of today disabling a handful of enchantments around the place that would normally alert Hecate House to our arrival. The breaks should hold long enough for us to slip in unnoticed."

Belle, for the first time, took proper note of their surroundings. With dusk setting in and the huge towering canopies of the oaks, the air was dark, almost purple in hue, with an undulating supernatural feeling. She immediately found her senses heightened like an animal, awareness sharpened to a weaponised point. Magic was in the air. The breeze was rushing through the nut brown leaves above, and the bare, spindly branches sounded like frantic whispers from every which way.

"We haven't much time. But they're all here, practically the whole coven if I'm not mistaken," Bonnie urged, gathering the four of them closer together so she could speak in hushed tones. "Your endarkenment ceremony is about to begin, love."

"It's this way." Rune gestured between two of the mighty oaks. She expected him to guide them farther into the woods, perhaps to a hidden doorway again. But stepping between the two trees, Rune dissolved to nothing as though he'd stepped behind an invisible waterfall, his whole presence rippling into thin air. His upper torso poked back out from nothing and nowhere.

"Probably should have explained. It's a glamour, a manipulation charm to hide the back entryway to the quad. You'd never find it unless you were looking for it. Come on."

He vanished again. Bonnie encouraged Belle through first, followed by Artorius before bringing up the rear, checking over her shoulder that nobody had taken a wrong turn in time to see four wicchefolk fade into nothing.

Breaking through the other side of the glamour, their surroundings changed.

"Is that it? No trials or tests?" Belle asked, astonished.

"I told you. It's a back way in," Rune said, dusting himself down. "Normally there'd be a maze of guarding enchantments in place, but fortunately, you've got me on your side." He flashed her a dazzling "Mr. Magical" worthy smile.

"You're telling me I went through hell and back through the front door, faced my darkest fears, almost drowned in quicksand, when I could have just waltzed through the fields and the woods like Maria von Trapp?"

"Who?"

"Never mind," Belle muttered grumpily. The new space around them was a shaded but verdant quad, manicured to a leafy pine-coloured perfection. The sound of running water echoed around the stone walls, all laced with moss that so perfectly traced the structures, it must have been placed magically. Fountains stood at various intervals along pebbled pathways, and a brilliant navy blue night sky peppered with stars hung low overhead. It felt tranquil and sleepy in a Gothic, languishing way. And just as Rune had mentioned, they entered between two large stone statues of Hecate, which took the place of the two oak trees.

"Nice place you got here, lady," Belle muttered to the statues. "Thanks for having us."

"You are so weird," Rune said, faintly bemused but, Belle noted, distinctly affectionate.

"Now where?" Bonnie asked.

"The courtroom," Rune answered. "Probably just in time to watch Morena revel in her own greatness and strike off Belle's endarkenment, all in the name of All Hallows' Eve."

They followed Rune as he wound them through the quad, the sky above disappearing as they headed downwards under a thicker canopy of lush leaves, eventually coming to a doorway built into the farthest wall. He swung it open with difficulty, the wood heavy and swollen with damp, cumbersome as it scraped across the quad's stony floor.

They arrived in the atrium underneath a vast depiction of the mythical Capricorn creature, goat-like with enormous horns. Across the room lay Bronwyn's office, with the giant metal silhouette of two witches hanging above.

Bonnie let out a gasp that sounded so horrified, Belle's instant reaction was to assume that her mother was hurt. She spun around but found Bonnie's eyes on the ceiling, a hand to her mouth in horror. Rune, too, was reeling, gazing at the domed roof in disbelief, brown eyes wide. Only then did Belle register it, too. What had once been a blanket of brilliance, the thick layer of physical magic charged across the entire stretch of the imposing dome, was gone. All that remained was the ceiling itself, a hollowed beige emptiness, void of everything but shadow.

"They've stolen it. All of it," Bonnie breathed.

Belle never saw her mother angry. It wasn't an emotion she leaned in to very often, but in that moment, a fury spread across Bonnie's face that was palpable. It radiated from her. Without warning, she charged towards the Libra doorway, blasting it open with a flick of her palm, so hard that it toppled from its hinges. They all ran after her.

Belle did a double take. It was as though she'd walked back in time to the very same moment she'd last been in this room. As though the same torturous scenario with her manifests was still taking place. The sage witches both stood at the high podium in the centre, the points of their hats dancing tall. The whole jury were in place, just as they had been before, filling both sides of the long pews that stretched towards the nexus. All had eyes closed, poised to that same immaculate stillness again. And the grand pendulum itself was stationary, as it had been when the storm erupted to conduct her manifests. The Gowdens were standing with arms outstretched, magic erupting around them in that same tidal wave force that she'd witnessed, but there was more of it. So much more. They were surrounded by it, their own fortress of incandescent magic enveloping them.

Belle dragged her attention to the jury, spotting Caspar first. Under their trance, his usual elegance and grace were gone. He was buckling, his breathing laboured, the richness of his skin faded to an ailing pallid greyness. The hollows of his cheeks were extreme, like engravings, his eyes set deep in skeletal coves. It was the same for every coven member. All seemed to be fading, an evanescent memory drifting away. Somewhere in the back of her mind, Belle heard Artorius stumble in shock, saw her mother sprint towards Caspar to try and catch him as he feebly swayed unconsciously.

"I wouldn't do that if I were you, Bonnie." Bronwyn spoke in her usual sweet tone, made sickly by the knowledge they now had. "I brought you to the brink once before, I can do it again."

"Let them go!" Bonnie shouted back, incensed. "What is this?"

"I'd have thought this would have been firmly in your diary, Bonnie. Your own daughter's retrial?" Morena tutted with a snarl. "They're all gathered here for her. They've all been waiting for you, Belle."

Belle felt hollow, nauseous. They'd used her retrial, aligning the moons with her mentorship, as an excuse to gather everybody here together. To ensure that everybody was at Hecate House on All Hallows' Eve.

"You tricked the whole coven! This was never about me. You just needed them all here, while the veil is at its thinnest, so that you wouldn't fail at . . . whatever it is you're trying to do."

"Oh, Belle, poor poppet. Not the brightest, are you, my love? Isn't it obvious?" Bronwyn smiled. "We're starting again. I dare say we've waited long enough." She chuckled, hands clasped together. "A new coven. Shaped for success and strength. No more hiding. After all, Selcouth itself has always unanimously agreed that my sister and I are the worthiest magic holders. Everyone else has sadly made such a mess of something that could be so perfect. It's only right that we should begin again, take the magic back for ourselves and do with it what we see fit. Once we have gathered all the magic shared amongst Selcouth, we'll consider who it is really best held by. Witches and warlocks who won't sully it or let it go to waste."

"You cannot do this." Artorius stepped forward as boldly as he could, and Belle felt her heart break in two at the sight of the frail old friend whom she'd become so reliant on, looking so small against the overbearing backdrop. He shielded his eyes from the brightness of the magic, faltering at what was unfolding before him.

Bronwyn let out her signature chuckle again; it felt impossible to Belle that she'd ever considered it endearing. "Well, look at you, Arty. Still clinging on to one last hope that you'll be a part of the gang again?" She laughed. "Pity. I'm afraid you're about as much of a feature in Selcouth's future as you were a part of its past. Just not quite up to scratch, you understand." She wrinkled her nose in a monstrously sweet way.

"Sisters . . . Why?" he called, sounding impossibly sad. "Where did this venom stem from? You are not the girls you once were."

"I should hope not," Bronwyn went on. "Those girls were woeful. They should have stood up for themselves from the beginning. Rather than letting Father ever tell us who was and wasn't worthy in our family. That oaf Savaric, especially. Removing him from the picture was the best thing I could have done. I never regretted it for a moment."

Belle was surprised to see Morena falter almost imperceptibly, the magic emitting from her palms flickering just the smallest amount. In a moment, it was back to its solid, controlled form. Perhaps she'd imagined it.

"And isn't that exactly what you're doing now? What you've been doing all of these years? Dictating who is and isn't worthy of a part of all of this?" Belle shouted, the hypocrisy enraging her.

"Silence, you utter waste of precious sorcery," Morena spat. "How dare you factor yourself into this! This is far greater than a fool like you could ever pretend to understand."

"Don't you dare. Ever. Speak to my daughter that way!" Bonnie thundered, her rage careering through the room. Before Belle could stop her, Bonnie threw her right palm up towards the sky and brought a crashing ripple of magic from the Gowdens' swirling supply towards them in a vehement gesture, breaking apart the barricade, the shock so sudden that they were both almost knocked off their feet.

Morena quickly adjusted herself and sent one back in return, the strength of the wave so enormous that Belle could feel it resound in her lungs as it hit. Another was sent roaring back in the Gowdens' direction, but it didn't come from Bonnie. Belle's head flung around just in time to see Rune's magic cascade across the courtroom, mighty enough that the pendulum shuddered as it resonated against the bronze.

"Isn't this just adorable?" Bronwyn giggled, though a thunderous temper was clearly visible behind her eyes, fracturing the façade. She gathered the magic back around her as though knitting together a string between her palms. "A mother and daughter act, a useless old sidekick and the handsome, hapless hero? I couldn't have written it better myself."

"And what does that make you both? The villains? Or just a pair of bitter, self-aggrandising old hags who anointed themselves as better than everybody else to feel powerful? You said it yourself, Bronwyn. 'The truth always outs in this coven.'"

"Call me a hag one more time, girl," Morena spat.

It was only then that Belle noted the pendant hanging around Morena's neck over her cloak. A sooth stone, but Morena's own was still encased in the ring she wore. As her eyes fell upon the jewel, once encased in a delicate shell brooch, it turned from grey to radiant gold, connecting to her. Her own stolen sooth stone. She could have exploded for the rage that burned inside her.

"Won't everybody please just take a breath?" said Artorius. "This is going to end in—"

"Enough from you, little brother! You're still unwanted, even now." Bronwyn cast out a palm specifically towards Arty.

Her spell threw him into the air at impossible speed, and he landed in a heap against the courtroom wall. His small body didn't move.

"No!" Belle cried out. She ran to him, a bundle of oversized jacket, glasses knocked to the floor.

"Arty, are you okay? Can you hear me?" Belle quickly manifested a pillow to place under his head, the best she could do in that moment, and said a silent wish to whatever it was that witches were supposed to believe in. She turned back to the scene just in time to see her mother send another blow in response, the effort visible across her face enough to break Belle's heart by itself. A chaotic storm of magic flew in every direction across the courtroom, ricocheting from the brass pendulum. The noise was enormous, too. Thunder cracks, implosions of what Belle could only assume to be the atmosphere itself, as the women's powers broke through normal planes of speed and light. It smelled distinctly of burning.

She called as loud as she could over the crashes, "Rune, stay here! Get everybody to safety. Whatever it takes," Belle yelled, struggling back to her feet to run to him, dodging flying bolts of magic. "Mum and I will deal with these two."

"You're sure?" he shouted back, manipulating a sphere of solid magic between his palms, which he sent careering towards the nexus. "I'm going to bring it down, the pendulum. It's what all of the magic is attracted towards, like a magnet. If that comes down, it should break the spell they're holding over the coven, at least temporarily. It'll be chaos, but—"

"Got it," Belle yelled, not even attempting to understand what he'd just said. It sounded good.

"And Belle, I didn't mean it." He swallowed hard, holding her with a stare. "You were wrong."

She rolled her eyes. "Just for a change, is this really the time?"

"Not like that . . . I mean, *I* was wrong to agree with you when you said we shouldn't have kissed. It was the best possible thing. You're the best possible thing."

Her heart gave a kick.

"Be careful."

Without thinking, she grabbed one of his hands and held it for just a fraction of a second. Their palms brushed, the static of magic snapping between them as they separated. She dashed to her mother's side, shielding her eyes as best she could as Bonnie battered the Gowdens again with shocks of magic.

"Mum!" she shouted, straining her voice. "We need to get them out of the courtroom, into the atrium, to move all the magic away. Rune will protect the coven members."

"It sounds like you have a plan, darling." They were screaming at the top of their lungs but still only barely able to hear each other as the room began to crumble around them, unable to withstand the forces of five witches at war, the unbalanced magic. Huge chunks of ceiling, wall, shelving and fireplace were crashing to the ground now, books flying at all angles, stone splitting open and sending a thick choking dust into the air.

"When do I ever have a plan?" Belle replied. "All I know is that when Rune brings the pendulum down, we run. They'll follow us. It's personal. They're hell-bent on it."

"I do love our girly time together, Belle," Bonnie shouted back sarcastically as a huge stone boulder missed her head by inches.

"It's coming down," Rune yelled, pulling the pendulum out towards them, seizing it from its hinges. "Get out!"

Bronwyn shrieked, "Rune, do not—"

The pendulum came crashing down, tearing chunks of the room with it. Belle chanced one last look at Rune, which she hoped said everything she hadn't managed to. Then she grabbed her mother's cloak and ran with all her strength out of the courtroom doors and into the atrium. As they'd suspected, Bronwyn and Morena immediately shot after them, without so much as a glance at one another. The Blackthorns were their main targets, that much was clear.

"It's because it's ours, if you're a stickler for the rules," Bonnie called to her daughter across the huge celestial floor as they held their stance, thick clouds of dust from the ruined courtroom already spilling out and filling the atrium.

"What is?"

"The coven should have gone to your nan when Savaric was killed. Artorius wasn't old enough for endarkenment, so it would have gone to her next. Luckily for the Gowdens, she had absolutely no interest in claiming it," Bonnie explained.

"That unanimous vote from the coven when they showed up years later . . . seems rather convenient, thinking about it now," Belle added.

Bronwyn and Morena came bursting through the enormous Libra door, clambering through the rubble, the bronze scales above ricocheting against the stone with a deafening metallic clang.

"You're making this much more difficult than it needs to be, Bonnie," Bronwyn called, raising her hands to drag out the magic from the courtroom behind her in an enormous train of stars. "Rune will not survive in there, returning so many witches back to their full form. They've all been drained of their magic. The effect will drain his own before he can revive even a handful. What a terrible waste."

Belle felt ablaze with anger and fear for Rune. Bronwyn swept towering, deep walls of the magic back around herself and Morena as they took their place opposite the Blackthorns.

"And you'll both be dead in a matter of minutes," she said casually.

"So, what's even your plan?" Belle shouted. "Bump off every single member of this coven? Don't you think that looks a little suspicious?"

"Freak accidents happen at the hands of magic. Granted, one of this scale hasn't been seen for quite some time, but—"

"And then what? Start all over again, rebuild a coven only of witches that you consider worthy? Or keep it all to yourself? Because where are you planning on finding anybody good enough, if it's not Bonnie Blackthorn, Rune Dunstan, Caspar Strix, Artorius Day—any number of the good people you're currently sacrificing just behind you?" Belle was screaming now, a passion so rapidly swelling between her veins that she could feel its temperature physically changing under her skin. "Who are you to tell anybody whether their version of magic is worthy?"

"I am the sole worthy witch!" Bronwyn screamed at such a pitch that Belle startled.

She saw Morena falter again, too, dropping her half of the magic, shooting her sister an uncertain look.

Bronwyn screeched. "Thirty years of age, and you don't know the first thing about magic. You know nothing, girl. You *are* nothing."

"Not anymore," Belle roared, her voice strained and hoarse, anger turning to certainty. "My magic is mine. It's greater than you'll ever know."

She wasn't certain that this would even work or what would really happen if it did. But she was certain of herself in that moment. That she was worthy of it. That she was good enough to those who mattered. And it was worth a try.

"Vividus Animo." One of her earliest lessons.

Bonnie glanced sideways at her daughter, eyebrows knitted together, immediately understanding. *"Vividus Animo,"* she echoed, laying both of her palms onto Belle's outstretched hands to make their magics join together, to double them in strength. The room rumbled. An earthquake beneath their feet, the walls trembling as though Hecate House itself was fearful of what was to happen next.

It couldn't be happening. It couldn't have worked for her, magic like this. Could it? From the corner of her eye, Belle noticed Taurus first. The giant bronze bull kicked a front leg against its back one, scuffing its impossibly sharp horns against its hindquarters. The bull leapt to the floor, as real as any other animal that Belle had ever witnessed but five times the size.

Then came the huge pincered Cancer crab, its pointed claws like impossible razor blades as they scraped down the stone walls of the atrium, clicking its way under Blackthorn magic towards the

Gowden sisters. All twelve of the horoscopes above each door of
Hecate House followed suit, each one animating to life, instantly
drawn in a fury to the two witches currently in charge of a cascading
force of magic that was bringing their ancient home to the ground.

The scorpion's acutely sword-like tail. The lion's vicious jaw.
The aimed arrow of the Sagittarius centaur swinging directly towards
Bronwyn, ruthless in its defence. Even the Gemini sister witches
turned against their human counterparts. Together, the whole zodiac descended on the sisters in a frenzy. The Gowdens, with frantic
looks passing between them, had no choice but to turn their attention away from the Blackthorns. They tried in vain to blast the zodiac away quick enough. But while one creature was sent reeling
backwards, another took its place, battering them relentlessly with
unbridled acrimony.

But it wasn't enough. Belle and Bonnie glanced at each other nervously, straining to keep the spell knitted. For now, they were separated by the destruction, but the sisters would outwit the zodiac. It
was only a matter of time before their seemingly endless supply of
stolen magic, surplus to their own natural strength, would overpower Belle and Bonnie. There had to be something more, with
everything that Hecate House held within its walls. Residing on the
ley lines, the very nexus itself.

"Fire to earth, earth to fire," Belle muttered to herself. "Create
that which thy most admire." The allegory for Earth Sorcery.

"What, love?" Bonnie struggled to hear over the chaos.

"Water to air, air to water. Powers for the firstborn daughter.
Mum, that's it!" Belle shouted in disbelief. "My challenge, the elements. This is it." The elements had all been present for her manifests. They were all present at the nexus, the point where all came
together. Artorius had been right, the grimoire had been trailing
clues like breadcrumbs all along.

She started small. That palm-sized glow of warm sunshine that she'd practiced in the greenhouse. The tiny bursts of rain that she'd made pour from her fingertips. The breath of air that she'd managed to manipulate and control, just enough so that it cascaded across the garden to bend the blades of grass at her will. Fire was easy enough, a witch's bread and butter. And they were so, so far underground. Earth was all around her. She just had to summon it, all at once. It had happened in the entryway tunnel, when her heart had needed it, but she had no idea how she'd made it happen. It had been within her all along, and Hecate House would answer her.

Against the cacophony surrounding them, Belle closed her eyes and tried to summon just the smallest moment of focus and peace while Bonnie and the zodiac shielded her as best they could. Remembering everything she'd learned for so many moons. Needing, more than ever, to trust herself, trust her instincts, trust her magic.

But nothing came. The air, water, earth and fire all stayed small within her palms.

Bonnie stayed locked in combat with Morena, but Bronwyn burst through the gloomy warfare like a thunderbolt, sending two solid flashes of magic directly at the enormous Pisces fish, both the size of a whale, thrashing violently. It hit them both square in the torso, and the bronze creatures emitted a strangled dying-animal noise that Belle hurried to protect her ears from.

"Give it up, Belladonna. You're nothing." Bronwyn looked possessed, a madness dictating her every move as she edged forwards. "There is only one magic that deserves to survive this night, and that is mine. You will not ruin this when I have waited so long."

"You can't, you can't . . ." Tears were coming as she willed the elements to do something, anything, at her call.

"You shouldn't have survived this long, the unremarkable disappointment that you are. It's a miracle you've beaten any of it—my protection block, astral manipulations, my *Subfuror Incantare*, even the poison, and taking that damned stone of yours . . . Do you know the lengths I've gone to, the ways I have pushed the boundaries of my powers to prevent us from getting to this point?" Bronwyn wandered closer, beating crashes of magic away as she walked. "I only set out to make you see that none of this is really for you. To scare you enough that it nudged you into giving up this world for good. Only the inevitable, I thought, to *prove* to you in black and white that you don't deserve this. That magic isn't meant for you."

She spat those last words. Without taking her eyes off Belle, Bronwyn sent the Sagittarius centaur ricocheting into the wall, smashing its bow and arrow from its grasp. Belle's arms flew to cover her face as bronze shards splintered through the air.

"I should have just left you to fail your EquiWitch and be done with it, like Morena wanted. Trusted that her silly little spell to send your summoning letter awry would be enough to ensure you didn't show. But I couldn't take the risk. Then your early manifests showed dangerous promise, memories of power and ability that could have been enough to convince you one day that you were worthy. That's when it occurred to me that I could kill two birds with one stone. Setting you up for failure with my halfwit brother would ensure there could be no doubt the second time around. An unprecedented second failed EquiWitch could never be contested, you would no longer be a threat to our leadership. And it would guarantee no possible future debate regarding Arty's past, present or future.

"But you just kept passing the challenges, the grimoire was supposed to ensure you couldn't . . ." Bronwyn's disbelief was audible. "It wasn't supposed to come to this. The stupid pair of you refusing to acknowledge the warning signs. I had to escalate . . . I had no choice." Belle thought she saw the sage witch waver in conviction, just barely.

"You've caused me great trouble, girl. And where does that leave us? What more will it take? With all of your loved ones trapped here, just moments from death. In fact, silly me"—she laughed, her usual chuckle now something sinister and twisted—"not all of your loved ones, my mistake. In all of the excitement, how could I forget? There's one missing out on the party, isn't there?"

With a mere flick of her palm, Bronwyn spun a vortex of magic towards the centre of the room.

Through the blurred whirlwind, Ariadne materialised, dressed in her pyjamas behind the sparks, brought directly into the middle of a battlefield she had no business being in. She squinted against the blinding forces of magic, gazing around in utter bemusement before catching sight of her best friend.

"Belle?"

"Ari!"

"What more will it take, Belle? Who else are you going to endanger? Surrender your magic," Bronwyn yelled over the pandemonium that filled the atrium.

"Stop it! Send her back, this isn't fair! She's not a part of this."

"Let your magic go!"

"I can't! I—"

"Then know that this is your fault. I told you all those weeks ago, love only leaves you vulnerable—if you allow it to endure."

Bronwyn moved so quickly that it took Belle a moment to even realise where the blast of magic had come from. The ground beneath Ariadne's feet, the point where the astrological sun wove together with the whimsical moon in the dazzling mosaic, surrounded by the stars and gilded with gold. It slipped from beneath her, erupting into pieces as Bronwyn cast a final, enormous barrage of stolen magic, exhorting everything she had, whatever it cost. In the fury, Ariadne was thrown up high above them, tossed like a rag doll to the very top of the domed ceiling. She came tumbling down in a rush.

Belle watched her in slow motion.

Her twin flame, the mirror soul that she would always swear was splintered from her own. She saw it all as Ariadne fell. The moments that they'd laughed until their faces ached with joy, the moments that she'd missed before they'd even ended, because she knew they were too impossibly precious to last long enough. It was all that she could see.

Her arms flung open, as though her insides were being ripped from her by something invisible, every sinew and muscle strand aching at the effort to feel it all, feel everything all at once. To be enough for everyone she loved. There it was again. It felt like her bones would snap. Like her skin would burst.

Then came magic.

First, the rush of a tidal wave which sent them all flying apart at such a speed that Belle struggled to catch her breath, drowning in gulps of foamed, frothed sea whipped to white. With it, a wind that ripped through the room in a tornado vortex, sweeping everyone and everything up in its wake with rubble and dust. A projection of fire from the ends of her fingertips that singed her skin, the sensation so raw that she could barely even register it. The ground beneath her feet, the walls and the ceiling shook violently, tremors vibrating everything in their wake as the earth itself moved under her magic.

But finally, a blinding burst of sunshine. So great that it consumed everything else. Golden and warm on her face. The sun had come. The clouds had gone.

Her final thought was Ariadne. How it wasn't fair. How she couldn't suffer here amidst all of the dark and dismal chaos created by something that she was powerless against, that she was too good for, that Belle couldn't possibly associate with her best friend.

Belle's skull was reverberating, her shoulders were torn, her spine shouted and her limbs felt like lead. But somewhere in the back of her subconscious magic instinct, she summoned her. Transferred Ariadne to her arms so that she knew she was as safe as she could make her.

And then it all stopped. The sun disappeared and everything turned black.

33
Magic

THROUGH HER THIRTY years (plus thirty-something moons on top now, but she didn't need to count them anymore) Belle had experienced some mighty hangovers. Particularly past the age of around twenty-six, when her body had decided that more than one or two glasses of wine was a terrible idea and that dancing in heels was not the natural art form it had once been. But this one beat them all. The hangover from a witches' battle was something else.

"You have got to stop calling it a hangover, you fool," Rune said, biting down on his lip to stop himself from laughing. "You're doing yourself somewhat of a disservice."

"It sounds a little too self-aggrandising to call it what it was," she replied, trying to sit up in her bed before promptly realising that it wasn't a good idea. Her head throbbed and her arms buckled under her weight.

"Easy, tiger," he growled softly. "Back on the pillows, please. How are those cuts looking?" He sucked in a breath as he eased the duvet away from one of her legs and saw the cross-stitch of wounds and bruises that had embroidered themselves along almost every inch of her body. He had yet to leave her side since pulling her out of the rubbled remains of the Hecate House atrium. Although they had certainly both taken their fair share of damage, the injuries that he and Bonnie had sustained were nowhere near as bad as Belle's, having thrown up their protection circles just in time before the place came down. Belle had been too intent on saving Ariadne from the fall to turn her attention to herself.

"Oi, I'm still pretty." Belle laughed, looking distinctly unpretty in that moment and quite possibly smelling even worse.

"Who told you that?" Rune smirked. They caught eyes, and he swallowed hard before averting his gaze to adjust the duvet again.

"Maybe we could try a bath again," Belle said. "Wait, I didn't mean we. As in 'we try a bath.' As in 'we could try a bath, specifically for me.' As in—"

"I think you have head injuries," Rune muttered, reaching the back of his hand against her forehead to check her temperature for the millionth time that day.

They had attempted to navigate a bath for Belle two nights ago, during which, after much awkward back and forth, Rune had won the argument that she didn't have the physical or magical strength to wash her own hair. She'd joked (half joked) that, in that case, he'd have to do it for her. And surprisingly, he'd agreed in a very gentlemanly way. Neither had cared to mention that a spell could have been used. There'd been a lot of magically manifested bubbles involved for dignity purposes, and he'd been surprisingly gentle. For all the front he'd ever put on towards her, for all of the rehearsed lines and sly flirting, the whole thing had actually made him rather shy in the moment.

"In fact, you have everything injuries. You summoned the elements together all at once. You saved us all—your mum, Ariadne, me, Artorius—not to mention the entire coven, who—I'm not supposed to tell you this, but I know you'll hate the surprise—are currently preparing to throw a celebration in your name for saving Selcouth."

"That was your doing, not mine."

"Hardly," Rune scoffed. "All I did was gather the magic back after Bronwyn and Morena vanished and return it to the rightful owners. I was basically the glorified paperwork guy. You laid the groundwork. And by 'groundwork,' I of course mean 'entirely destroyed the joint.'"

Belle frowned. "I still can't believe those hags got out."

He stroked her face with a barely-there touch. "We don't know that for certain. The place was a ruin, the coven are still clearing the chaos. Even if they did make it out, they'd be in a bad way, their cauldron pledge ended once Selcouth banished them. They're gone," he said firmly.

Belle accepted it reluctantly and thumbed the fabric of the duvet. "How's Ariadne doing today?"

"Fully back on her feet, thanks to you, cushioning her fall like that with the transference spell. I assume it's a given that she's driving me half mad with questions. I have no idea how you function as flatmates together."

"Best friends, eh? Can't live with 'em, can't live without 'em," Belle said in a horrible attempt at a New Jersey accent.

"You are insane," Rune said matter-of-factly while fighting a grin. "Can you manage to get dressed? There's someone waiting to see you at Lunar. Three guesses who. He has something that you need to see." Something in his face gave away that he knew exactly what it was.

"If this is that photo album again of his trip to Minorca, I'll honestly . . ."

She eased herself out of bed with a little help from Rune, both of his hands delicately placed on her waist to lift her and take the strain off her muscles. Everything ached as she moved, but with the help of a few healing potions, it was starting to feel manageable.

"Eyes off the prize, Dunstan."

"It's an instantaneous transformative spell. I won't see anything," he said indignantly, rolling his eyes and turning on the spot to face the wall, crossing his arms. It required significantly more effort than usual, but Belle flicked a finger towards her wardrobe to slide out a suitable outfit. She hadn't told Bonnie or Rune or Artorius that they had all individually ruined the news of Hecate House's surprise celebration during their bedside visits. Not an endarkenment but a congratulatory gesture. She was just relieved that this time, their summoning letter wasn't something to descend into a minor life crisis about. No more fear.

The coven, having all been rescued from imminent death, not to mention realising that their entire recent history was based on shameful lies, were altogether rather grateful. Not only to Belle but to Bonnie, too, and to Rune. They'd also granted an immediate pardon and coven apology to Artorius just hours ago, after each member of Selcouth received a co-signed letter from Bonnie and Caspar outlining the full extent of their discoveries.

With another finger flick, Belle freshened herself up and transformed her pyjamas into the celestial-patterned dress that the enchantment had selected. It was a shame that such a pretty piece had to be accessorised with a patchwork of plum-coloured bruises, but at least she wouldn't have to explain where they'd come from. Everybody knew. Literally everybody. Even Violet, Monica and Jim, although their version of events involved less witch anarchy and more falling down an entire flight of stairs into the tube station.

"That's a new one for the collection," Rune said, gesturing to a blooming petal of mauve and purple-blue across her collarbone.

"They really just keep on coming, don't they?" Belle replied, staring down at it.

Giving her a furtive glance, Rune leaned forwards and planted the softest, most delicate of kisses directly on top of the new bruise. Then, impossibly gently, he held her chin between his forefinger and thumb, the same spot that always held his magic, and kissed her. Belle, folding her fingers around the lapels of his jacket to bring him closer, felt her knees almost buckle, and this time it wasn't down to her injuries.

"You're looking better," he said, still holding her. "Can I get you anything?"

"A coffee, please. Big one," Belle said, attempting a grin but wincing as the inside of her split cheeks screamed in pain.

"You got it."

With small, timid steps, unconvinced just yet by the reliability of her own balance, Belle took the short walk to Lunar Books, a journey they were familiar with together now, only this time it was with a closed gap between them, her hand slipping so comfortably into Rune's that she swore it was the perfect fit. They squinted against the rosy November morning, chilly air biting at their faces beneath the spray of trees that had begun to change now from citrus oranges to richer browns.

"Did Caspar have any luck finding the Selcouth grimoire?" she asked. While she'd been recovering, Rune had been working closely with Caspar and Bonnie, raking through Artorius's endless reams of research to find remaining answers.

"He did. And it was still there, the loophole. We expected that it would have vanished, some kind of complex glamour that she'd created to fool you. But no, it was still written there, raven ink and all. How did Bronwyn manage to make an addition to the book if it was for her own gain, rather than for the good of the coven?"

Belle shrugged. "I can't tell if you're asking me for a genuine answer or if you're doing the usual dramatic, mysterious build-up to make me swoon somehow."

He laughed. "It's the latter. How am I doing?"

"Not too shabby."

Rune stopped and turned to her, their shadows melting together at their feet. "Bronwyn might have intended for the loophole to lead to your downfall, but the grimoire accepted it as lore because fate knew that it would result in you staying with Selcouth. Everything that happened was for the good of the coven. You were for the good of the coven." He lifted her chin to meet his gaze again. "But mainly for me."

Belle arrived at Lunar to the familiar welcoming jangle of the bell hanging above the door and breathed in the inviting scent of the fresh pastries that mingled with the new-book smell and plumed once again through the whole shop. Her shop. Danishes, croissants, savoury twists and apple cider donuts were ready and waiting in rows of golden glaze on the bakery cart next to the shiny new coffee machine. One of her first decisions for Lunar had been to bring back the steady supply of cinnamon buns and cappuccinos, and Mr. Ricci had been all too happy to team up on the idea, delivering everything early each day and already bringing a host of new commuting customers each morning as a result.

"Those are not for you." Belle rolled her eyes when she found Ariadne ripping apart the flaky sweetness of a bun for breakfast while she chatted to Artorius, the pair of them perched on alternate arms of an armchair.

Bonnie was moving from one end of the shop to the other, switching on the dotted table lamps with a train of tiny sparks as she went, with Wolfie contentedly snoozing on the rug in front of the till. Jinx had also been brought along for the occasion this time and was doing her level best to battle the end of a string of fairy lights hanging from a book trolley.

"There have got to be some benefits to being friends with the boss." Ariadne shrugged, dusting grains of sugar from her fingers. Belle's mother and her best friend had been taking it in turns to arrive at Lunar bright and early every morning while Belle rested and recovered, accepting the baked goods deliveries and passing on her slightly delirious, half-asleep instructions to Monica and Jim.

"So, really, if you think about it"—Artorius reclaimed Ari's attention—"a non-wicche branch of the coven could indeed prove rather useful, if you'd be interested in such an endeavour."

Ariadne looked mostly perplexed but was taking it in her stride. Bonnie and Belle had attempted to explain as best they could over the handful of days since the showdown, but it was more of a pencil sketch than a fully fledged masterpiece thus far. To her credit, Ari had been surprisingly quick to accept the existence of magic itself. The fact that Belle had not conjured a perfect life of riches and fame for them both was her biggest sticking point so far.

"Thanks for the offer, Mr. Day. I'll have a think . . ."

"Hi, Arty," Belle said, shuffling towards them at a speed that even he would have beaten. She dumped her bag on the desk next to the till and leaned against the oak for extra support.

The old man had escaped Hecate House relatively scot-free after being flung across the courtroom, just some bruises along with a fractured wrist, which he now wore in a pink sling to perfectly match his hat. Belle had marvelled at the miracle of his survival when she came to, sure as soon as she woke that she'd lost him. But things made a little more sense when Rune reported finding her sooth stone still attached to Morena's necklace, strewn just across the floor from his collapsed body. Alvina's *Praesentia Pretego* had flourished for her younger brother, too—a Day sibling bond built back together—although how it had got there remained an interesting question.

"Belle, it's wonderful to see you on your feet, my dear!" Artorius exclaimed, trying his best to rise to meet her.

"Don't get up. I hear you have a surprise for me," she said, fully expecting to spot the photo album in his bag. Instead, her stomach sank as she spotted the unmistakable corner of her grimoire poking out. "I'm not sure I'm ready to see that."

Despite everything that had happened, despite the wonder of the elemental magic that she had managed to perform in the moment, Belle still couldn't help but feel as though she'd failed herself. She knew it was stupid to care about redundant challenges after everything she'd achieved instead, but it was impossible to ignore. Naturally, she couldn't help but pay attention to the tiny negatives amongst the enormous joys. It was the last dream that she would ever allow to slip away from her.

The elemental magic would have certainly been enough to appease the Earth Sorcery allegory. That meant there had only been one allegory left unlit when Halloween met midnight and November arrived. She had failed her chance at endarkenment by one measly Incantation challenge.

Not that the coven were planning to adhere to the rules that the Gowdens had instated for her endarkenment, anyway. The whole process was to be updated, but still. It almost felt as though she'd disappointed the grimoire, which she'd been told time and time again was the truest source of a witch's worthiness.

Artorius gave her a smile. "I must insist that I return it to you. For safekeeping. You know as well as I do that nothing in that attic of mine is ever very easy to find again once you put it down. Has a mind of its own, that place. Have a look."

He handed her the great leather-bound book, the weight of it a struggle in her weak, bandage-covered arms but a strange comfort to have back in her possession. It fell open on that first page of pencil lettering that she'd scribbled as a brand-new witch.

What do you hope this new blessing of magic means for you, witch?

To be special. To like myself and be confident. To be happy.

She smiled to herself. "What am I looking for, exactly?"
Artorius beamed and, with a small gesture of his hand, guided

the pages along until they found whatever it was that he was evidently so interested in. The Incantation allegory.

As it fell open, Belle gasped, almost dropping it. The looped calligraphy letters turned from raven black ink to glowing warm amber. The page was lit from within, a tiny fire behind every word. "I don't understand," she stuttered, hardly daring to believe it for herself.

Bonnie laughed. "Ariadne. You summoned her."

Belle was baffled. It must be an admin error. Did grimoires suffer admin errors? "What? When?"

"After Bronwyn, that gorgon, brought her into Hecate House for no reason other than revelling in your misery," Bonnie said bitterly.

"Just before she fell to the ground, you summoned her to you. You cushioned her fall and took most of the blow as you both went down together," Rune said proudly.

Belle looked across to Ariadne, who was grinning smugly.

> So to prove good thine incantation,
> Rewrite the mind's own dark narration.
> Spirit, soul and spell to start,
> Summon that which is thine heart.

"You love me, bitch," Ariadne said. "I am 'thine heart.'"

Belle let out a slightly hysterical, extra-loud splutter of a laugh. "Only because I thought everyone else was already dead. Ow!" She clutched at a rib. "Don't make me laugh. Please."

Bonnie was grinning from ear to ear. "You passed, darling. You summoned Ariadne just before midnight on Halloween. The grimoire lit up just in time. You did it." She threw her arms around Belle, squeezing tightly before remembering that her daughter was a patchwork quilt of injuries.

"If we didn't have reason enough to celebrate already, then we sure do now," Ariadne called, shimmying towards the coat stand to grab her scarf and hat. "Come on, Jim will be in soon for opening, and I don't want to have to explain to the poor bloke why there's a giant Irish wolf-hound in the shop."

"You don't even know what all of this is about!" Belle said, straining to catch her jacket, which was sailing through the air as Ariadne chucked belongings at random.

"You can tell me on the way to your party."

Bonnie threw up her hands and rolled her eyes. "That was supposed to be a surprise."

"I'll drive, as it were," Rune said in his usual cool tone, turning up the collar of his coat.

"Marvellous, marvellous," Artorius muttered happily, scooping up Jinx.

"Are you ready, sweetheart?" Bonnie asked, easing her daughter over to stand beside them.

Belle took their hands, the five (plus cat and dog) standing in a chain to travel under Rune's transference. Jinx was purring to a volume that was verging on supernatural. Ariadne, on Belle's right, asking Rune whether he'd consider an alternative jacket for the winter months, which he instantly dismissed. Rune, on the end, looking across to her like he wouldn't ever want to look at anything else. Her mother, on her left, clasping onto her hand with a look that couldn't have been prouder, never applying pressure or expectation to her daughter but providing a love that was fiercely true and endless through all weathers. And Artorius, on Bonnie's end, politely extending his arm for her to take. A man who had been alone for so long welcomed into the life of friendship and family he had longed for, another grandparent whom she had serendipitously found for herself.

All under the glow of the fairy lights, wrapped in the pages of Lunar Books.

The radiance of her sooth stone heated against her chest, a feeling she would never tire of. Ever-loving.

"Ready."

All of this. Imperfect but hers. That candle flame of potential which had once felt infinite, then faded to being carried away on a wisp, now burned brightly, brilliantly again. She could feel it. Prioritising herself had brought it back, hand in hand with everything she needed, reaffirmed everything she already had. She had found true magic and would hold on to it tightly with both hands.

Acknowledgements

There is so much magic in my life. To my family and friends, I count my lucky stars for all of you.

Thanks to my beautiful, magical mum. For endless trips to Bebington library, for bedtime stories that I still vividly remember, and for making sure I heard that I was capable of anything and everything. You did such a good job. Ed, for always supporting, and Sam, just for being my six-foot little brother. Nan Pan and Far Nan, who I am certain must be tweaking the wheel of fortune in my favour somewhere. I miss you every single day. Everloving.

Adam, the one who brings magic to my every day. Thank you for our beautiful life that revolves around laughter and love above all else. I have never known anything like your positivity, patience and kindness. You are the best of the very best, and the little world we have built together is perfect magic to me. I can't wait to marry you.

Flo, who wrote approximately half of this book by walking her paws across the keyboard. Never far away, my forever familiar.

The easiest character to write for this book was Ariadne, because she is a wonderful, insane combination of the dazzling friendships I have grown up with. Hannah, Emma, Steph and Bradford, it says a lot about how enriching a friendship is when you can live off its goodness and laughter for six months at a time. Ours was a girl-hood shared.

The Thundergirls, who shared every minor meltdown over this book (and the rest of life) in glorious, alarming Technicolor. I don't know what I would do without you and our obsessive, emotional support group chat . . . It's a lifelong thing, I fear. And Jenny, my tini-est yet greatest and most chaotic cheerleader, even when on the other side of the world.

Lucy Brem, my wonderful editor. I am absolutely convinced now that something otherworldly brought us together to write the magical comfort read we both needed. Thanks for your steadfast support from the first read, your endless patience and your genius suggestions; we have made something so special. It's an enormous pleasure to get to work with you, especially when we roll a six in Dishoom. Thank you to the whole dream team at Pan MacMillan, who have made wishes I didn't even dare to say out loud come true.

An especially spellbinding shout-out for the edition across the pond! Ridiculously cool. Thanks to the magical gang at Berkley who make miraculous things happen from thousands of miles away, particularly my editor, Anne Sowards. I am still so touched that you believed in Belle's story, and I feel incredibly lucky to have your support, expertise and enthusiasm behind *Rewitched*.

Finally, my online gang of pals across roads, lands, skies and oceans. We are best friends who might never meet but who have so much in common and find so much comfort in one another. I can never thank you enough for making me feel less alone back then, and for granting me the privilege of hanging out with you, in your home, for so many years ever since. I hope that reading this feels like a love letter directly to you, and reminds you of everything you deserve to know about yourself, because it was always supposed to be just that.

LUCY JANE WOOD is an online content creator, avid reader, and coziness-seeker from the Wirral, UK. These days, you'll find her living in London, giant coffee in hand, and being headbutted at any given time by her cat.

VISIT LUCY JANE WOOD ONLINE
LucyJaneWood.co.uk
▶ YouTube LucyJaneWood
⊙ LucyJaneWood
𝕏 LucyJaneWood